Hasten to Me

ADRIENNE WOODS

Pass It On
Publishing

Dr. Kelley started toward the elevator when as it opened, his eyes were captured by a woman of immense beauty. She was a petite woman, around five feet, two inches compared to his, six foot, five inches. She had a curvaceous figure with full breasts and nice sized hips. Definitely a sight for his tired eyes.

"Good afternoon," he surprised himself by saying. "I love that perfume that you're wearing. I'm sorry, where are my manners? Hi, I'm Dr. Kelley. I'm not trying to pick you up or anything, but that perfume is positively intriguing. What is it called?"

"Thank you and my name is Jackie. This perfume was made specifically for me and my sisters. It's called Alluring because the fragrance reminds one of two people making love intimately on a bed sprinkled with rose petals, as their fragrance permeates the room."

"Perhaps if that is the intention, you won't mind if I do this." He hit the stop button on the elevator and Dr. Kelley, completely acting out of character, reached out and pulled Jackie ever so gently into his arms, allowing her enough time to pull away if she so desired. His mouth brushed hers ever so gently on the lips as he lightly kissed the corners of her mouth. Then meeting no resistance, he began to devour her mouth. It was as if he was having an out of body experience. Kissing her was like spontaneous combustion. The very flames licking at his insides were enough to devour them both. With each taste of her lips he wanted more. He sought to gain entrance into the soft crevices of her mouth.

With a sigh she opened up to him as her hands rose to encircle his neck. She kissed him without any inhibitions. Hot. Wild. Heated. Kissing the doctor was like a tidal wave raging to shore. His lips totally devoured her senses making her forget that they were in an elevator, alone, making out without any coherent thought as to stopping.

Novels by Adrienne Woods

360°, A Journey Awaits
Friends First, Joined by Love

Adrienne Woods, an avid reader since the age of three, credits her love of reading to her late grandmother, who would read her parables/stories from the Bible when she was little. A true romantic at heart, she loves to write stories that exemplify strong family relationships, an abiding faith in God and the belief that one can overcome any adversity. With five siblings, it's easy to see why her novels portray such strong family bonds.

Adrienne currently resides in Greensboro, North Carolina where she lives with her husband and her daughter. She is a graduate of North Carolina Agricultural and Technical State University, and holds a Bachelor of Science Degree in Accounting.

This novel is a work of fiction. The characters and events portrayed in this novel were created from the author's imagination and are purely fictitious.

Hasten To Me

ISBN-13: 978-0-9815849-4-2
ISBN-10: 0-9815849-4-2

Printed in the United States of America

Pass It On Publishing/ February 2009

ACKNOWLEDGEMENTS

Giving all the honor to my Lord and Savior, Jesus Christ, I thank you for all the gifts and blessings that you have bestowed upon me.

To my husband, my hero, and to my daughter, my rock and sounding board; thank you for all of your love, patience and support!

To my family and friends, thank you for your encouragement and feedback!

The Baileys

Discover exciting and intriguing romantic sagas where the hero/heroine through faith, overcomes adversity while producing a legacy for future generations.

Steven Bailey
m
Erma Johnson

Malcolm Bailey
My Love, My Destiny

Anita Bailey
Last to Love

Traci Bailey
Insatiable Thirst

David Bailey
Lay It on the Line
Summer 2009

Ryan Bailey
Ryan's Retreat

Jackie Bailey
Hasten to Me

Chelsea Bailey
m
Maxmillian Teal
360°,
A Journey Awaits

Taylor Teal

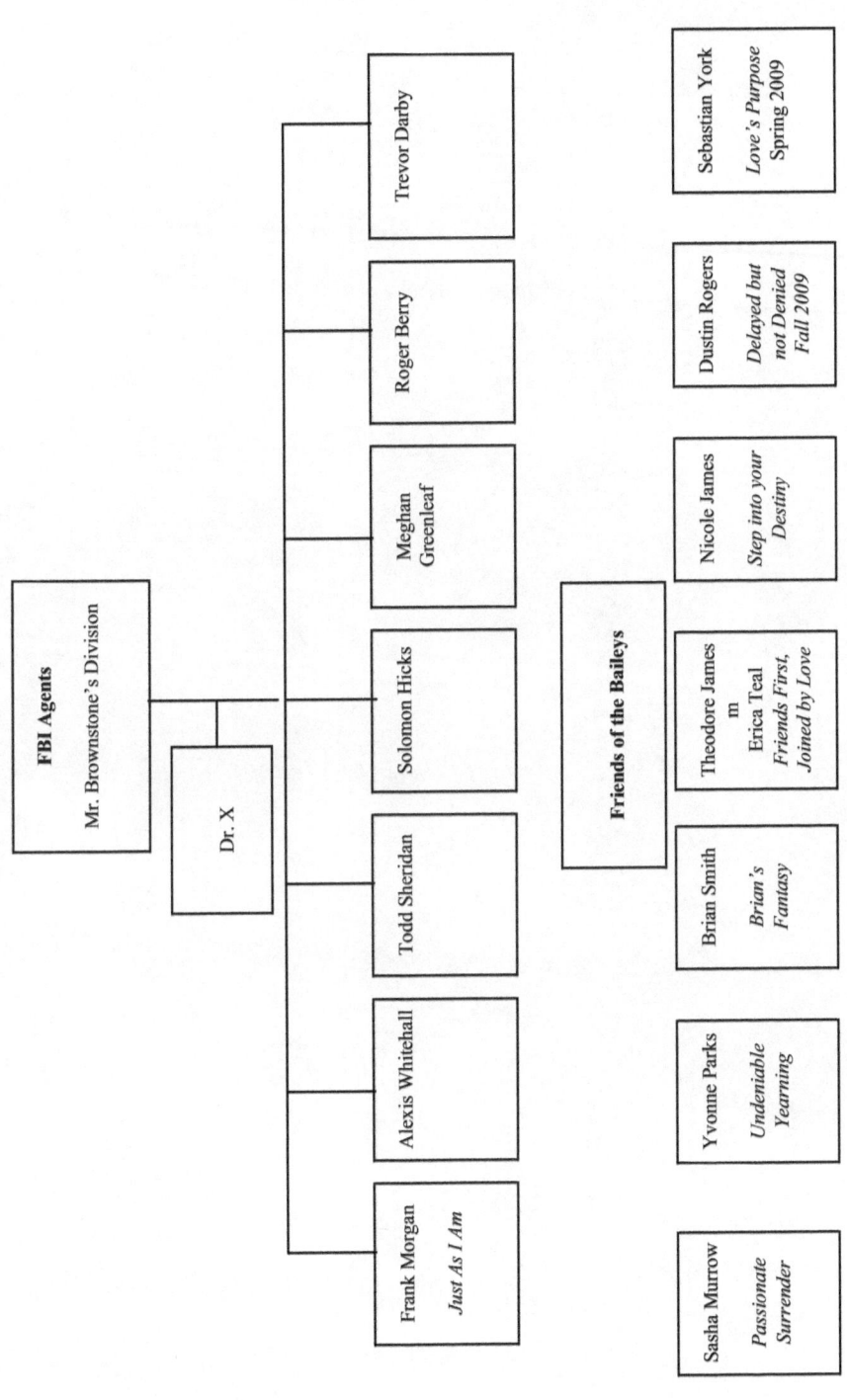

FBI Agents

Mr. Brownstone's Division

Dr. X

Frank Morgan
Just As I Am

Alexis Whitehall

Todd Sheridan

Solomon Hicks

Meghan Greenleaf

Roger Berry

Trevor Darby

Friends of the Baileys

Sasha Murrow
Passionate Surrender

Yvonne Parks
Undeniable Yearning

Brian Smith
Brian's Fantasy

Theodore James
m
Erica Teal
Friends First, Joined by Love

Nicole James
Step into your Destiny

Dustin Rogers
Delayed but not Denied
Fall 2009

Sebastian York
Love's Purpose
Spring 2009

Prologue

Walking into the conference room, Maurice noticed that all the partners were present along with the CEO of the firm. With measured steps, feeling like he was walking to his own execution, he surveyed his opponents to see if he could ascertain the full import of the meeting.

Breathe deeply. Exhale. Don't let them see you sweat. No one knows the truth.

Looking towards the door, he attempted to gauge the time it would take to flee. No, that wouldn't work. They would know then that he was guilty. Better to try to bluff his way out of the situation. He wouldn't know what he was up against until everything was out in the open.

Glancing briefly outside the large expanse of windows that lined the right side of the conference room, to see if any police cars were waiting to escort him to prison, Maurice visibly relaxed for the first time since entering the room. There wasn't any indication that any police cars were on the premises. The conference room they were in gave a frontal view of two parking lots that spanned the front side of the building.

His attention was drawn to the president of the corporation as he took his place at the podium and started to speak. "Let's get started, shall we? Maurice, because of the behavior of your portfolio, you are hereby being put on probation. Unless we see a significant increase in the value of your client's portfolio, your partnership is in jeopardy of being terminated. You have ninety days to turn your client's stock around in order to retain your partnership. At the end of the ninety days, an evaluation will be given based on the analysis of all the stocks that you handle. Subsequently a vote will be taken by the other partners regarding your future."

"Thank you Mr. Taylor for giving me three months to improves my client's stock portfolio. You won't be disappointed."

"This meeting is adjourned and we'll regroup in ninety days."

After Maurice left the conference room, all but one of the partners remained. The CEO looked at Chris, his long time friend and his senior partner. "Chris, what do you think is going on? I've looked at the stocks that were chosen and they are high performing stocks. Hell, most of these stocks I have myself. Do you think that this is a case of embezzlement?"

"I don't know Anthony. I've looked at the ledger sheets myself but I can't find where any dummy companies were set up nor can I find the account where the money is being deposited."

"How long do you suspect this has been going on? How long has Maurice been a partner?" Anthony asked with his elbows resting on the table supported by his crossed fingers underneath his chin.

"Maurice has been a partner for about four years now, which is why we can't explain his decline in productivity. While he was working as a regular stockbroker, he had an uncanny habit of picking the best stocks and earning the best returns. That's why he made partner so soon."

"When did you notice that his productivity began to decline? Did it start right after he became a partner?"

"No, not right away. His decline in productivity seemed to start during his second year of being a partner. His portfolio value up until that point, was the highest, then little by little, he became complacent. He didn't work as hard as he used to, and his results showed."

"Chris, pull all the records for all the stock activities for Maurice's portfolio since he made partner. You may have been looking for a dummy corporation in the wrong year. Was your concentration for the bogus corporation just on the current or past year?"

"We initially started with the current year then we expanded our investigation to the previous year. We were unsuccessful in our search to uncover any wrong doing."

"What does your gut tell you?"

Answering without hesitation, Chris replied, "That he's diverting funds to an offshore account in his name or in a company's name that he owns."

"I'm going to contact my friend Trevor that works for the government, who has been known to uncover offshore accounts that no one else can locate. Hopefully, he'll be able to trace Maurice's moves and uncover the stolen funds. Right now without further proof, I'm not sure what magnitude of a dollar amount we're dealing with."

"It could be crippling to the company depending on how long he's been operating in this fashion. I'll let you know what happens, but in the meantime, keep a close watch on what he does and where he goes. Do you still have friends on both sides of the law?"

"Yes. I'll put the word out on the street that you're seeking information. We should hear something soon."

Going back to his office, Maurice breathed a sigh of relief. *Whew! He wasn't going to jail. All he had to do was replace the funds in his client's account before his probation ended and he could wipe the slate clean.* Now it was time to settle down to work. He had ninety days to implement his next plan of action for starting his own firm and for reinvesting his clients remaining funds to come up with monetary value that was at stake, if a thorough investigation was completed.

Leaning back in his chair, he pondered his options. Who could he borrow that type of money from? How much would the bank let him borrow considering that he had just purchased a million dollar house and signed a lease for office space in the Bank of America Building in downtown Charlotte for the next five years?

Most of their liquid cash had gone into putting down a sizable down payment, roughly half of the purchase price, for their new house so that their remaining mortgage would be a lot easier to handle. If he liquidated all of their combined assets, his and his wife's, that would probably garner around three hundred thousand dollars. If he cashed in their insurance policies, that would give him another two hundred thousand dollars.

Far short of the money that he had reassigned.

Pulling out his cellular phone, he dialed Ricky, his childhood friend that knew some people in low places. Perhaps he could tell him where he could borrow about two million dollars.

Chapter 1

After moving into their new house, in the Christenbury Hill subdivision in Charlotte, North Carolina, Maurice decided that he would go back to work while his wife, Jackie, stayed home to organize the house with the help of the new maid, Alva. Maurice thought that the maid was necessary to help with the organization of the house, and also with the extensive entertaining that he planned to do now that his firm was successful.

The third day after moving in, they received a visitor. A client stopped by to see Maurice, thinking that he could catch him at home that week instead of at the office.

Walking up the driveway towards the open garage door where the two women were sorting boxes, Robert cleared his throat to make his presence known before he introduced himself. "Excuse me, is this the Holmes residence? I'm looking for Maurice Holmes. Does he live here?"

Thinking that a neighbor was stopping by to welcome them to the neighborhood, Jackie stepped forward as she wiped her hands on a nearby cloth. "Yes, this is the Holmes residence. How may I help you?"

The man stepped forward as he extended his hand. "My name is Robert Smith and I'm one of your husband's clients and your neighbor at the far end of the street. I just wanted to stop by and welcome you to the neighborhood. Is he here?"

"No, I'm afraid that you've just missed him. He went to the office for a couple of hours. Do you want me to call him?"

"That's okay. I'm sure that I'll catch him at another time." Extending the gift wrapped box in her direction, Robert replied, "I don't want to intrude. I'm sure you have plenty of work to do. Please accept this gift from myself and my wife and again welcome to the neighborhood." Turning around, he walked back towards the waiting car.

Jackie stared after him. Something was wrong or felt out of place. It was odd that the man didn't mention which house he lived in nor did he bring his wife with him. Usually if someone new moved into the neighborhood, if you were a married couple, you would greet them together. Plus, clients didn't often stop by unannounced; only if they were invited.

What was going on, she wondered? Shaking her head, she decided that she had too much work to do to worry about it. She would ask Maurice about the guy when he came home. Maybe the guy was someone the used to work with as a client and wanted to come on board with her husband's new firm.

Shrugging her shoulders, she turned to the maid, Alva, and together they resumed working.

Later that evening, Jackie questioned Maurice about the guy showing up at their house to welcome them to the neighborhood.

"Honey, one of our new neighbors came by today. He said that his name was Robert Smith. He didn't come with his wife though. I thought that was a little strange. Is he one of your clients?"

Since Jackie was busy cooking as she was talking, she missed Maurice's startled expression. He was taken aback that his enemy had found him so quickly. He thought that by moving, he could gain at least a two to three month reprieve.

"Oh, sweetheart, who did you say stopped by; a neighbor? Which house does he live in? We must make time to stop by and thank them. Maybe it's another client that wants to come on board with the new firm. I told you that this would happen." Maurice stated absently as he was pondering how to get ahead of the eight ball that he seemed to be behind.

"I don't know which house he lives in. He didn't give the address; just stated that he lived down the street."

"Whenever he comes into the office, I'll get that information and then find out where he lives. Once we settle in, we can get to know our neighbors."

Secretly he was a little apprehensive. Robert was putting on the pressure. He needed to get the money that he owed him first, before someone got hurt. Now that he knew where they lived, he didn't have much time. This visit wasn't a social visit.

"Oh, by the way, he left a gift. You might want to open it, and then I can catalogue it with the rest of the gifts and send him a thank you card."

"Uh, uh. I'll take care of that honey." Making an excuse to his wife that he had work to do, Maurice went to the room that he had designated as his home office to come up with a plan for the money. He was running out of options and running out of time.

Downtown, in a prominent business building that housed Maurice's investment firm, a fire was being started on the floor directly above where his office was located. Careful not to leave any evidence, the arsonist left the scene of the crime as soon as the flames ignited. The fire would be untraceable because the arsonist was good at what he did and thus far, had not been caught. Luckily the building was outfitted with a new sprinkler system, which helped contain the amount of damage done to the facility.

When the police and the fire department arrived and investigated the premises, they were able to ascertain that the fire was started because of an electrical spark due to faulty wiring, in one of the fuse boxes. After the fire was contained and eventually extinguished, the police contacted the building's tenants and requested that each of them come down to survey the damage.

Three weeks later…

As Jackie was working yet again in the garage, sorting out the few remaining boxes, the doorbell rang. It was funny how at the old house, no one wanted to visit them but once they move into a more prestigious neighborhood, it seemed as if their home had now become a revolving door. Yet again, visitors would show up wanting to see Maurice. She wondered which one of them it was this time.

Knowing that Maurice would not answer the door if he was knee deep in work in his office, Jackie entered the house through the door that connected the garage to the house. Intercepting Alva, who had stopped preparing dinner to answer the door, Jackie insisted, "Thanks but I've got it Alva. I don't know why my lazy husband can't answer it. I'm sure he heard it. You go ahead and fix dinner. I'll get it."

Walking down the hallway to the front door, Jackie glanced through the transom to identify the visitor. Cautiously, she asked, "Can I help you?"

"Yes, ma'am. You're Jackie right? I'm Toby, one of your husband's old childhood friends." Extending his hand, he waited patiently for her to make the next move.

Warily she briefly shook the gentleman's hand before releasing it and asking over her shoulder, "Alva, could you get Maurice from his office, please?"

Inviting Toby into the foyer, Jackie closed the door. "Toby, Maurice should be here shortly. Would you follow me? We can go into the family room. So far, that's the only room, we have furnished at the moment. Our furniture has yet to arrive."

Once they moved into the new neighborhood, Maurice refused to take any furniture from their old house. She had been forced to sell several antiques that she had owned, simply because he wanted all new furniture in the house. She couldn't understand why she wasn't more firm to demand that her things remain. That was something she wasn't good at. Consequently, she usually let Maurice have his way.

Walking into the room, Maurice pulled up short in alarm, upon noticing the stranger that sat in their family room. Who was this guy?

Before he could voice his objections, Toby stood and embraced Maurice; tightly enough so that he could not pull away. Whispering softly, Toby suggested, "Play along or your wife will witness a murder right here in her very own house."

"Toby, Toby, is that you? How did you get here so quickly? I wasn't expecting to see you until sometime next week."

"Well, since you moved to my area, I couldn't wait. I had to come and see you for myself, to make sure it was really you. How long has it been since we've seen each other?"

"It's been a minute. Why don't you come on down into the basement and we can catch up? I'm sure Jackie doesn't want to hear our old stories." Turning towards the door, he left the room with Toby fast on his heels.

Once they were in the basement, Maurice turned on Toby with a heated expression. "What are you doing here? I told Robert that I would have the money. It's just taking slightly longer than I expected."

As soon as the words were out of Maurice's mouth, Toby landed a punch to his middle; straight to the ribs. "Let's get one thing straight. You don't call the shots. Right now you are so far behind the eight ball, it's not even funny. Do you have the money?"

Blustering, Maurice, tried to bluff his way out of answering.

Grabbing Maurice by the neck, he threw him across the room, into the chairs that sat opposite the large table that took up a good portion of the back wall. A loud bang could be heart all over the house. "I'm here to deliver a message from Mr. Smith. He wants his money within ten days or you'll be sorry."

Jackie, hearing the commotion, went to the top of the stairs that led to basement. "Honey, is everything all right?"

Hearing a faint grunt in response, she became worried.

Walking down the stairs into the basement, with a sharp knife in her hand, just in case she needed backup, she gingerly approached the wide open expanse of the basement.

"What's all the commotion about down here?" she asked looking from one man to the other.

"Nothing sweetheart. Just two old men roughing each other up since we haven't seen each other in a while. You can go back upstairs."

Looking around the room skeptically at the furniture that was overturned, she wondered what was really going on.

"Okay, just try not to ruin the furniture, Toby."

"No ma'am. I need to leave anyway. I just stopped by to congratulate you and your hubby over here on your success. I'm sure since ya'll live here now in Charlotte, we'll be seeing more of each other. Isn't that right, Maurice?"

Looking at Toby and trying not to wince at the pain he was experiencing in his ribs, Maurice replied, "Not if I see you coming first." Laughingly, he retracted, "Just kidding," when he saw the look of menace enter Toby's eyes.

With one final punch on the shoulder that had Maurice's step faltering, Toby left.

After seeing Toby to the door, when Maurice returned, Jackie, standing in the doorway to the kitchen asked, "Do you want to tell me what that was all about?"

"No, I don't. It's nothing for you to worry about," Maurice yelled in a voice full of frustration as he walked back towards the basement.

Jackie reached out to stop Maurice from heading into the basement by grabbing his arm, as she demanded, "Are you in some type of trouble?"

Feeling at the end of his rope, turning so swiftly that he surprised her; Maurice rounded on Jackie and pushed her hard into the wall. "Don't ever question what is going on with me. If I want you to know something, I'll tell you."

Upon hitting the wall, Jackie crumbled to the ground in pain and blacked out. Opening her eyes several minutes later, she wondered what was wrong when she saw her husband looking worriedly at her with fear in his eyes. Glancing around the room, she noticed that she was lying on the floor. How had she gotten into that position? "What happened? Why am I on the floor?" she decided to ask.

"I was going to the basement to cool off when you followed me. When I abruptly changed my mind and was coming back to you to apologize for my churlish behavior, I turned so quickly that you didn't notice. My momentum from turning must have knocked you sideways into the wall. I'm so sorry. Are you hurt?" Maurice asked shakily. For a minute there, he thought that he might have killed her from the shove. It wouldn't have been his intention. He loved his wife. It was just that at times, she pushed the wrong buttons that sent him into a rage.

"Yes, I think so." Struggling to stand, Jackie winced in pain. "I must have hit my side pretty hard."

"Sweetheart, why don't I run you a bath where you can soak, then afterwards you can lie down and I'll clean up everything in the kitchen."

With shocked disbelief, Jackie shook her head to make sure that she heard her husband correctly. He was offering to clean up? That was a first! Thanking him, Jackie started to walk upstairs to their bedroom to lie down when she felt Maurice's arm encircle her waist. "Ouch." Immediately, he withdrew his arm.

As they entered into the bedroom, he picked her up into his arms and placed her onto bed. Walking into the master suite's bathroom, he ran her bath, then picked her up from their bed and gently unrobed her as he placed her into the soothing, heated, bubbling water.

"After you've soaked for an hour, call me and I'll come to help you out." With a kiss to the top of her head, he flipped the remote switch to the fireplace, as he left the bathroom, closing door behind him.

Downstairs, Maurice breathed a sigh of relief as he slumped against the kitchen counter. She didn't remember his shove. All she would remember from this night was that he had offered to clean up and had taken care of her. Maybe it wouldn't hurt for them to go out of town for a couple of weeks to escape the heat. He was working on a plan to get the money, but he needed more time.

The next day when it was time for Jackie to leave for work, as she was getting into the car, she noticed that one of her tires was flat.

"Great, now I'm going to be late for work."

Going back into the house, she alerted her husband, who still remained at the house. "Honey, I've got a flat. Can you come and change my tire?"

Maurice went outside to inspect the tire. "Did you run over something yesterday on your way home?"

"Not that I remember. Just a lot of speed bumps in the parking lot."

"Why don't you take my car, since I know you're running late for work and I'll take care of this for you today?"

Kissing her husband, Jackie wondered why he was being so nice. Ordinarily, he would have asked her to wait for AAA to come and change the tire. Shrugging her shoulders, she got into his BMW and went to work.

As his wife pulled out of the driveway, Maurice called the police to let them know that someone had slashed his wife's tires, sometime between midnight and daybreak. When the police asked the location of the car, Maurice advised them that their cars were parked in the driveway because they still had a lot of boxes to unpack after their move. The police lieutenant informed him that someone would be by to test for fingerprints.

Of course, when the police came and dusted for fingerprints, it was not a surprise that they couldn't find any. Maurice knew that they wouldn't. This was just another message from Mr. Smith.

He had to think of something that would buy him some more time; to get Mr. Smith off of his back. Going back into the house, Maurice reached into his wife's closet and pulled out a handbag that she seldom used. From the handbag, he retrieved a loose diamond that was nestled in a small velvet pouch. Dropping the diamond into another pouch, he replaced the handbag and left the room.

Maybe the diamond will buy me three more weeks, he thought. If so, it would allow him enough time to prepare for one more heist and then he could disappear to one of the Caribbean islands and live happily ever after with his mistress.

Dialing Mr. Smith's number, Maurice was finally connected to him after a series of checkpoint questions.

"I don't have your money yet, Mr. Smith, but I'm working on it. Can you give me three more weeks?"

"What's going to change from now until then?"

"I'm working on selling some stocks and bonds and getting the money from my wife's trust fund. It's going to take that long to get the money."

"What do you have now that would sway me to wait and not kill you?"

"Uh, uh, I have some diamonds that I can give you."

"What type of diamonds? Where did they come from?" Mr. Smith asked with interest. He had just been on the receiving end of a jewelry heist gone awry. Someone had been watching his men and had ambushed them when they made one of the largest heists in history, to the tune of twenty million dollars in stolen diamonds. Now the diamonds were gone, and he didn't have a clue, who had outsmarted him.

He had paid the Unita rebels a lot of money to steal the diamonds. Obviously, someone else had paid them more. Maybe his luck was about to change.

Was the culprit Maurice? Could he be responsible for the jewelry heist ambush? Was he that smart? Where did he get the money to pay the rebels? Did Maurice use the money, the two million dollars, that he had borrowed from him to steal the diamonds? If that were the case, there was no way that he would let the man live. First, he doesn't pay the loan back; then he steals from him. He had to go!

Chapter 2

Ten days later....

At dinnertime, late one Thursday evening, when Jackie was dining alone, yet again, because Maurice was stuck with a client at the office, another visitor showed up at their new house. It was funny to see the number of people that had recently starting showing up just to check out their new house. Granted it was very nice, but it didn't warrant the attention that seemed to continue to grow with each passing week. Some of the same people that never used to drop by their old house were making it a point to visit, to signify over their good fortune.

Jackie took it all in stride in the beginning and would laugh about the number of visitors with her husband late in the evenings when they were alone. Due to their busy schedules, they were like two trains passing by, going in opposite directions. Usually their opportunity to catch up on each other's daily activities was at night, when it was time for bed, which led her husband to demand that she change her shift hours as a nurse so that she could spend more time with him. Due to the argument that ensued after that demand, it wasn't any wonder that Maurice had taken to spending more and more time at the office because she wouldn't give in to his demands. It was now three weeks later and he was still mad at her.

Something had to change.

She would have to do something special to let Maurice know that she had finally capitulated and gotten a job as a private duty nurse that would start in about three weeks.

The repeated ringing of the doorbell brought her out of her trance. She cautiously glanced through the peephole at the door, hoping that the number of unexpected visitors had stopped, especially the ones that insisted that they wanted, no needed, to see Maurice immediately. She started to worry that perhaps the business wasn't doing so good. Making a mental note to ask her husband about their state of affairs, she walked from the dining room to answer the door. She had given the maid the evening off.

Noticing that the gentleman that had previously come several weeks ago was back, Jackie, with a sense of uneasiness, opened the door. *What was his name,* she questioned? *Paul, Peterson?* Finally, his name popped into her head at the last minute. *Smith? That's it! Smith is his last name.*

"Hello. How are you this evening, Mr. Smith?"

"Not so well Mrs. Holmes. I seem to have a problem that only your husband can solve. I hate to bother you, but is he home?" Mr. Smith asked as he absently twirled a twig between his fingers.

"No, he called about thirty minutes ago to tell me that he was still at the office."

"I'm sorry to inform you that I've been by there and he's not there. The security guard said that he left there around four o'clock and hasn't been there since. Do you have any idea where he might have gone?"

Worriedly, chewing on her bottom lip, Jackie could not fathom where Maurice could be. "I'm sorry but if he isn't at the office, I'm sure that he just got tied up and is on his way home, especially if he knew you were going to possibly stop by."

"Are you sure that you're not trying to cover for him? I'm going to ask you one more time, if he's at home. He owes me some money and I'm here to collect it." Pensively looking at Jackie, Robert stared intently into her eyes. He would hate to hurt such a pretty woman, but business was business.

With a shocked expression that couldn't be faked and a startled gasp, Jackie backed up in fear. "Why would he need to borrow money from you when his business is doing so well?" She asked in disbelief.

"I'd rather not get into that with you, but sufficient to say that he owes a approximately two million dollars."

"That's impossible," Jackie shrieked!

"You seem like a nice person, ma'am. Take heed to this warning. If I have to come here again, tell your husband that he will not like the consequences." Breaking the twig that was in his hands into two pieces, he extended the broken tree limbs to Jackie.

"Please deliver this to Maurice. Have a nice day."

Spinning on his heel, Robert walked back down the driveway, got into his car and drove off at a very high rate of speed. He usually didn't visit people more than once when they owed him money. Usually the second visit resulted in a severe punishment. There must be something about Maurice's wife that caught his attention because by now, Maurice would be dead.

She appeared to be clueless about their current financial situation. Knowing the type of person that Maurice was, Robert decided to offer him one last caveat in exchange for half the money that he was owed. He was willing to negotiate the amount of money that Maurice owed him only if his wife would sleep with him.

Knowing that Maurice would not be able to repay him, Robert savored the thought of spending time with his next conquest. He was a man that usually got what he wanted, no matter what the cost.

Jackie stared in horror after Mr. Smith as he drove away. Did the breaking of the twigs mean that they were in danger? What had Maurice done to warrant that type of threat? What kind of man was Mr. Smith? Was he a loan shark? A drug dealer? Who else lent people two million dollars and dropped by their house to collect?

Picking up her telephone, she frantically dialed her husband's cellular phone. The phone went unanswered for five rings before a female voice answered, slightly breathless. Thinking that she dialed the wrong number, she apologized for the call. Too distraught to look at the faceplate for the number that was actually dialed, she simply redialed her husband's number. This time after three short rings, the call was transferred to his voicemail. Punching in the 911 code that was only used for emergencies, she sat back and waited for a return call.

A response was not immediately forthcoming.

Pacing back and forth in her home, Jackie didn't know what to do. Should she call the police? What harm would that do? Would they put Maurice in jail or her as an accessory, even though she knew nothing? What was their financial situation really like? These thoughts kept running through her head, over and over again.

Deciding to be decisive for the first time since she married Maurice, she picked up the telephone to dial their bank to see how much money was in their account.

Going into the sitting room that was part of the master bedroom suite, Jackie sat down at her desk, and opened her laptop computer, to pull up their financial information online. After logging onto the bank's site she entered her login name and password. Slowly their accounts were listed on the screen, but beside each account number, a caption read, "Account Closed".

What in Hades was going on, she wondered? How could their accounts be closed? Where was their money? Frantic that perhaps they had been the victim of fraud, she immediately dialed the bank manager's telephone number.

"Mr. Carson, please."

"Just one moment ma'am while I connect you."

"Mr. Carson, how may I help you?"

"Mr. Carson, this is Mrs. Holmes. I was online checking my accounts when I noticed that my joint accounts with my husband have been closed. Could you tell me when and how this happened without my approval?"

"Mrs. Holmes, as a joint account holder, if one party withdraws money from the account, the other parties' signature is not required. It is unfortunate that your husband withdrew your funds but the bank acted according to its policies and procedures. Is there anything else that I can help you with?" Mr. Carson answered in a heavily sarcastic voice.

Holding her ear away from the telephone, Jackie could not believe her ears. What was wrong with this man? Was he having a bad day? Why take it out on her? She was the one with the problem. "Excuse me, Mr. Carson, there must be some mistake. If you would take the time to look at my account you will see that there are certain restrictions on the account that must be followed for any large withdrawals."

"Mrs. Holmes, the end result remains the same. Your husband could withdraw the funds legally. I suggest that you talk to him about the situation. I'm sorry that I cannot help you. Have a good day." Click.

"Oh no he didn't!" Jackie exclaimed as she furiously dialed the telephone number for the bank's president.

In an agitated voice, Jackie asked, "Could you connect me with the president of the bank? I have a complaint about the branch manager."

"Of course, one moment please." Music could be heard in the background as the call was put on hold before being transferred.

"Mr. McAlston. How may I assist you?"

"Mr. McAlston, this is Jackie Holmes and I need to discuss my account with you if you have the time."

"Sure Jackie, take all the time you need. How's your father?"

"Fine, sir. Remember the trust funds that my father setup for each of his children at your bank because of your longstanding friendship?"

"Yes, and to this date, none of you have used those funds. Do you need to withdraw some of those funds for a business venture?"

"No. I was checking the balances of my accounts online and noticed that my accounts had been closed and my trust fund had been totally depleted. Since I hadn't initiated any changes in my accounts, nor had I authorized my husband to do so, I was wondering if you could tell me the date the joint accounts were closed, and the amount that was withdrawn along with the name of the person that withdrew those funds."

"I'm not sure what's going on but that would be impossible at my bank. We have secure measures in place to prevent this from happening. Could you give me the account numbers along with your social security number, while I bring up my computer system?"

After providing the requested information for their accounts, Mr. McAlston was able to verify the status of the accounts. "Jackie, it appears that your husband came into the bank this past Monday, to withdraw these funds and to close out all of your accounts. The amount that was withdrawn was two hundred and fifty thousand dollars. He also cashed in two certificates of deposits, totaling another two hundred and fifty thousand dollars. I don't however see a transaction record where the funds were withdrawn from your trust fund. A notation on the account indicates that you were in the process of purchasing a house and wanted to use the funds for a sizable down payment. Congratulations."

"I'm curious how could my husband withdraw the funds from our joint account and then close the account without my presence, let alone my signature?"

"Um, Jackie, it is not our policy to release funds to only one person on the policy of a joint account. Let me verify what occurred on that day. Could you hold on a second so that I can pull your file?"

"Sure."

Mr. McAlston went to the closed accounts file cabinet to retrieve the Holmes files. Funny, that file was missing. It was customary procedure that when a file was closed, that all pertinent information be included in the file and that the file be placed into the secured cabinet by the close of the day. No exceptions.

Pressing the intercom, he paged his secretary. "Stacey, please bring me the Holmes files if they are still on your desk. The account was closed this past Monday but has yet to be filed."

"Sir, I haven't seen the files. I make it a habit to make sure that all closed files are secure at the end of each business day."

"Who was the personal banker that handled that transaction?"

"Rasheeda Montgomery, our top personal banker."

"Please check with her to locate the files. I have Mrs. Holmes on the telephone, wondering why a joint account was closed without her being present to sign the papers, especially due to the dollar amount involved. It appears that either someone else came in with her husband to forge her name, or one of our personal bankers decided to break policy. Either way, we are at fault. I need the files ASAP."

Punching the line that was on hold, Mr. McAlston took a deep breath as he tried to formulate in his mind, the correct way to divulge to a client and his best friend's daughter, that his bank had made a mistake.

"Jackie, thank you for waiting so patiently. Are you at home? Can you come down to the bank? The personal banker still has the file on her desk and I need to figure out what is going on."

"Certainly, Mr. Alston. I should be there within thirty minutes. Thank you for taking the time to help me."

After hanging up the telephone, his secretary walked into his office with the Holmes file. "Sir, here is the file that you requested. When I asked for the file, Rasheeda seemed a bit jumpy. Instead of the file being locked away in a drawer, she actually tried to pretend that she didn't pull the file from her personal briefcase. Something suspicious is certainly going on."

"Stacey, please have Monday's video tapes pulled for the entire day. I need proof that something underhanded or shady took place before I can fire her. This merger that we're attempting would make this bank three times the size that it currently is. We can't afford for one person to mess that up. Additionally, we need to see if other corruption has occurred that we are unaware of."

Stacey left to personally walk to the Security office. According to the office grapevine, Edward had the hots for Rasheeda and would do anything for her on the off chance that she would go out on a date with him. That's why she wanted to provide the element of surprise when she asked for the tape. Simply because he wouldn't have time to react.

Putting her security badge to the coder on the door, she gained entry into the Security Room. Looking at the camera's always fascinated her. Walking towards the bank of television screens that monitored the bank's activity, Stacey smiled.

"Hello Edward, Scott. We've got a rush job for you from Mr. McAlston. He's doing an audit on a few of the bank tellers this week. Can you pull the tapes for Friday and Monday? I'll wait for them."

Going to the files, Scott retrieved the files before Edward had a chance to move. "Here you go Ms. Stacey. Could I please get your signature on this clipboard?"

Signing the paperwork, Stacey smiled after accepting the tape. "Thanks Scott. By the way, were both of you here on Monday?"

"No ma'am. I was off. Only Edward was here. Did something happen?"

"Not that I'm aware of. Mr. McAlston keeps a record of the security team that was on duty the day of the audit. Again, thanks and I'll get these back to you as soon as possible."

As Mr. McAlston perused the file, he noticed that indeed there were two signatures on the required paperwork. Inspecting the file further, he noticed that the signature on the paperwork did not match the signature on the account's signature card. Red flag number one. It would be interesting to see who actually showed up with Mr. Holmes to sign the papers. That would be red flag number two.

A knock on the door indicated that Stacey had returned with the tapes. As Stacey loaded the tape, he reviewed the file to see when the transaction was made, so that they could fast forward the tape to that timeframe.

"Stacey, the time transaction on the withdrawal is twelve fifteen in the afternoon. Right during rush hour. Could you fast forward the tape to eleven thirty? Rasheeda would have needed to prepare the documents in advance so let's push the time frame to thirty minutes prior and see what happens."

"I took the liberty of pulling the tape for Friday also, in the event she prepared the documents a day earlier."

"Good thinking, Stacey. Her good for nothing husband has withdrawn all of their money out of the bank and managed somehow to withdraw the money from her trust fund as well."

At her gasp of surprise, Mr. McAlston grimaced in agreement.

"Stacey, please meet Mrs. Holmes at the elevators and escort her here, please. She's going to view the tapes with us."

At her startled look of surprise, Mr. McAlston shook his head. "If her husband withdrew this money from their joint account without her permission, she could press charges. We really do not need that type of publicity right now. Hopefully, the culprit responsible for the banks part in this fiasco doesn't know what Mrs. Holmes looks like to give them a heads up that we're suspicious."

Chapter 3

As she was riding the elevator up to the Executive Wing to the President's office, Jackie was a little apprehensive. Would she be able to recoup her money? Would she have to hire an attorney to get it back? What game was her husband playing? Why had he secretly withdrawn all of their money and put it into a separate account? Was it just for the house or was there another reason? Was he cheating on her? How had he accessed her trusts fund?

Fragments of an earlier conversation drifted through her mind as she waited for the elevator doors to open, of an unknown woman and her husband's voice in the background. She could not remember if she had met the woman at some charity event, a luncheon or if she met her one evening while they were entertaining. If she could put a face to the voice, she would then be able to pinpoint where the conversation took place. She never forgot a face.

Thankfully her thoughts were derailed when Mr. McAlston's secretary walked towards her as she stepped off the elevator. She didn't like the path that her thoughts were taking.

"How are you Jackie?" Stacey asked as she hugged her friend as she walked with her down the corridor to her father's office. "If you'll follow me, we can review the tapes together of the day your husband made the transaction."

Opening the double doors to the President's office, Mr. McAlston rushed to greet Jackie with a hug. "I'm sorry that we have to meet in such unfortunate circumstances. Come right on in and we'll get started so that we can get to the bottom of this."

Stacey, pushing several buttons, rewound the tape to show Mr. Holmes entering the bank with a woman, who was posing as his wife. The woman on the tape was of a similar height but that's where the resemblance ended. On the tape, the woman was approximately five feet, six inches tall in heels, with large breasts on a slim build, which appeared to be phony, even to the naked eye. Her complexion was the same, smooth brown skin without any blemishes, along with a long flowing mane of dark brown hair with reddish highlights.

Jackie, looking at the screen had to admit that the woman could pass for her is she was slightly larger.

Mr. McAlston was thinking the same thing, but also had a perplexed look on his face as he tried to think of the person that the woman on the tape reminded him of. She would be a dead ringer for Jackie if she was more curvaceous, more voluptuous. Jackie had turned into a beautiful, full-figured woman that was sexiness personified in Mr. McAlston's opinion. She had a husky voice that immediately put you in the mind of a sultry jazz singer. Her hair was shoulder length with attractive highlights that complemented her features.

Instead of wearing the provocative dress like the woman had on in the tape, that left little to the imagination, the woman before him had on a pantsuit with a red, lacy camisole top that peaked through the suit jacket that made a man want to rip off her jacket to see what was underneath that kept tantalizing him.

Mr. McAlston shook his head. What was wrong with him? He was a happily married man, not to mention the fact that he was fantasizing about his best friend's daughter; his young daughter at that. Chalking the experience up to simply appreciating a woman's figure, he refocused his attention on the matter at hand.

"You can see from the tape Jackie, that someone impersonated you to complete the withdrawal."

"How could the transaction go through without proper ID and without comparing that person's signature to the signature card on file?"

"That should never happen, Mrs. Holmes. We take our jobs here very seriously and follow strict guidelines when withdrawing large sums of money and when closing accounts. The only way this would have been possible is if that person was working with someone here at the bank."

"Are you telling me that one of your employees didn't follow procedure or was he/she responsible for actually helping my husband steal my money?"

"I'm merely explaining how things could have transpired without having the actual facts. Let's look at the tape more closely to see if the person impersonating you looks familiar to you or to us, meaning someone that works here at the bank."

The tape showed the couple, completing the paperwork in one loan officer's office after the woman signed whatever paperwork was displayed in front of her. Zooming in on the offices, they were able to see the couple leave Mr. Carson's office and then go and sit in Rasheeda's office even though she had not yet arrived at work.

Looking at her watch, the woman began talking. Mrs. Holmes, silent up until that point, asked that they play the tape with the audio turned on so that she could hear the voice and possibly identify it. As they listened to the tape, the woman explained that she had to go to work, and therefore since all the papers were signed, she would see them later.

Ten minutes after the woman left, Rasheeda walked into the bank, straight to her office. Immediately Jackie noticed the woman's shape, which only resembled the woman from the tape, height wise and by the complexion. With only a moderate sized chest, she couldn't be the accomplice. Just when she was about to give up, Stacey voiced her opinion.

"Why don't we listen to what Rasheeda and Mr. Holmes talk about before the transaction is finalized?"

As soon as the woman called Rasheeda started talking, Jackie experienced an epiphiany. That was the voice she heard on her husband's phone when she dialed his cellular number after Mr. Smith left their house with the threatening message of what would happen if he didn't receive his money.

Oh, *so he could possibly be cheating on me,* Jackie thought. She didn't have time to process the information fully as another clue was presented to her befuddled mind.

Rasheeda stepped around her desk to present the check to Maurice, lightly stroking his arm back and forth, the action spoke of a closer relationship than one of banker and client. The closer came when Jackie looked at the woman's shoes. They were a leopard print, black and red shoe that would have went well with the red provocative dress worn by the woman on the tape. It didn't however go well with the brown and blue suit that Rasheeda had on.

Looking at Stacey, who had rewound the tape, they instantly came to the same conclusion. The personal banker was the same woman (without the breast enhancements), that walked into the bank with her husband to close out their accounts.

Jumping up from her seat, Jackie started towards the door in a rage that the woman thought that she could get away with stealing her money. Before she could do anything drastic, Mr. McAlston grabbed her by the hand.

"Jackie, let me handle this. Let me apply pressure to her, that way, we can find out what Maurice is up too. That's the only way we will get you get your money back."

"No, Mr. McAlston. No disrespect intended. I need to handle this myself. I've lived with him telling me how to dress, when we first started dating; telling me how to behave when he entertained his clients. I could never do anything to his satisfaction. His food was never cooked like his mother cooked it. The list is endless. I felt it was my duty as a wife to help my husband succeed. When he spent so much time with me in the beginning, he had a plan. I was so stupid to believe that he loved me so much that all he wanted to do was spend time with me. Now I realize that his intention was to control me by distancing myself from my friends. For my self-esteem that has been eroded for so long, I need to finally handle my business."

Walking out of the room, Jackie marched to the elevator to go down into the lobby to confront her demons and to take control of her future.

Mr. McAlston calmly settled back in his seat. It had been a long time coming. Finally! Jackie was coming into her own. The blinders that she had on for the last five to six years regarding her husband were finally off.

Stacey looked at her boss who also happened to be her father and shook her head in disbelief. "Are you just going to let her go downstairs by herself? What do you think is going to happen when she confronts her?"

"Stacey, she needs to do this. She has to take control of her life. This is the first step to fighting for her freedom. Please go down, just to make sure that Rasheeda's office door is closed while they are talking. Once Jackie is finished, send Rasheeda and the branch manager up to my office. We need some answers and right now they are the key to recouping Jackie's trust fund."

Just as Rasheeda was getting ready to leave for her lunch date, the branch manager told her that she had one more client to service before she could leave.

Knowing that she couldn't meet her sweetie for their date, she pulled out her cellular phone to call him to cancel or delay their lunch date. With her back turned towards her office door, she didn't hear Jackie when she entered her office.

"Yes, can you connect me to Maurice Holmes, please?"

"Maurice, honey I can't meet you for lunch today. I have a last minute client."

Walking forward, Jackie waited until Maurice answered the phone before she snatched it from Rasheeda's hand.

"Maurice, that's right, Rasheeda can't meet with you for lunch today. I'm her last client."

Trying to get her phone back before all hell broke loose; Rasheeda lunged for her phone, after realizing who her last client was.

Jackie rushed on, "She's going to be tied up for a while, so you might want to cancel your late evening dinner plans also. She's going to be with her boss trying to explain how you closed all of our joint accounts and how she helped you swindle money from my trust fund."

"Uh, who is this?" Maurice asked into the phone, afraid to believe that the person on the other end was his wife. How did she find out?

Click. Jackie hung up on her husband.

"Now for you." Drawing her right hand back, Jackie punched Rasheeda squarely in the eye, and then followed with a punch to the nose, before leaving the office. "That should teach you to never snatch the phone from someone and that there is retribution for sleeping with someone's husband, while not immediate, it comes never the less."

Rasheeda stood motionless in shock. She couldn't believe that Jackie had actually hit her.

Her work done, Jackie calmly turned around and walked out of the office and out of the bank fuming; to hurt to cry.

The people that had gathered around outside Rasheeda's office due to the raised voices, actually cheered when Rasheeda walked out of her office, with a black eye, screaming at Jackie as she walked out of the bank without looking back. Since Rasheeda had always acted so uppity, the people were glad someone had brought her back down to earth.

At that moment, the security guard, Scott, walked up to Rasheeda who was attempting to run out of the bank after Jackie. Before she could make it to the door, Scott stopped her by stepping in her path. "Ms. Montgomery, Mr. McAlston wants to see you in his office."

"What does he want? I need to fix my face. Tell Mr. Carson that I'm going home for about thirty minutes. I can't see customers with my eye looking like this and my nose bleeding.

That heifer had better be glad that it's not broken. Just wait until I get out of this meeting. I'm going to press charges."

"Ms. Montgomery, Mr. McAlston wants to see you now. If you're not there within the next five minutes, you might as well kiss your job goodbye."

"Where is Mr. Carson?"

In the blink of an eye, the reason why Mr. McAlston wanted to see her clicked in. Putting two and two together, with Jackie's visit, and now with Mr. McAlston wanting to see her; it had to be about the closed accounts. *Well they couldn't trace anything back to her,* she thought, *especially the monies being depleted from the trust fund.* She had been very careful. If anything, everything would point towards Mr. Carson.

With her life in disarray, Jackie walked to her car, silently telling herself not to cry; that her husband wasn't worth it. To say that she was completely surprised would be an understatement. To say that she should have seen the signs: like working late hours, clients coming in at odd times then her husband would have to cancel dinner plans, the telephone ringing in the evening and someone hanging up whenever she answered, the frequent trips out of town; the list was endless. She berated herself for being so stupid.

Getting into the car, she drove aimlessly around town for several hours before her emotions got the best of her. She pulled her car into a nearby park and leaned on the steering wheel. Finally the tears that she had held at bay for the last two hours, coursed down her cheeks. What was she going to do now? Was her marriage worth saving? Could she forgive her husband? Why did he cheat on her?

She thought that things were going great. They had a nice house, her husband's business was going great, or so she thought. Their marriage had a few ups and downs but she didn't it was anything that they couldn't work out. Her husband had asked her to quit her job because he needed her to entertain his clients, which had been a cause of contention between them. She had finally decided to compromise and had applied for a job as a private duty nurse so that her schedule would be flexible. What more did he want?

The only other problem that existed in her marriage that she was aware of, was Maurice's inability to satisfy her. She had recently broached the subject with her husband about experimenting with different positions in bed, but to no avail. He steadfastly refused to consider that he wasn't the "Mac Daddy" in bed. Of course, now she knew why Maurice really didn't care whether or not he performed in bed; he was getting laid somewhere else. Finally, Jackie was able to realize that her husband was just as selfish in bed as he was out of bed. Their entire marriage had been based on a lie.

Muttering a brief prayer to God for guidance, Jackie contemplated her next move.

Chapter 4

Maurice left his office immediately after his wife hung up on him. If he didn't get the situation under control, by obtaining her silence, there wouldn't be enough of them to find to bury. On his way home, he noticed that his brakes were starting to squeak. He made a mental note to put the car in the shop. With everything that was on his mind, he didn't notice the coincidence with the car's brake failure.

If the police got wind that numerous crimes had been committed, then Mr. Smith would not hesitate to eliminate him. Driving at a fast pace, Maurice was thankful that he didn't get stopped for speeding. Pulling into the driveway, he pressed the button to raise the garage door.

Walking into the house, he dropped his keys on the counter and proceeded straight to his study. There he began to pace back and forth, waiting anxiously for his wife to come home. He even tried dialing her cellular number every ten minutes to see when she was coming home. After his calls went unanswered, he then telephoned Rasheeda at the bank. Getting her voice mail, he threw up his hands in frustration. *Where could she be? What was taking her so long to come home?* Maurice asked himself.

Taking a drink from the mini bar that he had setup in his study, he sat down upon the sofa to contemplate how he was going to convince his wife that the money he withdrew was put to good use for their future. Furthermore, he had to devise a plan to explain how the bank was at fault for the missing money in her trust fund.

Snapping his fingers, a thought hit him. Fear had always worked well with Jackie in the past; no need to change tactics now. If she thought that her family was in danger, she would do anything to keep them safe. All he needed was just a little more time for the coast to clear before he could fence the rest of the jewels on the black market. After the jewels were fenced, he wouldn't need his wife anymore. She would have served her purpose.

After she arrived home, and pulled into the garage, Jackie noticed that Maurice had already beaten her home. *I guess he's come to apologize and attempt to woo me back into submission,* thought Jackie. *Too bad he's in for a rude awakening.* She just wanted to go into the house and grab some clothes for the next couple of days, without any drama, before deciding what to do.

Maurice, anxious to start his damage control plan, met her in the garage, ever the contrite husband. "Sweetheart, where have you been for the last couple of hours? I was worried about you."

At her look of total disdain, and with a, "Humph", Jackie continued into their house.

Maurice, directly on her heels, grabbed her arm to turn her around to face him. He knew that he had his work cut out for him. Since the cat was literally out of the bag, he had some explaining to do. "Honey, can we discuss this? Things aren't always what they seem. There are a few things that I have to straighten out for you."

"What could you possibly have to say that could explain that the money in our joint accounts has been wiped clean and that my trust fund has been depleted?" Jackie asked angrily. "All with the help of that hussy you are sleeping with?"

"First of all, I'm not sleeping with Rasheeda, Jackie. Where did you get that idea? We have working lunches set up once a quarter to go over our investment portfolio. She was only calling me to cancel our quarterly lunch date." Maurice glibly lied.

"I beg to differ. Could you explain why she answered your telephone, the day that I called you, frantic that Mr. Smith had stopped by, threatening your life?"

"What the hell are you talking about?"

"I called you that day but you didn't answer. She did. I recognized the voice. I guess you were too busy enjoying yourself. Cell phones are a great tracing device. They record useful information, like the last outgoing number dialed. Thinking that I had gotten the number wrong because I was a little shaken, I immediately dialed your number again, but you were wise enough then to let the voice mail pick up. Too overwrought, I didn't put two and two together."

Realizing that he had gotten caught, Maurice still continued to lie his way out of the situation, becoming angrier by the second. "That doesn't prove anything. So a woman answered my phone. It doesn't mean that we were having an affair."

"No that in itself doesn't, but when I reviewed the tapes and saw you withdrawing our money and someone other than me posing as an accessory, that pretty much sealed the deal. I am going to the police to press charges as soon as I pack my bags."

He couldn't afford for her to go to the police. Too much was at stake. If they found out about her money then they would find out about the other money as well. He would have to hide her away for a while until he could beat her into cooperating.

Rushing towards Jackie as she started to leave the room, Maurice grabbed her from behind and delivered several punches to her face, then slammed her into the wall. As she fell to the ground, he then proceeded to kick her in the stomach until she cried out in pain. Enough to hurt her but not enough to kill her.

Jackie, at first, cowered on the floor in shock that her husband had hit her.

"Do you think that I will actually let you go to the police? I have too much at stake. This has been planned very carefully and you're not going to mess it up. I have Mr. Smith right where I want him. I just need a little more time before my next payoff and then he'll be out of our hair. Now get up so that we can discuss our next move rationally."

Looking disdainfully at her husband's outstretched hand from her position on the floor, Jackie remembered another such time when he had to help her up. Jackie asked rhetorically, "Is this what happened the last time I confronted you about Mr. Smith? I didn't really get in your way, did I? My subconscious knew you struck me, but I was too shocked to believe that you could do something like that to me. Now I know better."

Standing with his legs spread slightly apart, Maurice towered over his wife, unknowingly leaving himself in a very vulnerable position. "It's your fault that you make me so angry," he yelled. "Sometimes, I can't control what happens when I get this angry. As for the other time, I didn't do anything. You ran into me as I was turning around. You just happened to be in the way, running your mouth, as usual. It was a good thing that I didn't do any more damage than shove you against the wall. That's what happens when you get out of place."

With deadly accuracy and with all the force that she could muster, Jackie raised her leg and struck Maurice in his crown jewels.

Maurice collapsed to his knees; moaning in pain.

Scrambling to her feet, Jackie ran to the door, only to be dragged backwards by Maurice, who had somehow recovered enough to grab her foot. Jerking hard, she tumbled to the ground, grazing the side of her face against a table in the process.

Panting very hard, Maurice uttered, "Now that I have your attention, here's what I expect you to do. You are going to pack our bags for a two week vacation. Enough time for the heat to die down a little bit. If you decide to leave and go to the police, I want you to remember this; you will be responsible for the deaths of all your siblings and your parents. Mr. Smith has knowledge of each of their whereabouts and their daily activities. He will not hesitate to kill each of them if he thinks they are hindering him from attaining his money. Do you want that to happen? Do I have your cooperation?"

At Jackie's nod of yes, Maurice confiscated Jackie's cellular phone from her pocketbook, along with her keys and the remaining money that she had in her purse. Leaving nothing to chance, to ensure his wife's cooperation, Maurice reached into their bureau drawer to retrieve the gun that he had purchased for protection against Mr. Smith.

With her husband's back to her, in agonizing pain, Jackie crawled on her knees to the door, determined to escape. With her throbbing head and the ache in her jaw, she couldn't see straight. Shaking her head slightly to clear the cobwebs, to refocus, she reached for the door. Just as she was opening the door and slowly rising to her feet, she stopped in her tracks when she heard the distinct sound of a gun's bullet whizzing by her head.

Directly in front of her, a bullet now rested in the corridor's wall.

That bullet was meant for her! Her husband was crazy! Self preservation kicked in. *I don't want to die but I need to get away from this bastard. How can I do that without him killing me,* she thought?

"I meant what I said Jackie. We will be going on vacation for the next two weeks so get used to the idea. There is no escape unless you prefer death. The next time I shoot this gun, I won't miss."

"If you kill me, then you won't get to enjoy all that you've taken from me. You would be the number one suspect. Right now you may think that you hold all the cards but I'm praying that God will rescue me."

"Why don't you save your breath about what your God will do? I'm in control here. Go pack our bags. We have two hours to make it to the airport." He walked with her to their bedroom while she packed their clothes for their getaway.

Planning to use the house telephone when Maurice wasn't looking, Jackie was biding her time in order to escape. In excruciating pain, she managed to slowly pack their clothes.

Pleading for some relief of the pain, she told Maurice that she was going to soak in the Jacuzzi tub for about an hour.

"That's fine. I'll be right here when you finish." Sitting on the bed in their massive bedroom, Maurice telephoned the airlines to confirm that his flight to Aruba was still on schedule. Instead of taking Rasheeda for a little fling, he would just substitute Jackie. It didn't make a difference as long as his needs were met. Just maybe he could enjoy both of them in Aruba.

In the bathroom, Jackie started the water for the Jacuzzi. With the door cracked slightly, she was able to hear Maurice on the telephone. She couldn't tell whether he was using the house phone or whether he was using his cellular phone. Taking a chance, picked up the telephone in the bathroom, Jackie was horrified when she didn't hear the dial tone. Were the lines cut?

She had no way of contacting anyone to help her out of this nightmare!

Trying to calm her rapidly beating heart before she hyperventilated, she sat on the side of the tub and put her head between her legs. Agonizing pain shot through her body.

Breathe, she kept repeating to herself. *You can get out of this. It may just take a little time. Perhaps at the airport, I will have a chance to escape.* Sinking into the bathtub her main thought was soothing away some of the hurt that her husband had inflicted. She knew that she had a few bruised if not broken ribs. She would have to bandage them if she was going to be able to walk with any degree of normalcy.

Driving on the highway, as he was getting ready to take the airport exit, Maurice pressed on the brake pedal to avoid hitting the car in front of him that had come to a complete stop for no reason. When the car didn't slow down, he became somewhat alarmed. What was wrong? Why wouldn't the car stop? With barely enough room to swerve, he was able to ride the median without side swiping the car.

Looking over at her husband, Jackie thought that maybe he was trying to throw her out of the car. This man had completely gone mad, she thought, hugging the door and the seatbelt at the same time while praying for her safety.

Glad that he was able to prevent that accident, Maurice's concentration was on getting them to the airport in one piece before they missed their plane. Deciding to take the long-term parking lot to avoid having to make sudden stops, Maurice veered off the road to that exit. Pumping the brakes to stop at the stop sign produced no results. Pulling up the parking brake produced no results.

"Oh my God, the brakes have gone out! I knew I should have had them checked the other day when they seemed to go to the floor." Maurice exclaimed. Thinking quickly he let his foot off the gas, decelerating the car until it came to a complete stop. Thankfully, the road to long-term parking was similar to a highway. They weren't in danger of hitting anything. When the car finally came to a stop, he breathed a sigh of relief.

Too scared to move, with her chest heaving in fright, Jackie didn't think to escape until Maurice had grabbed the gun in his hand. He dared her to escape. Pulling out his cellular phone, he called AAA to get the car towed to a local garage. The airport shuttle bus then took them to the airport terminal.

Rasheeda was ushered to Mr. McAlston's office by the security guard named Scott, some thirty minutes later. After his departure, Mr. McAlston's secretary escorted her to the conference room.

Mr. McAlston did not hesitate to get right down to business.

"Rasheeda, would you care to tell me what the commotion was all about in the lobby?"

Without knowing how much Mr. McAlston knew, Rasheeda decided to play dumb. "Sir, a client's wife came in to confront me because her husband and I have quarterly lunches to discuss their portfolio." That was sticking as close to the truth as she could manage on such short notice.

"Oh? I was unaware that our bank offered that convenience for our clients. When did this bank start that policy?"

"Well, uh, Sir, I thought that if I could meet face-to-face with my clients on a regular basis, then they would gain a better understating of how I work and have some input in the decisions that are made regarding their portfolio."

"I see. Is Maurice Holmes is the only client that you have implemented this policy with?"

Okay things were not heading in the right direction. *How can I turn the tables on Mr. Carson and make him the fall guy?*

"Yes sir. I wanted to see how the program was progressing before adding any additional clients," Rasheeda offered quietly. "Pulling open her palm pilot from her pocketbook, Rasheeda used her stylus to open her calendar to see which clients were scheduled to come into the bank within the next couple of days. "I have Mrs. Adams and Mr. Sellers on my schedule for next week to start the quarterly meetings."

"Tell me, how long have you been seeing Mr. Holmes?" Mr. McAlston slyly questioned.

"With all due respect Sir, I don't think that's any of your business."

"Actually it is, Ms. Montgomery. When you started using your business credit card to book your quarterly lunch dates with Mr. Holmes, it became the bank's business. I believe that you misunderstood me, Ms. Montgomery. Let me rephrase my question. How long have you held your quarterly meetings?" Pulling out a computer printout of the business expenses for the past year, Mr. McAlston perused the file before laying it down in front of Rasheeda.

"I believe we've held them for the last six months. Mr. Holmes wanted to start his own firm, so we worked together to secure funding for that venture."

"I see. Just to reiterate our policy Ms. .Montgomery, here at McAlston Bank and Trust, personal favors are not bartered in order to gain nor retain clients. I also wanted to ask a few questions about the clients in your portfolio that have chosen to close their accounts. Could you explain what led them to sever all ties with us? Specifically, would it be possible for you to explain what occurred the day that Mr. Holmes closed his accounts?"

"Sir, I'm not sure what happened that day, it was so long ago."

"Perhaps I can refresh your memory. Stacey, could you run Monday's tape for me, please? Ms. Montgomery, please watch closely so that you can explain your actions."

As the video started rolling, the only reaction they were able to get out of Rasheeda, was an imperceptible widening of her eyes when Mr. Holmes walked into the bank accompanied by her, portraying to be his wife. How did they get the tape? Eugene was supposed to have destroyed it.

Watching her in disbelief, Mr. McAlston had to admire her poker face. She gave nothing away. All they had was circumstantial evidence, which wasn't enough to send her to prison for embezzlement. They needed more time in order to figure out her scheme. Until then, he would need to keep her close by, in order to set a trap for her and gain valuable information.

"Ms. Montgomery, can you identify the woman in the video? Did you follow proper procedure to verify the woman's signature with the signature card on file when the accounts were closed and the trust fund monies were released?"

"I believe proper procedure was followed sir. Mr. Carson handled the monetary transaction himself. If you'll look in the file sir, his signature is on the papers as well as mine. I just closed the accounts sir after he had distributed the funds. Unfortunately I assumed that he had verified everything. Is there something wrong sir?" Rasheeda asked innocently.

"Unfortunately, the proper procedure was not followed. After auditing several files, this one failed our audit test because the closing signature does not match the signature on the signature card. Since we're in the process of merging with another bank, all of our procedures must be strictly adhered too. We're having a meeting individually with all of our employees to make sure that our written polices are reflected in our everyday work. Thank you

Ms. Montgomery. Keep up the good job and remember, what you do for one client, you must do for all of your clients. I expect you to implement that policy with your other clients within the next sixty days."

"Yes sir."

After Rasheeda walked out of his office, Mr. McAlston quietly conversed with his daughter. "I wonder what her next move will be? Stacey, make a copy of that tape and send it to Mr. George at the police station to be kept as evidence on the case that we're building. Also please send Mr. Carson to my office when he returns from lunch so that we can get his version of the story. It appears that she's willing to use him as the scapegoat."

"Dad, how will Ms. Montgomery's fraudulent actions affect the impending merger?"

"In a negative way, I'm afraid. We probably will have to pullout of the merger or delay it. We don't know how many other clients were swindled out of their money nor do we know the number of people involved. Mr. Carson, of course is involved as we've seen from the video but someone else had to be working with them."

Picking up the telephone, he made contact with one of his friends that owned an auditing firm. "Sammy, I need you to audit the bank's books."

"Steve, we were going to do that during Phase 2 of the proposed merger. Why do you want to do that now?"

"We've just uncovered an employee scheme to defraud the bank. This takes precedence over the merger. We will either have to postpone it or delay it. When can your team arrive?"

"Steve, I can have a team come in tomorrow. You do realize the negative impacts this will have on the merger, right?"

"Unfortunately, I do but this is out of my control. I will just have to find another way to grow the bank, after I put in stronger safeguards to prevent this from occurring again."

"I know just the firm to do that. There's this new company called Secrets, who I'm told are the best in the security business. They come highly recommended. You should give them a call. If you'll hold on, I'll get the number for you."

"Thanks!"

Rasheeda, after escaping the bank with her job intact, drove home immediately and began putting plans in motion for the next phase of her million dollar getaway, as she commonly referred to her swindling project. Placing the call to her sister she hoped that with her assistance, her plans would be finalized.

"Cherita, I need a favor."

"Hello to you to big sister. What's up Rasheeda? I don't hear from you for several months and now you need a favor. Why should I help you?"

"Because I'm burnt out. I've been working so many hours at the bank, trying to improve my clients' portfolio, that I'm bone tired, fatigued, can't sleep and desperately in need of a vacation."

"So take one. You probably haven't taken any this year knowing you and your penchant for tying to make it to the top at all costs, even working yourself to death."

"That's just it. I can't take a vacation. We're in the process of merging with another bank and I don't have time. I need to be on top of my game just in case the top people of the merger decide to cut staff."

"All the more reason for you to stay. Quit stalling. What's the real reason you need me to play you? We haven't done that since we were in college."

"Okay, no sense trying to fool you. Actually everything I said is true. I have been working a lot of hours, but the main reason I wanted you to sub is that I'm getting married. Maurice and I are eloping."

A true romantic at heart, Cherita squealed into the telephone. "Why haven't I met Maurice before now? How long have you known him? How long have you been dating?"

"Slow down. I can't answer your questions if you keep asking so many. We've been dating for almost a year and a half, and I love him. He's smart, witty, owns his own investment firm and he treats me like a queen."

"Okay, if he's all that, why hasn't the family met him?"

"I didn't want the family to meet him because ya'll always complain about my taste in men. You always say they are no good, selfish leeches. So I didn't bring him around. This time I found a good man."

"So when are you eloping?"

"On Friday. So I need for you to come to drive down tomorrow so that I can brief you on everything, but you can't tell Mother."

"What's in it for me? You know that there will be hell to pay once she finds out."

"How about twenty thousand dollars? That will be a good down payment for you on a small office so that you can start your own graphic design firm."

"Wow, this guy must be rolling in money for you to offer me this kind of cash. Is this legal?" Cherita asked skeptically.

She had known Rasheeda all of her life and had been on the receiving end of some of her plots that had gone terribly wrong. The very idea that this could be another scheme with her ending up in trouble caused Cherita a moment of fear.

"Come on Cherita. It's legit. All you have to do is help clients with their banking issues and problems. That should be a piece of cake for you. Just remember when you were a branch manager at Wachovia. Plus, how long do you think it will take you to save twenty thousand dollars? Years at the pace you're going. Freelance is okay but you've got to setup an office and establish your presence if you want to get the big bucks.

Torn between her desire to start her own firm, and the past knowledge of being the brunt of her sister's antics, made Cherita hesitate. Rasheeda's last comment about her career helped her to reach a decision.

"Okay, I'll help, but only for two weeks. I want the money upfront, in cash."

"Done. However, you'll have to stay at my townhouse."

"Why?"

"You have to give the appearance of being me, remember?"

"Is your place clean or does it look like it did the last time I visited?"

"I'll hire a cleaning service to come in, okay? What time will you get here?"

Her sister lived in Washington, D.C. so it would take about six hours for her to reach Charlotte.

"I'll leave today and spend the night in a hotel and come by your place in the morning."

"Fine. I'll see you then. Drive safely."

Hanging up the telephone, Cherita wondered what she was getting herself into. Would she be able to survive the fallout?

After disconnecting the call with her sister, Rasheeda jumped up from the bed with glee. Little sister Cherita would help her in ways she couldn't even imagine.

Cherita was her total opposite. She was nice, cheerful, helpful yet somewhat reserved. In addition to being smart, she was a people person. If the interviews with the merger team took place while she was gone, Cherita would win them over. She would increase her portfolio simply because she was a whiz at making people feel comfortable and knew as much as she did about banking and stocks and bonds.

Plus, she would provide the perfect alibi when she decided to kill Mr. Carson because he was becoming a liability. Eugene on the other hand, still had work to do.

Picking up the telephone again, Rasheeda made two additional calls. The first one was to Eugene.

"Eugene, sweetie, I need a favor."

"What type of favor Rasheeda, and what do I get out of this?"

"Oh, I'll make it good for you sweetie. I need you to confiscate the bank's tape from last Monday and then erase it. It should be in Mr. McAlston's office. He was reviewing it today. Then take Saturday's tape and copy it onto the erased tape. That way, it'll look as if the wrong tape was put into the backup drive."

"Okay, that sounds easy enough. What do I get?"

"What do you want?"

"I want you to make love to you again and this time I need five thousand dollars. I need money to help my mother who is taking care of my sister's kids."

"Then consider your request granted. How about if I stop by tonight to give you half of the money and once you have accomplished your task, then I'll give you the other half?"

"That sounds like a plan. In fact, since I'm still at work, why don't you bring all the money and I'll give you the tape and just make a copy here for the bank."

"Sugar, that's music to my ears. Just make sure that no one sees you, especially Scott. I'll be by your place at midnight when you get off. Be ready and waiting for me because I can't wait to be with you."

Rasheeda then dialed Maurice's cellular phone. When he didn't answer after five rings, she hung up only to dial again five minutes later.

Oomph, his wife must have made it home. They are probably having an argument right now. Deciding to push the envelope, she called him again.

Chapter 5

Dialing Maurice's cellular number again, Rasheeda was surprised when he picked up on the first ring.

"Hello."

"Hey baby, it's me. How are things going?"

"Not good. We're just getting ready to go to the airport for a little impromptu vacation for two weeks."

"I thought that the vacation was going to be for us. What happened?"

"A little change of plans. Jackie's threatening to go to the police. That's why our plans have changed. I'm taking her to Aruba until the heat dies down. You're welcome to join me there. I can find a local to watch her when we get together."

"Do you want me to take care of her there?"

"No, we need her alive for a couple of weeks at least until we fence the rest of the jewels. I have everything planned, so don't worry. Have I ever let you down?"

"Not at all. I'll catch a flight out tomorrow and call you when I land. Ciao."

Cherita, after arriving in Charlotte later that evening, checked into a hotel and unpacked. To wipe away the grungy feeling of having spent the last six hours in a car, she took a quick relaxing shower. After dressing, she went down to the front desk to ask the hotel clerk for directions to the nearest library.

The trip to the library was to brush up on her banking and finance knowledge as well as to read any information on the companies participating in the upcoming merger. She wanted to be prepared for any business meetings that might occur regarding the merger.

As she was walking into the library, she spotted a gentleman heading towards another section of the library. Just from that quick glance, she smiled appreciatively. He was well dressed, with a body like Shemar Moore, but with a smooth, silky, midnight black complexion and curly hair.

She could just imagine her hands running through his curls. Shaking herself out of a trance that she had lapsed into, she continued towards the area where the newspapers were located. After reading several papers, she realized that there wasn't enough historical information readily available on the racks. She needed to research the history of both companies and in order to do that; she would need to go to the microfiche room.

Gathering her pocketbook, she located the designated room and was surprised to see the same gentleman that had previously caught her eye when she entered the building.

In order to investigate possible deposits into offshore accounts, Trevor needed Maurice Holmes account number and name of the bank, to be able to trace any activity. Since he didn't have that, he would have to hack into the SWIFT database; a repository that housed all offshore banks account code names and account numbers. Once the account codename and the account number were located, he would then be able to isolate the bank where the funds were deposited.

Typing several commands on his computer, at first he wasn't able to get the information that he needed. *Mr. Holmes had covered his track well,* thought Trevor. Not to be outdone, Trevor dug a little deeper, using his computer expertise and several random logarithms for possible codenames. After about thirty minutes, he was able to identify several alias codenames that Maurice Holmes had used.

With that knowledge he was able to locate several bank accounts that Maurice Holmes had used for his deposits. It was now time to trace all of the transactions to see if he had illegally gained the funds by swindling the clients at Cymballas.

With all of the transactions that appeared on the screen, Trevor knew that he was in for a long night. Minimizing one screen, he was able to start another program, called TraceMe that would monitor all transactions; any deposits or withdrawals of the accounts that were being traced and log them into the system. The best part about the program was that it would be invisible to any onlookers, offshore banks and foreign governments. When he originally developed the program for the government, his superior had requested additional programming so that if any of the accounts were part of a government investigation, an alert would flash across the screen.

Deciding that he needed a break, he ran his program, CoverMySteps, to disguise his trail from potential hackers that tried daily to circumvent the government's monitoring radar. Just as he was about to shut down his system, an alert flashed across the computer screen.

The accounts listed above are being monitored by Caleb Maine, a Jewelry and Gem (JAG) FBI agent, based out of the New York field office.

Trevor with his limited knowledge of the JAG program, decided to do a little more research. Logging onto the FBI site, he was able to learn that the JAG agents were responsible for investigating jewel robberies that often times involved multiple states and or countries. That's why the FBI was involved; they had the jurisdiction across the nation to bust the jewel thieves, which normally had ties to organized crime. The primary group that was listed on the FBI site was the South American Theft Group (SATG).

Reading further on the site, Trevor noted that the JAG program worked closely with the Jewelers' Security Alliance, the Jewelers' Mutual Insurance Company and the Gemological Institute of America to bring the thieves to justice. It was time for him to contact this Caleb Maine, but first he had to run all of this by his superior, Mr. Brownstone.

While he was on the FBI site, Trevor logged into the mainframe computer to leave a message for Mr. Brownstone that he needed to speak with him about the case that he was working on and asked if he could meet with him at ten o'clock the following morning. Knowing that an answer would be forthcoming within the hour, Trevor decided to leave and get something to eat.

Before he could meet with Mr. Browstone, he needed to identify all the players in the game. Since he was going out, he would head over to the local library first to see if their microfiche had information regarding any major jewelry heist that would have occurred recently, then afterwards, he would grab a bite to eat.

Arriving at the library, he went directly to the microfiche room to review old newspapers from around the world, mainly South Africa, Australia and Switzerland. After several hours he was able to locate some information about three heists that occurred within a ninety day span in South Africa and in Australia.

One heist involved the DeBeer mine in South Africa, one of the leading diamond exporters in the world and the rebels that tried to overtake the company. Roughly eighty percent of the world's diamonds came from the DeBeer mine. It was widely known that the rebels that had taken over a few of their smaller mines and ran their operations like sweatshops. The rebels' goal was to take control of the largest diamond manufacturer by any means necessary; usually with the help of heavy weapons.

The rebels who had been somewhat successful up until this point, threaten the miners, mostly poor Africans, who tried to make a decent days work with very long hours for very little money in the dangerous caves. The work was dangerous because the diamonds were plucked out of the cave walls, manually with chisels and picks and placed in barrels that ran along a conveyor belt. Workers were made to climb ladders to reach the diamonds and precious gems that were at the top of the mines. Heavy equipment couldn't be used because the areas in the mines were so narrow. Health issues were also cause for additional concern because of the drilling dust that was prevalent in the mines which could lead to the lung disease, silicosis. Due to the lack of proper ventilation and over exposure to heat, it was a miracle that anyone could work under those conditions.

As Trevor continued to read the article, he gasped in horror, at the atrocities that were occurring in Africa, all for the sake of selling diamonds. The rebels had set off an explosion in the caves in Catoca, during the height of the working day, which resulted in thousands of workers being killed. The explosion had been timed just right, around two o'clock in the afternoon, so that the morning and midday's barrels of the jewels had already been sent out of the caves. The barrels were in the process of being loaded into the trucks to be taken to the company's warehouse.

According to the article, the trucks that were carting the jewels had been hijacked and all the drivers had been killed. The explosion and the hijacking could never be pinned on the rebels. The case remained open and was currently still under investigation by Caleb Maine.

Printing the story, Trevor continued to research the information and articles on the second heist to see if there was a common denominator. As he was gathering information on the last jewelry heist, he looked up from the microfiche machine when several people walked into the room; one studious gentleman with a handful of books and a very beautiful woman with a drop dead gorgeous body.

Arrested by her beauty, he stared at her until she was seated at the machine closet to the wall. As she took her seat, she was interrupted by the studious gentleman, claiming that the machine in front of her was already taken. Not one to cause an argument when there was another available machine, Cherita picked up her belongings and moved to the next machine, beside Mr. Gorgeous, as she dubbed the fine gentleman, that had stared at her so intently when she entered the room.

When his eyes had connected with hers she felt a warm shiver of excitement cascade down her spine. *If he could do that with just a look, what would it be like to have his hands and lips upon hers,* she wondered.

"No way to find out," her conscience reminded her. "You are sworn off men, remember?"

Heading the warning by her conscience, Cherita settled at the machine, pulling out a tablet to jot down pertinent information pertaining to the merger and the financial history of the bank. As she gazed at the machine, she noticed that the screen was now black. Perplexed that the machine now seemed to be malfunctioning, she turned around to see if there were any staff members in the room. When her quest for help came up empty, Trevor decided to offer his assistance.

"Is there something wrong that perhaps I could help you with?" Mr. Gorgeous asked in a melodious voice. "I'm sorry, that was rude of me. My name is Trevor and I would be happy to help figure out what's wrong with your machine."

Glancing briefly into one of the most gorgeous faces that she had ever encountered, Cherita had to blink twice to clear her head before she could answer. "Thank you. Yes, you may. When I came into the room, all the machines seemed to be working. Now this one seems to be on the blink. I wonder why it stopped working. My name is Cherita by the way."

She briefly clasped the hand that Trevor had extended.

An unexpected current of electricity raced through Trevor's body. With a quick indrawn breath, that was barely perceptible, Trevor willed Cherita to look into his eyes to see if she felt it too. Having never felt that jolt of electricity before, he was taken aback. Why now? Why this person? Was she even single? With her looks, Trevor knew that he didn't stand a chance. She was probably married or engaged. There was no way that someone that fine could be unattached.

Immediately dropping his hand, Cherita pretended to search for something in her pocketbook. She didn't want Trevor to know how his touch had affected her. It was just a simple reaction, she told herself. She new that nothing would come of it; that no matter how much her mind wished, that that she couldn't attract the attention of a handsome, successful gentleman. History had always proven to be her enemy.

Men didn't want a full-figured, voluptuous woman. They always preferred her twin, Rasheeda with the tall, slim, willowy body. She was tired of competing for attention, first from her parents, then for friends, then for men; only to have them taken away from her, once Rasheeda knew that they were interested in her.

A pretty face was all they saw, not the whole package. Tired of being second best, Cherita decided that at least for one evening, she would get to enjoy the company of someone that at least seemed to appreciate her as a person.

"Let me take a look at it." Bending over the microfiche machine, Trevor pushed the plug tightly into the wall. The microfiche screen lit up once again. "Cherita, I believe your machine is working now. It was probably just the cord in the back that was loose. If I can be of any further assistance, please let me know."

Giving Trevor her one hundred watt smile, Cherita responded, "Thank you Trevor. Please don't think that this is a pick-up line, but if it's not too much to ask, can you show me how to use this machine? It's been awhile since I've had to use one."

Just the opening that he needed, Trevor thought. "Sure. If you'll scoot over here just a bit, I can walk you through how it works."

Sliding her chair next to his, Cherita leaned over slightly so that she could watch as Trevor demonstrated how to utilize the more modern version of the microfiche machine. Inhaling the scent of the exotic perfume that Cherita was wearing, Trevor was momentarily at a lost for words. Whatever perfume Cherita had on was simply divine. Shaking his head in an effort to refocus, he completed the demonstration.

"Thank you Trevor. Would it be presumptuous of me to thank you by offering a cup of coffee?"

"Not at all. I was just about to ask you the same thing. Is there any significant other that would object to us sharing a cup of coffee?" He asked, hoping that he would get an honest answer. Glancing at her hands, he checked to see if a wedding band was present. At least she wasn't wearing one and didn't have any visible signs of ever wearing one. Good.

"No, there isn't anyone that would object to us having coffee although I'm sure that your wife or girlfriend wouldn't appreciate you going out with another woman, even on a platonic date."

"I haven't been that fortunate to get married and unless you're applying for the job, I don't have a girlfriend or a significant other either. Can we go somewhere else to have this conversation?" Trevor asked, as he gazed around the room to see the gentleman at the other computer, clearly eases dropping on their conversation.

"It would be my pleasure. There's a coffee shop, Koko Mo's, around the corner. They even offer live jazz on occasions."

"How much time do you think that your research will take to look up?"

"Probably about thirty to forty five minutes. Are you almost finished with your research? I don't want to impose upon your time. If you need to leave that's fine." Cherita said, already distancing herself. Maybe this was Trevor's way of canceling their date.

"No, I'm not canceling our date."

How could he read her mind?

"I'm just trying to be conscientious and thinking that whatever brought you here had to be important. I simply wanted to give you enough time to accomplish your task."

"Are you always this nice?"

"Yes, I try to be." Smiling Trevor responded with a wink.

"Don't tell me I said that out loud! Sometimes, my thoughts are relayed into words even when I don't mean for them to be spoken aloud. I'm going to just sit here and wait for the hole in the floor to swallow me up. You might want to step aside so that you aren't taken too." Cherita then turned to the machine and began searching for the information on the merging bank.

Laughing hilariously, Trevor couldn't help liking everything about Cherita. She pleased him. She had a sense of humor, seemed down-to-earth, told the truth, even when it was unpopular, obviously was a professional, and was very beautiful. He wanted to learn as much about her as he could.

When his laughter subsided, he touched her shoulder to regain her attention. Another blaze of heat seared his hand. *Okay, the first touch wasn't my imagination.* He knew that Cherita felt it too, as her body unconsciously shuddered at his touch.

"Cherita, you have a good sense of humor. I like that."

"I wasn't trying to be funny," she responded in a small voice.

Looking earnestly into her eyes, Trevor quietly stated, "Never be afraid to say what you feel towards me. Since it's obvious that neither one of us is interested in getting any work done, why don't we go ahead and have that coffee?"

"Promise me that you won't get offended if my mouth talks before my brain can catch up?"

Throwing back his head, Trevor laughed again. Standing up, he pulled out Cherita's chair so that she could stand and gather her belongings.

Once she had gathered everything, with his hand lightly resting at the bend of her back, he escorted her from the library. Walking towards her car, a silver Lexus 450, Trevor explained, "If you'll lead the way, I'll follow you in my car to Koko Mo's. That way you can leave at any time if you feel uncomfortable."

"Thank you." Reaching up on her tiptoes, she placed a kiss on his cheek.

Driving the short distance to Koko Mo's, they pulled into the parking lot and parked their cars. Once they were inside the coffeehouse, they were pleasantly surprised to see that there was a jazz band playing that night. Tables and chairs had been moved to provide the band a stage.

After finding a table in a secluded corner of the room, they were able to sit down after placing their orders for a light appetizer of chicken wings and a triple chocolate cake dessert along with two exotic teas. Feeling the vibe of the music that was playing, Trevor couldn't resist asking Cherita if she wanted to dance. That would be a great excuse to get her into his arms, at least for a little while.

"Care to dance?"

Leaning towards him, Cherita whispered, "We can't. They don't have a dance floor."

"Why do you think that they removed the table and chairs to create an open space, directly in the front where the band is playing?" Trevor patiently asked.

Realizing that he was serious, Cherita smiled. "Okay, you got me. What makes you think that I can dance, though?"

"The way that you walk tells me that you have an inherent sexiness about you that says you would move well to any beat that you're given."

"Are we still talking about dancing?"

"That depends. Please dance with me. I feel a desperate need to have my arms around you in public, so that I can remain the gentleman that I've shown you I am."

Enjoying the repartee, Cherita was totally unprepared for Trevor's directness. *Did this gorgeous man just say that he couldn't wait to get his arms around ME?*

Holding out his hand, he stood and waited patiently for her to accept what was flowing between them.

Once again he read her thoughts. "Yes, I find you very attractive and stimulating. When we get back to the table, I would like for you to give me your telephone number so that we can continue seeing each other, if you desire. If there's one thing that you will find out about me, as you get to know me, is that I'm very direct and honest. I try not to play games with people's feelings and I hope to be treated likewise. I want to get to know you better. Before you say anything, let's just dance and you'll see what I mean."

Is this man for real? Cherita wondered.

Seductively, he whispered in her ear, as she stood. "You must work on that inner voice. Dance with me and I'll show you just how real you make me feel."

They blended into the couples that were already dancing to the music on the makeshift dance floor. Pulling her close, Trevor swayed to the beat. In perfect rhythm, they slow-dragged. It was as if her body was made specifically for him.

He wondered if this was how Max and TJ felt, when they first met and became attracted to their wives. Having been around Max and TJ for the last ten years, he was at a point in his life where he wanted what they had; the love of a good woman who loved him beyond measure.

A wife that he could come home too. A marriage that was strong.

Of course he didn't want to go through what they had to go through to finally be happy with the woman of their dreams.

As the song ended and segued into another more up-tempo dance, Cherita and Trevor remained on the dance floor.

"Show me what you're working with," she demanded, laughing as she finally relaxed, and began to have fun.

"Oh, it's like that now?" Instead of doing the latest dances, Trevor pulled her tighter into his arms then released her into a full swing, only to twirl her back towards him, without even missing a beat.

Flowing effortlessly with his moves, Cherita threw back her head to enjoy the moment. With her upturned face, Trevor, bent towards her ear and whispered, "Don't ask for anything that you're not prepared to receive." Ever so quickly, he lightly placed a kiss on her lips.

What started as a quick peck to tease Cherita, turned into something neither one of them had bargained for.

A fire so fierce raged through Trevor's veins. He felt as if he were being consumed. Never before in his life had he felt the need that was coursing through his veins. As the blood rushed throughout his body, so did the impact of Cherita's kiss.

With his tongue wrapped around hers, Cherita felt an ache begin to build within her that only he could assuage. Never before had she been so fully aware of a man. Her body hungered for more of his touch.

The crescendo of the music broke them apart, as well as the need to breathe air into their deprived lungs. Swinging back into the rhythm of the music, they continued to dance, closer than ever before. Looking around, Cherita noticed that other couples were behaving just as they were. Most were simply just staring into their significant other's eyes with passion and love.

In a voice that was hurried and breathless, Cherita asked, "What else to do you have to show me?"

"All that I am. Anything that you want to see. Am I feeling this all alone?"

With an intense stare into his eyes, she shook her head no.

Grabbing her hand, he led her back to their table. "Do you want to wait for the food and eat it here or do you want to go somewhere else?"

"I hate to be a killjoy, but I skipped breakfast, since I was on the road, and I'm really hungry."

"Then feed you I shall do. I'll be right back." Going to the counter, he paid for their food. Luckily, God must have been shining on him because their food came up just as he was about to go back to the table.

Cherita watched as Trevor walked away. *What was she doing, she wondered?* She was about to go somewhere with a total stranger.

For just a little while, maybe she would know the meaning of being comforted, of being loved, for the person that she was, of having something without it being taken away from her. Experience had taught her that you had to grab the precious moments in life whenever they occurred, because they were fleeting and didn't come around very often. However just this once, she wanted a little piece of heaven.

Setting the food on the table, Trevor smiled. "Are you still with me?"

With a hand clasped to her forehead, mimicking a near-faint, Cherita resorted to humor to ease her nervousness. "Barely. Do you think that I'm going to let all that food go to waste? Not as hungry as I am. Feed me Trevor, feed me!" Cherita sang in the voice of Seymour from *The Little Shop of Horrors*, a movie that she grew up on.

With his hand on his hip, Trevor retorted, "You've still got jokes. So it's like that? You don't want me for my money nor my good looks; just for the food that I can buy for you. Well, eat up little Seymour Jr."

Cherita placed a provocative kiss on Trevor's lips. "For this night, I want everything that you have to offer."

"In that case let's hurry up and eat. You're going to need all of the energy that you can get, so behave; otherwise the patrons here will see a different show than the one they paid for."

After saying grace, Trevor dug into his food. Eating became difficult for Cherita due to Trevor's leg constantly brushing hers, since they were sitting so close together in the tight confines of the booth. Feeling his muscular leg against her thigh, caused an intensifying need to build within Cherita, so much that she stopped eating after taking several bites of her appetizer.

Sensitive to her mood, Trevor gazed deeply into her eyes. "What's wrong? Is the food not to your liking? Is it not done enough? Tell me what it is and I'll fix it for you."

Standing, he gathered her plate into his hands and was about to take it to the counter when Cherita grabbed his hand. "The food's not the problem," she explained with a slight tremor in her voice.

"What is it? Do you feel sick?"

Embarrassed, Cherita mumbled that she was ready to leave.

Lifting her chin with the tip of his forefinger, Trevor gazed deeply into her eyes to see if he could decipher what had gone wrong. She was with him up until the point of when they started eating. Was she having second thoughts?

"Talk to me. Tell me what's wrong."

Whispering in a soft voice, Cherita exclaimed, "Umm, I can't concentrate on eating with your leg rubbing against mine without wanting to taste every inch of you."

Coughing, Trevor choked on his food at her response. "Is that any different than me wanting to be the chicken that you are savoring with each bite? I think that it's time we leave. Where do you want to go? To your place, to mine or to a hotel?"

"Whichever one is the closest."

Chapter 6

Pulling into The Courtyard by Marriott's parking lot, Trevor reflected a moment on what he was about to do. Never before had he slept with a woman on the first date. His mother and father had raised him to respect women, but the fire that Cherita started inside of him couldn't be quenched. Throughout their impromptu snack, small flames had been started with every touch of her hand, every laugh, every smile. In fact, it was burning out of control, licking at his insides, ready to ignite with just a simple touch.

Cherita, who had pulled into the parking space beside Trevor, wasn't having similar thoughts. She wanted to experience her heaven here on earth for the very first time, with Trevor. Stepping out of the car, as he held the door open for her, Cherita smiled. "Thank you. You are such a gentleman."

After closing her car door and making sure that her vehicle was secure, Trevor turned to face her. "Hopefully you'll feel the same way in the morning. Am I to take it that you've never done this before on the first date?"

"How did you know? Am I that transparent?" She asked worriedly.

"Believe it or not, I have never felt this urgency to become one with another person, so soon after meeting them, in my entire life. It's as if my body is already acquainted with yours. See, it's instinctive. I can't help but touch you." Trevor explained, as his hands rose to cup her face, slowly allowing the distance between them to close, as his lips unerringly found hers in a provocative mating of their tongues.

If this is a line, then I'm falling hook, line and sinker. I want to just bask in the moment a little while longer.

Knocking on his superior's door, Trevor advanced into his office, slightly early for their ten o'clock appointment.

"Trevor, what were you able to find out about the embezzlement case for Cymballas Corporation?"

"Mr. B., I think that Max should be a part of this meeting. It involves someone close to him."

Pressing the intercom on his desk, he asked his secretary to page Max to join him and Trevor in the conference room. After walking into the conference room, Mr. B secured the room with a radio frequency that prohibited their conversation from being overhead or intercepted. "Trevor, you seem a little preoccupied. Is there something wrong?"

"No sir. Just have a lot of things on my mind."

Less than five minutes later, Max walked into the conference room with a smile on his face, once he saw Trevor. Greeting him with the "brother's handshake," they both sat down at the long table, facing their boss.

"Mr. B, Max, as you both know, I've been working on the embezzlement case for Cymballas Corporation for the last couple of weeks as a personal favor to a friend. It seems as if one of their top investment bankers is embezzling or rather diverting money from the client's portfolio to several offshore bank accounts. This person who had performed at the top of the company, made partner very quickly in the firm and then became greedy and chose to help himself to other people's money."

"After reviewing the stocks that were chosen for the clients, it was deemed that the stocks had performed well. Based on the market, there wasn't any reason for the client's portfolio to be decreasing. Of course the corporation chose to confer with the investment banker to see if there were other extenuating circumstances that would attribute to the decline in value in his portfolio. No answer was forthcoming, so they placed him on probation, thinking that I would have enough time to find some evidence that would point to the crime. The gentleman must have gotten scared that he was going to go to jail, because miraculously, those same clients portfolio seemed to increase overnight. The following week, this gentleman resigned and started his own firm."

Mentally skimming his mind to see why that Corporation's name sounded so familiar, Max questioned aloud, "Trevor, what's the name of the gentleman that's responsible?"

"Max, it's your brother-in-law, Maurice Holmes, Jackie's husband." Throwing up his hands, he requested, "Wait before you start asking questions; there's more. He's not working alone. It appears that he has an accomplice, a personal banker by the name of Rasheeda Montgomery, who works at McAlston's Bank and Trust. She appears to be spooning money from the banks clients into the same offshore accounts. For the last two years, Maurice and Rasheeda have diverted about five million dollars into these offshore accounts."

Remembering that McAlston's was Chelsea's family main banking institution, Max became concerned. "Trevor, do you realize that most of Chelsea's family uses that bank? It's owned by their father's best friend, who is an upright, honest citizen. If I'm not mistaken, Frank received a call yesterday at Secrets for us to review their security measures due to possible employee theft. Hold on a second so I can confirm that the bank is the same one."

Max pulled out his cellular phone and contacted his partner at the Bureau and for their security company Secrets. After a couple of pertinent questions, Frank confirmed that McAlstons was indeed the bank that had hired them to review their records and their security measures.

Hanging up the telephone, Max explained what Frank had relayed to him.

"No, I hadn't gotten that far yet. What I discovered though causes the plot to thicken. As I was locating the owner's names of these offshore accounts, I discovered that these same accounts were being used to fund money to the Unita Rebels, who the papers claim were responsible for the jewelry heist at the DeBeer mine in Africa a couple of months ago."

"The jewelry heist was valued at about twenty million. Caleb Maine, one of our agents in the JAG program based out of New York, is working on this investigation. Unfortunately, at this time, the cops and the FBI have not been able to prove that the Unita Rebels were responsible." Mr. Brownstone offered.

Pacing back and forth, Max was astonished that his brother-in-law had the guts to do something of this caliber. He didn't come across as being that smart. Having never liked the way he treated his wife's sister, he was determined to make him pay for his transgressions. He would do everything within his power to make sure that Maurice didn't drag Jackie's name into the mud, or attempt to frame her for crimes that he committed.

"Let's video conference Caleb and John, his boss, in on this conversation to see if they can shed some light on the investigation." Dialing the telephone number to the New York office, John came onto the line immediately.

"Sam, it's good to hear from you. How's Mrs. Brownstone?"

"Wonderful and how's your family and the kids?"

"Great. How can I help you today?"

"Can you get Caleb Maine to join you on this video conference call?"

"Sure, it'll take a couple of minutes. Let us call you back once we're got everything setup."

Ten minutes later, Mr. Brownstone's secretary transferred John's call to the conference room.

"John, let me introduce everyone. You already know Max and this is Trevor, our computer genius."

"Trevor, it's great to finally put a face to the name. Your help has been invaluable to our team on numerous occasions. Gentlemen, this is Caleb Maine, our best agent in the JAG program."

"It's an honor for me to meet both of you. Your work ethic is impeccable and I've chronicled your progress for quite some time."

"John, let me explain what we're after. A few weeks ago, Trevor began tracking the offshore accounts for an embezzlement case. Yesterday after some additional investigating, he discovered that the offshore accounts in question tie back to the accounts that are being used to fund the Unita Rebel activity in Africa. We have reason to believe that the person for the embezzlement case is one of the people responsible for the jewelry heist. Can we combine our forces and work together on this case?"

"I'm glad that you asked Mr. Brownstone. We've been tracking the sale of the jewels for the last six months but only a handful of the diamonds have surfaced. Trevor's expertise will come in handy on this case." Caleb responded, alert to the tense body language that both Max and Trevor were displaying.

"Caleb, we need to explain a few other issues with this case, just so that you know what you're walking into. It appears that my brother-in-law, Maurice Holmes, of whom I'm not particularly fond of, is one of the suspects in this case. Since I've been so busy working on another major case, trying to catch the Chameleons, to save our operatives in the field from being killed, I haven't been around the family for any extended periods of time in order to pick up on his behavior. I apologize."

"No apology needed Max. Thank you for being honest about your connection to the suspect. What do you want us to do now?"

"Trevor, why don't we plan for you to work undercover on this case? I need for you to pose as a gentleman needing financial guidance for his portfolio at McAlstons. When you have access to the personal banker's office, why don't you run your program to trace her keystrokes and determine which accounts she's swindled the money from? That way we'll have more concrete evidence of the embezzlement."

"Caleb, it might be a good idea for you to pack your bags and visit Charlotte for a while. That way with all of us working closely together, we'll be able to close this case. My instinct tells me that another heist is being planned soon. If we follow Maurice close enough, I guarantee that he will lead us to the mastermind behind the jewelry heist as well as to the diamonds."

Conferring quietly with his boss, Caleb didn't object to working with two of the youngest and brightest agents in the field, as well as visiting his family in Charlotte.

"I'll take a flight out tomorrow and check in with you guys then."

"Thanks Caleb. Max and Trevor, check in daily. I've got to discuss some other things with John, so I'll touch base with each of you tomorrow."

With their marching orders, Max and Trevor left the conference room.

"Max, can I talk to you a minute?"

"What's up Trev? You seem a bit preoccupied. Is something wrong?"

"Can I ask you something personal?" Since Max had pulled him from the depths of a world of crime, mainly as a computer mercenary, hacking into computers worldwide for a fee, Trevor had always looked upon him has his mentor and friend.

"Trev, you know that you can ask me anything." Max was concerned at the unrest in Trevor's expression when he gazed into his troubled eyes,

"How did you know that you were in love with Chelsea?"

"When I first met her, I knew that she would be important in my life. I didn't how, but my heart knew. I couldn't keep my mind off her. Then when I finally decided to do something about it, regardless of what protocol dictated, I knew she meant the world to me. She matched me in so many ways. Her intellect stimulated me, her caring and unselfish love soothed me, her humor encouraged me in dire situations, not to mention she stirred my soul. Making love to her is like heaven here on earth; something that I had never felt before until I met her. Trev?"

Trevor gazed off into the distance, thinking that Max had pretty much explained what he had experienced the night before with Cherita.

His flashback...

Moving quietly, hardly making a sound, Cherita inched her body away from Trevor's. No easy task, since their limbs were still entangled with each others, as if they slept that way every night. Leaving the cocoon of his warmth caused her a moment of uncertainty. Was she doing the right thing? Should she stay and face him in the morning? How would he act? How was a person supposed to act, the morning after?

There was a reason why she didn't know the answers to her questions. The night had been one of many firsts; the first time that she had slept with a man, on the first date or otherwise, the first time that she had experienced an orgasm, no make that multiple orgasms, and the first time that she had fallen in love. Was everything that she had experienced over the last couple of hours normal? How could she be in love with someone that she had just met? She didn't believe in love at first sight.

Deciding that she needed time to come to grips with her emotions, she eased out of bed, gathered her clothes and tiptoed into the other part of the suite. Hurriedly she began to dress, only to freeze upon hearing his sleep laden, husky voice from the doorway.

"Where do you think you're going?" Trevor asked as he leaned against the doorframe, with only his jeans hugging his body. He had only donned them to save her from embarrassment in his haste to stop her from leaving him.

"Uh, I need some time to think," she replied honestly.

"Can't you think, lying in bed beside me, with my body cradling yours? With my lips ever so gently raining kisses all over your sweet body? With my hands following every path, touching and caressing you, bringing your body to a fever pitch? With me entering you from behind, in an attempt to assuage the fire that just keeps building, never dying down? Then when you think that you can't take anymore, as you drift off to sleep, I remain inside of you, strong and heavy, willing and waiting for you, to respond. What's there to think about except how we make each other feel?"

Inside of answering his questions, she asked one of her own. "How did you know that I was gone?"

"I was awake, savoring what we had just shared, trying to see if I should subject you to my desires or let you sleep, when you got up. I watched you try to sneak away, willing your mind to reconsider; to come back to me."

"I can't handle this! I can't handle you! You are a figment of my imagination! You are not real!" she screamed on the inside, as she searched for her bra and her panties. To intent on clothing herself so that she could escape, she didn't hear Trevor move until it was too late.

As if he heard her innermost thoughts, he moved directly in front of her to still her movements. Putting his finger under her chin, he lifted her downcast face to meet his eyes. "Yes, what we felt was real. Yes, you can handle anything that I throw your way. You proved that over the last four hours. Why run from it? Why not see where this leads?"

Without touching her with his hands, he let his lips speak their own intimate language. He surrounded her with his heat by lightly stroking her skin with tender kisses to her shoulder that was still bare. Next, he began an assault on her senses.

She quivered from his touch. *Move*, she told her muscles, before you...

Her mind could not formulate another thought, as he showered her neck with the same soft, whisper like caresses, making her head roll backward to rest on his shoulder. Tilting his head to the side, he captured her mouth in a steamy, mind-blowing, searing kiss. No longer content to use only his lips, he gently placed his hands on her breasts, stroking them, kneading them, bringing them to a harden peak yet again.

Her body, seeming to have a mind of its own, rubbed against his already aroused shaft, in a circular motion, each action emulating everything that he had taught her. At his swift intake of breath, she knew that he wanted her with an intensity that surpassed their previous mating.

Backing against the wall, he braced himself as he picked Cherita up from behind, and drove into her. She clenched around him, drawing him even further into her satin heat. Moving with instincts as old as time, Cherita met him stroke for stroke. Like a madman, he kept thrusting into her, again and again; unto they both screamed each other's name as they rode the waves of ecstasy.

When Trevor awoke, as the sun peaked above the horizon, Cherita was gone. Scrambling out of bed, Trevor reached into the pocket of his pants, searching in vain for the card that Cherita had given him with her telephone number on it. Coming up empty, he searched his wallet. Sighing with relief, he pulled out her card and immediately dialed her number.

When her voicemail clicked on, Trevor left a message. "Cherita, this is Trevor. You left before I woke up. Why? We could have watched the sun rise together. Call me, please, when you get in so that I won't worry about you making it home safely." Trevor ended the call after leaving several telephone numbers where she could reach him, just in case she had thrown his number away.

At that point there wasn't any sense staying in bed so he showered, dressed and then settled the bill with the hotel. It was only when he was finished checking out that he remembered that Cherita was in Charlotte, house sitting for two weeks at her sister's place.

Slapping his hands into his fist, he muttered a sarcastic comment out loud, "Great! You have the most fantastic night of your life with a woman that's witty, beautiful, smart, has a sense of humor, and you have no way of getting in touch with her to start dating her properly."

"Trevor. Trevor." Max had to repeat his name twice before he got his attention. "Care to share what's on your mind?"

"I met a woman last night that evoked emotions in me that I've never felt before. Everything that you've just said, is how she makes me feel. That's what has me so blown away; I don't believe in love at first sight. I'm trying to figure out if she was real or a figment of my imagination."

"What's her name, where did you meet her and are you telling me that you slept with her on the first date?" Max asked in surprise. As long as he had known Trevor, he was very conscientious about the women he slept with. Usually, it was several weeks, sometimes months before he took that crucial step. This was out of character for him.

"Her name is Cherita and she's visiting her sister for two weeks in Charlotte. I met her at the library while I was looking up information on the jewelry heist. After I helped her with the microfiche machine, we hit it off right away. Then we had a cup of coffee at Koko Mo's; her way of thanking me. One thing led to another, and we ended up at The Courtyard. It was surreal; like there was a fever rushing inside my blood that had to be quenched. When I woke up, she was trying to disappear, I guess, having second thoughts about sleeping with a virtual stranger. I know what she was thinking, because I have an uncanny knack of reading her thoughts. It had been happening all night long, as if she had spoken aloud. Am I crazy?"

Patting Trevor on the back, Max smiled. "Welcome to the wonderful and sometimes painful world of Love. Chelsea and I have moments like that too. When do we get to meet her?"

"Your guess is as good as mine."

At Max's questioning glance, Trevor grimaced.

"Once I caught her trying to put her clothes on, I had to convince her to stay. Then we made love again and I fell asleep. When I awoke the second time, she was gone. I didn't get the telephone number of her sister's place, only her information for her house in DC."

"Did you call that number to see if she gave you the correct or a bogus number?"

"Yes. It's her number and I even have her address. Unfortunately, that's not doing me any good for the next two weeks while she's in Charlotte."

"What do you plan on doing? From what you've explained, I don't think that you can wait that long to see her. I remember only to well, those feelings. I used to break my neck, coming to see Chelsea from Georgia. Are you going to investigate her to get the information that you need?"

"No, I'm no longer the kid that you rescued, hacking his way into every known computer just for money. I won't resort to investigating someone that could potentially be my soul mate. I guess, I'll just have to look for her the old fashioned way by visiting every library in Charlotte if need be, for the next two weeks. Until then, I'll leave a message every day hoping that she'll return my call. If that doesn't work, I'll camp out on her doorstep in Washington, once we've implemented the trap for the personal banker at McAlston's Bank and Trust. If I fail, then and only then, will I use whatever means necessary to find the woman who has somehow captured my heart."

Hitting Trevor on the shoulder in encouragement, Max reminded him, "Sounds like you've got it bad. Welcome to the club. Let me know if there's anything that Chelsea and I can do. Even though my plate is still pretty full, trying to look for the Chameleons, I'll make time if you need me."

"Thanks, that means a lot to me. I'll let you know if anything happens."

Chapter 7

Late in the midnight hour, Isabelle, Jackie's aging grandmother, had a dream that Jackie was in trouble. Waking up from a deep sleep, she sat straight up in the middle of the bed in fright. Breathing heavily, she was barely able to gasp air into her lungs. With a rapid heartbeat, she slowly eased out of bed. *He's abusing her. Water. I need some water, or something to calm my nerves.* Going into the kitchen she prepared herself some tea to steady herself.

Hearing someone in the kitchen, Isabelle's daughter, Jackie's mother, Erma, went downstairs to see if something was wrong. Her mother had come to stay with them after becoming very ill the previous year. "Momma, why are you up? What's wrong?"

"I had a vision that Jackie's in trouble. Her husband's abusing her." At her daughter's gasp of surprise, Isabelle, tried to offer some assurance.

"I don't think that it's been going on for too long. Have you heard from her since she moved? I don't trust that husband of hers. I never have."

"Yes ma'am. I've talked to her but she didn't sound good. I was planning a visit this weekend but I can't reach her. None of the other kids have heard from her either. That's strange. She's usually in touch at least every other day with one of us. We'll just get in the car tomorrow, very early, and drive to Charlotte to see her. If you're right, she's coming back with us and I'll let the boys handle Maurice."

Having been up for the better part of the night, because Chelsea had slept restlessly, due to her belief that something was wrong with Jackie, Max decided to get some work done. It must be a heredity thing, since both her mother and grandmother had called during the night with the same dream or thought. He didn't know what was wrong, but he intended to find out.

Easing out of bed, he went into his office to work. As he was working on the case, something didn't seem right. He kept going over everything in his head. Why wouldn't Jackie return any of their calls? Even if she went on vacation, she would always let someone know. Pulling his cellular phone out he contacted Trevor.

"Trevor, I hate to disturb you at this hour but something's going on. Jackie is in some kind of trouble. Chelsea, her mother and grandmother, all had the same dream last night about Maurice abusing Jackie. No one has been able to contact her and she didn't report for work this morning. Can we meet at eight o'clock at your house?"

"Yeah, I really didn't sleep that much myself."

Going back into his bedroom to check on his wife, he saw that she was still restless. Slipping back in bed, he held her close in his arms and slowly she was able to relax and together they drifted off to sleep for a few more hours.

The next morning, Max decided to try an idea that came to him while he was sleeping. Picking up the telephone, he asked Trevor to meet him at the office within thirty minutes.

Due to the dangerous nature of their jobs, as a safeguard for all of their family members, including his wife's extended family, Max and Trevor had installed a program similar to Goggle Earth to run daily, where a satellite would zero in on all the addresses within a database and monitor any external activity. The program would take photos, at various intervals, within a twenty-four hour period, of all the people entering and exiting the house. This information would be stored on a computer server at Secrets headquarters, available for retrieval at any given moment.

Logging onto the computer in the conference room at the office, Max was able to remotely retrieve the information from his server. Typing in several commands, he inputted Jackie's address and the current weeks date range into the computer, to visually show all the activity that the program was able to capture. After reviewing the activity, they noticed Maurice escorting Jackie out of their house, with a gun to her back. Checking the date stamp on the program they were dismayed that the photo was taken two days ago.

Knowing that time was of the essence, they had to act fast in order to find her alive.

Ending their meeting with Mr. Brownstone after they updated him with the new information, Max and Trevor immediately caught a flight to Charlotte from DC to survey Maurice and Jackie's house for clues as to where her husband had taken her. Trying to contact the airlines was useless. Ever since the tragedy of September eleventh, no longer could the airlines verify if a passenger was on board or not. Max and Trevor hoped that Jackie was able to devise a clever way to conceal a clue that would help lead them to her.

Leaving no stone unturned, they searched the entire downstairs of the house before moving their search upstairs. Looking at the damaged walls, they could see signs that a struggle had occurred. Feeling angry and frustrated, they sped up their efforts to locate anything that would lead to their whereabouts.

Deciding to start in the master bedroom, they continued to see patterns of a struggle. Max, looking closely at the struggle pattern, noticed a stray bullet in the wall, leading out of the bedroom. He didn't know if other rounds had been fired or if his sister-in-law was hurt or wounded. They had to find her alive!

Walking into the master bathroom, Trevor noticed the makeup on the counter. At first glance, he knew based on what they saw in the house that Jackie had been beaten pretty badly if she needed to cover up some bruises. On closer inspection of the countertop, he noticed a pattern in the makeup.

"Max, I think I've found something. Come into the bathroom."

Hurrying into the bathroom, Max looked at the shavings that Trevor was pointing too. "I believe that she was trying to give us a clue to their destination. It looks as if it's Aruba."

"Even though its kind of fuzzy, I agree."

Getting on the telephone, and by pulling some connections, Max had some agents to discreetly check into the local hotels in Aruba, to see if they spotted the couple. Since there were a plethora of hotels in Aruba, it would take some time before they would be able to identify the correct hotel.

After several hours, the FBI agents located the correct hotel after talking to a bellhop named Antonio, who happened to be at the desk when they were inquiring about the couple. He took them outside, explaining that the couple had not been seen since check-in. He told them that he had observed the couple, but nothing seemed out of the ordinary but assured them that he would keep an out for the couple.

A was to escape at the airport did not present itself. Jackie went to go to the ladies room with the hope of enlisting the help of an airport worker in or near the restrooms but didn't have any luck. Maurice simply followed her into the restroom, claiming that his wife was sick and that no one should enter the restroom so that he could help her with her morning sickness. All of the women present left the bathroom with handclaps, saying that she was lucky to have such a conscientious husband.

From then until it was time to board the plane, Maurice kept a close eye on her and never let her leave his side. Once the plane landed in Aruba, they were able to secure a cab to take them to the hotel. At the hotel desk, as Maurice was checking them in, a distinguished, well dressed man came up to Jackie and lifted her off her feet with a bear hug and a kiss to the cheek.

Exclaiming in surprise, and wincing in pain as he swung her around in a circle, Jackie smiled briefly when she recognized Stan, one of her best friends from her sophomore year in college. At lease he was her best friend until Maurice ran everyone away.

Things are always clearer in hindsight.

Hearing his wife's gasp of surprise, Maurice turned around to see that a strange man was hugging his wife. Hurriedly striding over to his wife, Maurice demanded, "What's going on here? How dare you let some stranger hug you!" Angry at her perceived lack of respect, instead of waiting for an introduction, Maurice grabbed Jackie by the arm and marched off toward the elevator, with a "Let's go."

Jackie meekly allowed herself to be pulled away, unwilling to draw anyone else into the nightmare that she was living, in case Stan got hurt by the gun that Maurice was still carrying. Looking back over her shoulder, she sent Stan an apologetic shrug with a hint of desperation in her eyes.

Still standing where he left her, Stan was surprised by Jackie and Maurice's actions. It wasn't as if he was a total stranger. Sure he hadn't seen one of his best friends since she got married but he there was no need for the histrionics that her husband pulled. Stan wondered why Jackie allowed him to lead her off like that. The old Jackie would have taken him to task for such behavior.

When Maurice and Jackie got to their room, he went off on her as soon as the door was closed. Dropping their bags as his wife walked further into the room, Maurice rushed up behind her, grabbing her by the neck and choking her while he screamed. "How dare you let some man grab and kiss you in my presence?"

Using her elbow, Jackie punched him in the side. The surprise hit was enough for her to run into the bathroom and stay there until Maurice came to his senses.

"Jackie, you can't stay in there forever. I'm sorry for choking you. When I turned around and saw that man hugging you, I lost it. I'm going to leave right now in order to cool off. I'll be back in a couple of hours. You don't have to stay in the bathroom. Please come out."

In order to cool off and not hurt her anymore, Maurice left his room and went to the room that Rasheeda had texted him was reserved for her. Since she had not arrived yet, he relaxed in the room while he talked to her on his cellular phone.

"Baby, where are you? I thought that you would be here by now."

"I had to tie up a few loose ends with the video tape of the day you closed your accounts at the bank. Therefore I wasn't able to get a flight out tonight so I won't be arriving until tomorrow morning. Here's what I have setup though. Since we've used this hotel before, I have established a few contacts there. Tomas will be the gentleman guarding your wife while we have some quality time together."

"When will he be available?"

"He's actually there right now. If you go back to your room, he'll introduce himself. I've also taken the liberty of making sure that your wife is not able to make any outgoing calls from your room."

"You think of everything. I can't wait for you to arrive."

After talking for another hour, Maurice deemed it was time to go back to his room.

When Maurice left the room, Jackie waited for ten minutes before unlocking the bathroom door. Rushing to the telephone, she tried dialing her sister Chelsea's number. After repeated attempts and several fast busy signals, she dialed the hotel operator; only to be told that they were having problems with their circuits and that no outgoing calls could be made at that time. She advised Jackie to try again tomorrow.

Feeling like she was in the twilight zone, Jackie left the room in search of the only person she trusted to help her, totally unaware that someone was following her every move.

Deciding that she needed a stiff drink, she walked into the restaurant's bar, hoping that Stan would come in while she was there by herself. After waiting for two hours, Stan arrived as she was leaving.

Noticing that a strange man had been watching her since she left her room, Jackie got nervous and wondered if the stranger has been paid to watch her movements. Not willing to take a chance that the stranger would go back and tell Maurice that she was talking to someone, she spoke to Stan, gave him a brief hug, and slipped a note into his jacket pocket.

Perplexed, Stan watched Jackie as she left, wondering what was going on. He waited until she disappeared from sight with the intention of following her until he noticed that a man was shadowing her; as if he was clocking her every move. Stan thought that she must be married to a jealous jerk if he was that insecure that he was having his wife followed. Thinking that the situation with Jackie was best left alone, he proceeded to enjoy his vacation.

Maurice returned to the room before Jackie was able to make it back to the room. When he didn't find her in the room, he went into another rage, thinking that she was off somewhere with the man that greeted her at check-in.

When she came into the room, he was right behind the door, in the bathroom, so that she didn't notice him when she walked in. Coming out of the dark bathroom, he punched her as she walked further into the room.

Tired of being hit, she grabbed the lamp that sat on the desk, and threw it at him. It missed Maurice and crashed to the floor. The light bulb in the lamp fell to the floor and broke in the process. Too angry to let a broken lamp stop him, Maurice raced across the room and attempted to hit his wife again.

Jackie reached down to the floor in the nick of time and grabbed a piece of the broken bulb. Swiping at her husband, who was advancing on her, she brought her hand up and cut him across the face, narrowly missing his eye. As blood spewed forth, Maurice howled in pain.

Jackie, swiftly as her legs would allow, ran to the door to escape.

Opening the door, she ran straight into the stranger's body that she saw in the restaurant. Catching her with his arms to stop her forward movement, he applied force to the pressure point in her shoulder, thereby knocking her unconscious as he propelled her backwards into the room.

By that time, Maurice had located a towel to stop the bleeding. "I need you to stay and watch her, while I see about getting my face stitched up."

"No problem. Let me make a few calls to get a doctor over here, that won't ask any questions."

Sure enough, a doctor arrived within ten minutes and took care of Maurice by applying ten stitches to this face.

"Tomas, can you watch her throughout the night? I want to get some rest in Rasheeda's room."

"Sure mon, no problem. I'm here for whatever you need me to do. You are paying me quite well."

Several hours later, after Jackie had regained consciousness and had eaten a light meal, she went into the bathroom, to sleep. She didn't feel comfortable sleeping in the presence of a stranger and she was afraid that Maurice would attack her in her sleep in retaliation for cutting him.

During her sleep, she had a nightmare that someone was after her. That she was tied to a pole and someone was standing over her, mocking her, saying that she would never get out alive.

That person was holding a small device in their hand, similar to a remote control switch. As the person departed the warehouse like space, he or she, kept taunting her. Towards the end of the dream, all she could see was a massive explosion and a building crumbling to he ground.

Shivering, her body drenched in sweat, Jackie woke up crying, with tears streaming down her face. The dream seemed so real, so vivid. *Is this how Maurice plans on getting rid of me,* she thought?

It had been awhile since she last had one of the dreams. It was a gift that her family shared when someone they loved was either in trouble or dying.

She had to find a way out before her husband succeeded in killing her. The dream, she believed, was a premonition. Tomorrow, she had to escape; whatever it took.

Praying to God to cover her while she slept and to help her escape her crazy husband, she was finally able to fall back to sleep.

The next morning, Maurice woke up early, sending Tomas away, as he walked back into his room as if nothing had transpired the night before. "Jackie, I need you get dressed because we're going down to breakfast. We need to portray the loving couple."

"What makes you think that I would go anywhere with you?"

"This gun right here," he stated as he pulled it from his waistband, "tells me that you will do anything that I ask. You have exactly fifteen minutes to get ready. Don't push your luck."

Taking the fastest shower known to man, she was ready within her allotted time. Donning shades she covered the bruises on her eyes. Putting on a wide brim hat, she was able to cover the bruises on her forehead.

Walking slowly to the breakfast area, grimacing in pain, she sat down at the table. In the crowded restaurant, Stan, who was seated several tables away in the distance, observed the pain that Jackie seemed to be in. As an emergency room doctor, he was trained to pickup on the small details that helped him diagnosis the signs of an abused woman.

Watching the couple's interaction, he knew that something didn't quite add up. Deciding to intervene with an apology to the husband for the hug at check-in, Stan proceeded to walk to their table, when he was interrupted by a telephone call.

Taking the call outside the restaurant, it was several hours later before Stan was able to ponder on that morning's observation. Later in the day when he was sightseeing, as he was reaching into his pocket for his digital camera, he discovered a piece of paper with writing on it.

Curious, he opened the paper to see what was on it. The note read, *Please help me* and was signed with the initials *JBH*. Racking his brain, he wondered who JBH was. He was clueless to the identity of the person that had written the note. Tucking the note into his pocket, he headed back to the hotel in search of the person who would have left him the note.

He stopped at the desk, to see if there were any messages, thinking that the person that had requested help would leave another message. When there wasn't a message left for him, he decided to lounge at the pool. Maybe the person would materialize again requesting help.

He rejected the idea that the person needing help was Jackie because he didn't know her married name. Introductions were never made because her husband started acting a fool the previous day. However, the more he thought about it, she was the obvious conclusion. She was the only person it could be, because no one else knew him that he was in Aruba.

Having been a good friend to him in college, helping him study for exams and encouraging him, she was one of his best friends before her husband got rid of everybody that was close to her. Over the years, he had forgotten what Maurice's last name was, because he had never liked him. Stan knew that he had to do something. He just hoped that she hadn't caught hell when he had kissed her innocently on the cheek the day before.

Thirty minutes after resting by the pool, drinking a virgin daiquiri, he saw her enter the poolside area, fully dressed with shades on and a wide brimmed hat. She chose to sit several feet away from him on one of the many lounge chairs; unusual for lady with a body like that to be covered so completely. She must be covering up some bruises. Tempted to ask her to sit beside him, Stan hesitated when he noticed the bodyguard several feet away.

Getting up, Stan walked towards Jackie, who frantically shook her head as if to dislodge the hat she was wearing. Stan knew that she was warning him to back off. Taking her advice, to prevent further harm from happening to her, he kept walking until he reached the hotel desk.

"Excuse me. I'm looking for the bellhop Antonio that assisted me with my bags at check-in yesterday. Is he on duty today?" The bellhop had told him that if there was anything that he could do while he was on duty and if the price was right, not to hesitate to contact him. He needed money to help his mother and sisters with their day to day living expenses.

"Yes sir. I'll see if I can find him." The hotel clerk paged Antonio and it was only five minutes or so before he showed up.

"Dr. Stan, the desk said that you needed me?"

Pulling the bellhop outside into the parking lot, Stan asked Antonio for a favor. "Antonio, I need a favor?"

"What do you want me to do, Dr. Stan?"

"I have an old college friend here at the hotel. She just checked in with her husband yesterday. I made the mistake of greeting her like we always have in the past, with a huge hug and a kiss on the cheek, and her husband got very irate. I believe that her husband is abusing her. Just now, she could barely walk and her skin is discolored with deep bruises. I need to get her away from that bastard. Can you help me get a message to her?"

"Dr. Stan, is that your professional opinion or do you want this woman for yourself?" The young man asked intelligently.

"My professional opinion. We were good friends during college, nothing more. I can't however in good conscience leave her to fend for herself."

"What is your friend's name?"

"Jackie Bailey, although I don't remember her married name, but she's married to a guy named Maurice."

"Yes, I know Mr. Holmes very well. He comes here quite frequently and usually stays in Room 2501, but I didn't know that he was married. Whenever he comes here, he's always with a very nasty lady by the name of Rasheeda. She must be his mistress. I believe that you're right about the husband abusing the wife. Today we had a compliant about the noise coming from their room, last night. The person who complained said that they heard what sounded like a lamp being thrown, a woman being hit, and a man cursing because he had gotten cut.

"So will you help me?"

"Yes. I do not like men that hit women. They should be cherished."

"I feel the same way. Let's go inside. She's the one sitting on the lounge chair fully clothed."

"But she's beautiful!" exclaimed Antonio.

"Yes, I know. Beautiful but broken. Here's what I've planned. I want you to give her this note and wait for a reply. It simply asks her if she is being abused and wants to escape. If she says yes, then tell her to order room service around three o'clock when your shifts are about to change. You will deliver the food to their room and help her escape through the connecting door to the adjacent suite."

"Dr. Stan, that won't work. Mr. Holmes' mistress usually reserves their regular suite and the suite next to theirs because they are rather loud when they do their thang, if you know what I mean. I have an idea though. Some of our connecting suites have an additional small storage room and soundproof walls that can be utilized at the customer's discretion."

"What do you mean? How does it work?"

"We recently installed the sound boards, as sliding walls, which makes the room soundproof, since we have so many concerts here in Aruba and a lot of the musicians stay at this hotel that oftentimes rehearse late into the evenings, preparing for a concert. To ensure their privacy and to reduce the noise level from these "mini rehearsals", sliding sound boards walls were erected in the storage space to soundproof each room. The "walls" encompasses each side of the storage room, thereby making both suites soundproof, and provide a secure, insured space to store expensive equipment."

"Your friend could hide in the storage area behind the sound board wall. To the average onlooker, it looks like cement but it isn't."

"What happens if someone opens the connecting door?"

"They will only see the wall, not what's behind it. There's a special switch that mechanically moves the wall back and forth."

"Has Mr. Holmes' mistress checked in yet?"

"No sir. She's not due to check in until this afternoon, around four o'clock."

"Is there any way that you can put her in another room until tomorrow? Whatever it costs, I'll pay. It will be worth it to save Jackie's life."

"One hundred American dollars should do the trick for the desk clerk. He has a gambling debt, so it shouldn't be too hard to convince him to change the room."

"Do you have any other friends that can occupy her husband and the bodyguard until she's escaped?"

"Yes sir. Just leave everything up to me."

"Antonio, here is three hundred American dollars. Get Jackie to safety and I'll give you five hundred more American dollars."

Grinning broadly, Antonio promised Dr. Stan that all would go well. "Now I need to give her the note. If anyone questions me, I'll simply say that I wanted her autograph."

When Jackie saw Stan leave, her spirits fell. He wasn't going to help her. What else could she do to escape? She didn't have any money and she didn't know who to trust. Did Maurice have any other hotel staff members on his payroll? Tears started to roll down her face.

"Ma'am is everything ok? Could I get you anything?" A young bellhop asked as he moved directly in front of her, thereby blocking the view from any onlookers.

Looking up in surprise, Jackie shook her head no, while wiping away the tears with her hands. As she wiped away the tears, her shades slid up and the bellhop noticed the dark bruises around her eyes. His heart went out to her. He had two sisters and would hate it if someone abused them like the tourist here was being abused. The bellhop extended a towel to her.

"Please take this. I think that you will find everything that you need inside." Talking softly, he continued, "I can help you. Dr. Stan sent me. I'm to take a message to him for you. Read the paper quick before I have to leave."

Jackie opened the towel while unassumingly removing her hat. Once her hat was removed, it shielded her actions from anyone watching her. After reading the instructions, she nodded yes emphatically to Antonio.

That was all he needed. Bowing to her, he stated, "Make sure you follow the instructions to the letter so that we can take good care of you while you're here."

"Thank you!" The bodyguard came over to see why the bellhop had stopped to talk to her.

"Why was he here talking to you?"

"He asked if there was something wrong; if I had any sun burn, since I'm the only one here that's fully clothed. He simply gave me the remedy for sun burn. Do you want to see it, she asked?" Grabbing the other paper that was included, she flashed it towards the bodyguard.

Bowing her head in prayer, she thanked God that help was on the way.

Chapter 8

Two o'clock rolled around and Jackie, having gone back to her room, was anxious. She kept thinking of all the things that could go wrong that would prevent her from escaping. Holding on by a thread, she just kept praying that all would go well.

Following the instructions on the paper, Jackie ordered Room Service for an afternoon snack. Thirty minutes later, they called to confirm the delivery within the next thirty minutes. Not long after she finished talking to Room Service, Maurice came back to their room. "Tomas, take a break. I'll be in the room for a while."

"Yes sir. When do you want me back?"

"Around four o'clock. I have a meeting that I need to go to at that time."

Tomas walked out of the room, making his way down to the bar for an afternoon drink. He wished all of his jobs were as easy as the one he was currently working. Ordering a tequila, he tossed the shot down in one swallow. If Maurice didn't want to make love to his wife, then he certainly would. He was almost certain that Maurice was meeting his mistress. Maybe once he left the room, then it would be time for him to get his.

Ordering another shot, he turned his stool to watch the women that were lounging by the poolside. On second thoughts, maybe he would get lucky here, he thought, as one woman walked up to him and began whispering naughty things into his ear.

Maurice's cellular phone started ringing as soon as Tomas left the room. Walking to the other side of the room, near the window so that his conversation could not be overhead, he answered. "Maurice."

"Baby, I'm here! However, there seems to be a slight problem with the room. It's going to take them about thirty minutes before I can get into the room. Come and keep me company."

"Where are you now?"

"At the front desk."

"I'll be right down." Punching in Tomas' cellular phone, he didn't get an answer. Cursing softly because Tomas was unavailable, he waited to leave a message. "Tomas, change of plans. My guest has arrived earlier than expected. I need for you to return to the suite immediately."

Pacing around the room at the delay, Maurice tried once again to contact Tomas. On the fifth ring, he answered.

"Yes?"

"Change of plans. I need you to come back to the room. My guest has arrived earlier than expected. I'll probably be gone for the next three hours. How long will it take you to arrive?"

"I'm around the hotel. I'll be there within the next ten minutes."

True to his word, ten minutes later, Tomas knocked on the door. "Tomas, Room Service should be here within the next thirty minutes. Make sure that they are the only one that come into this room."

"Okay sir." Maurice left soon after delivering his instructions.

As Tomas opened the door for Room Service, with his back to the room, a partition in the wall opened to reveal Dr. Stan. He grabbed Jackie and pulled her into the storage area behind the sliding walls. The partition slid back into place within mere seconds. When Tomas turned around, she was gone.

"Jackie, where are you? I know you're in here." Where could she have gone? He wondered. He searched the suite for Jackie, looking under the bed, to no avail. Thinking that she must have locked herself in the bathroom, he knocked first, yelling, "Open up," before picking the lock. No one was in the bathroom.

"I fell for the oldest trick in the book. She must be in the bottom of the room service cart," he said to himself. Dashing out of the room, he bumped into several guests as he raced after the hotel employee with the room service cart.

The person maneuvering the Room Service cart moved quickly down the corridor, taking a sharp right and barely missed being clipped by the elevator doors as they closed. Once inside, the Room Service attendant hit the stop button to pause the elevator for five minutes. Antonio, who was hiding underneath the cart, untangled himself as the stood up. He then climbed onto the cart and removed the ceiling panel as he escaped through the elevator shaft. Once the ceiling panel was replaced, the Room Service attendant started the elevator and proceeded to another floor to resume his daily activities, before sending the elevator back to the lobby.

Thinking that the Room Service attendant was going straight to the kitchen, Tomas, ran down the corridor to take the stairs. Taking them two at a time he was able to catch the Room Service attendant when he came into the kitchen. After questioning the young man, he finally confessed that he had been ambushed. Other than offering that information he was unable give a description of the person that ambushed him.

Frustrated, Tomas hurried back to the room still looking for the missing wife.

Dr. Stan, who waited for Jackie in the storage room, handed her some of the maid's clothes to put on, which would help her blend in with everyone else. With his back turned, she slipped the clothes on over her short set. Hurriedly he flipped the switch to slide the walls back to escape through the connecting suite.

Just as they were stepping out of the storage area, the door opened. Hugging and kissing, Maurice and Rasheeda backed their way into the room, wrapped up in each other's arms like newlyweds. To busy frantically tearing each others clothes off, they didn't see the man or his companion, until they were almost naked.

At Jackie's gasp of surprise, they finally noticed that they were not alone in the room. Caught, it was too late to slide the walls back or to hide. Dr. Stan immediately stepped in front of Jackie to shield her body. Bending forward he kissed her passionately, with single-minded intensity; totally devouring her lips.

"Pardon me. I see we're not the only ones using this room. Don't mind us, we were just leaving." Holding his blazer open, Dr. Stan protected Jackie's identity as they swiftly ran out of the room, slamming the door behind them.

Giving them a cursory look, Maurice nor Rasheeda was inclined to go after the couple. They had better things to do than chase after a couple who were catching stolen moments while still on duty. Time to report them later, when they were finished.

Racing towards the elevator, Dr. Stan and Jackie dashed inside, praying that they would make it to the lobby undetected.

As they rode the elevator to the lobby, Jackie donned yet another disguise, that of a pregnant woman. Taking the maid's uniform off and bawling it up, she stuffed it under her shirt. Looking four months pregnant, with a billowy hat on her head, and sunglasses to cover her eyes, she was the perfect image of a normal tourist going out on a rendezvous with her husband.

After Dr. Stan and Jackie escaped outside to the parking lot, a cab was waiting to take them to safety. Driving downtown, Dr. Stan advised the cab driver to stop so that they could go into one of the stores. After paying the cab driver, Dr. Stan hailed another cab, representing another cab company, making it difficult for someone to track them, as he gave directions to the airport.

Having trusted Dr. Stan thus far, Jackie didn't question why they had changed cabs. She was tired and exhausted after having the nightmare and being up the majority of the night, scared and defenseless.

"Stan, how can I ever repay you for rescuing me? Thank you for your friendship! How did you know?"

"I see a lot of this in the Emergency Room with women with unexplainable bruises or broken limbs. They come in, get treated and go back to the same guy that hurt them. They refuse to leave him, much less, testify against him. I also volunteer at a women's shelter on a weekly basis, not to mention growing up with a father that treated my mother as his personal punching bag."

"I'm so sorry if this brought back painful memories for you."

"Can I ask you a question? Why didn't you leave him? How long has it been going on? Do you still love the bastard and are you going to press charges?"

Seeing her hesitate, he became angry, thinking that all his efforts to rescue her had been in vain.

Putting her hand on his arm, she turned to face him. "I don't think that I can. No hear me out," she pleaded when he was about to interrupt her.

"Maurice held me at gunpoint to come to Aruba. He owes money, about two million dollars, to a loan shark, I believe. That person has made three trips to our new house in Charlotte over the last two months. Ironically or by design, now that I think of it, Maurice was only at home one of those times. He got beat up a little on the second visit. The only reason it wasn't worse was because I went into the basement, trying to figure out what all the fuss was about."

"How did he play that off?"

She continued as if he hadn't spoken. "He shoved me against the wall after the guy left the house when I asked him what was going on. I must have blacked out because I didn't remember what happened until the second time. After the third visit from the loan shark, I was scared and wanted to help so I called my bank only to find out that he had closed all of our accounts and had even withdrawn all the money from my trust fund with the help of that heifer, his personal banker, that you saw him making out with back at the hotel. I confronted him with the truth and that's when the abuse really started."

"The second altercation which came after demanding my money, ended up with a couple of broken ribs and several bruises. I believe that was day before yesterday. He then told me that if I went to the police, the loan shark would kill everyone in my family. Since he saw that I believed him, for added insurance he pulled the gun on me and here we are."

Pulling her closer to him, Dr. Stan asked another hard question, sensing that she wasn't finished. "Did my greeting cause you to suffer?"

Her refusal to comment gave him the confirmation that he needed. Muttering a string of expletives, he vowed to make Maurice pay for every bruise that he had inflicted on Jackie.

"Can you just get me to a phone so that I can contact my family to let them know that I'm alright? They haven't heard from me in a couple of days, so I know they're worried. I also need for them to wire me some money to pay for my airfare home."

"Jackie, listen to me. You've got to press charges; otherwise he'll just keep coming back. If the loan shark wanted to hurt Maurice, he would have already done it. He must have something that he wants or is involved in something that's about to go down. We have to get the FBI involved in this. I have a cousin that's an agent that can help us. Let me see if I can contact him, then we'll plan our next move."

"Why are you going to so much trouble to help me?"

"Maybe its to make up for what I couldn't do for my mother, since I was so young when it happened. Plus you were one of my best friends that encouraged me when I needed it. I wouldn't be where I am today without your support and your tutoring. Plus I'm hoping that now that we're reconnected, you'll put in a good word for me with your sister Ryan." Holding up his hand, he responded, "Don't ask. It's a long story. By the way, have I told you that you're a helluva kisser and that if I wasn't so taken with your sister, I would wait for you to get over Maurice and pursue you for myself?"

"You're not so bad yourself. If I could just bottle what you have and market it, I could make millions." Laughing they embraced as only true friends could do after their ordeal.

Tomas, hesitant to contact Mr. Holmes with bad news, knew that he couldn't put it off any longer. He was unable to get any information from the Room Service attendant. After questioning the entire staff, he came up empty. Jackie was gone. Someone had helped her to escape. *Perhaps all was not lost*, he thought as he dialed the number to Mr. Holmes second room. There was still time to catch them at the airport.

Maurice, annoyed that he forgot to turn his telephone off, leaned over to grab the offensive instrument from his pants pocket. He had other things on him mind when he entered the room with Rasheeda. Recognizing Tomas' number, he immediately answered the call. It must be important because Tomas knew not to interrupt him.

"Mr. Holmes, I hate to disturb you, but something unfortunate has happened." He proceeded to explain how his wife had escaped. After listening for about ten minutes to Maurice's tirade, Tomas interrupted him.

"Mr. Holmes, if we hurry, we can still catch them at the airport. The next flight to the States does not leave until eight o'clock."

"I'm on my way." Leaning over Rasheeda, he kissed her quickly and explained that Jackie had slipped away and that he was going to the airport to bring her back.

Tomas, Maurice and five others, raced to the airport to capture Jackie and her accomplice, before they boarded the plane back to the States.

Jackie and Dr. Stan, who were waiting anxiously at the airport during the two hour delay before their flight was scheduled to take off, thought that it was wise to stay in their disguise, as a married couple expecting a child. They had just left one of the cafés, and were heading towards the waiting area until their plane's departure. With the large number of people surrounding them, they figured it would eliminate anyone from discovering them.

Unfortunately, they didn't count on Maurice catching up to them and recognizing them as the couple making out in his room. They thought that he would be too busy to stop his amorous pursuits to look for them.

Maurice and his crew cautiously converged upon the US airport section designated for flight departures to the States. Maurice's attention was arrested by the vision of a pregnant woman leaning forward to grab something from her handbag that was resting on the floor. As she reached into her bag, he noticed a charm bracelet on her arm that was identical to the charm that he had given his wife on their fifth wedding anniversary. With an imperceptible nod, he motioned for Tomas and his men to grab the woman and the man next to her.

Jackie reached into her purse and pulled out her compact mirror which would allow her to pretend that she was repairing her makeup when actually she was on lookout for the enemy that could approach them from behind. Dr. Stan was surveying the crowd from the frontal angles for anyone that looked like they were watching them.

In the distance he could see a group of men that were headed in their direction. Dr. Stan did not recognize them as being from the hotel. To be on the safe size, not knowing what Maurice may have planned when he discovered Jackie was missing, Dr. Stan softly whispered for Jackie to be prepared to follow his lead and run like their life depended on it.

As the men neared them, Dr. Stan grabbed Jackie's hand and together they quickly darted between the tourists that were walking about, as they swiftly power walked along the concourse to another gate, hoping to lose the men that seemed to be following them. Glancing briefly over his shoulder, Dr. Stan confirmed that the men were in fact rushing to catch up with them. As they rounded the corner, leading to the next set of gates for the other airlines, they saw Maurice and his men rushing towards them from the opposite direction.

Back in Charlotte, Trevor who was frantically trying to match the hotel guest list with anyone that Jackie may have known previously, either in high school or in college, finally found a match. Stan Jones name popped up as a close friend in college who had several classes with Jackie. He later went on to become a doctor. This had to be the person that was helping her. How else would she escape with no money?

With precious little time left, Trevor was able to access the government's public database for cellular telephone numbers to find Dr. Stan's number. While he was calling Dr. Stan's telephone number, Max was able to load his picture into the system to download it to his men's telephones so that they could confirm Jackie and Stan's identity. His men communicated to him that they had them within their sights.

Without knowing which men were the good guys, Dr. Stan made a decision to bank left to the other concourse, hoping that they could disappear to a storage room if they were lucky. All of a sudden he saw one of the first set of men with a cellular phone to his ear just as his phone started ringing. Without breaking their stride, he answered his phone.

"Dr. Jones, my name is Max, a Federal Bureau of Investigation agent as well as Jackie's brother-in-law. I have four men in your immediate vicinity that are ready to take you to safety. One has his cellular phone up to his ear looking directly at you. I understand from my men that Maurice is nearby. If you'll just keep walking towards my men, they'll act like they are taking you into custody, thereby eliminating Maurice and his men from capturing you. By the way, if you could refrain from mentioning that I'm an agent I would appreciate it, for my family's safety. If you need further evidence, give the phone to Jackie and she'll verify who I am."

Dr. Stan immediately passed the phone to Jackie as they continued to walk towards the FBI agents. With his hand on her arm, he moved them expeditiously towards the federal agents.

"Hello?"

"Jackie, its Max. Are you okay?"

"Max! Thank you, God! How did you find us? Can you get us out of here?"

"Dr. Stan knows what to do. I'll meet you when you land in Miami."

Maurice and his men pulled up short, when the federal agents surrounded Jackie and her accomplice and handcuffed them, before escorting them off in another direction of the airport, although some remained and were headed in their direction. He couldn't afford to get apprehended by the police in another country; there was too much to lose. Getting arrested for domestic violence wasn't a part of his plans.

Shooting bullets into the air, Maurice's men were able to create a diversion, by causing the tourists to panic with hysteria, which allowed Maurice enough time to escape from the airport. The federal agents were unprepared for the chaos that followed to handle the situation properly. Their orders were to get the woman and the doctor to safety at all costs. Unfortunately that meant, letting the culprit responsible, escape.

There was always more than one way to accomplish a task. Perhaps Jackie's rescue would provide the temporary diversion that was needed to keep Mr. Smith off his back for a few weeks. In the short term, it was impossible for him to go back to the States, at least back to Charlotte.

Maurice settled back as the car made its way back to the hotel; back to Rasheeda, who he hoped was ready and waiting for him. Revising his next sequence of actions based on the present set of events, he decided that they would camp out at Rasheeda's twin sister's home in DC; well out of harm's way. No one would think to look for them there.

When the plane landed in Miami for their layover, Jackie said a silent prayer, thanking God that he had saved her; that he had sent several people to her rescue. As she exited the plane, and walked the short ramp through the airport gate, she was enveloped in a tight hug by Max. After thanking the doctor for his heroic efforts, they were both escorted to a private room, just inside the airport. Jackie assumed that there would be questions to answer.

Upon entering the room, she was shocked to see all of her relatives crowded into the small room. Max had taken the initiative to fly all of them down to Miami so that they could be assured that she was alright. Amiss the hugs and the greetings, Jackie introduced her knight in shining armor, Dr. Stan Jones, to her family. More hugs and kisses were circulating as they thanked him from the bottom of their hearts for rescuing their beloved.

Unfortunately seeing the tall, handsome gentleman with their sister, caused at least one person in the room, a moment of anxiety. Ryan, with her heart in her throat, only had eyes for Stan. It had been awhile since she had last seen him, and based on what she had done, she didn't think that he would be receptive to any overture that she would make. Subsequently, Ryan tried to ease past Stan while her brothers were thanking him. To her dismay, she didn't get very far.

Ryan's two brothers, very attentive to their sister's emotions, noticed the way that Ryan was trying to discreetly make her getaway without talking to he doctor. They wondered what was up with that. Taking note of the love and misery that was shinning in her eyes that she was unaware of, they decided to give the doctor a break, only because the same emotions were shining out of his eyes. Knowing their sister, they could only guess what she had done to derail her romance.

As she kept inching away, the doctor took his own action, by lightly grabbing her arm, to stop her evasive movements. "Excuse me gentlemen, I need to talk to Ryan." Without another word, he walked away.

"Were you going to just leave without at least saying hello?" He asked as he gazed into her eyes with the passion and torment that had hounded him since she had chose her career over their relationship.

"I was trying to before you stopped me. I didn't think that you would be receptive to anything that I had to say after what I did." Taking a deep breath, she kissed him on the lips and hugged him fiercely. "Thank you from the bottom of my heart for saving my sister. I'm glad that you returned safely without being hurt."

As he raised his arms to engulf her in a hug, she ducked and walked away. With a tormented spirit, he could only watch as she went to join her sister. Max, who was ever watchful of people and their reactions, noticed the brief exchange. Walking over to the doctor, he tried to give him some advice.

"I take it that you and Ryan have some history together."

At his affirmative nod, Max continued. "Loving the women in this family is oftentimes hard and frustrating but well worth it in the end. Don't give up. Just try to find a way around whatever it is that's coming between you, if you really want her."

"I do, with my heart and soul."

"Then don't let anything stop you from reclaiming her heart."

Walking to another portion of the room, Max telephoned Caleb who was supposed to meet them in Charlotte the next day.

"Caleb, this is Max. We have a change of plans. We've just been alerted that Maurice is in Aruba. He kidnapped his wife and forced her to go to Aruba along with his mistress. Jackie was held a gunpoint and had a bodyguard watching her when he wasn't around. An old college friend helped her escape."

"Max, I'm in Aruba right now. My cousin Stan, called yesterday requesting help to get out of the country. He's the old college friend that helped your sister-in-law, Jackie to escape. Since I couldn't get there quick enough, one of our operatives in training, Antonio, helped them to leave the hotel safely."

"Any sign of Maurice or his mistress?"

"No. By the time your operatives had gotten Jackie on the plane and circled back to the hotel, they had checked out. Antonio verified that Maurice did not come back to the hotel. He tried to follow the taxi that Rasheeda left the hotel in, but he lost her on the freeway because of an accident."

"They're probably going underground. Any particular reason Antonio was at the same hotel?"

"A few pieces of the missing jewels have been sold in Aruba on the black market. We've traced some of the transactions to this area. Antonio is working undercover as a bellhop to keep his eyes and ears open for any information that could lead us to the fencers. How did you figure out that they were here?"

"Let's just say that several family members had the same dream that she was in trouble so we drove to Charlotte and checked out their house. There were signs of a struggle. Jackie was smart enough to leave some cosmetic shavings with the written word Aruba, although faint and fuzzy, on the countertop. From there, Trevor did the rest of the work."

"What's the next step on your end?"

"We are going ahead with the plan for the bank. Trev is going to setup his program on the personal banker's computer and then we'll process that information to see the number of clients involved as well as the dollar figure that's in question. It might be a good idea for you to come to Charlotte when you're finished in Aruba. We plan on going back through the surveillance photos on the computer since Jackie and Maurice moved into their house.

She had previously mentioned that a lot of company had recently visited their house. You should be there when we do this; you might recognize some of the people as being on your watch list."

"My family owns a jewelry store in Charlotte. I'll see if my parents can take a vacation for a couple of weeks. It will give me time to design some jewelry as well as keep an eye on things and establish a legitimate cover. I have a feeling that this case is far from over. Even if we catch Maurice, we still need to locate the mastermind behind the jewelry heist. I don't believe that it's Maurice. Is there anyway that we can transfer the funds from the offshore accounts that Trevor found, which will force him to sell some of the jewels?"

"We'll work on the timing of that when you come to Charlotte. Let me know when to expect you."

Chapter 9

On the flight back to Charlotte, Max and Trevor ironed out the details regarding Trevor's undercover task. It was determined that he would setup a trap to gain information on how Rasheeda Montgomery embezzled the banks funds and hopefully gain insight as to how she helped Mr. Holmes deplete his wife's trust fund.

However, in order to gain that information, Trevor needed access to her computer so that he could install a tracking program. The tracking program would record all the keystrokes that had been entered on her computer. At the end of each day, the keystrokes would be downloaded into a database and stored on Rasheeda's computer.

Once Trevor ran the sweep of the database each night, by logging remotely onto her system, he would wipe the database clean. As the keystrokes were recorded, a webcam would video the entire room, thereby providing a visual of any person or persons that would be considered an accomplice. Additionally it also provided a clue as to the clients whose portfolio was in jeopardy.

Two days later, at eleven o'clock in the next morning, Trevor strolled into the bank, looking every bit the young, successful, sinfully handsome gentleman, in search of a local bank that could help him to diversify his funds. Only too eager to help, Mr. Carson, the branch manager, always on alert for novice investors, directed the gentleman to his favorite personal banker and friend in crime, Rasheeda Montgomery.

As Cherita set out to do her sister's job, her fellow coworkers were shocked at the transformation in "Rasheeda's new attitude". She was more approachable, more helpful than she had ever been. They were wondering amongst themselves, when the old Rasheeda would resurface.

Could the day get any worse? Cherita asked rhetorically when she was finally able to take a break at work. She had been met with opposition at every turn ever since her first day at McAlstons. Something didn't feel right. The tellers at the bank were looking at her like she had grown another head. She was being as pleasant as she possibly could be, yet they still were a little standoffish and would barely cooperate with her when she was forced to interact with them for her client's sake. One had even questioned what happened to the other Rasheeda that they were used too.

To make matters worse, one of the security guards had cornered her in the hallway that lead to the break room. He had brushed up against her like they were lovers. She had slapped him for reaching out to touch her breast, but he had only laughed.

"So you don't like my touch now? After all I've done for you?" He asked, breathing heavily in her face.

"Keep your hands to yourself. Not here, while we're at work," Cherita replied, trying to play along, hoping he would give her an indication what he was talking about.

"Oh, so that's how you want to continue playing this, huh? It's okay for me to see you after hours where you're a freak in the bedroom, but while we're at work, you're Ms. Prim and Proper. What if I don't want to play by your rules anymore?" Eugene, the security guard asked as he leaned closer, so close that she could smell liquor on his breath. It was way too early in the morning for him to have had a drink.

"I've got something that you need so you had better be nice to me," he said as he attempted to put his arms around Cherita.

Stepping one of her high heels onto his foot, she was able to put some distance between them. Forgetting the roles she was playing, Cherita demanded, "Don't ever touch me again without my permission." Hurrying off to Rasheeda's office, she tried to calm her nerves.

The ringing of the telephone reminded her that for the next two weeks, she was here to do a job. Picking up the telephone, she answered, "Ms. Montgomery." She didn't like lying so she was only going to answer to Ms. Montgomery. That way, she could have some semblance of peace for her conscience for the next two weeks.

"Ms. Montgomery, this is Mr. Carson. I have a Mr. Hawkins here to see you. He's a successful businessman trying to diversify his funds. He's a novice at investing, so give him the royal treatment. I'll usher him into your office." Without waiting for Cherita's response, Mr. Carson hung up.

"What was the royal treatment? Cherita wondered aloud?"

Going to the file cabinet, with her back turned away from the door, Cherita gathered the forms that she would need.

Mr. Hawkins walked into the room so quietly, that she didn't hear him. It was only when she felt the quickening of her pulse, the shivers that coursed down her spine did she realize that she wasn't alone in the room.

As a breath of air caressed her cheek, she was completely mesmerized when a soft, husky voice enveloped her as a pair of arms encircled her from behind. Only one man could make her feel like this. She knew that she had to be dreaming. Without a word, she had left him. How did he find her? He had called several times but she hadn't responded.

With a kiss to the side of her neck, Trevor turned Cherita to face him. "Why haven't you returned my calls?" He felt her shiver as instinctively she leaned her head back to give him greater access to her neck.

Turning, she gasped in shock. "What are you doing here?" She asked in a shaky voice, as she tried to move out of his arms.

"I've called you numerous times. Why didn't you call me back?" Trevor asked as he sat on her desk, with Cherita positioned between his thighs. He was glad that the closed blinds provided them some privacy. "Did you not want to see me again?"

At the startled, instinctive shake of her head, Trevor smiled. She wanted him.

Unwilling to encourage him any further while she was living a lie, Cherita tried one last time to dissuade Trevor's advances.

"Trevor, I've got a lot to do within the next two weeks. Can we pick up this conversation then? I won't have any free time until then."

A knock could be heard on her office door. Trevor moved around the desk to take his seat. He didn't want to compromise her job. A man with the name tag of Mr. Carson, Branch Manager, stuck his head in the door.

"Rasheeda, could you come into my office for a minute? Sir, if you could excuse us for a minute, I would appreciate it. She'll be right back to service your needs."

Cherita didn't have a choice but to follow Mr. Carson from the room.

Trevor was pole axed, as he sat in the chair. The man had called her Rasheeda, not Cherita. She was the suspected personal banker that he was after. What type of trick was she playing on him? Angry with himself for letting a pretty face and figure get under his skin and ingrained in his heart, he proceeded to perform the task at hand.

Taking out the flash drive from his pocket with the programs that he needed to load, he added them to the banks system. Then he checked the system to see if it had remote connectivity. Writing down the computer's IP address, he had all the information that he needed.

Sitting back in the chair, he waited for Cherita's return, or whatever named she called herself.

Five minutes later, she entered the room. Looking at Trevor, she read the anger, the hurt and the disappointment in his face. As much as she wanted to erase the mistrust that she saw in his eyes, she couldn't. She had to remember the role that she was supposed to play for the next two weeks. Her heart wanted to confide in him but she couldn't. She had given her word.

Something didn't add up. As angry as Trevor was, his heart knew that she had been completely honest with him the night that they had spent together. She had given him her telephone number and her address. He had verified both to be correct. For every question that they had asked each other, both responded with the truth. So why would she answer to another name? Was she in on the plot too? He had to find that out before they could go any further.

His job meant everything to him. He had a duty to uphold.

It wouldn't be long before he found out whether or not their glorious night meant anything to her. No better time to start than the present.

Looking directly into her eyes, he asked, "Are you in some type of trouble? Your branch manager called you Rasheeda. Is that your real name? If so, why did you lie to me?"

"Trevor, I mean Mr. Hawkins; you came here for a purpose. Can we get back to that purpose please, and leave the personal questions to a more appropriate time?"

"No, that's not satisfactory. Before you can handle my funds, I need to know if I can trust you." Deciding to use another tactic, he asked, "Did the other night mean anything to you?"

Without thought or hesitation, Cherita replied honestly, "More than you'll ever know."

Trusting his instincts, Trevor read the sincerity in Cherita's eyes and let the personal questions subside. Thirty minutes later, armed with all the information that was needed, he stood to his feet. Placing his hands on the desk, he leaned over towards

Cherita. "This isn't over between us. I won't disappear. If you're in trouble, I want to help you. I can't stand deceit. Please call me when you're ready to be completely honest with me. I won't accept anything less than a committed relationship." With a gentle caress of his hand to her cheek, he left.

"Max, this is Trevor. I just left McAlston's. We need to talk. Call me when you get this message." Heading to his apartment, Trevor was about to break one of his own rules. He told himself that he wouldn't investigate Cherita but his instincts were telling him that something was definitely wrong. She was jumpy and seemed scared, yet was adamant that nothing further happen between them until her two weeks expired in Charlotte. Why two weeks?

Replaying everything in his head as he drove to his apartment, Trevor had run every possible scenario through his head, from Cherita being a crook and running from the law, to her taking the fall for something her sister did.

Letting himself into his apartment, Trevor immediately walked into his office. Settling down to the computer, he ran a series of steps to remotely connect his computer to the computer at McAlstons. Using his proprietary software, he was able to log into the system without being detected. On his screen, the web camera was replaying the events of the day, as if it were a video. The web camera took pictures of the person sitting at the computer, while another program recorded the keystrokes.

The playback began with the Branch Manager sitting at Cherita's desk typing commands into her computer. He would get the keystrokes later. What was more important was the next scene unfolding before him. Cherita had just walked into her office. She appeared to be mad that the Branch Manager was utilizing her office and let him know as much. The Branch Manger then tried to console her by pushing her back on top of the desk.

Trevor's blood started boiling. How dare this man touch his woman! Grabbing his coat and his keys, he was about to walk out of his apartment and head over to the bank before Cherita's voice stopped him.

Pulling her knee upward as hard as she could, she hit the Branch Manager in his golden jewels. "What is it with you people at this bank? I am not your present to unwrap. You do not, I repeat, do not, have the right to touch me! If you so much as breathe on me again, I will sue you for sexual harassment. Now leave my office!" Walking to the door, she fully expected the Branch Manger to leave.

Unfortunately some things don't always happen as planned.

Instead of leaving, the Branch Manager angrily pulled her against his body, with her arm bent behind her back.

"What the hell?" Trevor asked himself as he continued to look at his twenty-two inch computer monitor.

"Listen to me Rasheeda, and listen closely. Whether or not you like it, we're partners. I've slept with you and I'll sleep with you again, anytime I like it. Unless of course you want me to go to the CEO and owner of the bank as well as the police and tell them how you've swindled money from your clients. How would you like that?"

Not knowing what to say, she just stared at him. What was he talking about? What had Rasheeda gotten her into?

Meeting no resistance, he leaned forward to kiss her but Cherita was too quick for him. With a jab to his midsection and a hit to the nose, she opened the door of her office, waiting impatiently until Mr. Carson left.

Okay, something was definitely wrong! Cherita was definitely a virgin until the other evening when they slept together. So what was the branch manager talking about? More specifically, who was he talking about? He didn't know but he intended to find out and when the opportunity presented itself, he would make the branch manager pay for manhandling his woman. Checking his messages, and seeing none from Max, he decided to do a little more investigating.

After Cherita walked out of her office, behind Mr. Carson, her intention was to go home and cool off. She was so mad that she didn't think that she could deal with any more customers at that moment. To be accosted twice in one day was too much for her. She felt violated.

While she was walking to the door to leave the bank, she was assessing her options. She could leave and deal with the problem later or she could stay and face it and figure out what was going on. She chose the latter. Doing an about face, Cherita turned around and proceeded to walk back to her office.

Sitting down at her desk, she replayed the day's events over in her head. So far, she knew that her sister was sleeping with two men, both of whom were stealing information from the bank. The question was; what were they stealing and was anyone aware of their crime? She didn't want to go to jail for someone else's misdeeds.

The second sequence of events that she kept thinking about was the file on her computer that Mr. Carson was entering information into. Pulling the keyboard to her, she attempted to find the file. Speaking out loud, she posed a question, "Okay Mr. Carson, you needed my computer, but for what?" Bringing up several programs, she wasn't able to find the file at first. Then looking in the computer's directory, she tried to find the file that had been recently updated by looking at the computer's date for the file details.

"Bingo. You mentioned Royal Treatment and here is a file with that exact name. Let's see what was so important in this file." Opening the file, a message ran across the screen. *The encryption on this file has not been reprogrammed. Please add the encryption to protect your privacy and then close the file.*

"Okay, it's obvious the file can still be opened. Let's open it and see what's in it." In the file, Cherita found a report that listed numerous client names, their account numbers, and monetary deductions. The report even listed another account number where the funds were deposited into. Looking at the account number, she knew that it was an offshore account.

What should she do with the information? Go to the police or the FBI? Should she tell the president of the bank? Was her sister involved in this willingly or was she forced to participate?

Searching further on the computer, she found detailed notes that her sister had kept, logging information on Mr. Carson. It seemed that yes, they were working together and that obviously they didn't trust each other.

Pulling out two flash drives from her office desk, Cherita copied both files. She put one in an envelope and mailed it to Trevor; the other she mailed to her house address in D.C. She didn't know why, but her heart felt as if she could trust him. Leaving her office, she made a quick trip to the Post Office to mail her packages before returning to work.

When she returned to work and logged onto her computer, she checked the Royal Treatment file to see if Mr. Carson had returned to finish what he had started. Sure enough, he had. The file was now encrypted.

Just when she thought things couldn't get any worse, she was proved wrong.

Two days after the incidents, a plainclothes policeman showed up at the bank, requesting that she follow him downtown for questioning. Confused, she asked why. As he rattled off a list of her alleged crimes, Cherita had a sinking feeling in the pit of her stomach that her sister had set her up.

Protesting her innocence, she tried to tell the policeman that she wasn't the person he was looking for, but to no avail.

As the doors to the jail cell closed, Cherita considered whom she should call. If she called her parents would they believe her and bail her out? If she called Rasheeda, would she come or let her rot in jail? Or should she call Trevor? He did say that if she was in trouble, he wanted to help her.

Could she trust someone that she had just met and spent one glorious night with or trust her sister, that she had known all of her life?

Was she willing to risk the love of a lifetime for a sister that had obviously set her up to take the fall for a crime she knew nothing about?

After six hours, she finally came to a decision. All her life she had lived in the shadows, waiting for someone to love her for herself, not for who they wanted her to be. As the youngest, born only five minutes apart from her twin sister, her parents had always treated her as an outcast; as if they only wanted one child. Treating her differently became a way of life for them. At a young age, Cherita had learned to become invisible. Even though they were identical in appearance, with the exception of their body structure, her parents couldn't see fit to love her like they loved Rasheeda.

If Trevor could see beyond her face and her figure to look into the depths of her soul, she was willing to take a chance on love.

Yelling for the policeman on duty, she received her allotted call. Luckily, she had memorized the telephone numbers that Trevor has given her; to his apartment in Charlotte, his house in DC and his cellular number. Hopefully, he would answer her call.

Chapter 10

Max had to divide his time between tracking down Maurice and tracking down the Chameleons, who were the assassins that were killing government agents overseas. A trap had been set for the Chameleons, spearheaded by Mr. Brownstone, Max's boss. The only people that knew about the trap were the two teams that reported directly Mr. Brownstone; Max and Randolph's team. Someone within their organization leaked the information which caused the entrapment to go wrong, with fatal results. After the details were ironed out, each left to talk to their respective teams to apprise them of the situation and how things were supposed to play out.

Leaving the building, Randolph had a few decisions to make; which of his sources would he contact to handle this new turn of events. He had people in various metropolitan cities in his pocket; lawyers, judges, policemen, and loan sharks that were so deep into his pocket that nothing was impossible. All of these people benefited from the strip clubs that he illegally owned.

It was time to get the heat off of Maurice, who could indirectly lead the agency back to the loan shark, which would ultimately lead back to him. He wasn't about to let all of his hard work go down the drain. Millions of dollars was at stake and he wasn't about to let anyone disrupt his cash flow! He just had to redirect the agency's efforts; get them focused on a bigger issue. Maybe he could kill two birds with one stone.

Picking up the telephone, he called Mr. Smith.

"I've got a job for you. I need you to immediately leak some information to your contacts in the following areas: Canada, Belgium, France, Spain and Africa. We need a diversion to draw the heat off the agency's investigation into the jewelry heist. Tell your contacts, that the agency is setting a trap for the group called the Chameleons. If their head leader wants a jump on Max, he has less than a week to get to the States. The trap will take place this weekend.

"Consider it done. Have the Feds been able to locate Maurice and the jewels?"

"Not yet. He's gone into hiding. When do you expect to wrap up this loose end?"

"My men are still looking for him. So far, they haven't come up with anything either. He's left Aruba. The trail is cold but I've got a plan to smoke him out that we can put into place as soon as your diversion is over."

"I don't care what your plan is as long as it gives me the desired results. We both know that we can't afford for Maurice to start selling the jewels or interrupt another jewelry heist. I need those jewels and I want Maurice eliminated."

After hanging up the telephone, Mr. Smith called, Leon, his right hand man into his office.

"Leon, let's talk. Any word yet on Maurice's location?"

"Not yet, boss. He's gone underground. I believe that we underestimated him. After he left Aruba, we lost his trace. We don't know if he went to another island or came back to the States."

"You're probably right, however his greed will be his downfall. I don't believe in coincidences. Who can you call and put pressure on that will give us some information?"

"I can call our government contact that can use their system to see if he's used any credit cards but I think that the only person that can give us information is your FBI agent."

"You're right. Before he stepped in, we had been planning the jewelry heist for well over a year. Shoot, it took that long to find enough people that could infiltrate the DeBeer's Company. No wonder they own most of the mines in South Africa. They have a virtual monopoly on the entire area. Getting someone to work for them is like getting someone to work at Fort Knox."

"That's why only ten of our people were actually able to infiltrate the company instead of the fifty that we had sent. Most of the workers couldn't stand the rigorous working conditions."

"What did they expect?"

"They were not in it for the long haul. Forty of the men quit within the first two months; claiming that the conditions in the mines were not worth the money that they were getting paid, nor worth what they would reap, once the heist was successful."

"I believe what really scared them was the rebels that would show up at the mines to steal the diamonds and would kill everyone in sight."

"That's the part I don't understand. We were paying the rebels to help us with the jewelry heist. We paid them a million dollars in cash and supplied them with enough weapons to take over a country. That's what the Unita rebel leader wanted; to overthrow the government."

"So what went wrong? Did Randolph pay someone else that he knew was expendable, to double cross us?"

"I believe that perhaps Randolph, the FBI agent, was trying to play both ends so that he could get the jewels and keep the money. Nothing else makes sense. Sitting here, I've been trying to go over in my head, what went wrong with the jewelry heist. How we ended up getting ambushed..."

The jewelry heist...

The heist had been planned carefully for well over a year. It took that long to infiltrate the DeBeer Company's operation. Roughly eighty percent of all the diamonds came from their mines which were located in various cities like Botswana, Sierra Leone and Angola, just to name a few.

Only ten workers were able to successfully infiltrate the company and remain there until the heist. Most couldn't stand the working conditions in the mines because the work was hard and dangerous, not only physically but also health-wise. If exposed to an excessive amount of the dust in the mines, a person could contract a deadly illness called silicusis, a lethal disease that attacks the lungs.

Forty out of the fifty men that Mr. Smith had sent to work for the DeBeer's company, quit the first or second month, claiming that the conditions were not worth the money that they were getting paid or what they would reap once the heist was successful. When asked what conditions other than the dust was the problem, the workers would complain that the rebels would come into the mines and raid them at least six or seven times a year to steal the diamonds. The rebels were ruthless and would kill anyone that got in their way.

It was this information that prompted Mr. Smith to alter the original plan for the jewelry heist. He would get the rebels to provide security and help him to steal the diamonds in return for cash money and weapons.

Traveling to Africa, Mr. Smith had his work cut out for him. The leader of the Unita rebels was known as a vicious leader. After gathering information about the leader in several cities, Mr. Smith decided to ask for a meeting with the leader, proposing to help him in his quest to overthrow the Angola government. According to the general public's knowledge, the government was able to stave off his last attempt to overthrow their government by raising funds in excess of what he was able to come up with.

The leader, late one evening, summoned him at gunpoint to his compound. He was handcuffed and blindfolded as he was led to the leader's quarters. Once inside, the handcuffs and the blindfolds were removed. With twenty men guarding the leader with semi-automatic weapons, a person would be foolish to try anything. He, on the other hand, just wanted to make it out of there alive.

"I understand that you think you can help me with my cause."

"Yes. I'm prepared to offer money in exchange for your weapons expertise and knowledge of the terrain for a jewelry heist."

"How much money and which company are you targeting?"

"I'm willing to offer two million dollars for the robbery of the DeBeer's company and a percentage of the diamonds."

"Make that one million in cash, one million in weapons and a percentage of the diamonds and you have yourself a deal," the leader requested. To himself, he thought, this time the government wouldn't be so lucky when he managed a coup; he had almost six hundred million dollars to get rid of the current president.

"Consider it done."

Mr. Smith and the Unita leader, talked late through the night, laying out the specifics of the jewelry heist of what was needed from both sides.

The day of the heist...

The rebels were set to cause quite a stir at two of the larger local mines which would be used as a smokescreen for the real heist which would take place at the headquarters where the vault was located.

Due to the increase in rebel activity, guards were posted at the mines to protect the diamond production. With a walkie talkie, the rebels initiated the first sequence of events. An explosion went off near the first mine, which of course caused immediate panic. The guards, not knowing what to think, took cover and fired their weapons towards the massive gunfire that was aimed towards them. It didn't take them long to figure out that this was no ordinary rebel attack; they were outnumbered.

The rebels surrounded the mine, shooting from various locations, killing the security guards that were protecting the outside. Some of the guards then on the inside made their way outside to help with the chaos. After the rebels eliminated the truck drivers, they pushed them out of the trucks and sped away with the jewels, which had been loaded for their mid-day pickup.

Simultaneously at the DeBeer Corporate Headquarters...

A construction crew was busy at work, clearing the land next to the DeBeer Headquarters for a future office complex. A permit from the government, only allowed the use of the explosives as a means of tearing down the old building, for only one day. With the timing being impeccable, the land was cleared and a tunnel was created underground that would give the crew access to the DeBeer Headquarters.

Once the explosion was successful and the old building was falling to the ground, Leon and his group moved into place. He had just received a text message on his cellular phone that the first sequence of events at the mines had also been initiated.

Going to the set of seven electrical panels, the electric testers that were normally used to gauge the amount of electricity was connected to one breaker on all of the panels. Once applied, the men rushed away for cover. Instead of testing the breakers, the instrument actually applied a surge of electricity, five times the amount that the breaker could withstand, thereby causing the breakers to overload. This massive overload of circuits caused the transformer to overload at the downtown electric company.

Everything went black on the inside of the headquarters. Five minutes later, backup transformers on site were turned on. The building was flooded with lights. The DeBeers had spent extra money to install these transformers in case the main transformer at the electricity plant malfunctioned. Thankfully, since they had purchased the extra transformer, they only had to use them once. When they received the electricity bill after that incident, they were astounded at the cost. Using the transformers there, had quadrupled their electricity bill.

Having anticipated the operation of the backup transformers, Harry radioed Leon that the backup transformers were powering up on the grid at the electrical company. Using a similar process, the backup transformers were permanently disabled. Leon then confirmed that everyone had made it into the building.

The foreman for the plant as well as the plant manager assumed that the crew working on the office complex had inadvertently knocked their power out. They immediately contacted the electrical company to see how long it would take before the situation was resolved. The electrical company estimated that it would take approximately one hour to rectify the situation.

After confirming that all the employees were safe, the foreman took a head count and escorted everyone to the cafeteria using a heavy duty flashlight.

The thieves were able to circumvent the security system, using some of the FBI's advanced computer technology, to open the door leading to the room where the vault was located. There was a three step procedure in order to open the jewelry vault. One had to successfully pass the retinal scan using either the Chief Executive Officer or by the President's retina. A fingerprint scan had to be garnered by the Chief Operating Officer, and a voice recognition scan was only viable if it came from a descendant of the DeBeer family.

The voice recognition for access to the vault area was previously acquired by Rasheeda at a party in New York, when she slept with one of the high ranking officers. The retinal scan and the fingerprint scan were collect by attaching a computer device, called Picture This, directly to the security device. Once the Picture This device was attached to the security apparatus, it would make a 3-D sketch of the last person that had successfully completed the required scan.

As soon as the sketch was complete, the image would be sent back to the apparatus creating a perfect match, thus opening the vault. Everything was working perfectly. Stage two with the security scans was now complete. The thieves were able to access the vault.

The jewels were placed into special velvet pouches and were hidden in undetectable pockets in two vests created specifically for the heist. Unknown to Mr. Smith, Swarovski crystals were placed underneath a small amount of authentic diamonds in each pouch that the robbers replaced in the vests. Instead of twenty million dollars in diamonds, that Mr. expected, the vests contained only about ten thousand dollars in jewels. The rest of the jewels went to the person that gave the rebels the largest amount of the bounty; Maurice.

The vests would enable the workers that had left the cafeteria to go to the restroom, to remain on site after the robbery. This would prevent the security staff at DeBeers from thinking that a robbery had taken place, and that it was an inside job.

Once the electricity came back on, the security team's first task was to check the vault. After the vault was found to be intact, they then searched all the employees, fearing a possible robbery. When the security team didn't find any evidence of a robbery, they alerted the police and the FBI. All employees were then told to remain on the premises until the police was able to question them.

Shaking his head, Leon exclaimed, "Robert, as soon as the men answered the questions by the police and were released, the FBI agent that was working undercover, met with all of us to make the exchange."

"What we didn't count on though, was the duplicity of the FBI agent. He had to be working with someone to make the exchange for him so that it would look like a setup. Someone that we wouldn't think would be involved. Someone that would be in Randolph's debt and someone that he could eliminate once the heist was over."

"That person would probably be someone that owes us money, so that the crime would look like a loan shark protecting his turf and not an FBI execution."

"Right. Maurice Holmes is the one that has the diamonds. Randolph knew where Maurice got the diamond that he used as a deposit on the two million that he owed me. Of course, now everything makes sense to me. Maurice owes me money because he swindled money from his clients that he had to repay. He suddenly comes up with a diamond to keep me off his back. He's goes into hiding so he doesn't have to pay me any additional money right away."

"Plus since we're planning another heist, this one bigger than the last, Randolph isn't in any rush to get his cut because if he was, the man would be dead by now. With all of the resources of the government at his fingertips, he claims that he can't find the man."

"He's planning on using him again for the next heist. If we find Mr. Holmes, we find the diamonds. I think there's a way to beat him at his own game."

Back at Headquarters...

Max headed over to his DC apartment after the meeting with Mr. Brownstone. Hitting the touch screen on his telephone for each member of his team, and then pressing talk, he was able to hold a conference with his entire team.

"Everyone, Operation Shutdown is scheduled to kick off this weekend. Our team and Randolph's team will be working on this case together. The Chameleons are set to takeover the Canelli drug territory. Our informant has already requested a meeting in an abandoned warehouse just off the I95 interstate. In exchange for ten million dollars, they get control over the territory and the last shipment of drugs are due to the port this weekend. That's when we take them down."

"How do we know that they will fall for this," asked Meghan?

"Word on the street has Nate, Michael's brother, buying up drug territories in various states. I believe he's trying to stage a coup over Michael. They've always had this rivalry as long as we've been tracking them."

"Here are the plans." Max proceeded to discuss every scenario possible for their operation and verified that everyone knew their responsibilities. When he was finished he made plans to fly to Greensboro to see his wife, Chelsea.

Chapter 11

Operation ShutDown...

Chelsea's telephone rang as she was leading Taylor to the car after being picked up from the daycare.

"May I speak with Chelsea Teal?"

"This is she," Chelsea answered as she was buckling Taylor into her car-seat.

"My name is Mr. Cooper. I'm sorry to inform you that your husband, Mr. Teal, has been in a minor accident leaving from the airport, and has been rushed, as a precautionary measure, to the hospital."

Chelsea, upon receiving the news, took a deep breath to calm her nerves so that she wouldn't terrify her daughter, Taylor.

"How bad is he?"

"Ma'am, he's going to be okay but we need for you to go directly to the hospital."

"Can I speak with him to make sure he's alright?"

"No ma'am. We're trying to stabilize him. I'm sorry but he's in and out of consciousness."

"Oh my God. What hospital are you taking him too?"

"The closest is Wesley Long. How long will it take you to arrive?"

"About twenty minutes. Please do whatever you can to save him." Putting the car in drive, she pulled out of the daycare parking lot and drove down the street towards the highway. With her BlueTooth, she was able to dial Erica, Max's sister to let her know what was going on.

"Erica, I just got a call from a Mr. Cooper, advising me that Max was in an accident on his way from the airport. I'm on my way now to Wesley Long."

"Oh no! I'm on my way. Did you get Taylor from the daycare?" When her sister-in-law didn't answer, she yelled, "Chelsea, Chelsea!" She still didn't get a response. All she heard was a loud crash and the wail from her niece.

"Mommie................"

Chelsea's car was hit from behind. It was a small bump but nonetheless she was still a little shaken from having to keep the car from hydroplaning and turning over. As soon as she recovered enough to open her eyes, she checked the back seat to make sure that Taylor was okay. After confirming that she was alright, she noticed two things. One, an ambulance was parked directly in front of her and two men from the ambulance were at the side of her car, knocking on the windows.

Slowing rolling the window down, she remarked, "Gee, how long was I out for the ambulance to have arrived so quickly?"

The next thing she knew, she felt a small pinprick in the side of her neck then everything went blank. When she awoke, Taylor and her were in a dark building, presumably an abandoned warehouse, filled with office equipment, tied to a pole, with a bomb in a suitcase, two hundred yards across the room.

Quickly Erica dashed down the hall, crying, almost hyperventilating as she ran into her husband's office.

"TJ honey, Chelsea called and said that Max was in an accident on his way from the airport. Then I heard a loud bang, as if Chelsea was in an accident. She had Taylor with her and all I heard was a loud scream from Taylor before everything went silent."

"Calm down honey. Let's check with the hospital to see which one they took Max too. Keep trying to get Chelsea on the telephone."

"Chelsea said that Max was being taken to Wesley Long."

TJ hugged his wife close, as he called the hospital. They didn't have a record of a Maxmillian Teal being admitted to the hospital. When asked if they had admitted a Mrs. Chelsea Teal from a pileup on the freeway, the receptionist replied that the pileup was just a fender binder and that no one needed immediate hospital help. TJ became alarmed. His next call was to Frank.

"Frank, this is TJ. Something's wrong. Chelsea received a call stating that Max was in an accident and on his way to the hospital. The hospital hasn't checked anyone in by his name. While Chelsea was talking to Erica, she heard Taylor scream and a big bang, which sounded like they were hit while driving in the car. She may have been the victim of foul play because the hospital receptionist said that the pileup on the freeway was just a minor bumper to bumper accident. No one was hurt."

"TJ, listen very closely. I need for you to keep trying to contact Chelsea and get her location if possible. I'll keep trying to reach Max. Please don't try to go to her. It's too dangerous. Let us handle it. This may have something to do with the case that Max is working on, if you know what I mean."

"Okay. I understand. I'll follow your instructions to the letter."

Frank tried multiple times to reach Max. It seemed as if Operation ShutDown was starting sooner than expected with drastic results. Somehow the Chameleons had gotten to Chelsea on her way home. Max was going to be furious with himself.

Finally, on the fourth try, Frank was able to contact Max. "Max, where are you?"

"I'm just got home from the airport. I called Chelsea to come and get me but I was unable to reach her. I thought that I would spend the day with her before we started Operation ShutDown."

"Max, brace yourself. I believe that Operation ShutDown has already started." Frank proceeded to tell Max what TJ had relayed to him. Hearing his best friends broken cry, nearly tore him apart. He knew how much his friend loved his wife.

Composing himself, Max muttered a string of expletives, mad at himself for putting his wife and child in the predicament that they were in. He had to find them alive to apologize for putting them in a position to be hurt because of his job. That's why he never told his wife his primary occupation; to prevent someone from holding them hostage to get to him.

"Frank, come and get me. We'll end this once and for all, after I've rescued my wife and child." Going to the backyard, he whistled for Angel, their black Labrador Retriever, to come inside. She was a good hunting dog. If anyone could find their scent, Angel would.

Just as expected, the Chameleons were ready for Max and his team when they showed up at the warehouse, later that evening. Gunfire could be heard everywhere. Max, along with Angel, rushed into the building from a side entrance, determined to find his wife and child, even if it meant that he would perish. In the distance, he could hear the exchange of gunfire between his team and the enemy, as well as several explosions.

Using an echo wave, his voice was distorted as he called out Chelsea and Taylor's names. If the enemy was in the building, they would not be able to pinpoint his location because the sound reverberated throughout the warehouse. To prevent anyone from entering the building behind him, Max setoff small explosives as he went. In the back of the building, Chelsea could hear Max's voice, frantically calling them. She couldn't answer because she was gagged and so was Taylor. They couldn't move either because their hands were tied to a pole.

Hearing a moaning sound, Angel dashed ahead of Max to the area where the sound was coming from. Max renewed his efforts to make it to the back of the building, upon hearing Mr. Brownstone's voice from his computerized watch, yelling that the building was about to blow.

Running swiftly in the direction that Angel had fled, he exchanged gunfire with the enemy as he rounded a corner. Because the building was on fire and time was running out to save the people that he loved, Max rose from his crouched position, dove over several pieces of furniture and made it to the entrance to the last room in the warehouse. As he ran through the door, he could see all that he held dear to his heart, tied to a pole; immobile. With several rapid rounds of fire aimed behind him into the wide expanse of the warehouse, Max ran into the room, intent on reaching his wife and child and releasing them at all costs.

Chelsea, who had been praying, screamed to Max to watch out. The warning was too late as an evil man came from behind Max and shot him. The bullet caught him in his side, and he fell to his knees. In excruciating pain, with all of his might, he tried to crawl to his beloved, only to be shot again. When he tried to rest for a few seconds, the building exploded.

Satisfied that the explosion had killed his nemesis, the Chameleon left town. Dialing the designated number, Michael, left his message. "It's finished. The operative and his wife and child have been eliminated."

The funeral was held several days later for Max, his wife Chelsea and his daughter Taylor. The Bailey and the Teal family could not believe that their loved ones were gone. Every television news station ran the story of how a local attorney and her daughter, who were kidnapped in broad daylight on a major highway, met with an untimely end. The story even ran on CNN.

Maurice happened to be watching television when the story aired on CNN. Looking at Rasheeda who was sitting on the couch, he exclaimed, "This is just the break that we need. I can show up at the funeral and get her address so that I can supposedly apologize for my behavior, as well as give her the money that I took out of her trust fund. She'll take everything that I say at face value because she'll still be in the throes of grief."

"When is the funeral?"

"According to this story, it's on Saturday. We'll leave on Friday and drive up to North Carolina."

"Good, I need to get a few things from my house. By that time, Cherita should be in jail, so we won't have to worry about her."

At the funeral, with so many people in attendance, Maurice attended the funeral but was unable to get talk to Jackie because she was never alone.

Both Erica and Jackie blamed themselves for Chelsea and Taylor's death. Erica thought that if only she had talked Chelsea out of going to the hospital until she had verified whether or not Max was admitted, or if she had called 911 to go to the scene of the accident, then maybe her best friend would be alive.

Jackie took it the hardest. While in Aruba, during her captive days, she had a premonition that someone would be captured and that death was eminent. Due to the distress she was in after her husband's abuse, she chalked the premonition up to a warning from God of the events that was to come. She didn't however equate the vision with her sister.

If only she had, she could have saved Chelsea and Taylor. After the funeral, severely despondent, grieving deeply, Jackie moved to Georgia. She hoped that with time, she would be able to come terms with being responsible for causing her sister's death.

As soon as the funeral was over, the next day, Jackie submitted several resumes to hospitals in Atlanta, Georgia and in Miami, Florida. She needed to escape from everyone; from all the hurt, her guilt and from the pain of losing her beloved sister. Again, Dr. Stan came to her rescue. He offered to contact one of his friends, who was the Chief Hospital Administrator, in a hospital in Atlanta, to secure a job for her.

Two days and a telephone interview later, she had a job. Packing only what she needed, she left Greensboro and moved to Atlanta. She asked her sister, Ryan, to take care of packing all of her things from her house in Charlotte. She never wanted to step foot in that house again. Ryan assured her that she would take care of everything and put her things in storage.

To the world, Max, his wife and child had died. To the select few that knew the truth, Max was recovering in a secluded hospital. The secrecy was necessary because the Bureau had a mole. The mole was responsible for the failure of Operation ShutDown. Someone that worked closely with Max and Randolph's team was responsible for Max being shot.

Trevor, who was mentally and physically exhausted, having spent the past two days at the hospital, willing Max to return to the land of the living, finally went home to get some rest. Frank, his coworker and friend, was his relief, after wrapping up some loose ends on the explosion that had killed Max's wife and daughter, and possibly Max's will to live.

All he needed was a hot shower and a bed for the next twenty-four hours. He hadn't gotten any rest, except for catnaps, for the past forty-eight hours. Walking into his apartment, he threw his keys and his phone on the foyer console and started towards the bedroom when his phone rang. Thinking that it was

Frank at the hospital, with bad news about Max, Trevor swiftly grabbed his phone.

"How bad is he?"

"What? Trevor, I can't talk long. Can I take you up on your offer of help?"

"Cherita?"

"Yes. I'm in jail. Can you come and bail me out and I'll explain what's going on at McAlstons Bank?"

"I'll be there in half an hour. Can you hold on till then?"

"As long as I know that you're coming. Thank you," she whispered.

Picking up his keys and pocketing his phone, he ran out the door and exceeded all speed limits as he drove downtown to the Mecklenburg County Jail. Flashing his Bureau badge, he was able to cut through the red tape quickly and succeeded in getting Cherita's release in less than half an hour. When she was brought from the back, for her release, she quietly gathered her possessions and waited for him to finish signing all the paperwork.

"Sir, she's being released into your custody."

"Thanks for expediting her release."

Trevor then escorted her out the door to freedom. Both were silent until they reached his SUV. As he opened her door, Cherita turned to face him before she got into the car. Just as she was about to thank Trevor, he gathered her possessively to him and with a voracious appetite, kissed her passionately upon the lips. Consumed by the kiss, Cherita's body instinctively rubbed against his.

Breaking off the kiss, since they were still in the parking lot, Trevor stated, "I'm hanging on by a thread, so behave. Let's go home and we'll talk."

Home, such an unfamiliar word. Where was that? Cherita thought, having never felt the peace that one thought of when they thought of home.

"Are you hungry? Do you need me to stop and get you something to eat? How long has it been since you last ate? How long were there?"

"I couldn't eat anything earlier. I've been there since around two o'clock."

Pulling into his apartment complex, Trevor parked his SUV and got out to open the door for Cherita. "Why did it take you so long to contact me? I could have had you out of there earlier!"

"I had to weigh my options. Is there something wrong Trevor? You look exhausted. Here I am adding to your problems. I'm sorry. If you can just drive me back to my sister's place, I'll let you get some rest."

"Yes, I am exhausted. I've been up for the last forty-eight hours. My best friend and mentor, was shot two days ago. Come on in and we'll discuss everything."

"Cherita, help yourself to whatever you can find in the kitchen. I need to take a shower if I'm to remain awake while we have our discussion." Leaning down, he placed a sweet kiss to her cheek before moving in the direction of the bedroom. Trevor returned five minutes later with a handful of items; a towel, a bath cloth, one of his shirts and a bathrobe.

"There's a shower in the other bedroom if you want to use it. I'm sorry that I can't help with your undergarments but I have a washer and a dryer. Feel free to use them.

Without another word, he was gone.

How could you not love a man that was so thoughtful; that he cared enough to think of your well-being first?

Looking in his refrigerator, Cherita found several ingredients to make breakfast while Trevor showered. He claimed that he hadn't slept; he looked as if he hadn't eaten either in those two days. After preparing an egg and cheese omelet, along with some bacon and grits, Cherita put the food into the warming oven. Then she hurried into the other room to take a quick shower; to wipe away the grunge that she felt being in a jail cell for well over six hours.

Changing into his shirt, she then made her way self-consciously into the kitchen. Since Trevor had not reappeared, she thought that she would check on him, to make sure that he was still awake.

Knocking on his bedroom door, she called out, "Trevor, I've prepared some food for you. Are you finished?" When he didn't answer or come out of the bedroom, she hesitantly opened the door. Finding the bed empty, she rushed into the bathroom to make sure he was alright.

Pushing open the door, she gasped in surprise upon seeing Trevor's magnificent body through the transparent glass shower enclosure. The sheer size of the shower enclosure amazed her. It was big enough for three or four people and had a wrap around bench on one side. Frozen to the spot, Cherita could only stare at Trevor as he stuck his head out of the shower.

"Did you need something?" He asked, watching Cherita intently.

"Um, yes. I mean no. I just wanted to let you know that I've made breakfast. Whenever you're finished, come on out."

"I would rather that you join me instead; not in repayment for bailing you out, but simply because I can't think of a better place for you to be, than enclosed in my arms as the water cascades over our bodies."

When Cherita didn't move to leave, or to join him, Trevor replied, "If you don't want to join me, give me five minutes. I didn't realize that I had been in here so long."

Cherita stood frozen to the spot, drinking her fill of his magnificent body that she could only see through the transparent glass.

Stepping out of the shower, Trevor's next words spurred her into action. "If you don't leave now, that discussion we talked about will have to be postponed until tomorrow."

Cherita backed out of the bathroom, determined that all secrets between them would be out and in the open before she let herself become intimate with Trevor again.

Reaching for the towel hanging on the warming rack, Trevor sighed in regret as he dried off and quickly dressed.

Entering the kitchen he placed a kiss on Cherita's lips as he looked at the scrumptious meal that she had prepared for him. "Thank you! You didn't have to go to this much trouble for me."

"It wasn't any trouble. You look like you haven't eaten in a few days."

"Some things become unimportant given dire situations. Let's eat, and then we can talk. Will you be staying the night or do I have to handcuff you to me to make you stay?"

Laughing at his joke, Cherita looked up to see if he was kidding. When she saw that he was completely serious, she stopped laughing. "No, I'm here for as long as you want me. No more running."

Seeing the sincerity in her eyes, Trevor nodded and proceeded to eat his first real meal since Max was admitted to the hospital. After their quick make-shift meal, he escorted her into the den for their discussion.

"Okay, can we lay all our cards on the table? Do you want to go first or shall I?" Trevor asked Cherita, giving her the option of hopefully, explaining what she was really doing in Charlotte.

"I'll go first. My name is Cherita Montgomery and I have an identical twin sister named Rasheeda Montgomery. We're the same height but she's slimmer than I am and also the firstborn. I'm a graphic artist and I live in Washington, D.C. The telephone numbers I gave you are my correct personal information. My sister is one of the personal bankers at McAlston Bank and Trust. She asked me to cover for her for two weeks while she eloped with her boyfriend, somebody by the name of Maurice, in exchange for twenty thousand dollars."

"I didn't suspect anything unusual because Rasheeda has always made good money. I did ask her however, if she was eloping, why the family hadn't met her boyfriend. She blew me off with some story about myself and our parents' opinion of the guys she's dated as being leeches. I agreed to help her because I want to open my own graphic design firm and need the extra cash.

Although I've saved about thirty five thousand dollars, the extra twenty thousand dollars would allow me to buy some additional equipment."

"During the past week at McAlstons, I've been accosted twice in the same day; first by the security guard, Eugene, then by the Branch Manager, Mr. Carson. Apparently Rasheeda is sleeping with both of them, either for their help or to keep them quiet. I'm not quite sure which. I reacted negatively of course to their overtures by slapping them and hitting them in their jewels, along with giving them a few choice words."

"Anyway to make a long story short, after the last incidence, I walked outside, ready to quit and go back home but decided to face the music. I found Mr. Carson in my office at my computer when I returned. After I kicked him out, I noticed an encrypted file that he didn't have time to protect or close when I caught him. The file has several of the banks client's names, their account number, dates and amounts withdrawn from their portfolio and deposited into an offshore account. I used to work in a bank so I'm pretty familiar with their operations. I mailed a copy of the file to you and one to my home address, just in case something happened to me."

As she paused, Trevor asked, "Is that it?"

"Yes," she said, looking down at the table in the den, afraid that he would think negatively of her for pulling a scam to earn money to open her own firm.

Putting his finger under her chin, he raised her face so that he could look directly into her eyes.

"Thank you for being honest. My name is Trevor Darby and I'm an FBI agent, specializing in computer security. Anything that is discussed tonight is strictly confidential. I was called by a close friend to investigate someone for embezzlement at his Corporation. Investigating that Corporation led me to Charlotte. I normally live in Washington, D.C. too. The person responsible for the embezzlement actually happens to be my best friend's brother-in-law, Maurice Holmes."

"My best friend, Maxmillian Teal, who's also an FBI agent and the owner of his own security firm, is currently in the hospital fighting for his life after an FBI operation ambush. But that's another story that I can't deal with right now. Unfortunately, neither of us suspected that Maurice was shady."

"Meeting you was purely coincidental, but by far the best thing that has happened to me. We suspected your sister but had not pulled a dossier on her because as far as we knew, she was still working at McAlstons. So I didn't have a picture or anything on her because we set a trap to meet her at the bank. That's why I was there. To put a program that I designed on her computer to figure out which clients were affected and how much money was involved. The program would also record her keystrokes and any conversations from that point forward, which would give us the opportunity to see if she was working with anyone else."

"You can imagine my surprise to see the woman I had spent a glorious night with, that ran out on me without saying goodbye, to be standing in front of me as the suspected personal banker that had committed several crimes. I couldn't believe it. I was angry with you for not being the person my heart recognized as its soul mate. When you wouldn't answer my questions but kept putting me off until your two weeks had expired, I began to suspect something."

"I then asked you if our night together meant anything to you. You responded honestly without hesitation. That's why I offered my help if you were in trouble. Short of killing someone, it didn't matter to me. I haven't always led a perfect life so who was I to judge you?"

"Then I loaded my program on your computer when you stepped out of your office. When I came home I watched the events that occurred after I left. I almost had a coronary when that guy grabbed you. I had picked up my keys and started out of the room until he spoke about sleeping with you. I knew, based on our night together that you were a virgin. That meant that something was wrong and that we were talking about someone else. I did a little more investigating at that point on your sister."

"For the record, if I'm really interested in someone, I don't investigate them. I had the motive and the opportunity when you left without a word and of course I have all the resources, but I chose not too. I didn't want that to stand in our way of developing a committed relationship. The information that I found on your sister you may or may not believe. I hate to be the bearer of bad news, but your sister set you up. She was in Aruba with her boyfriend Maurice. However, he's married to a wonderful person by the name of Jackie, Max's sister-in-law."

"Maurice and Rasheeda knew that we were getting close so they decided to hide until you were arrested. With some false evidence given to the police, you could have been convicted."

Quiet up until that point, Cherita exclaimed, "How is that possible when I have identification that says I'm Cherita Montgomery?"

"Because the police could say that you forged your sister's identity or something of that nature to make it stick. Getting back to your sister and Maurice, everything that you told me is true. They are working together, and so are Eugene and the Branch Manager, Mr. Carson. Each of them is doing something to help her. When Rasheeda and Maurice went to Aruba, he abused his wife and forced her to go with him. Luckily she escaped but they've gone underground. The offshore accounts that you mentioned are also tied to a jewelry heist. So you see it's not safe for you to be alone. If they find out that you know what's going on, they could harm you. Will you stay with me until then, so that I can keep you safe?"

"This is a lot to think about. Can I take some time to digest all of this?"

"Yes, take a couple of hours, or a day or two to think it over. Look, I know it's late and I'm beat. Promise me that you'll be here when I wake up." Trevor pleaded with his hands outstretched towards Cherita as he stood. He didn't know what he would do if he woke up again and she had disappeared.

Putting her hands in his, he pulled her to her feet. "I won't leave again without saying goodbye."

"Not exactly what I wanted to hear but I guess that's all I'm going to get for now."

Feeling an overwhelming urge to pull her closer, he placed his hands around her waist and brought her flush against his aroused body. With a desperate yearning, he captured her lips in a searing kiss that seemed to reach the very depths of his soul. As his mouth continued to feast ravenously on her lips, thrusting deeper into the opening that she provided for him, he picked Cherita up in his arms and carried her into the bedroom. Laying her gently in the bed, with one final kiss, he pulled the covers up over her body. With his hands clenched at his side, it took all of his will power to stop himself from joining her in the bed. Whispering goodnight he walked out of the room. He needed to rest for a couple of hours before he went back to the hospital to check on Max.

For forty-eight hours, Max's condition was touch and go. Surprising everyone, even the doctors, he walked out of the hospital five days later and went straight to work on finding the persons responsible for the deaths of his wife and child. Since it was reported that he had died in the explosion, Max was free to move about with ease; always in disguise though, when he searched through the ruble of the explosion site for evidence that would lead him to the responsible culprits.

After discussing the issues surrounding the embezzlement case with Max to give his mind some relief, they decided to do a video conference with Mr. McAlston to apprise him of the ongoing investigation and the ramifications it had on his bank. Upon completion of the conference, Mr. McAlston was taken aback at all that had transpired at his bank, right before his very eyes.

He was okay with Cherita remaining on his staff to keep up appearances for the sake of the case. She was a good worker and was a welcome change from her sister Rasheeda and her attitude. In her time there she had implemented new programs that had been very beneficial to the bank. She had even found another bank for them to merge with that was more cost effective and would provide a greater coverage in areas that they currently did not operate in.

A frantic voicemail message awaited Cherita when she got home from work the next day. Rasheeda left a message begging her to stay on at the bank for the next three to six months, because she was taking a hiatus and was traveling the world with her new husband. When Cherita tried to contact her sister, the call went straight to an automated answering service. It became impossible to reach her.

As she was leaving a message, her phone beeped with an incoming call. Hurriedly she left the message for her sister, and then clicked the phone to switch to the new caller. Unfortunately, the caller had already hung up. Retrieving her messages she smiled upon hearing Trevor's voice advising her that they had worked it out so that she was welcome to stay at the bank and work until the case was solved.

She owed him a debt of gratitude. Working would continue to allow her to save enough money for her dream. If she was going to remain in Charlotte, she had to go back home to get additional clothes and gather the rest of her supplies so that she could continue to service her existing clients.

Leaving a message for Trevor, Cherita decided to leave immediately for Washington and return the following day. Little did she know that what awaited her in Washington would alter the course of her life forever.

Tried, after driving for six hours, Cherita let herself quietly into her house. Hearing a faint thumping sound from upstairs, she walked quietly with a baseball ball to investigate the sound. As she approached the top of the stairs, she then started to hear moaning sounds like someone was in the throes of passion. Coupled with the clothes that were strewn from the top of the stairs to the master bedroom, it didn't take a rocket scientist to figure out that two people were making love in her house.

How did they get in? Who were they?

Inching closer to identify the intruders, Cherita stopped upon hearing what sounded like her sister's voice, discuss how well their plan was working and how she would plan it so that Cherita would take the fall for the upcoming murders. This talk was interspersed with more moaning sounds, when the male screamed, "Rasheeda!" in a hoarse voice. Her sister's answering cry, "Maurice, enough talking!" was enough evidence that Cherita needed to confirm the intruder's identity and to make her way quietly back down the stairs.

Since they were so loud, they were oblivious to anyone being in the house until the door made a noise when Cherita hurriedly closed it. Up until that point Cherita hadn't really believed that her sister had set her up. She felt sick to her stomach. She had been used.

Luckily she was in a rental car. Even if they stopped and looked out the window, they would not be able to identify who had come into the house. After driving for fifteen minutes to the other side of town, Cherita pulled into the parking lot of a Walgreens and purchased some stationary.

Sitting in the parking lot, she wrote a letter to Trevor.

Trevor,

You will find Maurice and my sister Rasheeda at my house located at 2604 McCall Lane, in Washington DC. I went home after I got your message to gather more clothes and to retrieve some material for my business so that I could continue to work on some freelance projects. I found them living there without my permission.

To my surprise, I walked in on them talking about my taking the wrap for the murders that would take place while hearing them having sex like two teenagers. They were so involved that I don't think that they heard me. I can no longer deal with the fact that my sister is a criminal, a home wrecker and a thief. It will be best if you never see me again.

I don't want to jeopardize the career that you love. Please don't attempt to find me. You would just prolong the inevitable.

My heart is dying.

Cherita

Sealing the letter, she then stopped by the post office to mail the letter to his Charlotte address. Thinking that she had caused Trevor and his friends too much pain, she disappeared and headed to New York. How could he love her after what her sister had put his friends through?

Chapter 12

Two years later...

Now that the FBI agents were focused on saving their operatives from being killed in other parts of the world, according to the information that was leaked to the press, Maurice felt it was a good time to retrieve the hidden jewels from his ex-wife.

It was now time to up the ante.

The time was right for him to fence some of the jewels to pay for the men that he would need for his next heist. Having gotten away with the first one, he wanted to score the coup de grace, so that he could retire forever. In order to do that, he had to travel to Georgia, to have a friendly talk with his ex wife.

During a break in her hospital shift, Jackie received a telephone call. Answering the call, she was surprised when she heard her ex-husband's voice.

"Hello Jackie. Please don't hang up. I need to talk to you. I tried to talk to you at Chelsea's funeral but you were surrounded by people."

"Were you afraid that Malcolm and David would get to you? What do you want Maurice?"

"I wanted to meet with you to apologize for my behavior and my indiscretions, and to see if you would take me back. I've come to my senses and I miss you."

Laughing, Jackie hung up the telephone. *What was he up to? This wasn't just an ordinary call. Did his mistress put him out?* Thinking nothing of the call, she went back to work.

Leaving work that night, she didn't see the man in the black clothes following her from the building to the parking deck. Luckily a few coworkers were walking with her so she wasn't in any danger.

The next day, Maurice called again. She refused to talk to him and told the operator for her floor that her ex was being a pain and that she didn't have time talk to him.

Okay my beautiful ex-wife. You don't want to talk to me. I guess I have to get your attention another way. We'll see how long it's going to take you to come to your senses and to connect the dots. Pretty soon, you'll be begging me to help you.

Putting the word out on the street that he needed a little surveillance, Maurice was able to hire two gang members to follow Jackie. If they could provide him with an address then he would give them five thousand dollars.

Just when Jackie thought she was getting her life back together, strange things started to happen soon after the telephone call from her ex-husband. She felt as if she was being followed. Taking different routes to work, she hoped that she would lose the person that seemed to be stalking her.

Careful of the people that she went out with for social occasions, Jackie didn't feel as if the stalker was any of them. Since she had been in Atlanta, she had met a lot of really nice guys but none that she wanted to have a committed relationship with. The old adage; once bitten, twice shy, was one that she now lived by.

At work, earlier that morning, she could have sworn that she saw her ex-husband asking for her at the nurse's station. Not waiting long enough to find out, she proceeded into a patient's room and completely forgot about his presence.

Getting off work that evening, she went home to relax. She had just gotten off a twelve hour shift and she was tired. Unlocking the door to her apartment, she stepped into her dimly lit foyer. Turning on the lamp as she walked into the living room, she screamed in fright when she saw all of her belongings sitting in the middle of the floor, torn completely to shreds.

Her entire apartment seemed to have been ransacked. Grabbing her purse, she ran out the door to her neighbor's house and called the cops.

Thirty minutes later they arrived to dust for fingerprints. Asking all of the usual questions, Jackie answered them as best as she could; no she didn't know of anyone that wanted to hurt her and no she didn't have any enemies, at least none that she was aware of. If she thought of anyone, she advised them that she would let them know.

Her neighbor and good friend, Cookie, wouldn't dream of her checking into a hotel, so she slept in her guest bedroom that night. To weary to think, she fell into a restless sleep. She would deal with everything the following morning.

Muttering a string of expletives after the report that was given to him, Maurice paid the gang members even though they were unable to find what he needed. It seemed as if she hadn't brought anything to Georgia with her, but the clothes on her back. Where was the rest of her stuff?

What has he to do? He couldn't just come out and ask her. He didn't know what her reaction would be if he saw her face to face. Would she put him in jail for abusing her? He wasn't willing to take that chance. He would just have to continue to follow her. Eventually she had to go to a storage unit at some point, for the rest of her things, now that everything was destroyed. Smiling, Maurice headed back to his hotel room.

Jackie wasn't scheduled a day off until two days after the ransacking of her house. Since Cookie had offered her apartment, she only needed a change of clothes for those two days. After contacting a maid service, her apartment was back to normal, albeit a rather sparse reflection of its former self but it was still home.

After musing over the events of the past couple of days, she was pretty sure that Maurice had something to do with her apartment being ransacked. It was too much of a coincidence with him showing up out of the blue, at the hospital. Nothing had been taken, which made the break-in more suspect. The question was, what was he after?

The ringing of the telephone interrupted her musings. Feeling cautious, she hesitantly picked up the telephone.

"Hello?"

"Hey honey. Are you busy?"

"I'm never to too busy to talk to you Daddy. What's up?"

"I was wondering if you could come home this weekend? There are some important things your Mom and I need to discuss with everyone."

With trepidation, upon hearing the gravity in his voice, Jackie asked, "What things Daddy? Is everything okay?"

"We'll discuss that when you arrive. Can you fly in tomorrow?"

"Yes, Daddy. I'll catch the next flight out."

"See you soon, punkin. I love you."

"I love you too, but Dad you're scaring me."

"Not my intention. See you tomorrow." Without another word, he hung up.

Hastily dialing her sister's telephone numbers, she talked to each one to get a feel for what was wrong but they didn't know either.

They had all been summoned home.

When Jackie arrived in Greensboro the following afternoon, she was met at the airport by her brother David. Hugging her fiercely, he welcomed her home. He had missed his little sister.

"David, do you know what this is about?"

"No one does. Mom and Dad are being real secretive."

"They are not getting a divorce are they?"

"Of course not. It must be something else. We were ordered to come straight to the house."

Pulling up in their parent's driveway, seeing that everyone else had already arrived, judging by the number of cars, they immediately parked and went inside.

Smiling, Jackie greeted all of her loved ones. Soon, Mr. Bailey walked into the room with a distinguished, older gentleman. After he hugged Jackie briefly, he got right down to business.

"Everyone, I'd like your attention. I've called this meeting today to discuss something very important. This is Mr. Brownstone, a government official that has come to discuss something very important with us."

Glancing around the room, Mr. Brownstone, immediately spoke. "There is no easy way to say what I have to say, so I'm just going to get right to it. Two years ago, your sister happened to be at the wrong place at the wrong time. She fell victim to a terrorist plot and was used as a hostage by that group of assassins that were stealing information from the government. Unfortunately at that time, in order to preserve thousands of other operatives in the field, domestically and abroad, Chelsea and Taylor were pronounced dead at the scene of the crime."

"What exactly do you mean?" Malcolm, the oldest questioned.

At the audible gasp around the room, and the tears that were forming in everyone's eyes, Mr. Brownstone rushed on. "I'm here today to let you know that Chelsea and Taylor are in fact alive and in need of your help."

A shocked expression was seen on everyone's face. Then came the anger. It was a test to see which brother would jack the man up first. David, being the one closest to Chelsea, got to Mr. Brownstone first.

"What do you mean she's alive? We saw the news. We even went to the site of the explosion. We searched and searched for their remains but didn't find anything. Nothing. We even had their burial. Now two years later, you want us to believe that she's alive? What the hell is your problem and why are we being notified today that she's alive? Why didn't you tell us this before?" David yelled as he choked Mr. B in his anguish.

"Sir, I'm sure that you are justified in trying to hurt me. However, let me put your mind at ease. Chelsea has been in a coma since the accident. She has just awakened with the help of her dog Angel, who was also recuperating. Because of the nature of the operation that caused the explosion and the lives of others, we had to wait until it was safe to contact you. We had to let you go through with the burial so that the assassins would think that they had succeeded in murdering them and one of our best operatives." Mr. B haltingly replied once he could catch his breath.

"I don't understand," said Chelsea's mother Erma.

"Do you mean to tell us that Chelsea was almost murdered because of a government plot?"

"No, she just happened to be at the wrong place at the wrong time. Now, getting back to the imperative matter at hand; Chelsea has amnesia. She doesn't remember her past life or who she is. She has been going through various tests to determine how much she remembers. So far, we know that she remembers her dogs' name and general information that she would know growing up and having gone to college. That means she doesn't remember her husband, her child or her family, (i.e. all of you)."

"If she doesn't remember us, how are you going to convince her to come home to stay with what to her would be total strangers?" asked Anita, Chelsea's oldest sister.

"I believe that if we work together, we can come up with a story that will sound plausible and convincing. Jackie, if you can rearrange your schedule to pick Chelsea up within the next two days, we can discharge her into your care, that is if you can get a leave of absence from the hospital in Georgia." Mr. Brownstone replied anxiously praying that everyone would come to some kind of agreement.

"Consider it done."

"Here are the instructions from the neurologist and the psychiatrist: (1) Don't reveal her name to her because it might cause irrevocable damage by jarring her memory back to the time of the explosion, (2) The family must pretend to Chelsea that her real daughter is actually her niece, and (3) since Taylor is such a precocious child, she must be told the truth. She will understand and "play" along with you until you tell her its okay not to pretend."

"What about Max? How are you going to keep this from him considering that he still comes by whenever he's in town to socialize with the family?" Jackie asked pensively.

"That won't be a problem. Max is a workaholic. Ever since the explosion, he has been working like a madman. He will be overseas for the next several months anyway working on a case," stated Mr. B.

"I think it's cruel not to tell Chelsea's husband that she's alive. My God, the man still loves her! He still goes to visit their burial site at least once a month. Every week if he's in town," said David angrily.

"If we tell Max, he will undoubtedly try to force her memory to recall the great love that they shared. Remember, Chelsea's last thought of Max, was of him attempting to rescue them and being shot in the stomach and side. Her last waking thought was him falling to the ground to his death or so she thought. We want Chelsea to come to grips with her memory normally. Therefore, we will place them in the same proximity for about six months to see if a relationship can develop naturally. If not then we will assign Max to protect her as one of our cases."

"How do you plan to arrange that?" Mrs. Bailey asked skeptically.

"If it's all right with you, Chelsea will recuperate with Jackie acting as her nurse right here at the family home. We'll simply tell her the basics of her former life, starting with her name as Paris Bailey. Since we are shortening her name, to her middle and maiden name, Chelsea Paris Bailey Teal, perhaps on some level she can identify with the name. She will be a long lost friend of Jackie's, from their college years at Howard. They were drawn together during school because of her similarity to Chelsea. Her personality was so much like Chelsea's that Jackie adopted her as another sister," said Mr. B, warming to his theory that him and his wife had hashed out the previous two days.

"Since Chelsea or rather Paris, as we have to refer to her until she regains her memory, graduated from college, she has worked on the West Coast in Los Angeles as a family attorney. Since their occupation will be the same, there shouldn't be any noticeable gaps in our story. Once she returned to her hometown, she enters a contest, sponsored by Max's business, for the next model for his new perfume, Alluring. Anita you will be responsible for getting Paris to enter the contest on a dare and since Max will be so taken with her likeness to Chelsea, he'll want to get to know her better."

"What does that have to do with Paris staying with us and how are we going to explain her likeness to Chelsea?" Traci asked.

"Well, Paris and Jackie were such good friends that when she came back to her hometown, she wanted to build a house and put down some roots. Since she didn't have any family left in this world except some extended cousins, your mother offered to let her stay in the family house until hers was completed. When asked about the similarities, your reply would be the old Southern expression, that everyone somewhere has a twin. If we let Paris know up front her involvement with Max, as simply good friends, then she will expect him to be around a good portion of the time."

"From Max's standpoint, I'll concoct some story about him keeping Paris safe because of a powerful businessman/drug dealer from the West Coast who Paris went up against in a custody battle. He threatened to kill her, hence her relocation to the East Coast. Since he lost, Paris' life is in danger. We'll use Max and his team to keep her out of harm's way. This will give Max an excuse to stay in constant contact with her and as the "case" unfolds, they should develop a relationship because of their natural love for each other. Hopefully, when all is said and done, they'll fall in love and Paris' memory will return and the subterfuge will be forgiven in time."

"Okay, when can we see her?"

"Tomorrow. Jackie will be the first one to meet her and will bring her back here. At that time, the entire family can meet her. I think it's best to just get the initial shock over with at one time. Then she can concentrate on healing and getting back to her normal life."

"One question, Mr. Brownstone, have you caught the person that was responsible for this?" asked Mr. Bailey, who up until this point had been very quiet.

"Unfortunately, that's the other problem that we still face. Max will be guarding Paris for real, however, not from a drug dealer from the West Coast, but from the assassins that planned the explosion."

"When did Max say that he would be back, Anita?"

"This weekend. He should be by on Sunday." Okay that means since today is Wednesday, we have to move fast. I'll brief him tonight during our regular talk."

"Mr. Brownstone, let me make myself clear. If we should lose Paris, or Chelsea, or whatever name you want to call my daughter, know that you'll have to deal with me. I won't be so forgiving the next time. What you don't want is a vigilante on your trail," stated Paris' brother Malcolm.

A knock sounded at the door, as soon as Mr. Brownstone had received everyone's cooperation and all their questions were answered.

Mrs. Bailey then excused herself to answer the door. After she opened the door, she stood frozen in shock. There stood a little girl that resembled her late granddaughter holding a beautiful stranger's hand.

Throwing herself immediately upon her grandmother, Taylor exclaimed, "Hello grandma! What took you so long to find me?"

Hugging her fiercely, Mrs. Bailey started laughing and crying at the same time. Pretty soon the entire family came to the foyer to see what the commotion was about. Taylor then ran to each aunt and uncle and greeted them by name with a hug and a kiss. Finally she reached her grandfather. She climbed onto his lap and sat there quietly for about two minutes, as if she remembered doing that thousands of times before.

Then with a kiss on his cheek she started talking nonstop about her adventure. All too soon after a hearty hug from her grandfather, Taylor got down and went to talk to Mr. Brownstone, one of her favorite people. With the help of his wife, the Brownstones had kept her for the last two years while Max and Chelsea had recuperated.

Not to exclude anyone, Taylor gave him a hug also. "Mr. B, I'm going to miss you and Mrs. B but I'm with my family now. I'll see if they can let me visit sometimes. Tell Mrs. B that I love her."

Everyone started talking at once before Mr. B held up his hand for silence.

"As you can see, this is Taylor. I would like to believe that my wife and I have raised her like you would have raised her for the last eighteen months. I'll take my leave now so that you can spend time with her and catch up. Goodbye."

Mr. Brownstone and his secretary left the Baileys house and returned to their base headquarters. Things were slowly starting to fall into place.

As everyone held separate conversations, Jackie pulled Malcolm and David to the side, into a secluded part of the house so that they wouldn't be overheard.

"Malcolm and David, I've got a couple of questions that I want to run by you. Can we talk?"

"Sure Jackie. What's up?" Malcolm asked.

"Two days ago, someone broke into my apartment when I was at work and ransacked my place."

"What?" They both exclaimed in unison.

"Were they at the apartment when you returned home?"

"Did you contact the police?"

"Yes the police was contacted and no they were gone when I got home. After dusting for fingerprints, the police didn't come up with anything. They believe that some gangs were responsible because a gang symbol was left behind."

"Did they take anything and why are we just hearing about it now?"

"No, that's the funny part. My thirty-seven inch LG television was still there and so was my computer. Other than pulling everything out into the middle of the floor, and turning over the furniture, I couldn't find anything missing. It was if they were looking for something and didn't find it."

"What about an answer as to why we are just finding out?"

"I've been working twelve hour shifts and stayed at my friend, Cookie's place, across the hall."

"The next time, call us immediately. We're just a little over two hours away by plane. Your well-being is too important to us to go through what we went through the last time you were in trouble."

"I know and I appreciate you guys."

"Why do you think that someone was looking for something?"

"The furniture wasn't slashed or cut up, only turned over. The same with my clothes. They were pulled out of the closet and dumped in the middle of the floor. However, my pocketbooks were completely destroyed."

"How so?"

"The lining of two of my favorite handbags were completely ripped out of the bag. On the street, someone could have gotten a lot of money for the Dooney & Burke handbag as well as the Louis Vuttion handbag."

"Maybe they were looking for cash?"

"Do you normally keep cash in your bags?"

"No, I never keep money in them."

"That doesn't explain why the linings were torn though. I don't believe this was a random attack. Last week out of the blue, Maurice called at the hospital one day and then showed up the next day looking for me."

"What the…!" exclaimed Malcolm.

"Shush. Keep your voice down so that you won't worry Momma. She has enough to deal with right now."

"Why would Maurice seek you out now? He didn't contest the divorce. As a matter of fact, he was never served with the papers because we couldn't find him."

"Either I have something that he wants or something of his got mixed up with the things that Ryan packed from the house when I moved to Atlanta."

"Did you talk to him?"

Rolling her eyes at her brothers, Jackie explained, "No I saw him before he saw me, when he was at the nurse's station asking for me. I had just left one of my patient rooms when I heard a voice that sounded like his. As he was talking, I peeped around the corner quickly to verify if that was him or not, then I ducked into one of the extra rooms. My friend at the desk covered for me."

"I guess we'll just have to take a visit to Atlanta tonight to see what's going on. If he came by your job, it's only a matter of time before he would be able to learn of your address. I'm sure that once he confirmed that you worked there that he had you followed."

Seeing Jackie's dubious expression, Malcolm and David became concerned when she didn't look them in the eyes.

"There's more isn't there?"

"Well.... I did feel as if I was being watched for the rest of that week, but I wasn't able to catch anyone. I changed my routes and my routines like ya'll taught us, and unfortunately didn't give it any more thought until the break-in."

"That settles it. We're heading out tonight to Atlanta to do a little surveying of the land."

"Please be careful. I don't want anything to happen to either of you."

Kissing their sister on the cheek, Malcolm and David went to say goodbye to their parents and siblings before they headed out.

Maurice drove cautiously down the street, in an unfamiliar Atlanta suburb, while trying to locate the apartment complex that his ex wife lived in. After locating the apartment complex, he pulled into the gated community and parked his car on the side, as if he was verifying the address from a piece of paper. In order to enter the complex through the gates, one had to have a security card or had to wait until a resident could supply a code to be entered onto the keypad.

Without the security card, Maurice didn't stand a chance of gaining entry into the complex. He patiently waited at the entrance, on the side, until a car passed through the gates. Quickly putting his car in gear, he floored the accelerator so that he could follow the car into the complex before the gates had time to close.

Parking the car, he looked around at his surroundings to make sure that he wasn't walking into a trap. No one seemed to be paying him any attention. Looking at the paper with the address written on it, Maurice proceeded to Jackie's apartment door. Knocking on the door, he waited for an acknowledgement. None was forthcoming.

He knocked again, this time a little harder. Just as he was about to turn away and head back to his car, Jackie's neighbor stuck her head out of her apartment.

Maurice took that opportunity to question the neighbor. "Excuse me miss. Do you know if Jackie is at home? I was supposed to take her to dinner this evening."

Cookie caught herself staring at the sexy, handsome gentleman. Wow, he sure was fine! Jackie didn't mention him. He must be an old friend because she had never seen him before.

"She's not in. She had a family emergency and had to go back to North Carolina. Who should I say stopped by?"

"I'm sorry to hear that. I'll call her to see if everything is alright. I'm an old friend of the family, just checking on how she's been doing, while I'm here in Atlanta for a business trip. Thank you."

Turning, he quickly made his way back to his car.

Shrugging her shoulders, Cookie went back inside her apartment. It was strange that the guy didn't want to leave his name. She made a mental note to contact Jackie and let her know that someone had stopped by looking for her. Going into the kitchen, Cookie continued to prepare her dinner for the evening.

Malcolm and David arrived at Jackie's apartment complex several hours later, around seven o'clock, after taking the first flight out of Greensboro to Atlanta. Scoping out the neighborhood, they didn't see any sign of Maurice or anyone that could be watching her apartment.

Using the key that Jackie gave them, they eased into her apartment. Because Jackie had the place professionally cleaned, they were unable to get a feel for how the intruders entered the apartment. Going to the door, David opened it to inspect the casings to see if a forced entry was apparent of if the person had picked the lock.

Pulling out a miniature magnifying glass, David held it closer to the doorknob, where the key would be inserted into the lock. There weren't any marks on the casing, so they didn't pry the door open. Scaring though was found on the lock, which would indicate that someone had picked the lock; obviously not a professional.

Cookie, who was coming home after an evening at the gym, was alarmed that someone was inspecting her friend's apartment. Had something else happened, she wondered? Even though they didn't look like policemen, they could be undercover cops. She owed it to her friend to find out since she had inadvertently given her friends whereabouts to the stranger that had come looking for her earlier during the day. Worriedly, she chewed her bottom lip in indecision as she approached her apartment.

Malcolm chose that moment to check on David. Seeing a woman who resembled the image that Jackie had relayed of her friend Cookie, her neighbor across the hall, Malcolm took the opportunity to question her.

"Excuse me Miss. I'm Malcolm and this is David Bailey, we're Jackie's brothers from North Carolina. We're here to investigate what happened here a few days ago. Jackie just informed us today that her apartment was broken into. We immediately took the next flight to determine what was going on. Did you see any suspicious people that day, hanging around the complex? Are you Jackie's neighbor, Cookie, by chance?"

This guy seemed legitimate but one could never be too certain. He even knew her name. "Do you have some type of identification? Better yet, can you get Jackie on the phone? I've been trying to reach her all day."

After showing Cookie his driver's license, she felt a little more comfortable. They had the same last name. When Jackie had filed for divorce, she retained the right to use her last name.

Malcolm hit the speed dial number for his sister and handed the phone to Cookie after he asked Jackie to confirm who they were and why they were at her apartment. Once she verified who they were, Cookie handed the phone back to Malcolm. Saying that he would contact her when they were finished, Malcolm disconnected the call.

Breathing a sigh of relief, Cookie asked the gentlemen to follow her to her apartment. Gesturing with her hand, she motioned for them to sit down on the sofa. Without wasting time she explained her theory.

"Gentleman, I apologize early for what I'm about to tell you. I think that earlier today, I may have inadvertently hindered your case."

"What do you mean?" David asked.

"A gentleman was knocking on Jackie's door, when I returned from the grocery store. Today is my day off. Anyway, he was knocking so loud that I stuck my head out the door to see if there was something wrong. He was so nice and courteous that I didn't see any harm in answering his questions. With hindsight, I probably should have been more cautious. That's why I've been trying to contact Jackie today to let her know what I had done and to warn her."

Malcolm pulled a picture out of his back pocket. "Could you tell me if this is the gentleman that was here earlier," he asked gravely.

Cookie took the picture from Malcolm and looked at it intently. "Yes, this is the gentleman."

"Was he alone?"

"As best as I could tell. When I told him that she wasn't here, he took off with a backward kind of "thank you" over his shoulder."

"What exactly did you tell him?" David asked.

Looking ashamed, Cookie murmured, "I told him that she had a family emergency at home. He then told me that he would call to check on her since he was only here in Atlanta for a business trip. Do you mind if I ask who he is?"

"Jackie's abusive ex-husband; Maurice."

At Cookie's wail of denial, Malcolm and David thought that they might have to administer CPR to the poor woman, as distraught as she was. Laying a soothing hand on her shoulder, Malcolm tried to offer assurance to Cookie. David went into the kitchen in search of something for her to drink.

"It's going to be all right, Cookie. Please calm down. Can you tell me what time it was when Maurice was here?"

"It was about three o'clock."

Muttering an expletive, David immediately pulled out his cellular phone to contact Frank at Secrets. "Frank, this is David. Malcolm and I are in Atlanta, searching for Maurice who was spotted here at Jackie's apartment. Unfortunately, her roommate told him that Jackie had a family emergency at home. That was around three o'clock. He's probably on his way now back to North Carolina. I need for you to put some security on Jackie. He's obviously after something."

"Not a problem David. Todd and I will handle it. When will you be back?"

"We'll be leaving in thirty minutes to drive back and we'll touch base tomorrow."

Chapter 13

The next day at the hospital, Dr. Kelley, Chelsea's neurologist, was trying to formulate the words to get his patient to understand why her release from the hospital would take place sooner rather than later. As he headed toward the patient's room, he received a call on his cellular phone from Mr. B.

"Hello, Dr. Kelley, how may I help you?"

"Dr. Kelley, this is Mr. Brownstone calling regarding your amnesia patient, Paris Bailey. We've made the final arrangements for her sister, Jackie Bailey, a registered nurse, to care for her until she is back on her feet. Jackie will be by today to get Paris. If anything should arise that seems threatening, I'll contact you immediately."

"Okay. I'm just on my way to see Paris right now to brief her on the events of her departure. I'll also talk to her sister today with any last minute instructions," said Dr. Kelley as he closed his cellular phone.

Dr. Kelley started toward the elevator when as it opened, his eyes were captured by a woman of immense beauty. She was a petite woman, around five feet, two inches compared to his own six foot, five inches. She had a curvaceous figure with full breasts and nice sized hips. Definitely a sight for his tired eyes. As the doors were beginning to close, he called out in his deeply masculine voice, "Please hold the elevator." He wasn't going to miss the opportunity to check out the beautiful woman in the elevator. If luck was with him, maybe he could determine if she was married or not.

As the woman held the elevator open, she smiled to herself and thought, *Yes, as good looking as you are, of course I will hold the elevator and anything else you might have in mind.* He sure was a hunk of a man. Six feet, five inches of pure black masculinity. With any luck, perhaps he was Paris' doctor. She had recently gotten to the point where she felt that she was ready to date again. No commitments, just light hearted dating.

As Dr. Kelley stepped into the elevator, the beautiful woman smiled at him and asked in a somewhat husky voice, "Which floor?" He noticed that her eyes were a light hazel brown. *Beautiful, bedroom eyes that a man could sink himself into.*

When he finally found his voice again, he stated, "The sixth floor." His heart began to beat erratically in his chest. In an instant he knew love at first sight had hit him hard. Her beautiful eyes had looked into his and it seemed as if she had looked into his soul and conquered all of his doubts about committing to the opposite sex.

Dr. Kelley shook his head as if to clear it. He looked at the woman out of the corner of his eye and admired the sweet smelling sensation that was her perfume. It was a mixture of a musk scent, coupled with a floral tone. He sniffed the air appreciatively.

"Good afternoon," he surprised himself by saying. "I love that perfume that you're wearing. I'm sorry, where are my manners? Hi, I'm Dr. Joshua Kelley." *Wow, did that sound like the weakest pick-up line ever, he thought.* "I'm not trying to pick you up or anything but that perfume is positively intriguing. What is it called?"

"Thank you and my name is Jackie. This perfume was made specifically for me and my sisters. It's called Alluring because the fragrance reminds one of two people making love intimately on a bed sprinkled with rose petals, as their fragrance permeates the room. Their hearts connect as one as the aroma of a hundred lightly scented candles shed light in the darkness of night." *Now why did I say that,* thought Jackie as she glanced at the floor in embarrassment.

"Perhaps if that is the intention, you won't mind if I do this." He hit the stop button on the elevator and Dr. Kelley, completely acting out of character, reached out and pulled Jackie ever so gently into his arms, allowing her enough time to pull away if she so desired. His mouth brushed hers ever so gently on the lips as he lightly kissed the corners of her mouth. Then meeting no resistance, he began to devour her mouth.

It was as if he was having an out of body experience. He never kissed complete strangers. He respected women too much. Somehow he couldn't seem to stop himself. Kissing her was like spontaneous combustion. The very flames licking at his insides were enough to devour them both. With each taste of her lips he wanted more. He sought to gain entrance into the soft crevices of her mouth.

With a sigh she opened up to him as her hands rose to encircle his neck. She kissed him without any inhibitions. Hot. Wild. Heated. Kissing the doctor was like a tidal wave raging to shore. His lips totally devoured her senses making her forget that they were in an elevator, alone, making out without any coherent thought as to stopping. When neither could catch enough air to breathe, he reluctantly let go of her lips. He still held her close so that she could feel his heart beating erratically, let alone feel his total arousal.

He looked down into Jackie's eyes. "You may not believe this but I don't usually go accosting women in elevators. I would apologize but then I would be lying if I said that I was sorry. I could not let you go without tasting you. My heart was speaking to me that we're destined to be together for all eternity. Do you believe in love at first sight? I do. I believe you're destined to be my soul mate. Tell me quick, are you married, have a significant other or are you currently seeing someone special? I have to know when I can see you again."

Dr. Kelley, whose mother raised him as a single parent, remarried late in life. He wanted the same everlasting love that his mother found with his stepfather. He wanted forever. He had not previously married because he was a workaholic. He wasn't willing to settle for less therefore he just dated when his schedule permitted. He could tell by the look in Jackie's eyes, as her passion slowly cleared, that she had been mistreated badly in the past, but Dr. Kelley was up to the challenge of proving her wrong. That there were still some good men left in the world that knew how to treat a woman as their queen. He knew that he could conquer Jackie's fears about her mistrust of men and prove to her that his love was everlasting.

By this time, Jackie was slowly coming back down to earth, to her senses. She had just kissed a man or rather been kissed senseless by a doctor in an elevator. But the romantic in her seemed to listen to her heart to know that yes indeed, she did believe in love at first sight, however her practical mind overruled what her heart felt. If he wanted her as his soul mate, he would have to work extremely hard to get her.

"No, I don't believe in love at first sight. I believe in lust at first sight, which is what we reacted too. No, I don't have a significant other. Why, do you have plans for us that I need to know about? Are you otherwise entangled or spoken for?"

"No, but I will be soon if you're willing to give us a chance," said Dr. Kelley.

Jackie thought of all the reasons why she should say no. She didn't relish the thought of developing a relationship with a doctor. She knew the demands made on their schedule. She knew how some of them treated the nurses that worked with them. She didn't know this man from Adam but oh la la, he sure could kiss.

Forget the vision that she had before he actually kissed her of them as a family with three kids. She hadn't yet come to trust her visions. Her visions had let her down when it came to her own sister Chelsea's demise, so how could she trust in it for someone that she had just met? The little voice inside of her that was an incurable romantic urged her to get to know the doctor and give him a chance. He certainly couldn't be as bad as her ex, the control freak.

So she did the only thing she could do; she said yes. "I'll give us a chance as long as I can have just one more kiss."

Dr. Kelley took Jackie in his arms again and savored the sweet smell of her perfume and the sensual look that crept into her eyes as she rose on her tiptoes in an attempt to kiss him. Since she was so petite he picked her up in his arms and brought her lips to his.

Time stood still. He felt as if he could die and go to heaven happy just because he had glimpsed his future in her eyes.

As he put her back down on her feet, he asked her for her telephone number. She readily gave it to him. Simultaneously, they both pushed the button to restart the elevator. The electricity crackled the air as their fingers touched the button at the same time. Each retreated to opposite sides of the elevator in an attempt to cool off.

Once the elevator stopped on the designated floor, Dr. Kelley turned to Jackie and stated, "This is the beginning of the love of our lifetime. Let's enjoy the ride." With a quick kiss he departed to the left of the elevator to take the time to walk aimlessly along the corridor in an effort to let his manhood adjust back to its normal size. *Thank God for doctor's lab coats*, he thought as he then retraced his steps to Paris' room.

Jackie turned to the right of the elevator. She had trouble finding Paris' room because she was in that much of a daze. It wasn't long before she realized that she had walked down the wrong corridor. She retraced her steps back to the correct corridor to Paris' room and taking a deep breath; she opened the door and walked in. To her surprise, the object of her desire was standing beside her sister's bed.

"Well hello again," said Jackie as she fully entered into the room with a huge smile on her face. What a way of ensuring that the object of your desire remained in constant contact. As Paris' doctor, he would definitely stay in touch.

Dr. Kelley turned around with a look of surprise on his face. "I assume by that smile that you're pleased to see me so soon?" Putting two and two together, he asked, "Don't tell me that you're our patient Paris' sister?" All of a sudden he laughed. Life was good. Now he had a way of keeping in touch just in case Jackie decided to get cold feet.

God sure has a sense of humor, thought Jackie. It wasn't everyday that a man told you that you were his soul mate and seemed so honest and sincere that you actually believed him.

Paris looked from one to the other to figure out what happened between them and who the lovely young woman was. *That's right; the doctor said she was my sister.* She looked closely at the woman who was supposed to be her sister. *Yes, they did favor. Finally! Someone who could help fit the pieces of the puzzle together. Thank you Lord for someone finally finding out where I was.*

"Okay you two, tell me what happened. How did the two of you meet and why are you both smiling so widely?"

"Paris, meet Jackie, your sister. She has come to take you to your family home to help you to recuperate. You have a lot of people that are glad you are alive."

Jackie walked over to the bed and gave Paris a big kiss as she hugged her tightly. With tears streaming down her face, she said, "Hey there baby sister. We've missed you. I'm so glad to see you." As Jackie continued to hug her sister, a brief flash of memory pulled at Paris' senses. She remembered other such occasions where hugs were handed out by this person.

Dr. Kelley immediately sensed a recollection from Paris. "Paris, there will be other moments like this where you will remember something from your past. It's okay. Don't try to block it. Let it come to you." As he stated his professional opinion, emotionally he wanted to reach out to Jackie and kiss away her tears. He didn't ever want to see her cry again.

In order to remain professional and not react the way his emotions were dictating him to, he resorted to humor. "Anyone up for a group hug?" Everyone laughed as Jackie and Paris separated in order to allow the doctor to complete the circle of hugs.

Paris said, "I remember other such hugs as this. Thank you."

"Do you remember anything else?" asked Dr. Kelley as he tried to probe deeper to see if anything else was lurking around in her memory bank.

"No, just that brief recollection," Paris stated dejectedly.

"Okay, it appears that your memory is trying to come back. Don't be alarmed if you start to have more of these brief glimpses into your former life. It's only natural. Just don't try to force your memory to return. Let nature take its course." This was said in jest but he meant for Jackie to catch the double innuendo in his meaning. He looked deep into her eyes to convey his meaning.

"Now that you seem comfortable with your sister, I must get to my next appointment. Here are my telephone numbers to reach me should the need arise, or if you just want to talk about any memory recaptures." He handed his business card to Paris.

Dr. Kelley then walked to Jackie's side and whispered, "As much as I want to kiss you, I won't embarrass you in front of your sister. Call me later, please." He then took his leave from the room.

"What was that about?" Paris asked with a smile on her face. She had never seen her sister so flustered in the presence of any man. She had worked with many top doctors at the best hospitals in the United States but none had left her this speechless. With a start of surprise, Paris smiled because she had remembered something else.

"Girl, you won't believe what just happened," said Jackie. She then proceeded to explain everything to Paris from the elevator to the present moment. "That man is just too fine, with a capital F and the best kisser I've ever tasted."

"So what are you going to do? Something tells me that not only will he be checking in on me but he's got plans for you as well."

"Paris, I had a vision in the elevator before he kissed me that showed us married with three kids. You know, usually, my visions come true. Just like the one I had about you and Max," she replied before she could stop herself.

Now look at what I've done. Jackie hurriedly tried to keep talking in order to cover up what she had just let slip. "Knowing my track record with men, Dr. Kelley will have to be extraordinary indeed in order for me to let my guard down. Men are not a priority on my list right about now. I can enjoy them but my heart never gets involved anymore. But if he makes love like he kisses, I can't wait for us to be a permanent item!" She laughed.

Paris laughed as Jackie stared to fan herself. "Jackie, who is Max and what is he to me?"

"Oh don't worry about that. Once you're back home, he's a guy I want to introduce to you. His company Sole Impressions has a model contest for a woman to be the next spokesperson for their new fragrance, Alluring. Incidentally, it's the fragrance I'm wearing today. It got me kissed senseless in an elevator with a fine doctor, who was before now a complete stranger. I'd say that this perfume will definitely be a hit, which is why they need a model that's mysterious, beautiful, sexy, sensual and innocent looking. You fit the description to the tee. While you take a mini vacation to recuperate you're going to meet a wonderful man, fall in love and live happily ever after."

"Jackie I see you're a true romantic at heart but we'll have to see about the rest. However, since I'm alive, I do intend to enjoy myself. Life is too short to waste on what ifs. Let's get this show on the road. Incidentally, are there many more like you? I just want to be prepared in case I meet any other nuts."

"Yes, girl there are six of us. You'll meet them once you return home." Jackie reached out and gave her another hug. "It's good to have you back."

Chapter 14

After Paris was discharged from the hospital, Jackie was free to take her home to meet the family. They arrived at their parent's house, later that afternoon. Pulling up into the driveway, Paris noticed all of the cars that were lined up on the street.

Taking a deep breath, she muttered to herself, "You can do this."

Putting her hand over Paris' hand, Jackie affirmed her comment. "Paris, only your immediate family is here to greet you. We thought that we would get it over with all at once since there's so many of us. No one expects anything from you; only the chance to show their love for you and to help you in any way that they can. Come on. Let's go inside."

Opening the door, Paris stepped onto the lush manicured lawn. A flashback stirred her memory of herself as a child running around barefoot on the lawn; at least until she found out that she was allergic to the grass. Smiling at the memory she followed Jackie into the house.

Mr. Bailey, while he had everyone together, said a heartfelt prayer, thanking God that his daughter had returned to them. Tears of joy and laughter could then be heard throughout the house, as everyone started talking at once. What a homecoming! It was more than Paris could ever have hoped for. Such love resounded within the room. She couldn't explain why she felt as if something or someone was missing. Counting her blessing, she thanked God for restoring her family to her.

Two hours later, after everyone had laughed, cried and prayed together, Jackie noticed that Paris was getting tired. She suggested that Paris take a nap before she rejoined the family. Taylor surprised everyone by volunteering to read Paris a bedtime story.

Without understanding the affinity that she felt for the little girl, who was Jackie's adopted child, Paris readily agreed to her idea. Hand in hand, they walked in the direction of the bedroom that Paris would use. More crying could be heard as they walked along the corridor. Paris smiled thinking that her family sure was emotional and very free with their feelings.

Dr. Kelley, after Paris' release from the hospital, pondered whether or not Jackie would contact him of her own free will. He had detected a sense of hesitancy within her. Without thinking about the proper dating etiquette of when to call, when not to call; Dr. Kelley had already dialed Jackie's telephone number. Hearing his call forwarded to voice mail, Dr. Kelley impatiently listened to the message.

"I'm sorry; we're unavailable at the moment. Please leave a message and we'll get back to you shortly."

Who exactly is we? Dr. Kelley questioned rhetorically as he hung up. Is that a term used on one's answering machine to deter people from thinking that they lived alone? She said that she was single. If she was involved in a relationship, would she have let him kiss her like that? Would she have given him her correct telephone number? He could tell by the husky voice that he had dialed the correct number. Shaking his head in disbelief, he shrugged. Why was he second guessing himself? He had taken the time to read the next of kin information for his patient, Paris Bailey, and the telephone numbers listed were one and the same.

Deciding that it was time to take control of his destiny, he decided to call Jackie back and this time he left a message.

"Good evening Jackie. This is Dr. Kelley calling. I wanted to see how you and your family fared today upon seeing your sister for the first time since the accident. Of course, I'll contact Paris to talk to her, but I'm just as concerned about your state of mind. Could you give me a call, tonight, when you get in? I'll be waiting for your call. Goodbye."

With that out of the way, the ball was now officially in Jackie's court. He just hoped that she would pass the ball back to him and continue their journey. A sense of tranquility settled over him as he dialed Paris' number. After a lengthy conversation, he determined that she hadn't overextended herself and that although she didn't remember anyone; she felt at peace and was looking forward to her family helping her to regain her memory.

The rest of the day passed in a swirl of activity for Dr. Kelley as he went on his rounds at the hospital. It was well after nine o'clock when he finally made it home. Immediately upon entering his home, he went towards the answering machine to see if a message had been left. The flashing light was indeed blinking on his answering machine, indicating that two messages had been stored in the memory.

Pressing the playback/rewind button, he listened to his brother Caleb, advising him that he would be in the area working on a case for the next six months and wanted to know if he could hangout at his place. His brother worked for the FBI in the JAG division as a gem's agent. Smiling, Dr. Kelley took out his cellular phone and called him.

"What's up doc?"

"I'm returning your call. I just got in. So when are you coming?"

"I'll be there by the weekend. Is it okay if I stay with you while I'm in town?"

"You know that anytime you need refuge, ma maison est votre maison."

"Thanks. Make sure that I have something to eat when I arrive. I know you. Your cupboard is probably bare. You work entirely too much."

"It must be a genetic trait because you suffer from it also. When are you going to slow down?"

"I've been thinking about slowing down lately. This case that I'm currently working on has taken a lot out of me."

Abruptly Dr. Kelley declared, "I've got to go. The love of my life is calling me. I'll see you late Saturday evening. Be safe."

Before Caleb could question his brother about his actions, the line went dead. Grinning, Caleb couldn't wait to tease his brother. Now he had an even better cover for showing up in Greensboro. He wanted to make sure that the woman his brother was so crazy about was legitimate and not after his money. Maybe this trip would also help soothe his tormented soul.

"Hello."

"Um, may I speak to Joshua Kelley?" Jackie asked anxiously.

"How are you doing Jackie? I'm glad that you returned my call."

"I wasn't going to at first but since you asked about my well-being first and then that of my family, I couldn't resist."

Joshua smiled. She had told him in those few words, how others had treated her in the past. He hoped to change that. Settling down on the chaise in his sun room, he asked, "Tell me about your day."

Excitedly Jackie exclaimed, "It was wonderful. Everyone was crying and laughing for pretty much the entire afternoon. Chelsea seemed to take it all in stride even when we didn't want to let her out of our sight."

"That's understandable given all that your family has gone through. How do you feel?"

"Thankful. My sister is alive and I've been given a second chance to apologize to her."

"What do you mean?"

"Are you sure you really want to hear this? It might change your opinion of me."

"Let me be the judge of that." Joshua wondered what could cause her to sound so regretful and distressed even now when her sister was going to be alright.

"I had a vision of someone in our family being hurt before the accident, but I didn't pay any credence to it. I didn't warn any of my family members and consequently I blamed myself for what happened to my sister for a long time." It was better to get the truth out in the open. If Joshua was a keeper, he would understand.

Choosing his words carefully, Joshua contradicted Jackie's statement. "There must have been extenuating circumstances going on in your life for you to have ignored your vision. Was that the first time that you recalled having one with dire consequences?"

"Yes, it was the first time where someone's life was in danger."

Joshua was sure there was more to the story than she was telling him. "Maybe after we've known each other better, you'll tell me about those extenuating circumstances. I was told by a wise older woman who happened to be my grandmother that a person who has such a gift is special, and that it takes time and wisdom to be able to accurately learn how to use it. Since you're still getting used to the idea of being able to "sense" things, there's a question I want to ask you. Did you have a vision when we first saw each other in the elevator?"

A discernible pause was detected before Jackie spoke again. "What makes you think that I had a vision when you kissed me?"

He countered with, "Would you pay attention to your next vision?"

"I'd be foolish not to, based on the potential consequences."

"Then it wouldn't be much of a stretch then for you to go out on a date with me, seeing as I'm your future husband, would it?"

"You're very sure of yourself aren't you?" laughed Jackie. "What makes you think that I want to get married again?"

"So, you've been married before. May I ask for how long?"

"About six years." Jackie waited, curious as to what his next question would be.

"Do you have anything against the institution of marriage?"

"No, my parents have been married for well over forty-five years."

"Are you still in love with your ex-husband?"

Jackie stated emphatically, "No!"

"The next question is kind of personal. If you choose not to answer it, I understand."

"Okay, what is it?"

"Do you have any children from your first marriage?"

"Yes and no."

"Come again?"

"I didn't have any children from my marriage but I was fortunate enough to adopt a child whose mother had died in an accident." If I stick as close to the truth as possible, I wont be caught up in a web of lies, Jackie thought. If he doesn't want to date a woman with kids, then I'll know shortly how he feels. When Paris fully recovers, then I'll explain the subterfuge.

"How old is she and how long have you had her?"

"She's almost six and I've only had her for a little while."

Quickly cutting to the chase, Joshua asked, "Since I've never dated a woman with children before, will you be patient with me as I learn what to do and what not to do?"

"Good answer, Joshua."

"When can we go out on our first date?"

"Joshua, you certainly don't waste any time."

"I always go after what I want, and I want to get to know you better. What better way to do that than date?"

"Why didn't you ask me anything about Paris? I'm sure that was your original reason for calling."

Smiling, Joshua delivered his surprise. "I've already spoken with Paris today and asked her all the doctor related questions. I called you because I'm interested in you and wanted to see how you were handling things. Don't think though that you've side-tracked me. I'm still waiting on an answer to my question."

"Okay, since you're so persistent, how about Saturday night?"

"Do you mean Saturday night; as in tomorrow?"

"Yes, is that a problem?" Jackie asked innocently.

"No. Will seven o'clock suit you?"

"Yes."

"Where would you like to go?"

"Surprise me."

"That's a pretty dangerous proposal don't you think?"

"Within reason of course."

"Until tomorrow then."

Maurice, in a nondescript car, drove slowly past the Bailey family home. With all the cars parked outside, he was tempted to just drop in and say hello, but since that might land him in jail, because of his past actions, he continued on down the street. He wanted to make sure that he wasn't being followed. After determining that he was the only one driving on the street, to be less obvious, he decided to park his car at one of the neighboring houses. Maurice then waited patiently for Jackie to come outside.

When she didn't immediately appear, he settled in for a long night. Since he didn't find what he was looking for at her apartment, he had to figure out where her other belongings were stored. In order to do that, he needed to follow her to her sister's house where he guessed she would be staying. The question was; which sister's house, Ryan's or Anita's?

Covering all of his bases, Maurice contacted Harry, who owed him several favors, to go by Anita's house to wait for Jackie's arrival. He would wait until all the cars were gone before he dropped by Ryan's house.

When a car slowly passed his going down the street, Maurice became concerned. Why would a car be driving in this prestigious neighborhood this late at night and not stop at any of the houses? Was it an undercover policeman patrolling the area? Or was it one of Mr. Smith's men; waiting for him to show up at his former in-laws house? Either way, he couldn't take a chance on being seen. Starting the car, he drove away before the other car could circle the block.

He would just have to beef up his surveillance routine for quicker results.

Pressing the speed dial button for Rasheeda, he let her know that he was headed home.

Chapter 15

Jackie telephoned Joshua at three o'clock the following day, to arrange to meet him at the restaurant, claiming that she had several errands to run for her mother that would delay her returning in time to dress and get ready for their date.

Although Joshua wasn't happy about the idea, as long as their date was still on, he was willing to let her slide, just this one time. He didn't like the modern idea of a man not picking up the woman that he was taking out on a date. Tonight, after their dinner was finished, he would just have to make sure that Jackie understood his feelings about the issue. Another thought immediately popped into his head; was she canceling on him?

Deciding to call her back, he punched in her number but was interrupted by a page on the hospital's intercom. His call would have to wait. Joshua offered a prayer to God that Jackie wouldn't change her mind and that she would me him at the restaurant as planned, later that evening.

Joshua arrived first at the Ruth Chris Restaurant and waited outside for Jackie to arrive. He didn't have long to wait. She pulled into the parking lot within minutes of his arrival. He loved a punctual woman.

Walking towards her car, he extended his hand to help her arise from her seat. Together they both walked into the restaurant.

Once they were seated and the waitress had distributed the menus and taken their drink orders, Jackie thanked Joshua. "Joshua, I want to thank you for agreeing to meet me here. A woman can't be too cautious when meeting a stranger for the first time."

"Thank you for coming. You look very beautiful this evening. I seriously thought that today when you called, you were trying to cancel and didn't quite know how to tell me that our date wasn't going to happen."

"Oh no. My mother wanted me to run a couple of errands for her that she wasn't able to perform herself due to a prior commitment. I had to transport my grandmother around today, and that's always an adventure. She usually has us running around all day and I didn't want you to have to wait on me."

Jackie came across as a very thoughtful woman that loved her relatives. She was endearing herself to him, more and more. "Jackie, I understand from Mr. Brownstone that you currently live in Georgia. Now that you've found your sister and will be responsible for her recovery, will you be relocating back to North Carolina permanently?"

"Yes. Since there isn't a time frame for Paris' recovery, I will have my things moved here. Life is too short to spend it away from the ones that you love. Although I've only been gone for a little over eighteen months, I have truly missed my family."

"I'm glad about that, because long distance relationships can be hard on a couple."

"What makes you think that we're going to have a relationship, much less become a couple?"

"Did I forget to tell mention when we kissed, that I fell in love with you at first sight and that my heart recognized you as my soul mate?"

"I vaguely remember you saying something like that, although I must confess, that my mind was still in the clouds from your kiss."

"I see that honesty works for both of us. I like that. Care for another demonstration?" Joshua asked with great expectation.

"We'll see how the evening goes before I make that determination."

"That's fair. It's up to me to prove how worthy I am of your kiss."

Jackie couldn't help it. She laughed until her sides hurt. Joshua was funny and seemed to say exactly what was on his mind. One would never have to wonder where he was coming from.

"How can you be so sure that I'm the one?" Jackie laughingly asked.

"I've been waiting for you for my entire life, so when I see what I want, I go after it." Joshua stated in a very serious tone.

"What if I don't want the same thing?"

"Then it will be up to me to help you reach the same conclusion; that I'm the one for you."

"Pretty much like proving how worthy you are of another kiss? How do you expect to prove that in one night?"

"I'll let you be the judge tonight when this date is over, whether or not I've proved myself worthy of a goodnight kiss. As for the other, once we start dating, you'll see that we are meant for each other."

"You're very sure of yourself and talk a good game. How do you even know that we're compatible?"

The waitress then brought their drinks and left to place their order. Once the waitress departed, Joshua responded to Jackie's earlier question.

"I don't know if we're compatible, but there's only one way to change that. What are your likes and dislikes?"

Deciding to humor him, Jackie said, "Okay, let's just see. It doesn't take much to please me. I'm a simple woman. I like to go to the movies, I like to go dancing, visit antique shops, go to concerts and I'm an avid sports fan. So any sporting event, I would enjoy. It's your turn. What do you like to do?"

"I'm an avid sports fan myself. Of course football is my favorite then basketball, baseball and finally soccer. I enjoy it so much that a couple of my friends and I play on a team."

"What type of team?"

"We get together when our schedule permits and play flag football. Do you play?"

"I said that I'm a lover of sports; not necessarily that I play any."

"Would you play with me?"

"That depends upon what my reward would be for playing?" Had they gone from talking about sports to something else entirely? "I'll keep that in mind for the next time that we play. We usually try to play on Saturdays when we're not working. As a matter of fact, our next practice is in two weeks. Would you care to join me?"

"As a spectator or as a participant?"

"A spectator of course. Once you see how much fun we have, I'm sure you'll want to join us."

"So what else do you like to do?"

"Given the opportunity, I try to attend at least one major NFL and NBA game a season, just to sit in the stands and soak up the atmosphere. Who is your favorite football team?"

"The Carolina Panthers, since we live in the great state of North Carolina. Who is your favorite team?"

"My favorite team is the Dallas Cowboys."

"I should have guessed but I won't hold that against you."

They spent the next thirty minutes debating which one of their teams was the best. The waitress then brought their food. As they were eating and talking about general topics, Jackie looked up, and thought that she saw her ex-husband in the restaurant. It was just a fleeting glance but she was a little startled and her conversation stopped as she turned around in her chair to figure out whether she was having a mirage or was he actually there.

That's weird. What's he doing here? she thought. Her next thought was if he was there, why was he in Greensboro and was it simply a coincidence that they were actually in the same restaurant. Getting paranoid, she then turned completely around to the other side of the restaurant looking for her cousin Pauletta to see if she had seen Maurice too.

Joshua, noticing her apprehension, quietly asked, "Is there a problem?"

Not wanting to mess up their date with the mention of her ex-husband, Jackie calmly replied, "No, I just thought I saw someone from my college days."

"I'm assuming it's a woman, otherwise I might feel slighted if you were looking for a gentleman that you went to college with."

"There's nothing for you to feel slighted about Joshua. I was simply looking to make sure of my friends identity before I went over and made a fool of myself."

Joshua could tell that she was slightly spooked so he tried to go out of his way to appease her mind. He felt that when she was ready, she would tell him what caused her apprehension.

Jackie on the other hand didn't want to let the evening end on a sour note or to have Joshua guessing as to whether or not she wanted to see him again, tried to revert back to her normal self. She went out of her way to be funny and entertaining and the rest of the evening went well for them, so much so that they didn't want the evening to end.

Joshua suggested that they go dancing or go to a jazz club where they could listen to the group, Mint Condition, in concert. One of her favorite groups, Jackie was pleased that he had been thoughtful to suggest going to the concert. With a somewhat subdued shout, Jackie leaned over and hugged Joshua.

"How are we going to get tickets at this late hour? Will we be able to pay at the door?" Jackie indignantly inquired.

"I already have tickets."

"Am I a substitute for someone since you already have tickets?"

Joshua replied, "No, you're not. You're my first and only choice. It's just that when I asked you out yesterday, I knew that they would be in town. My first thought was just to take you there then I second guessed myself, thinking that the group might not be one of your favorites. So instead, I wanted to have dinner first, so that you would be in a mellow mood, and if the evening went well, you would be inclined to go out with me again."

"What would you have done if I didn't like Mint Condition?"

"It would have been a shame to waste the tickets but rather than you suffer through it, we could have blessed someone in line with the tickets. I generally try to be as thoughtful as I can possibly be."

"Well at this point, I think you're getting an A in that department. I've really had a nice time."

"But our date's not over yet. Are you kicking me to the curb already?"

"Not at all. I'm simply expressing my feelings."

At that point the waitress came to the table to settle the bill. Joshua then pulled back Jackie's chair so that she could rise from the table. He had such impeccable manners. She liked that about him. Just as they were about to exit the restaurant, Jackie caught another fleeting glance of the gentleman that resembled her husband. His head was always turned so that she couldn't see his face fully.

Deciding to push that to the back of her mind, she chalked her thoughts up to stress. The break-in of her apartment was making her paranoid. She would however tell her brothers what she experienced this evening as soon as she got home.

Outside, Joshua asked, "Would it be possible for me to drive you to the concert and I'll bring you directly back here to pick up your car as soon as the concert is over?"

"I think that will be fine." While she was gathering her lightweight coat from the car, Jackie sent Pauletta a text message that they were going to the Mint Condition concert.

They proceeded to the concert and had a great time. Joshua had one more surprise in store for Jackie when the concert was finished. Since he had grown up with one of the members, whenever they were in town, Joshua always had backstage passes. He took her backstage so that she could meet everyone, which really blew her mind. They ended up staying for about an hour, talking, joking and catching up on old times. Finally, Joshua was able to pull her away and they returned to the restaurant's parking lot.

Pauletta had pulled into the parking lot right before Jackie and Joshua. She had even gone as far as to reenter the restaurant to make it look as if she was just leaving. They had the Dating Rules 101 system that they adhered to, which is why Pauletta was at the restaurant, on hand, watching over Jackie, just in case something happened. They had learned the hard way with their sister-in-law Erica, what could happen if someone was kidnapped from a restaurant.

Joshua escorted Jackie to her car, and settled her inside. "Could I follow you to your home to make sure that you arrive safely, since its so late? I don't like the idea of you driving by yourself, this late at night."

"No, I have a friend that I think I see coming out of the restaurant that lives close by and we'll follow each other home. I'll introduce you to her at a later date."

She threw up her hand and waved at Pauletta, who was coming out of the restaurant. Of course Pauletta, waved back. Joshua turned to see who Jackie was waving at, to make sure that there was someone there. Pauletta then made hand gestures asking if everything went ok. Jackie responded discreetly in kind.

Then as if sensing what was going on, Joshua smiled. Putting two and two together, he figured out that her girlfriend was there at the restaurant and that she was the person that Jackie was anxiously trying to find when they sat down to dinner. Her friend must have been checking to see if Jackie thought that everything was going to be okay.

Bending towards the open window, Joshua did what he had wanted to do all evening. He kissed Jackie with a desperate yearning. It seemed like forever since their first kiss. His body hungered for more of her touch.

At first Jackie was startled by the passion that he could evoke with just a mere kiss. Sinking deeper into the kiss, consumed with desire, she realized that his kiss, his touch, was enough to send sensations coursing throughout her body. It was as if this passion was second nature. It felt right.

Slowly breaking off the kiss in degrees, Joshua savored the taste of her lips. With one last whisper of a caress across her lips, he raised his head.

"Thank you for a beautiful evening. Will you call me once you get home so that I can feel at peace that you made it there safely, since it's so late?"

"I think that I can do that. Putting her hands up to his cheek, she caressed his face. "Joshua, thank you for a night to remember."

"Does that mean you will be willing to go with me again?"

"Yes, without a doubt, I would enjoy that."

"Then we'll discuss that when you call me once you get home."

Feeling like she was on cloud nine, Jackie drove home, smiling all the way. That man was lethal. His lips should be rated X. She couldn't wait to see what else those lips could do.

Maurice meanwhile was still driving up and down the neighborhood, clocking the time that Jackie spent away from her parent's house. Since she had left by herself, he didn't see the need to follow her. In the back of his mind thought, he knew that if someone came to meet her, he would do everything in his power to disrupt her happiness since it seemed that she could go on quite easily without him.

Just as she was pulling up into the driveway, he got out of his car, ready to run across the street to catch up with her, so that he could make her take him to the location where she had stored her things. As soon as he stepped out of the car, he saw another car slowly riding down the street. Was it the police or was it Mr. Smith's men? Without protection on him, he didn't stand a chance.

Jumping back into the car, he sped off. A high speed chase ensued. They were gaining on him until another car, cut them off several streets over. Catching a glimpse of the black Lexus, Maurice knew who was driving the other car. They would have hell to pay for endangering their life just to save his. He had everything under control.

As Maurice continued to the hotel that he was staying at, he replayed the last hour over in his mind. It would seem that Jackie had someone watching her. It was time for the kid gloves to come off. Things were escalating. He would have to use force to obtain the jewels.

Immediately upon entering the house, Jackie, went to her room and did a three way call with her brothers.

"Malcolm and David, I just left Ruth Chris Restaurant on a date with Joshua and I could have sworn that I saw Maurice fleetingly in the same restaurant. Pauletta was there too and she also thought that she saw him. She wasn't able to confront him though, when she went to investigate, because he had disappeared. Do you think that he's stalking me?"

"He might be. We asked Frank to have a car patrol the area while you and Paris are there, especially after what happened in Atlanta."

"What do you think he wants?"

"That, we can't answer until we find him."

"What should I do?"

"Never go out alone. Call one of us or wait until someone is free to go with you. Keep changing your routines; vary the routes that you go when you pickup Taylor from her after school activities."

"He hasn't made any threats yet but based on his history, I wouldn't rule anything out. We can't place a restraining order with the police here in Greensboro, because he hasn't physically contacted you here." David, the former FBI Relocation agent advised.

"What about the guy that you've just started dating? Do you think that he's up to the challenge of watching over you when we're not around?" Malcolm asked.

"Yes. He reminds me of each of you, but it's too early to determine if he has staying power."

"What's this guy's name by the way so that we can check him out?"

"His name is Joshua Kelley and incidentally he's Paris' doctor. That's how I met him; at the hospital. You'll have the opportunity to meet him quite often if I'm not mistaken. He seems to be under the impression that I'm his soul mate and wants to become a permanent part of my life. It doesn't help that I also had a vision of us, married with three kids when he introduced himself." Jackie replied, smiling broadly. What she didn't tell her brothers was how that had transpired. Some things a girl had to keep to herself.

"That's deep. History has proven that your visions and our ancestor's visions have come true, so I don't doubt that it will happen. Better you than me. We definitely have to meet our next brother-in-law."

"Whoa. We just started dating; don't scare the man off yet. I want to see where this leads. I'm not interested in marriage just yet, so he'll have his work cut out for him if he can convince me to go that route again. A nice, steady, committed relationship is all I can handle right now."

"Don't sell yourself short, Jackie. Just because you married a jerk the first time, doesn't mean that it will happen again. Take your time and love will find you again."

Her phone beeped with a call waiting for her to answer it. "Oh, gotta go. That's Joshua calling to make sure I got home safely. Bye bye."

Laughing, both her brothers hung up. It had been a long time since they heard their sister so excited about a man.

"Hello." Jackie answered breathlessly as she hurriedly pressed talk to answer Joshua's call that had shown on her telephone screen as the call waiting.

"I know that I was supposed to wait for you to call but I became worried when you didn't. Did you make it home safely?"

"Yes. I apologize for not immediately calling, but I got stuck on a call with my brothers. Thanks for interrupting them."

"I can let you go if you need to continue your talk with them."

"No, I'm all yours."

"If you meant that, we wouldn't be having this conversation over the telephone. Instead you would be in my arms, in our home."

Not knowing what to say, Jackie was silent for a moment.

"Can I ask you to do me a favor?"

"That depends. If I can, I will."

"Will you allow me to pick you up for our dates? I'm an old fashioned guy with good morals and values. It doesn't sit well with me, to meet you somewhere. I would feel more comfortable and I wouldn't have to worry about your safety if you were with me."

"Yes. Let me explain the Golden Rules of dating in our family. Rule Number One; on first dates, never allow the gentleman to pick you up. In case he's a jerk, you're not beholden to him to drive you home. You can cut the date short at any time. If he turns out to be a stalker, then he doesn't know your address. Rule Number Two; a family member or a friend has to accompany you on your first date."

Laughing, Joshua asked, "Was the young lady you were waving too at the restaurant, a friend or a relative?"

"She's my cousin, Pauletta."

"I'm glad that your family takes dating seriously. In my line of work, I've seen unfortunate experiences where dates have gone terribly wrong, with disastrous consequences, so I understand." Joshua added seriously. "Are there any other rules that I should know about?"

"There are lots of them; you'll just have to wait and see."

"My schedule will be kind of hectic this coming week because I have to attend a conference for three days but I'll be back by Thursday. Can I see you then?"

"Won't you be too tired?"

"Your beautiful presence will revive me."

Smiling, Jackie then joked, "Rule Number Two prevents me from asking you to come over so that I could cook you a home-cooked meal. That would really make a nice homecoming gift, wouldn't it?"

At Joshua's groan of defeat, she laughed even harder. "Do you know what I would give for a home-cooked meal?"

"If you act right, I'll invite you to our family's next cookout, where you get to eat Southern food at its best."

"I hope that's sometime soon. I love to eat. When does your family have cookouts?"

"Every holiday. Since Paris is back, we'll have one real soon."

"I know you will think that I have a one-track mind, but can I see you on Thursday?"

"What am I going to do with you, Joshua?"

"Love me, if I have anything to do with it. I'd better let you go. It's getting late."

Looking at the clock, Jackie exclaimed, "Oh my gosh! It's two in the morning! I'm sorry, I shouldn't have kept you on the phone for so long; you need to get some sleep."

"You worry too much. I truly enjoyed myself this evening. Sweet dreams. I'll see you soon."

David and Malcolm contacted Frank via a three way call. "Frank, I think that we need to step up the surveillance. Jackie thought that she saw Maurice at the restaurant that she was at tonight. It appears that somehow, he is watching the house because she met her date there as a precautionary measure."

"That might explain the cars that our men have seen on the street where your parents live. As soon as they drive down the street and get pass the car, that person takes off without them getting a good view of the driver. Of course they've ran the license tags, but it only comes up as a rental under an assumed name. Each night the car is a different make and model. So it looks like your former brother-in-law has an idea that we're watching him."

"Let me check in with Max to see how he wants to handle this with everything else that's going on. This might work to our advantage so that we can flush him out in the open. It's time to pull the plug on his operation."

"Max, this is Frank. I need to bring you up to date on what's happening with Jackie and her crazy ex-husband Maurice. He's now here in Greensboro. According to Malcolm and David, she saw him at the same restaurant that she was at, last night. Pauletta saw him too. Our men have caught three different cars in the vicinity of your in-laws, parked on the side of the street. Once our men pass the car, trying to id the culprit, the car immediately takes off down the street."

"Good. This was the break that we were waiting on. Hang on; let me get Trevor in on this conference call." Putting Frank on hold, he called Trevor. Depressing the switch on his phone, all three were connected.

"Trevor, this is Max and Frank. We've got a new development in Maurice's case. He's been spotted in North Carolina in the vicinity of my in-laws house, because Jackie is staying with them for a short period of time, taking care of a college friend that was in an accident."

"Do you want me to go ahead and transfer the funds out of his account?" Trevor asked excitedly.

"Yes. That way, he'll be forced to do something drastic in order to get some funds. I'm pretty sure that he's planning another heist, since the first one was so successful. We need to find the jewels though, before they make it to the Black Market."

"Give me about ten minutes after we finish and the funds will be transferred. If he operates out of necessity, he will begin fencing the jewels by the end of the week. I'll keep my contacts open to see if they hear of anything."

"Max, I'll contact Caleb and advise him what's going on." Frank replied.

"Fellas, we need to keep this between us. I believe that we have a mole; either it's someone on our team or someone on Randolph's team. Too much information is getting out that could only come from our teams. Now that I think about it, the only way the jewelry heist could have been successful was because one of our agents helped them pull it off. I need to map out the last couple of cases that we've worked on to be able to figure out who the mole could possibly be."

"Max, why don't the three of us get together on Saturday to make the timeline?"

"That's a good idea Frank. Why don't we meet at Secrets around eleven?"

"That's fine with me."

"That works for me as well. I've got to go. Duty calls." Frank disconnected his line as Randolph came into his office. His ending phrase was a clue for Max and Trevor that someone under their suspicion had just entered his office.

Max had been working out in the field overseas, trying to come to grips with the death of his wife and child. He had not been able to go back into the office because he felt that he was setup, but by whom, he didn't know. He had been working steadily for the past twenty-four months to find the persons responsible but to no avail. Now it seemed, that it was time to go back home to face his demons and let the cards fall where they may.

Chapter 16

While Jackie and Joshua continued to date, Maurice decided to remove the last obstacle that stood between his ex-wife and the jewels that she unknowingly harbored. He cooked up a scheme to deliver some racy photo's to the new man in his ex-wife's life that Jackie had taken of them while they were married because she was not being satisfied.

She thought that if she showed him what turned her off that together they could explore other techniques; they could improve their intimate relationship. Of course he had scoffed at the idea and had told her that it was her problem, not his. He had included a date stamp on the photos to pretend that the poses had been recent.

It wasn't hard to find the identity of Jackie's new boyfriend. All it took was a couple of dollars, a smile here and there and he had all the information that he needed. With the delivery of these pictures, Maurice knew that Jackie would be alone, once again.

Time for him to make his move.

Dr. Kelley received a package at work several weeks later. Curious as to what it was, he opened the package during one of his breaks at the hospital. After examining the package, he threw the envelope down in disgust. Muttering a string of expletives, he paced back and forth in his office. He couldn't believe what the pictures represented; what his eyes had just viewed. There had to be some mistake. Why would Jackie turn to someone else? Where had the package come from? All of these thoughts were running through Joshua's head. Unfortunately no answers were forthcoming.

Hurt by her betrayal, for the next week, Joshua worked double shifts. He tried to work himself to the point where he wouldn't remember Jackie, her touch, her smell, how he felt inside of her. At night, all he wanted to do was to collapse into bed and fall into a dreamless sleep. Fate, however, wasn't that kind to him. Whenever he actually made it to bed, he would lie awake, remembering how it felt just to be with her.

He actually made it through the week without contacting Jackie or returning any of her calls. Joshua knew that he couldn't continue to operate this way on fumes. The lives of his patients were too important. He needed some sleep and he needed clarification for the pictures in the package that he had received. The only person that could help him was the very person that had hurt him beyond measure.

For his peace of mind, Joshua decided to confront Jackie to understand what went wrong in their relationship. Pulling his cellular phone from the case that was attached to his belt, he dialed Jackie's number.

"Hello."

"Jackie, this is Joshua. I'm sorry for not being in contact with you this week, but I received some news that was distressing to me."

"Joshua, if that was the case then why didn't you share that with me? Has something changed in our relationship that I'm unaware of?"

"That's what I want, no need, to talk to you about, but I can't do it over the telephone. Can I come over this afternoon and talk to you about it?"

"Yes, if it's going to help us resolve this distance between us."

"I'll be there around three, is that okay?"

"Yes."

Quickly before he was tempted to say anything else, he hung up.

Jackie recaptured their dates that led them to this point...

The Sunday after Jackie's terrific date with Joshua, was her first chance to attend church in her hometown since moving to Atlanta. After the abuse she experienced with her ex-husband, she promised God that she would attend church on a regular basis if he saved her. It wasn't a chore to attend service since she had grown up in the church.

For a while though, during the few weeks after the abuse started, she had blamed God for allowing it to happen to her. She didn't understand why it was happening. As it continued she didn't feel that God was listening to her call for help after she was forcibly taken to Aruba. She stopped believing in Him.

Then when the abuse escalated, when it was at its worst, she had no choice but to rely on her faith to try one last time for a cry of help. That's when God answered her prayer and sent Stan to her rescue. She thanked him each day for hearing her cry but she still had her faults. She wanted a committed relationship but she didn't want marriage. God would have to continue to work on her to deliver her from her fear.

As Paris, Taylor and Jackie walked into church the following Sunday, she was surprised to see Joshua with a beautiful woman and a handsome man, who could only be his brother, since they looked so much alike. Jackie's concern though was the identity of the woman.

Caleb's concern was which of the women walking towards them his brother was smitten with. He hoped that the woman that he had been seeing wasn't the Holmes woman that they had rescued in Aruba. It wasn't hard to recognize the beautiful woman from the photo that had been given to the FBI. His brother didn't need to become embroiled in the current case that he was working on; he had a career to consider.

Catching Jackie's eye, Joshua pointed to the three empty seats beside him. Quickly they moved to take their seats since service was about to start. Joshua took that moment to shake hands with Paris and ask how she was doing. Then he held out his hand and spoke to the little girl, who he assumed was Taylor, and lastly, he gave Jackie a quick hug. With narrowed eyes, Caleb watched the scene unfold before him. The beautiful woman, on the other hand was more than curious who the ladies were.

When the sermon was over and the congregation was dismissed, Joshua led Jackie outside so that he could introduce his brother and sister, Caleb and Spencer. Jackie laughed at the memory. Here she was worried that the woman was a friend of Joshua's and it was actually his sister. She, who had never been the jealous type, saw the green eyed monster, at the thought of another woman with her man after only one date.

Okay, so maybe she *was* putting stock in the vision that she had of Joshua eventually being her husband.

Jackie was glad that today was her day off because she didn't think that she would get anything accomplished. Her trip down memory lane was all consuming.

Joshua became a fixture at all of the family holiday cookouts. Her entire family loved him because he was so genuine and seemed to really go out of his way to make sure that Jackie was spoiled and well taken care of. Her family was glad that she had found someone that treated her as his equal and seemed to love her unconditionally, even though she was hesitant to show her feelings; to afraid of being hurt again.

One particular date stood out in her mind. Joshua had asked if they could go out on a date that included Taylor. He loved kids and since she had adopted a child, he wanted to include her in as many of their dates as he could, so that she would get used to him and learn to love him. That request endeared him to her heart. If she didn't already love him, then that request would have put her over the top.

From that day forward, every other week, Joshua would make it a point to have a day set aside for Taylor, to spend with them together, usually at Celebration Station, Taylor's favorite place. Sometimes they would even drive to Charlotte and go to Dave and Busters.

As a surprise to Taylor, one Saturday, Joshua and Jackie took her on an outing to the Grand Prix Racetrack. Since Taylor was so good at driving go-carts, Joshua felt that she would love the experience of going faster than the cars at Celebration Station would allow, due to her age.

On previous outings, at least once every two weeks, they would all go to Celebration Station and Taylor would terrorize the little kids with her competitive nature. She would race everyone at the track and would win, never letting anyone pass her, on the small children's course.

When Taylor learned that she was going to ride the big go-carts, she was ecstatic. That day they had so much fun and had laughed so hard, it was the first time that being with Joshua actually felt like it was where she was supposed to be

After a nice two hour nap for Taylor, they took her to her friend Macie's house for a sleepover, which left Joshua and Jackie to their own devices for the evening. When Jackie got back to the car after seeing Taylor settled, Joshua asked, "Honey, what do you want to do for the rest of the evening?"

"I'd like to fix dinner and dessert for you. What's your favorite food?"

"Anything that you cook will be fine, but my favorite is lasagna."

"Then lasagna it will be. I need to stop by the store then to get the ingredients. Do you want to drop me off at my house so that I can get my car and you can meet me back at my house, say in two hours?"

"What's wrong with me taking you to the store right now?"

"I'm sorry. I'm not used to men wanting to go grocery shopping."

That simple statement gave Joshua more insight into her ex-husband's attitude. What a jerk.

"I've told you on more than one occasion that I'm not most men. Besides, there's pleasure to be had when one's cooking or preparing a meal."

"What do you mean?" Jackie asked with open curiosity.

"I'll show you when we get home."

Arriving at Jackie's house an hour later, Joshua helped her store the groceries that she had purchased. Turning on the compact disc player to play songs at random, a little jazz, some Latin music, and some R&B, Jackie started preparing the meat for the lasagna. Instead of going into the den to watch sports, Joshua stayed with her in the kitchen and actually helped her to prepare the meal.

"Honey, where's the pan for the noodles?" Joshua grabbed the lettuce, the cheese, the cucumbers and carrots from the refrigerator as he searched multiple cabinets for a pot.

"Look in the bottom cabinet beside the stove."

In the process of moving towards the stove, Joshua placed a light kiss on Jackie's lips. Pulling a pot out of the cabinet that Jackie had directed him to, Joshua put the noodles on the stove. Then leaning over Jackie as she stirred the meat, Joshua placed several kisses along her exposed neck, and then returned to the salad that he was making. Jackie was beginning to like this cooking experience.

"How is it that you're so good in the kitchen?"

"My mother thought that it was just as important for my brother and I to know how to cook as it was for my sister. That way we wouldn't be dependent on a woman."

"Remind me to thank your mother."

While she was at the stove, Joshua put the knife that he was cutting the salad with down on the counter. He then walked up to Jackie as she was stirring the meat, and embraced her behind, gathering her lush curves possessively against his body. She arched her neck to give him greater access, to deepen the kiss that he had initiated as her body melted into his. Pleasure coiled inside of her. Her body burned for his touch. Why deny herself?

Swaying rhythmically to the soft jazz music, Joshua inquired, "Does that mean then that you're thinking about a committed relationship?"

Jackie's answer was to turn around completely in Joshua's arms. Their gazes clashed but for different reasons. Jackie's smoldering gaze was full of pent-up passion that was waiting to be released. Joshua's gaze was reminiscent of someone longing for something that they couldn't have.

Each sought to convince the other with their lips, their mouth and their hands. Joshua's fingers brushed her smooth skin just beneath her breasts, caressing her, causing shivers to race down her spine. Finally cupping her breasts in his hands, he felt the trembling in Jackie's body as he stroked and massaged them. When touching was no longer satisfactory, his lips followed the same path that his hands had taken.

The quickening of his desire could be felt as he treasured her breasts with gentle kisses that grew more demanding as he pulled each nipple deeper into his mouth.

Arching her body still closer to his, Jackie gave in to the sensations that he was creating within her. As if she could read his mind, Jackie's warm soft hands caressed his body, causing a groan to escape from his throat. He had hungered for her touch for so long. Heat consumed them both as they continued to caress and kiss each other.

A boiling sound could then be heard as the pot with the noodles on the stove spilled over. Spinning Jackie away from the stove, Joshua rushed to turn it off. Laughing he pulled Jackie back into his arms for a quick kiss.

"That wasn't what I had in mind when I said that cooking could be pleasurable, but you entice me as no other woman ever has. I'm sorry for spoiling your dinner." To resist temptation, Joshua pulled out a chair in the kitchen and sat down.

"I'm much more interested in dessert." Jackie said as she turned off the meat that was now done. Walking over to Joshua she straddled his legs. With her arms around his neck, she placed a searing kiss on his lips. Needing no further encouragement, Joshua took their desire to new depths with a need that seemed to grow as his body became more aroused, if that were possible.

Without disengaging their mouths, Joshua hands, that were caressing Jackie's derriere, removed the lacy bra that he had previously unhooked. Jackie was stunned at the sensations that she was feeling. With only one lover, her husband, as a reference, she finally knew what it felt like to lose oneself in the emotion of the moment. Whimpering in ecstasy, she bit her lip to keep from crying out.

Raising his head, Joshua asked, "Shall we continue this or stop? If you're unsure, now would be the time to stop me, while I still can."

In answer to Joshua's question, Jackie simply stood so that she could remove her top. Watching her movements was very erotic. Feeling uninhibited, Jackie proceeded to do a little striptease act as she shimmied out of her pants. Never before had she felt as beautiful as she did right now with Joshua's eyes filled with a desire that he didn't try to hide.

Standing in only a black lacy thong and a pair of high heels, Jackie decided that one of them had on too many clothes. Pulling Joshua to his feet, she helped him remove his clothes. Uncanningly, Joshua realized that she needed to feel in control of the moment. She appeared to be astonished at the level of passion that she was feeling. If he ever saw her ex-husband, he would hurt him for the pain that she had evidently experienced at his hands.

Sitting back down on the chair, after retrieving protection from his wallet, Joshua pulled Jackie to him, so that once again she was straddling him. Jackie rubbed his arousal as it strained against her bottom, time and time again as she rocked and swayed to the rhythm of the soulful song that was playing. With a voracious appetite that was waiting to be appeased, Joshua gathered Jackie's shoulder length hair into his hands and brought her head closer, as their lips fused together in a searing kiss. Their mouths opened simultaneously as their tongues mimicked the love dance that their bodies would soon enjoy; each giving and receiving.

Another thrust of her hips against his arousal, quickened his breath, which caused him to release her mouth as he began to kiss his way down her body. Arching closer to the source of her pleasure, Jackie gripped the back of the chair, as Joshua pulled her swollen breast into his hot mouth. A cry was torn from Jackie, as Joshua's tongue continued to lave each breast, over and over, alternating between licking, squeezing and touching them, as he gently feasted on them.

Wanting to give as much pleasure as she was receiving, Jackie bent forward, brushing kisses into the crevice beneath Joshua's ear, eliciting a moan of delight from him. As she stroked his broad shoulders and chest, she transferred her lips to his nipples, encircling them with the moistness of her tongue, teasing them into tiny peaks of desire.

Joshua couldn't wait another second before becoming one with Jackie. Sliding his hands over her body, Joshua lifted one of Jackie's legs in the air, kissing his way from her thighs down the length of her legs as he removed her thong. Quickly he donned the protection that rested on the table. With great tenderness, he joined their bodies together.

Kissing her deeply, he gave her time to adjust to his size. Setting a slow rhythm he began to move, even though everything that was within him, screamed for a frantic pace. Plunging into her wet, satin heat, Jackie's sensuous movements caused him to increase their rhythm. Fastening his hands beneath her hips, he drove into her with quick, rapid thrusts that caused sweet sensations to being building, intensifying their need for each other. Anchoring her to him, Joshua experienced an insatiable desire that couldn't be quenched. Over and over, he thrust into her and she met each stroke with a passion that was overwhelming.

Her feminine walls clenched around him, signaling a powerful orgasm. Riding the waves of ecstasy, Jackie surrendered to the passion only he could ignite. Joshua felt his world splintering into pieces as he gave all of himself. All thought ceased to exist as they climbed together to that infinite pinnacle that seemed to be just beyond their reach. Higher and higher they embarked upon a journey of discovery, until their control was shattered by the rapture that spiraled into every nerve ending as they exploded together.

When they could finally catch their breath, Joshua stood with Jackie in his arms, asking, "Where is your bedroom, honey, so that we can experience that piece of heaven once more."

The ringing of the telephone jolted Jackie out of her reverie and brought her back to the present. Waving her hand like a fan, she still could feel the after effects of the lovemaking that she had shared with Joshua. She had never before experienced anything so wonderful, so fulfilling.

Reaching for the telephone, she said hello, but was met with silence. Thinking that someone must have had a wrong number, she hung up. Deciding that she had to get her mind off the upcoming conversation with Joshua, Jackie left her house to go to the mall to occupy her mind with a little shopping. If she hadn't been so preoccupied, she would have noticed the car parked across the street with the gentleman that had visited her house in Charlotte, which would have caused her a great deal of alarm.

Everyone in Mr. Brownstone's Division received an email in their Lotus Notes as well as a voice mail on their telephone, regarding an important, mandatory meeting that was scheduled for two o'clock. They were asked to clear their schedules if there was a resulting conflict. An excited buzz was in the atmosphere around the office. Rumors were rampant regarding the subject of the meeting.

Randolph was in his office celebrating. Finally all of his hard work had paid off. He was about to be named Mr. B's successor for the directorship. He couldn't wait until two o'clock so that he could begin eliminating all the people that had worked for Max.

Some people in the office had the same idea as Randolph. They thought that Mr. B was announcing his retirement while the other half of the personnel assumed that someone was being reassigned or fired. All in all, everyone had their own idea and some were even willing to place bets on the outcome.

Hidden cameras had been placed in the conference room for this meeting to capture both teams reaction to the forthcoming news. The pictures taken would later be used to isolate the persons that had showed an adverse reaction. Since all of the team members had been trained well, not to show any emotion, Mr. B and Max wanted to pick up on the non-verbal clues that would help them to identify the mole.

Two o'clock came swiftly. Everyone began to assemble in the largest conference room. Mr. Brownstone was at the helm as usual. After everyone was seated, Mr. Brownstone got right down to business.

"Thanks for rearranging your schedules. As you all are aware, last year I made an announcement that I planned to retire at the end of this year. Due to some unfortunate incidents, that retirement was put on hold when our operatives in the field, kept turning up dead, one by one."

"Then Operation Shutdown occurred with fatal results. Several civilians were killed as well as one of our leading operatives, Maxmillian. The deaths that occurred didn't sit well with me. I vowed then that I would stay on an extra year to bring to justice those responsible for their deaths."

"Are you saying Mr. B that you're staying?" Randolph and Roger asked simultaneously.

"Yes. I will complete the task that I set out to do; bring the Chameleons to justice."

A muscle twitch began to beat in Randolph's cheek; otherwise no emotion was present on his face.

"How do we propose to do that Mr. B? Are there any new leads? Max was the only one close enough to them to understand how they operated. He was even close to capturing them until he died in the explosion."

Ordinarily, Mr. B would have taken offense at the way that Randolph was asking questions. One would think that he was in charge, which Mr. B guessed was the way Randolph had begun operating; a law until himself. That had to change. He stood more to gain than anyone from Max's death. Maybe it was time to focus more on the team leader than on the individual members.

"You're right as usual Randolph. You would make a good director one day. The questions that you ask always probe for more information. We do have one lead for the Chameleons. Contrary to popular belief, we just got word that the lead is actually going to join us today."

Everyone started talking at once trying to figure out what was going on. No one was prepared for what happened next.

The door to the conference room opened and Max walked in and sat down in the nearest chair. Shock could be read over everyone's faces. Even Frank, Alexis and Trevor managed to look suitably shocked.

Muttering an expletive, Randolph divulged his hatred. "My nemesis is back from the very gates of hell. I thought that I had gotten rid of you."

Several startled gasps could be heard around the room. Although they knew that Randolph was very competitive of Max, they didn't think that he had the guts to try to kill him.

Max nodded his head towards Randolph, picking up on the hatred that was visibly displayed in his eyes.

Randolph then jumped up and started chuckling as he moved to embrace Max. "Just kidding Max. It's good to see that you're alive. Things haven't been the same."

Max strongly believed that things often said in jest were a person's real feelings. Randolph had just shown his hand whether or not he meant to. It was up to Max to find out how he operated and if he had anything to do with the explosion. Heaven help him if he was responsible or played a part in its outcome.

Mr. Brownstone took Randolph to task as soon as he sat back down after trying to embrace Max. "Randolph there is no room in this division for that type of attitude, hatred or misguided joking. I suggest that you check yourself and get over whatever it is that you have against your team member. After all you will be working together to bring in the Chameleons and I expect complete operation from both sides."

Looking at each of them, Mr. Brownstone waited for their compliance. Once received, he proceeded to outline the steps that they would take to revive Operation Shutdown. After two hours, he dismissed the group.

Max and Mr. Brownstone left the premises to have their discussion about his "comeback". "Mr. B, it seems that our mole could possibly be either Roger or Randolph. What people often say in jest are really their true feelings. Randolph has been my fiercest competitor since we were in training. I wouldn't put anything past him. Have we been able to pin anything on him?"

"No Max, that's the problem. He's clean as a whistle. I've had Trevor and Frank to investigate him, but he comes up clean every time that we think we've found something. Usually, he has a fall guy that takes the rap."

"How come we can't get any information from the fall guy?"

"Once we get the fall guy into custody, he's released on bail and ends up dead before we can get a confession."

"I think the time has come to catch him doing his dirty work. After searching the crime scene where the explosion took place, I've come to the conclusion that someone on my team or on Randolph's team was responsible for the Chameleons being there. It was too convenient. I don't think that Randolph is in contact with the Chameleons otherwise they would have found me by now. This time whenever they come, I'll be ready for them. Here's what I plan on doing..."

Mr. Brownstone and Max hashed out the details of how they planned to catch the mole and their plans for executing the revised version of Operation Shutdown when the time arose.

Once the plans were in place for Operation Shutdown2, it was just a matter of playing a waiting game with the Chameleons.

During the time that it took the Chameleons to make their move, through a contest sponsored by Sole Impressions, Max was able to meet Paris and develop a strong relationship with her. What Mr. Brownstone and Max didn't account for, was the quickness which the Chameleons would strike based on insider information. Instead of coming after Max directly, they went after Paris, his girlfriend and another extended member of Max's family, his sister-in-law, Jackie.

Chapter 17

How much more could one family take? That was the question that Mr. Bailey had when he received a telephone call one morning from Max, frantic that his girlfriend Paris had been kidnapped. Max had called him first, since Paris had stayed with them while she was recuperating from an accident. Therefore it was fitting that he call the Bailey's; Paris' closest friends, really they acted more like the family that she didn't have.

Although everyone had told him the story about Paris and her accident, his heart knew differently. Deep down inside, Max thought that she was his wife that had perished in an accident, or so he thought, but was alive and seemed to have amnesia. His theories were never confirmed though.

He was glad that his sister had sponsored a perfume contest for the launch of their newest perfume, Alluring, otherwise he would not have reconnected with Paris. She had recovered enough from her accident to move into a house that she had built and had started working again as a family attorney.

Jackie continued to monitor her progress and reported her findings to Paris' doctor, who was also her boyfriend, that although Paris was starting to remember small things, she had not fully regained her memory yet.

Max felt a sense of déjà vu all over again; only this time it was worse. He had just gotten back from being overseas for an extended period of time searching for the Chameleons. After meeting with Mr. Brownstone for the "surprise Max is alive meeting" with their division, Max had surprised Paris with a visit. She wasn't aware of his primary job as an FBI agent; only that he owned two companies, Sole Impressions and Secrets.

As soon as he had left her place for another meeting with the team members that he trusted, Frank, Alexis, Trevor and Solomon, Paris had been kidnapped from her home. He didn't know how that had occurred since he had two security guards stationed at the entryway to her home. Plus he was with her until she left for the office.

When was it going to stop? Why is it that everyone that I'm connected to always meet with disaster? Max thought. Together, Max, Paris' brothers and his entire team searched for Paris to no avail. With increasing fervor, Max proclaimed to himself that he wasn't going to lose her again. Setting up surveillance at her house he kept going over the sequence of events that led to her capture.

To say that someone wanted his attention was putting it mildly. The culprits always seemed one step ahead. He had to figure out a way to catch the mole in the organization as well as save his heart; his only reason for living.

It wasn't until later that evening, when he was talking with his partner Alexis, about the two great loves of his life and how they were so similar that he felt as if they were one and the same person; that they stumbled upon a theory. With the help of modern technology, they figured out that Paris was indeed his late wife, Chelsea. Filled with a sense of happiness one moment that his thoughts had been confirmed, he was distraught the next moment because of the subterfuge that only one man would be able to pull off; Mr. Brownstone.

With a deadly look in his eyes, he left to visit his mentor, his friend, and the man that may have put his wife in jeopardy.

After his visit with Mr. Brownstone, Max decided that he would visit Paris' home to try to find some clues that maybe they had missed earlier. Luckily Alexis and Mr. B had alerted Frank, his long time friend and business partner to follow him so that they could make sure that Max didn't do something drastic that might put himself in jeopardy.

On a whim, the next day, Max slipped into the home where his wife was kidnapped and wrote her a love letter, hoping that if she was still alive that she would be able to read it and know how much she was loved. While he was there, Frank joined him to keep an eye on the surroundings while Max did what he had to do. To his utter surprise, his wife Paris or Chelsea as he preferred to call her, showed up with her kidnapper.

Using an invention by Dr. X, they were able to temporarily subdue, Nate, one of the kidnappers. Unfortunately, Chelsea had a bomb around her waist that had to be diffused. Since Frank was a bomb expert, he was able to quickly diffuse the bomb. Chelsea was able to give Max and Frank information that they needed regarding the kidnappers operation which was controlled by the mastermind, Michael.

She advised them that the key to their identity was in a microchip that was secured in their ring. While Nate was still out, they replaced the chip with a blank one from a kit that they kept with them at all times. Max was then torn between his duty and the love he felt for his wife. Should he squire her away to safety or should he let her go back with the kidnapper and rescue her the next evening, when the head person played his last card? If he let her go back, he would be saving the lives of thousands of overseas operatives.

If he got her to safety, what kind of life would they have, always looking over their shoulder? The decision was made for him as Nate woke up from the temporary sleep that he was forced into. They couldn't inject him again without killing him. Max and Frank then hid in the bedroom closet while Chelsea took the initiative to go to Nate to keep him from discovering them.

The old saying, the best plans often go awry would aptly describe the turn of events the following day. Max and his team waited outside Sole Impressions, the kidnappers hiding place that they were able to decipher from the listening device placed along with the chip in Nate's ring. They were waiting for Michael, the mastermind of the Chameleons to say enough to incriminate himself, so that they could arrest him.

When the conversation between Michael and Chelsea took a harmful turn, Max stepped in against his director's orders, to apprehend him. Unfortunately, Michael had an ace up his sleeve that they didn't account for. Since he was known for changing his facial features, they were unaware of what his current identify looked like. Therefore, he was able to escape undetected with Chelsea in one of the waiting limousines, as Max had the building evacuated.

Michael, who was riding in one of the limousines that was going to the airport, had a secondary plan that would keep Max from stopping his departure. He placed a call to his men to initiate Plan B.

"Things are critical. We're on our way to the airport. Plan B is now in effect. Follow your orders and meet me at the airport within the hour before our scheduled takeoff."

Joshua arrived at Jackie's house precisely at three o'clock with a heavy heart. He wanted to give her the benefit of the doubt but the pictures spoke for themselves. Every inch of her body was imprinted upon his memory. There was no mistaking the woman in the picture. It was his heart; the woman whom he thought was his soul mate. He just wanted to know why; what drove her to cheat on him.

Hopefully they could clear up the misunderstanding before it was time for her to pickup Taylor. When she heard the doorbell, she took a deep breath and opened it to find a haggard man standing on her doorstep.

Immediately concerned, she grabbed Joshua by the hand and pulled him into her home. "What is it? What's the matter? Did you lose a patient today?"

This was the woman that he fell in love with; the one that put other's problems before her own. Here she was, ready to comfort him upon seeing his distress. Was this the real woman? If so, how could she do this to him? How could she rip his heart out?

His conscience reminded him, *"People are innocent until proven guilty. Mister, you might want to tread softly when you ask these questions. If you're wrong then it'll be easier to repair the damage that you're fixing to cause.*

"No, I didn't lose a patient today but thanks for asking. Jackie, I'm not sure where to begin. About a week ago, I received an envelope addressed to me at the hospital. At first I was curious as to its contents since it wasn't from any medical facility. When I finally got a chance to open it, the contents blew me away."

"That was around the same time that you began to distance yourself from me, correct?"

"Yes."

"But why?"

"That's the same question I keep asking myself. Why? Why would you do this to us?"

"Stop talking in riddles. What am I accused of doing?"

"I think that I can show you better than I can explain."

Opening the flap of the envelope, Joshua started to take the pictures out but decided not too. He then extended the envelope to Jackie. Taking the envelope, Jackie was about to open it when her cellular phone beeped with a text message that read; 9-1-1. Immediately after the beep, her telephone rang. Offering her apologies, she stated, "This is an emergency. I have to take this. Please excuse me for a moment." Putting the phone to her ear she answered the call.

"Hello."

"Jackie are you somewhere that you can sit down?"

"Yes, why?"

"I don't know how to tell you this but Paris has been kidnapped."

At her cry of denial, Joshua sprang forward to catch her in his arms before she collapsed, moaning, "No, not again."

The voice on the other end of the telephone could be heard screaming, "Jackie, Jackie…"

Picking up the telephone, Joshua advised, "This is Joshua. Jackie collapsed. No, not that kind, just in tears. She'll be fine. What's going on?"

Her brother David broke the unpleasant news. "We just found out that Paris has been kidnapped. We don't know the specifics yet but we'll keep you informed as soon as we know something. Take care of my sister, please."

"I will, don't worry. Just find Paris." Picking Jackie up into his arms, he settled down on the sofa, murmuring soft, soothing words as he let her cry. Eventually the tears dried up and she was able to compose herself.

"Honey, are you all right?"

"No, but I'm glad that you're here with me. Did David say anything else?"

"He said that they didn't have enough information but that Max and his team, along with your brothers were searching for her. They'll let us know something as soon as they can. All we can do right now is pray for her safety."

"You're right."

Bowing their heads, Joshua said a prayer for the safe return of Paris and asked God that he cover her from any hurt, harm or danger. When he was finished, Jackie caressed his cheek before rising from his lap. There were things that they needed to discuss and she wasn't sure of the outcome so it was probably best if she sat down in a chair. She didn't know if she could withstand two shocks in one evening.

"Joshua, maybe discussing our problems will help take my mind off of Paris. What was in the envelope that you brought with you?"

"Why don't you open the envelope and then we'll talk?"

Jackie's curiosity was peaked that Joshua wouldn't tell her what the envelope contained. Usually he was very straightforward. Grabbing the envelope off of the table, Jackie slid the contents out.

When she flipped the papers over, a small gasp of surprise could be heard in the silence of the room.

To Joshua, it felt as if that one gasp was an admission of truth that kept playing over and over in his head. Okay so she was the woman in the pictures. What did he do now?

"Joshua, how did you get these pictures?"

"Are you admitting that you are the woman in the pictures?"

"Yes, I'm the woman and this is my ex-husband."

"How is it then that the dates on the picture appear recent?" Joshua asked hurt and confused by the reality of the situation.

Flopping back down into a chair, Jackie just kept staring off into space for several seconds before making up her mind to tell Joshua the truth.

"First of all, these pictures were taken while I was married well over four years ago. My husband destroyed these photos or so I thought. We were having a difficult time in our marriage or shall I say, I was feeling unfulfilled. When I broached the subject with my husband that he wasn't satisfying my needs, he became angry but refused to go to a sex counselor."

"Since I cared about making my marriage work, I decided to video tape us making love so that my husband could see my reactions and could visualize the areas that he needed to improve upon. It was supposed to be used as learning tool but it became a bone of contention between us. He refused to acknowledge that he had a problem. According to him the fault was mine. That very evening, he stormed out of the house and supposedly burned the photos. Since he's the only other person to view the photos, until now, I guess he didn't burn them."

Bending down in front of Jackie, Joshua grabbed her hands. "Sweetheart, you have to know that there is nothing wrong with you. The fault was his and his selfishness. When we make love, it's so powerful, it's all consuming and it blows my mine away that two people could share something so beautiful. I've never experienced that before in my life. Do you believe me?"

"I have to, because with you I feel free to just be me. You give me your all and in return, I don't have to hold anything back."

"Actually you do, but we'll discuss that at another time. I want it all, your heart, your mind, your body and your soul. How is it then that your ex-husband knows about me and would send me something of this nature?"

"Can I ask a question first? Why didn't you jump to conclusions and go off on me when you were faced with some pretty damaging photos of me with another man?"

"It's because I love you. I was hurt, no, I was devastated when I initially received these photos. Remember, I've had a week to cool down. All I wanted to know for my piece of mind was what happened to us? Was it something that I had done to repulse you? Was it leftover emotions that you couldn't control? Basically, I was feeling used. I kept thinking how could you sleep with someone else when what we share is so wonderful?"

Leaning forward, Jackie kissed Joshua briefly on the lips. "Thank you for believing in what we have, even though I'm not as sure of "this" as you are. I'm frightened if you want to know the truth. I'm scared of making another mistake. Maybe it's about time that you understand my past and what I went through with my husband so that you know without a doubt that I could never love him nor sleep with him ever again. I just pray that you will still love me once you know the entire story."

"Honey, nothing could change that."

Jackie then proceeded to tell Joshua about the move to Charlotte; the visitors that she assumed were on the wrong side of the law, the embezzlement of her trust fund money and finally the abuse. The story took about two hours due to Jackie's sensitivity. Finally she divulged the latest problems with her ex husband.

"Joshua after I was rescued, I moved to Atlanta to start a new life. I had been gone for almost two years. On occasions as I was going to and from work, it felt like someone was following me. I could never pinpoint one specific person so I didn't go to the police. One day out of the blue, I received a phone call from Maurice, my ex, but I just laughed and hung up on him. The next day, he showed up at the hospital, looking for me. Luckily, I heard his voice and hid in one of the rooms. Then just before I received the call that they had found Paris, my apartment was broken into and ransacked. Obviously someone is looking for something that they think I have. I just don't know what it could be. Besides, all of my stuff is here in Greensboro in storage. Ryan took care of everything for me."

"Did you contact the police when your apartment was broken into? Did you file a restraining order on your husband?"

"Yes and no. I contacted the police but they said that the place was wiped clean; they were not able to get any prints, that it looked as if a gang had caused the break-in. I didn't file a restraining order for Maurice since he hadn't been abusive until after we had moved to Charlotte."

Standing, Joshua pulled Jackie with him. Tilting her chin so that she could meet his eyes, he demanded, "Do you have photos of the abuse that you've endured?"

"Yes, a friend that happened to be at the resort in Aruba took some."

"Sweetheart, you need to go down to the police station and file a restraining order on him and press charges for domestic violence and include stalking charges. I don't want you to become a statistic. For him to reappear after more than a year when he's stolen money from you and abused you, he has to want something major. Otherwise, he wouldn't risk going to jail. Why didn't you go to the police when you found out that he had stolen your trust fund money?"

"I didn't want to be accused of dealing with those unsavory characters and I didn't want to die. One of the guys that visited Maurice, beat him up and they played it off like they were just two friends, wrestling. When I confronted him, that's when the abuse started. Then another guy came to the house and threatened Maurice's life. I feared that if I went to the police and told them everything; that the guy, a Mr. Robert Smith, would come after me, since I could identify him. I didn't want to die so unfortunately I did nothing."

Gathering her to him for a hug, Joshua advised, "I'll ask my brother that works for the FBI, what you should do. Since he's in town now working on a case, maybe he can do a little investigating. Will you allow me to take you to the police station to file domestic violence charges and stalking charges so that at the very least you can get a restraining order? We'll worry about the embezzlement once I talk with Caleb."

"Do you think that Caleb will help? I don't think that he likes me."

"Whatever gave you that idea?"

"Could it be his aloofness at the church when we were first introduced and all the other subsequent gatherings? It's as if he's always watching me, like I'm a crook or something."

"That's his FBI training. He's taught to watch everyone and everything. He's probably watchful of you because he knows how I feel about you. That's just his big brother routine. He wants to make sure that you're genuine; that you're not after my money."

"I'm not going to dignify that with a response. A doctor is the last person that I wanted to get involved with. Just remember that. Now I believe that it's time to go to the police station."

A warrant was issued for Maurice's arrest after Jackie filed the papers and photos claiming domestic abuse and the recent stalking charges. A cop though, who was on the take on Mr. Smiths' payroll, discreetly contacted him about the warrant, advising him that he had better find Maurice before the cops did because he was going to jail for abuse.

On the way home from the police station, Jackie just wanted to be alone, so Joshua took her to get Taylor and dropped them both back off at her home. Against his better judgment, he complied with her wishes.

The policeman that was sent to watch Jackie's home that evening was having an argument with his girlfriend when he should have been watching Jackie's house. Had he been paying attention, he would have seen the two cars that drove slowly down the street as if seeking the correct address. When the cars stopped at different houses; one in front of him and one behind him, that would have raised two red flags and he could have radioed for help. Unfortunately, he didn't recognize anything and before he could utter another word, two guys walked up to the car and shot him in the head with a silencer.

Having slept fitfully the previous night, Joshua tried calling Jackie at five o'clock the following morning to see if she was okay. When he didn't receive an answer, his spirit became more unsettled. Even if she was asleep, as a nurse, he knew that she would wake up and answer the telephone, never knowing if she was needed at the hospital to fill in for someone. Joshua waited and waited for her answering machine to click on, so that he could leave a message that he was on his way over with breakfast. When it failed to pickup, Joshua ran to the room where his brother was sleeping and burst through the door.

As soon as Caleb heard the commotion outside of his bedroom, he reached under his pillow, grabbed his gun and was ready for whatever burst through his door. Joshua momentarily came to halt upon seeing the weapon in his brother's hands.

Speaking quietly but insistently, so as to bring Caleb's mind from wherever it had disappeared to, he stated, "Caleb, it's me, Joshua. I need your help. Something has happened to Jackie. I've tried reaching her on her home phone but she doesn't answer; all it does is ring, which is odd because usually her answering machine will pick up. I called her cellular phone and she's not answering that either. We've got to go over there."

When that statement didn't get the desired results, Joshua patiently tried one more time. "Man, my spirit has been unsettled all night long. I've been up since five trying to call her. She received bad news yesterday that her sister had been kidnapped, and instead of going to her parent's house she only wanted to go home after she picked up Taylor from her after school. I wanted to stay and comfort her, but she wouldn't let me." Waving his hand where it remained in Caleb's line of vision, he then responded, "We have a few issues to resolve that just cropped up this past week, but I love her and I'm concerned that something has happened. Let's go."

Coming out of his reverie, Caleb shook his head and put the safety back on his gun. "Sorry man, just a hazard of the job. Let me throw on some clothes and I'll be ready in five minutes."

"Whenever you want to talk about what you've been through, just know that I'm here for you, without judging you or what you've had to do, to stay alive." With that, Joshua went back down the hall, praying for both his woman and his brother.

True to his word, five minutes later, Caleb was ready and soon they were speeding towards Jackie's house. Caleb took the initiative to drive, suspecting that foul play was involved. Since both of them were gifted with the ability of sensing danger, he knew not to question Joshua's spirit. They had learned growing up, that their heritage was mixed; part Indian, part African American and Caucasian. Their parents had taught them as youngsters about each of their heritages. Taking karate lessons with their father and their father's best friend, Mac, who was a Cherokee Indian, they had learned how to listen to their spirit and to recognize when danger was imminent. Each of them held black belt degrees and could handle themselves well in the face of any adversity.

As they were riding, Joshua wondered if perhaps Jackie had another vision that she had disregarded, and therefore blamed herself, again.

Cautiously arriving at Jackie's house at five thirty, Caleb surveyed the street, noticing the police car that was stationed right across the street from Jackie's house. "Joshua, was that car there when you left last night?"

"Yes. After we left the police station, they had a car to follow us here. He was supposed to watch the house to make sure that she was safe due to the stalking and abuse charges that Jackie filed yesterday against her ex-husband, Maurice."

Joshua missed Caleb's startled look. Things must have progressed farther than he thought if Jackie had told Joshua about her ex-husband and the abuse that she had suffered. He would have to disclose to Joshua, the real reason that he was there, once they were able to wrap things up.

"Since it's still relatively dark, I'm going to circle the block and then I want you to drive back down the street. You're probably going to need to do your doctor duty to check the cop in the police car to see if he's still alive since he didn't stop us when we rode past the house. While you're doing that, I'm going to sneak around to the back of the house and go inside. Josh, please be careful."

"Caleb, watch your back. We don't know what we're up against. As soon as I'm finished, I'll be right behind you."

Joshua took over driving as Caleb exited the truck when they rounded the bend in the road and came abreast a stop sign. The bend in the road was far enough down the street from the police car that an on-looker would only see the driver's side of the truck.

Thankful for the darkness of the night, Caleb sprinted to Jackie's house. Before jumping the fence to her backyard, he donned his night vision goggles that he had retrieved from his backpack, to aid him in detecting any human forms. As he turned his head to survey the house, he didn't detect any movement in or around the house. He was afraid that they were too late.

Moving stealthily towards the backdoor, he noticed the door ajar. With the door being ajar, Caleb knew that the alarm was not armed; otherwise it would be going off. With his weapon in his hand, he entered the house. Searching the downstairs rooms proved futile. Taking the stairs two at a time, he looked into the first two rooms and found them empty. When he was about to go into the master suite, movement could be heard from the garage area and from the front door. Slipping into the laundry room, he hid until he could identify the persons that were trying to gain entry into the house.

Joshua, after parking the car one street over in the cul-de-sac right behind Jackie's house, dashed through her neighbor's backyard and came upon the police car from behind. Furtively, he made his way around the car, jamming the trunk with a special type of epoxy glue that would make it impossible to open, in case someone was hiding there. Carefully checking the insides to make sure that no one was waiting to ambush him from the backseat, he made his way to the passenger side of the car.

Peering closely into the vehicle, he noticed the bright, red blood that had been oozing for quite sometime, out of the bullet hole that had been placed squarely in the middle of the policeman's head. Placing his forefinger and middle finger to the policeman's pulse at base of his neck, Joshua confirmed that the man was dead. Since his body was still warm, it couldn't have been long since the injury had occurred, roughly less than three hours if he had to estimate the time of death.

More worried now than ever, he made his way hastily but carefully, to the garage where there was a side door into the house. Was Jackie and Taylor hurt? He couldn't think of the alternative. Could he have prevented this if he would have stayed to comfort her?

Barely with enough time to spare, Joshua used the spare key that was located beneath the bushes to enter the garage. The hairs on the back of his neck were standing up. Someone else was trying to gain entry into the house, via the front door. Was it her brothers or some other family member or had the killers returned?

Slipping into the house through the garage door, he paused momentarily in the mud room before leaning against the wall that led to the dining room. Making the sound of a cricket, he hoped that Caleb would hear him and know that he had made it into the house safely. As he heard the key turn in the lock, Joshua crouched low as he moved to stand behind the column that flanked the dining room. Ready and poised for battle, he was prepared to take down the person that had entered.

Chapter 18

After the tip from the police station, the police were not the only ones following Jackie to her house. Mr. Smith also had his men in place that evening to commence Plan B for the Chameleons. They waited for the middle of the night to strike so that there wouldn't be any witnesses. Once the policeman had been taken care, of they proceeded to the house. For trained professionals, circumventing the alarm system and picking the lock were child's play.

Jackie never knew they were in the house. Walking quietly up the stairs, they were able to kidnap their victims without incident. Since they were already asleep, a light mist of chloroform was sprayed in the air directly under their nose. This process prevented their victims from waking up. Therefore when the cloth covered with chloroform was applied to their face; they remained immobile and were taken without a fight to the waiting getaway car.

The drive to their next destination, took less than forty-five minutes. Without any fanfare, the men removed Jackie and Taylor from the car and placed them in the back of a van where an ominous looking gentleman was waiting for them. Prodding

Jackie awake with the heel of his foot, Leon started asking questions. "Where are the jewels?"

Slowly coming awake, Jackie screamed in fright as she looked around at her surroundings and at the gentlemen that looked expectantly at her, as if she had something to offer them. Fearing the worst, that they were going to accost her, she backed up in fright, looking for a way to escape. That's when she bumped into a small frame that was still sleeping. Glancing down briefly, she recognized that the body belonged to Taylor.

Ready to scratch the men's eyes out, she lunged towards the one closest to her and demanded, "What have you done to her?"

Laughing at the woman's feistiness, Leon answered, "Relax, she's still out from the chloroform that she was given. If you'll give us the information that we require, neither of you will be hurt. Just tell me where the jewels are and we'll be on our way."

"What jewels are you talking about?"

"The jewels that your husband stole from Mr. Smith. He wants them back."

Looking confused, Jackie rushed to answer, "I don't know what you're talking about."

"Lady, we don't have a lot of time. In precisely fifteen minutes, someone else will be here asking these same questions and they are not going to be as nice. Do you feel me?"

"I'm telling you the truth. I don't know anything about any jewels."

"Okay, let me see if I can jog your memory. Where is the rest of your stuff stored?

"What do you mean? Some of my stuff is still in Atlanta."

"We checked your apartment in Atlanta and we didn't find what we were searching for. Now you live here but the search in this house last night was also unsuccessful. Tell me where you store your other belongings or else we'll start with the child. I don't think that she would look as pretty maimed."

"Noooooo," Jackie screamed. "Please don't hurt her. I'll give you what you want. What are you looking for?"

"That's better. Once again, we're looking for the jewels that you must have stored in a storage unit here in Greensboro. We've searched everywhere else and came up empty. Tell us where it is."

"The only storage unit that I have is in Atlanta near the Lenox Square Mall. If you have my pocketbook, I can give you the key."

Throwing the bag to her, she immediately searched for her key ring. Sighing with relief, she pulled the key ring out and pointed to the one that was a storage key. Leon pulled the key off the key ring and handed the ring back to Jackie.

Now that they had retrieved the information that they needed, or so they thought, it was time for the exchange. He could hear two cars pulling up. Opening the door to the van, he stepped out and motioned for his men to pull Jackie and the little girl out.

They handed them over to the Chameleons as bait to get Max. What they didn't know was that the storage unit only held some extra furniture; no clothing, no handbags, no jewels. After the exchange was complete, Harry who owed Maurice a favor, left a message on his voicemail that they had retrieved the key to the storage area from his ex-wife.

Roger arrived at Jackie's house to wrap up the last details for Operation ShutDown2. Working both sides of the fence was easy work. Each side always wanted something and he was just the man to make sure that it happened. After all, he had a habit to support. *This case wasn't any different*, he thought. When Randolph called him with the devastating news that he knew about his habit, he thought his career was destroyed. However, when he offered to forget about his indiscretions in exchange for performing small odd jobs, he readily took the bribe.

To date, he had only performed two small jobs that involved giving Randolph the jump on some information that was privy only to Max's team. The requested information was a part of Randolph's scheme to gain the directorship when Mr. Brownstone retired. It was somewhat of a surprise when Randolph called earlier during the week to advise him of the next job that was required as part of their bargain.

His job was to kidnap Max's current girlfriend and deliver her to a predestined site for the Chameleons to hold as bait to lure Max to his death. He had bartered with Randolph that in exchange for his cooperation of completing the task, he wanted his assurance that his indiscretions would be forgotten. Randolph at that time had agreed. Roger knew that if Max ever found out that he was responsible, there wouldn't be anywhere on earth that he could hide. Max would surely hunt him down and kill him after all the pain and misery that he had gone through the first time at the hands of the Chameleons.

Therefore after successfully delivering Paris into the Chameleons hands, Roger thought that his debt had been paid in full. However, Randolph had other ideas. Earlier that day, he had received a call stating that Jackie Holmes needed to be kidnapped and given to the Chameleons in exchange for a large sum of money. He was to deposit half of the money into a specified bank account and keep the rest.

Willingly, Roger took the assignment so that he could continue his habit. Smiling, he came to the conclusion that it was an all around win/win situation for everyone; Randolph would get off his back and he would get the extra money that he needed for the women at the strip clubs.

In order to get paid though for this latest turn of events, he had to dispose of the policeman's body and sweep the house clean of fingerprints. Paying a couple of gang members to take the car proved quite easy. They would take the police car to their chop shop and transform it into another vehicle, complete with a fake vehicle registration number.

Roger waited in his car that was parked right behind the police vehicle for about five minutes before the two gang members arrived. Getting out of the car, the first gang member pulled the dead body from the police car and stripped him of his clothes. After undressing the cop, the gang member pulled the police clothes on over his; thereby making it easy to drive the police car without looking suspicious.

The other gang member proceeded to put the naked, dead man in a body bag. Picking up the body, he threw it in the trunk of the other car and they drove off.

Within minutes, Roger was inside the house. As he closed the door, and began wiping down all the surfaces, Joshua whirled through the air, landing a solid kick to the Roger's face. He immediately crumbled to the ground. Caleb rushed out of the closet where he had taken cover, ready to battle if the need arose. Although he had counted only one set of footsteps inside the house, one could never tell and had to be prepared for anything.

After walking into the living room, Caleb assessed the situation and laughed. "I see that you haven't lost your touch. It appears that you have everything under control."

Joshua, who was barely breathing hard, took that moment to look out of the window to make sure that no one else was lurking around. "Caleb, it appears that this guy isn't working alone. The police car that was outside when we came in, is now gone."

Pulling out his cellular phone, Caleb made a call to the agency to alert them of the evening's events. His superior confirmed that they would put a trace on the vehicle and visit several of the known chop houses in the area.

"Joshua, now that we know he's not working alone, let's try to get some answers from him." Strapping Roger into a chair, Caleb was getting ready to pour some water on him to wake him up, until Joshua stopped him.

During the process of subduing the intruder, something had fallen out of the intruder's pocket onto the floor. Walking forward, Joshua reached down to pickup the shiny object. Turning it over in his hand, he muttered a string of expletives.

Looking at his brother, who didn't curse under even extreme circumstances, Caleb felt his gut clench. He knew that whatever it was, he wasn't going to like it. "Josh, what do you have in your hand?"

"It appears that this guy, who was so conveniently wiping down all the surfaces in the room, is one of your people."

"What the...? That's impossible!" Rushing to his brother's side, Caleb looked at the badge to verify its authenticity. It was a real badge; just like the one that he carried. Calling his secretary, he had her to locate Roger's department and his superior. When he received the information that the man worked on Max's team and that Mr. Brownstone was his superior, he was shocked. They had previously discussed the possibility of a mole within their organization but didn't have enough evidence to pinpoint the right individual.

Now it appeared that they had their answer. Walking outside in the backyard, he was about to place a call to Mr. Brownstone when he noticed that he had an urgent message waiting for him. "Caleb, this is Mr. Brownstone. We need your help. Max's girlfriend Paris has been kidnapped. I believe this kidnapping is also related to the deaths of his wife and child. The case, Operation Shutdown that we were working on, has taken a drastic turn that I know is the result of the mole, which is either Roger, who's a member of Max's team, or Randolph, my other head team leader. We're setting up a sting operation to bring both of them in that entail setting up another jewelry heist. When you get this message, call me."

Dialing the number, Caleb contacted Mr. Brownstone and got his orders for the sting operation that would bring in the mole. "Mr. Brownstone how do you want me to handle Roger?"

"Put a tracer in his phone and follow him. He's obviously working both sides. We need to know his other contact, and how Randolph is blackmailing him."

"That's going to be a little difficult sir because my brother's girlfriend, Paris' sister Jackie, has been also been kidnapped. My brother and I are at her house now. That's how we were able to apprehend Roger. He came to the house to wipe it clean of fingerprints. Knowing that she's the love of his life, it will be pretty difficult to let Roger get away sir. We are equally matched in strengths but somehow, I'll make it happen."

One of the hardest things that Caleb had to do awaited him. Shrugging his shoulders, he waked back into the house to perform his duty. Even though it would kill him to watch his brother suffer, he knew that they didn't have a choice.

Roger at that moment was starting to come too. With a swift kick to the face, delivered by Joshua, he was out once again. He hoped that Caleb would finish whatever he was discussing with his superiors. Inflicting pain went against everything that he now upheld as a doctor but this was necessary, if it meant finding the love of his life.

Once Caleb returned inside, Joshua took one look at his brother's face and knew that duty prevailed in this instance. "Just give it to me straight."

"We have to get out of here and let him go. He's the key to discovering where Jackie and her sister Paris are being held. This guy is an FBI agent but he's crooked. He's working both sides. We need him in order to nail a much larger mole in the organization. Mr. Brownstone, the FBI director and his team is closing in on the persons responsible for their kidnapping. A sting operation is now underway at the airport. Once the culprits are caught alive, we'll get the location of where they are and rescue them. It's just a matter of time before we locate them."

With a calmness that made his brother wary, Joshua replied, "You're asking me to allow you and your department to handle this when ya'll are responsible in the first place for this occurring?"

"Yes."

"Give me one good reason why I shouldn't beat this man to within an inch of his life so that he'll tell me where Jackie and her sister are being hidden?"

"One, you're a doctor, who by profession has to uphold the Hippocrates Oath. Two, you're a surgeon and we can't have your hands being messed up to the point where you're unable to perform your surgeries. Too many people count on you to be at your best. And lastly, I'm asking for you to trust me. We've got a plan that's going to follow this guy and determine how this all fits.

Will you allow me to do my job and apprehend all that are responsible so that no further loss of life will occur?"

With another kick to the middle and an upper cut to the face, Joshua walked out steaming. Caleb raised his head to God and thanked him for his brother's acquiescence. Since the sun was about to rise, they hurried to their car that was parked down the block. Noticing that the police car was gone, Caleb stopped and checked to see if the body had been discarded. When the remains couldn't be found, he telephoned his contacts at the police station for someone to come out and check the scene of the crime.

On the drive back to Joshua's house, Caleb divulged the real reason why he was in town. "Joshua, I haven't been completely honest with you regarding the reason why I'm in town."

"Does it have anything to do with this case?"

"Yes, I'm afraid it does. I'm been working a case that involved a jewelry heist for the past year. Recently I was notified that another FBI agent had found a link to an embezzlement case that he was working on that tied the persons to the case that I'm working on. That's why I'm here, to assist in bringing both cases to a close."

"What does that have to do with Jackie's kidnapping."

"Her husband is the one that is being investigated for embezzlement of his former companies' funds as well as Jackie's trust fund. He's also thought to be the person that pulled off a jewelry heist worth twenty million dollars. Of course, he didn't do it alone; he had help from his mistress, a personal banker at a local bank in Charlotte and I believe the help of an FBI agent with strong ties to some very important people."

Muttering to himself Joshua exclaimed, "It all makes sense now. Why Jackie is so hesitant to make a commitment; why she's so unsure of herself; why she really doesn't trust anyone that professes to love her."

"If she talked about her abuse, then she must trust you more than she realizes. I was there in Aruba when she was being rescued. She has more heart and courage than a lot of people that I know. At first when you introduced her, I was a little skeptic. I didn't know if she was working with her husband or not. Initially, I thought that perhaps they just had a falling out until she gave up everything, and just walked away to start a new life. Then I didn't want you to get involved until she was over her ex. You deserved better than to be caught on the rebound."

"What changed your mind about her?"

"The fierceness with which she loves you. Taking me to task one day was the beginning of my respect for her. Although she could tell that I didn't like her, she was honest enough to admit that she wished we could get alone for your sake but that if we didn't, then she was willing to love you in spite of your families' behavior. She didn't realize what she had said but continued with, as long as you wanted her and treated her right then she was yours."

"That's my baby. I'm going to have to deal with her phobia of commitment. I want to marry her but I can't do that as long as her ex-husband continues stalking her."

"What do you mean?"

Joshua then relayed the same information that he had stated when he first asked for Caleb's help when he had burst into his room, only to stare into the barrel of a revolver that was aimed at his head. He talked about the pictures and the police warrant.

"Do you still have the pictures?"

"Yes. I'll show you when we get home."

As soon as they pulled into Joshua's driveway, his beeper went off. Dialing the hospital, the receptionist told him that he was needed at the hospital, for emergency surgery on a government official that was being flown in. "Gotta go. The hospital has an emergency surgery. The photos are in my office in the front drawer."

"I'll try to trace the photos to see where they were printed. Hopefully, that will give us a lead to where Jackie's ex-husband is hiding."

Backing out of the driveway, Joshua sped to the hospital, attempting to focus his mind on the surgery at hand.

Caleb spent the rest of the afternoon visiting printing shops to understand if the photos were printed on any specialty paper. If he was lucky perhaps he could also isolate the printing company that had processed the photos. Since the photographs were explicit, the number of companies producing such photos should be quite small which would enable him to eliminate a lot of the printing companies on the list that he had prepared.

After a few discreet questions to several owners, Caleb was given the name and address of the printing company that specialized in producing explicit or x-rated photos. To avoid being arrested for pornography, the owner of the company was more than happy to comply with the name and address of the person that had requested the processing of the pictures. He gave Caleb, Maurice Holmes' name and an address for him in Washington DC.

Caleb headed out of the printing shop after threatening the closure of the owner's business if he contacted or alerted Maurice Holmes that someone had inquired about the photos. Sitting in the front seat of his SUV, he used his laptop to access the Bureau's computer for the exact location of the address. After typing in the address, he was able to identify that the house belonged to a graphic artist by the name of Cherita Montgomery.

Typing in a few additional commands, he was able to dispatch a team of agents to keep the address under surveillance. An additional email to Trevor would initiate the next phase, with the transferring of funds from the offshore accounts. This would force Maurice to escalate his retrieval of the jewels or else pull another heist. Either way, they would be ready for him.

Rasheeda, after reading the information that was coming across the wire, made a hasty call to Maurice to alert him that the Feds were on to them. She told him not to return to Cherita's house in Washington, D.C., because it was being watched. Instead, she advised him that it was imperative that he locate the jewels within the next seventy-two hours or run the risk of being arrested by the Feds; it was only a matter of time before they solved the case. Her next instructions were for him to check into the Doubletree hotel under one of the names that she had supplied him with and she would meet him there within the seventy-two hour time frame after she had finalized her business.

Time was of the essence. Her partners were busy tying up loose ends by killing Maxmillian Teal, the government agent, who was close to uncovering their real identities. Once he was eliminated, and after verifying that the next set of confidential documents were shipped to their boss, they were all scheduled to leave the country later that evening. The problem was, she didn't want to go with them. She wanted to stay with Maurice. It was nice having roots; having someone to come home too. However unless she scored big and was able to offer her partners a buyout, she would have to leave with them.

They would understand once she gave them the two million dollars to match their current job. She could then live in anonymity until another job was needed or until she got bored, whichever came first.

Now that their location had been compromised, Rasheeda knew that she had her own loose ends to wrap up. She had to get rid of Mr. Carson and Eugene at the bank. They knew too much and would be able to testify against her.

Later that evening Rasheeda paid a visit to Mr. Carson. Immediately she began the process of damage control; apologizing first why she had been unavailable to him and then explaining why she had been acting funny at work.

After her speech was finished, Mr. Carson began to put the pieces of the puzzle together. He thought that she was trying to cheat him out of the money that they had swindled. He then threatened to tell the police all about their scheme.

Switching to elimination mode, Rasheeda cajoled him into changing his mind by offering him an additional half a million dollars and by sexually arousing him, while at the same time stroking his ego, telling him how much she missed him. Mr. Carson couldn't resist Rasheeda. He grabbed her as she was standing by the window and started furiously kissing her and caressing her body. Overwhelmed by his passion, he didn't notice that she wasn't responding with her usual fervor. She was glancing out the window to time Eugene's arrival.

Earlier that evening, Rasheeda had broken into Eugene's apartment and had planted evidence of her affair with Mr. Carson; photos, dates and times of their trysts, and prerecorded conversations between them of how stupid Eugene was to do anything that she wanted him to do.

Breaking away from Mr. Carson before he got too carried away too soon, Rasheeda whispered that she needed to slip into something more comfortable. While in the bathroom, Rasheeda planted the same photos that she had used in Eugene's apartment in other areas of Mr. Carson's house. She also planted the tape recorder that she had used to record the conversations about Eugene that was sure to drive any man to retaliate with violence.

When Eugene returned home from work that evening, nothing seemed amiss to him. He followed his after work ritual every evening by coming home and taking a shower, then fixing him a couple of beers as he winded down and relaxed for about an hour. After he had finished his ritual and was dressing, he began to notice a picture here and there in every room.

Stunned to think that someone had been in his apartment, he immediately grabbed his gun that he used at work. Walking from room to room, he didn't see the culprit, he only saw additional evidence that Rasheeda had played him for a fool. Picture after picture was posted in various rooms of her and the bank manager in several compromising positions. That in itself didn't set him off.

On the table in the kitchen there was a note, laying on top of some bills that said, *Listen to this if you want to know where your woman is right now.* Beneath the note was a tape. Taking the tape, Eugene walked into his bedroom to hear what was on the tape.

Playing the tape on his component system, he listened as Rasheeda and Mr. Carson talked about all the money that they had swindled from the banks clients and how she had only slept with Eugene to take care of the tapes for her. In the background of the tape, as they were talking, moaning could be heard that escalated as the conversation continued until that was all that was left. Eugene's mind supplied the ending for the remainder of the tape.

Then a man's voice could be heard saying, "If you want to see for yourself if this is true, stop by 5512 West Common Street. She's there right now."

In a jealous rage, Eugene tore out of the house and drove over to Mr. Carson's house to confront him. Identifying the parked car on the street as Rasheeda's, Eugene sat in the car and planned their demise. From across the street, he could see Rasheeda's reflection in the small opening of the sheer window drapes. She appeared to be naked and in the throes of passion.

Rasheeda, noticing that Eugene had arrived as she glanced out the window, decided to add a twist to Mr. Carson's foreplay. "Can we try something a little different tonight?" She asked innocently.

"Anything you want just as long as you let me inside of you," he stated as he pulled her onto his lap. He continued to fondle and kiss her body.

Leaning over to retrieve her purse, Rasheeda pulled out a gun.

"Whoa, where do you think you're going with that?" Mr. Carson asked as he bolted upright in the chair, grabbing Rasheeda's arms in the process.

"Oh, this?" She asked, as she looked at the gun. "I want you to rub this all over my body with the barrel of the gun. It's not loaded. Let me show you how to do it." She placed the gun in his hand as she guided it over her body while fondling his arousal. In case he decided to try anything, she could grab him and control his actions.

To an outsider, it appeared that their passion had risen to new levels since she was mimicking the act of love. Up and down her shadow continuously rose.

Eugene got out of his car and ran across the yard to stare into the window.

Rasheeda, hearing the sensors chime that she had painstakingly planted earlier during the week, awaited Eugene's arrival. The sensors gave off a slight musical wind chime sound, similar to the wind chime that she had hung on Mr. Carson's porch. Preparing for the inevitable, she changed positions so that Mr. Carson was now facing the window.

Provoked beyond belief at the sight before him, Eugene fired four shots into the window, killing Mr. Carson instantly. Rasheeda then aimed the gun that Mr. Carson still held in his hand and shot Eugene in the head, who was still standing in the yard, frozen in shock. As he crumbled to the ground, Rasheeda sprang into motion. Running to the bathroom, she hurried into the black clothes that she had placed near the door. She needed something dark so that she could blend into the night.

Rushing out the back door, she waited until the neighbors came out of their house to investigate the shots that were heard before disappearing into Mr. Carson's neighbor's shrub. Unfortunately, Mr. Carson's neighbor had purchased a new dog, a pit bull that made it impossible to go through the yard without killing it. She had no choice but to mingle with the crowd and then escape when an opportunity presented itself.

Hurrying around the corner, she bumped into one of Mr. Carson's neighbor's as she was coming out of her house to join the media frenzy. Several harsh words were delivered by the lady that had come barreling out of her house. Sensing that she could get her fifteen minutes of fame on television, she tried to instigate a fight.

Rasheeda, attempting to avoid an altercation, showed the lady her gun that was resting in the waistband of her pants. Quickly the woman gasped in disbelief before hurrying to the news reporter to divulge what she had just learned.

By the time the report had gotten the ladies story, Rasheeda had swiftly disappeared into the night.

Later she would contact the rental car company to report that the car had been stolen. The car that Eugene noticed in Mr. Carson's driveway, just happened to be the same make and model that she drove but with rental tags.

Now it was time to give Nate and Michael their money so that she could remain with Maurice. Upon arriving at the hotel, she immediately checked in, carrying her laptop with her. After safely securing a wireless connection, she checked one of her offshore accounts. Staring aghast at the computer, she was shocked to discover that her account balance was zero dollars.

How was that possible? Even Maurice didn't know about this account! What was going on? There was a message waiting to be read, that was attached to the account. Opening the message to see if the offshore bank had located the problem, Rasheeda read, *If you want your money returned to your account, meet me tomorrow at seven o'clock at Kelley's Jewelry Store, with the diamonds.*

What diamonds? They didn't have them yet.

As Rasheeda pondered how they were going to get the jewels so that she could regain her money, a similar email message was being sent to Maurice's bank account.

I know what you've been doing for the past year; money laundering, extra martial affairs, jewelry heists, just to name a few of the improper things that you've participated in. To keep me from going to the police, meet me at Kelley's Jewelry Store in Charlotte, tomorrow at seven o'clock. And bring the jewels with you.

Chapter 19

The Chamleons' kidnappers had used chloroform again to knock Jackie and Taylor out while they drove to their second destination; the airport. Upon their arrival, they were rudely jostled awake. As they came too, she looked around but could not see anything because of the blindfold over her eyes. She surmised that they must be at the airport due to what sounded like planes taking off or landing nearby.

As soon as the vehicle they were riding in stopped at what looked like the side entrance to an airport hanger, Jackie had the foresight to ask if she and Taylor could go to the restroom. She was petrified because she couldn't see a way out of their current situation. The kidnappers had taken her handbag and emptied it before returning it to her, when they apprehended them so she didn't have her cell phone or any money or identification.

They had no means of communicating to the outside world where they were. The only thing that they had with them when they were taken was Taylor's backpack with her Bratz dolls, her IPOD and each other.

Because Taylor sported her IPOD in a case connected to her waist resembling a doll accessory, it was virtually undetectable unless she had her earphones in her ear. The kidnappers had grabbed the backpack for the little girl, just in case she became uncontrollable.

The kidnappers walked Jackie and Taylor to the restroom and surveyed it to make sure that the restroom was empty. Since it would have looked peculiar for the kidnappers to remain in the restroom with them, they stood at the entrance like they were guards protecting a royal princess. This maneuver prevented other people from entering the restroom.

The kidnapper called their boss while the lady and the little girl used the restroom. "Nate, everything is fine. They are using the restroom. We secured the restroom before they entered, by holding one of the maid's hostage. Don't worry, we have everything under control."

"Just make sure that they don't escape through a window or something."

"We won't. We'll let you know when we've reached the designated area."

After scanning the room, Jackie noticed a small door located adjacent to the last stall. Hopefully the door led to a closet. She immediately motioned for Taylor to be quiet and walked quickly to the door to see if it was open or if it could be used as a hiding place.

The closet was actually wider than it appeared and it was also very crowded with a large industrial garbage can and a large mopping station. Unfortunately it was too cramped, height-wise, for an adult to completely stand up in.

Experiencing an epiphany, Jackie picked Taylor up and put her in the trashcan. She then turned the latch on the window that was located in the back of the last stall to make it appear that they had escaped. Since the window was hard to open and made a cracking sound, she flushed the toilet to disguise the noise that the window made.

Taylor motioned for Jackie to move slightly to the side so that she could aim her IPOD that she had retrieved from her backpack, at the opening to the closet. By touching the click wheel several times and then aiming at the door, Taylor was able to create a makeshift hologram of another room within a room to disguise the fact that they were hiding in the broom closet. Once she was finished she put it back into her backpack. She didn't want the kidnappers to take it away from her. With her mouth open in shock, Jackie then shut the door to the closet and used the mop handle to secure the door.

When minutes passed and they didn't come out of the restroom, one of the kidnappers became very nervous and stormed into the restroom oblivious to any stares that he received. The only thing that the kidnapper saw as he examined the room was the empty bathroom stalls and an open window at the back. He banged his fist into the wall leaving a large hole as he walked back towards the entrance. He was angry with himself for letting them get away by playing the oldest trick in the book on him. As he was about to leave, in the mirror he noticed what appeared to be a small door in the corner. He then turned around to go and inspect the door, when a lady security official walked in.

"Sir, may I ask why are you in the ladies bathroom?"

With a quick response, the kidnapper repeated the story that was their cover, "I'm the guard for the Royal Princess Sana Al Shabah of Kudjesha, a small village in Kenya, Africa. Unfortunately, the royal princess has somehow managed to escape my presence and I have been checking all the restrooms to see if she is hiding in one of them."

The security guard took note of the damaged wall and replied, "I'm sorry but our rules state that men are not allowed in the ladies room regardless of the circumstances. Therefore you will have to step outside so that the people waiting will also have an opportunity to utilize the restroom. However, I'll be more than happy to search the restroom for the missing princess."

Radioing for help, the security guard took the precautionary measure, just in case the man became violent. To the intruder, the call sounded as if a page was going to be sent out over the airport's loudspeaker to alert everyone that someone was missing. Because the intruder didn't want to alert anyone that would be looking for the kidnapped individuals, he hurriedly agreed with the security guard that he would indeed welcome her assistance.

"Uh, that page is not necessary. We can't afford for the opposition to get wind of the fact that our princess is missing. They might attempt to overthrow the throne. If you can search the room and let me know if you find her I would greatly appreciate it. I'll just be standing by the outside door in case you need me." The kidnapper then moved his shirt slightly to the side to let the security guard know that he would use the weapon located in the holster on his pants if she didn't act according to his plan.

Immediately the security guard walked to the door with the kidnapper and allowed the remaining individuals to enter into the restroom. Since there weren't enough stalls, some individuals were repairing their makeup or just chatting with fellow friends while they waited their turn. The security guard took that time to ease towards the closet that the man was so interested in. Upon entering the restroom, she had noticed that something didn't look quite right about the door in the back.

Since she was an undercover federal agent working as a security guard, she knew that possibly the missing child and aunt were located in the closet in the rear. Thankfully, Frank and Max had the foresight to call in for extra help from their team members. Two of the other ladies in the restroom were fellow agents also. As they secured the front of the ladies room, she walked towards the closet and attempted to open the door. As she reached out her hand to touch the door, an image dissipated in front of her and she was left staring at a different view of the closet than before.

"What the ....? Cindy, can I borrow your lipstick please? I must have misplaced mine before I came to work.

This message was the code for, please come over here and help me decipher what just happened...

Since Taylor and Jackie were situated at the back of the closet they could not hear what was actually going on in the bathroom. However they did hear the kidnapper forcibly hit the wall with his hand. They immediately started praying to God to deliver them from the hands of their enemy.

Throughout the entire ordeal the only one that was calm was Taylor. When asked why she wasn't frightened, she replied, "My daddy will come to get me." Jackie thought that she was talking about her deceased father again.

Previously Jackie had squelched all notions that Taylor had about her dad being alive, but considering their current circumstances, she decided to probe Taylor's memory further. Jackie asked, "Honey, how can your dad save you if he's dead?"

At that moment Taylor, being the precocious child that she was answered, "How can Max be dead if we saw him the other day?"

With an open mouth, Jackie asked Taylor why she thought that Max was her father. Taylor then proceeded to tell her aunt what she remembered about the explosion and the events that happened afterwards and why she was now with her instead of with Max. She even told Jackie the conversation that she had with Mr. B the day of the funeral.

As Taylor finished the story, Jackie could only stare at her in wonder. She enveloped Taylor in a gigantic hug. "So all this time, you've known that Max was your father and yet you didn't tell any of us? Why? We just found out only a few weeks ago."

"Mr. B said that everyone would be in danger if word got out that Max was still alive. So he had to go undercover until he caught the bad guy. To protect everyone, I couldn't tell a soul. However every now and then, Mr. B would give me updates. Since I remember what he went through trying to save us at the explosion, I know that God has favor with him. He'll rescue us, you'll see or else he'll send one of his men."

"Taylor, does Max know?"

"No. Mr. B said that he and my mom have amnesia and that I can't tell them because it would harm their memory. He said that their memory has to return on its own. I sure hope that it returns soon. Although I love living with you Auntie, I can't keep this secret much longer."

"Whoa. Wait a minute. Who exactly are you claiming is your mother?" Jackie asked thinking that this information coming from a six year old was way too crazy. The family had decided not to tell Taylor that Paris was her real mother until her memory returned. They didn't want Taylor hurt if Paris didn't remember that she had a child.

"Paris, Max's girlfriend. Well it's not too hard to figure out Auntie. She looks just like my real mother except her eyes are different and her hair is different. Look, I've got a picture right here in my IPOD. I carry it with me at all times, especially when I get lonely and want to talk to her. If you can somehow reach into my bag, I can pull out my IPOD and show you."

Jackie leaned forward amid the muck in the trashcan and reached her arm around Taylor to the bottom of her bag and pulled out the IPOD. She handed the IPOD to Taylor who immediately located the picture in question.

"Taylor, how did you get this picture in here? I thought that these were just for downloading music."

"Well, Max gave me the IPOD on my last birthday because I was always singing whenever he came to visit over Paris's house. But I think that something is wrong with it because there are some gadgets on this IPOD that aren't in the instruction guide."

"What do you mean?"

"For instance, this button here, I don't know what it does. Little did they know that the IPOD that Max gave Taylor was a prototype of one of his inventions that was designed specifically for children and teenagers. His security company, Secrets had partnered with Apple to make the world's first musical device that also served as a telephone and walkie talkie. Max had developed this device so that he could protect the ones that he loved from the catastrophe that took his wife and child away from him. Taylor's IPOD was different from the one that was to be put on the market though. Her IPOD included a two way receiver, along with a homing device that could be used to locate her in the event that she somehow got lost.

"Let me take a look at it please. You know with the way that your Dad loves gadgets, I'm sure that it serves a purpose only he would think of." Jackie took the IPOD to examine it but could only find the place where telephone numbers could be entered under the contact menu.

"Have you ever tired to put in your friends telephone numbers?"

"Yes. I've put in the families numbers and a few friends. Let me show you."

"Okay. Do you have Max's number or can you pull up David's number?"

"Sure. Max told me that if I ever got lonely and wanted to talk to him I could call him at anytime. I think that he likes me a lot even though right now he doesn't know who I really am."

"Honey you know that Max really loves you. I don't think that he could possibly love you any more. Let's just try this button with the click wheel set to the telephone numbers to see what happens." As Jackie selected Max's number and pushed the button on the bottom panel, the IPOD started to dial the number listed. In disbelief Jackie stared at the IPOD as it was trying to dial the number. "Please, please," she whispered, "answer". It rung five times. Just when she was about to hang up, someone answered.

With careful observation from the sky by Trevor in a helicopter, Max was able to follow the only cars that had the potential to hide a body without detection. A harrowing rescue followed on one of the major highways. In the end Max prevailed and the woman that he loved was once again in his arms.

From his pocket, Max heard the faint ringing of his telephone. "Baby, can you grab my cell phone from my pocket? Please make sure that you do it discreetly and do not put down the weapon in your hand, just in case, our friends that are behind us start to shoot again."

"I've got it! Hear it is."

As he glanced down at his phone, he saw Taylor's IPOD address on the screen. "Taylor? Hello, Taylor? What's wrong honey?"

"Max! This is Jackie. Where are you? Can you come and rescue us? We're trapped! By the way how did you invent this IPOD?"

"Slow down Jackie. What are you talking about? Please explain what happened for you to have Taylor's IPOD." Jackie proceeded to explain the course of events that led up to them getting kidnapped. "Max, I think that the batteries are getting low. The screen keeps going in and out!"

"Okay Jackie, listen very carefully. The IPOD has its own homing device. I need you to activate it. Here's what you need to do. Press the click wheel until you get to the word help. Simultaneously click the word help and press and hold the two buttons on the outer surface of the IPOD. That will activate the antenna. You will see the antenna rise from the top of the IPOD. Do not block the antenna. It has to pick-up your signal otherwise we won't be able to find you."

A bullet whizzed by Max's ear. The enemy was getting closer.

"Max, what was that noise? Are you all right? Are you in some type of danger?"

"Jackie, I can't talk right now. There are some people chasing us but help is on the way. Put Taylor on the phone, please." Jackie pulled Taylor closer to the phone.

"Hello Daddy. Are you coming to get me this time?"

"Sweetheart, I love you with all my heart. Yes, Daddy's on his way. Just hang tight until I get there okay? I've got a surprise for you." He handed the phone to Paris.

"Hi Scooter. Mommy loves you too."

Taylor squealed a loud squeal! The only person that called her Scooter was her mother! Her memory was back! Jackie hurriedly placed a hand over her mouth. Hoping that no one heard her, she motioned for Taylor to be quiet. At the sound of the squeal, the security guard with weapon poised in hand, hurriedly opened the door to the closet to find two individuals huddled together in fright.

Meghan motioned for Cindy to bang the bathroom door on its hinges hopefully disguising the noise from the squeal. They needed to buy time in order to search their palm pilot for photos of missing people related to their case. A perfect match. Meghan identified herself softly to the lady and the child.

"Hello, my name is Meghan. I'm not sure what just happened but do you think that you can project another picture over this section to disguise us talking?"

"Sure," said Taylor, after finding her voice once she recovered from the shock of having the door thrown open. Then she aimed the IPOD at the opening and once again, the bathroom was transformed into a tranquil scenery, filled with lush plants and waterfalls. The waterfalls sounded like the running water from the bathroom faucets.

"If I'm not mistaken you're Jackie and Taylor, right?"

"How did you know who we are? I didn't think that anyone knew we had been kidnapped."

"Well, let's just say that you have friends in high places. Right now let's worry about how we're going to get out of here. We'll answer all your questions later."

Meghan motioned for Cindy to stand guard at the opening of the closet so that she could take care of the kidnapper. She radioed for extra help in case the kidnapper tried anything. Then she stuck her head out of the door to see if the two guards were still near the vicinity of the bathroom. Since they were, she stepped out of the bathroom to talk to the two guards once she noticed that her backup was making their way towards them.

"Sir, I believe I have figured out how the princess may have escaped. It looks like she used the top of the toilet to climb out of the window in the last stall. There was a ribbon hanging onto the top part of the window sill. Can you identify this?" asked Meghan as she pulled a ribbon out of her pocket.

The kidnapper could not remember whether or not the little girl had one on or not. All he could remember was that she had pigtails. "I don't remember her having a ribbon on." With menacing steps, he pulled his gun on Meghan and asked, "Are you trying to play me? Did you help the girl; I mean the princess get away?" The other guard had eased away from the doorway to block any onlookers from interfering with the situation.

Just then the backup agents came into view with guns drawn as they rounded the corner, just before they reached the area in question. "Sir, we're going to have to ask you to drop the gun or we will be forced to retaliate." With deadly accuracy, the federal agents had their laser guns trained on the kidnapper's hearts. Sensing defeat, the first kidnapper swung Meghan around by the waist as he fired the shot towards the other federal agents.

The shot went wide due to Meghan's quick thinking as she threw a forearm to the kidnapper's ribs. Chaos happened all at once. The two backup agents felled the kidnapers with one clean shot to the head. Since all three agents had worked together for so long, Meghan knew to lean forward out of the kidnappers arms so that when her friends retaliated, they would have an unobstructed view of their target.

Operation Shutdown2 came to its conclusion as Max and his team overpowered the Chameleons. The assassins ended up turning on each other when Nate attempted to take Michael and the agents close to him out. The FBI agents then killed him instantly. Michael escaped being killed because he hit the floor, intent on crawling his way off the plane. When a cease fire had been called, Michael's arrogance caused him to challenge Max, knowing that with his ethics, he wouldn't shoot him in cold blood.

Michael continued to bait Max as he walked closer to the exit, lying about being intimate with his wife while she was captured. Max, who had reached his limit, then lunged forward and proceeded to beat the crap out of him until Frank and Solomon pulled him off, lest he beat Michael to death.

Frank, who stood in front of Max trying to calm him down, wasn't paying attention to Michael, who with his last ounce of energy, grabbed a gun from a holster attached to his leg and fired a shot. Max, with his quick reflexes, pushed Frank out of the way while simultaneously reaching for the gun in Frank's. With one quick shot, Max killed Michael just as a bullet hit his chest.

Chapter 20

The doctor came forward at that time to see what all the commotion was about. He knew that he had a top FBI agent on his ward that was supposed to be top secret, so that didn't explain what the noise was about. He was tired, weary and haunted by a face that he thought he would never see again. He hadn't been getting any rest for the last couple of days because his soul mate, Jackie was still missing.

As he rounded the corner, to tell the people that they were in the wrong area of the hospital, his eyes were only able to focus on one person, Jackie, his soul mate. Right there before his very eyes.

He blinked to make sure that she wasn't a mirage. He even closed his eyes then opened them, only to rub his hands across them again. No she was still there, warily looking at him too. Forgetting that he was a professional doctor, on duty. Forgetting that he was in a room full of strangers. Forgetting that possibly she may have moved on, he purposely started walking towards her with the single intent of holding her and kissing her and thanking God that she was alive and well.

He didn't have to walk all the way. Jackie started walking to meet him halfway and then proceeded to run into his arms with tears streaming down her face. For the second time that evening, a loud cry was heard as a man held the woman of his dreams. His soul hungered for her. His mouth sought hers with an intensity that had other members of the family fanning themselves just from the heat they were generating. If it had not been for Solomon cracking a joke, there's no telling how long that kiss would have lasted or to what depth their passion would have taken them too. Her family was never going to let her forget this, thought Jackie as they slowly broke apart.

Dr. Kelley cleared his throat as he spoke to both families. "Please excuse me. I apologize for getting side tracked." Everyone laughed at his statement. No one seemed to mind the public display of affection since they knew how he felt about Jackie.

"Max is going to be fine. He's undergoing some x-rays now and all appears to be fine. Dr. X will come out in about five minutes to tell you what happened. As a matter of fact, here he comes now. Jackie, can I speak with you for a moment?" asked Dr. Kelley with outstretched hands.

Without a moment's hesitation, Jackie walked with him out of the waiting room into the hall. With another heartwarming hug, Dr. Kelley pulled Jackie into his arms and simply embraced her, holding her to his heart.

"Will you forgive me for dropping you off at your home and thereby putting you in a position to be apprehended?" He asked looking into her eyes.

"Honey, it wasn't your fault. I'm the one to blame. I was the one that needed some time to think. Please don't blame yourself. I wouldn't be here right now if you hadn't gone to my house to check on me. From what I hear, you and Caleb handled things and are responsible for Taylor and I being found. Thank you!"

Over the intercom, a page could be heard for Dr. Kelley's presence being requested in the emergency room. With a quick passionate kiss, he murmured, "I've got to go. Can I see you when I get off? Better yet, make that tomorrow since I don't know how extensive the injury for the person in the waiting room is?"

"Just hasten to me, whenever you're free." With another kiss, Jackie walked away before she was tempted to plead with him not to leave her alone ever again.

Entering the waiting room, her sister Ryan walked up to her with a grin on her face. "Are you ready to go home or do you want to sit around and wait on your man so that ya'll can finish where you left off?"

Smiling Jackie replied, "Don't hate. After my harrowing experience, I don't ever want to be separated from him again. You'll see. Your time is coming. Our family is known for their passion. Look at Mommy and Daddy over there. Go to Max's room and you'll see him and Paris making out. It just took me awhile to find my real passion in life."

"So what do you want to do to pass the time until Joshua is finished working for the evening?"

"I want to go to your house and freshen up, then come back and wait for him. Taylor will be with her parents and I really don't want to be left alone right now. First though, I need to have a word with Frank and Solomon about another case that they are working on."

"Okay, when you're finished, we'll be ready to go."

Jackie and Ryan headed over to the circle that Frank, Solomon, David and Malcolm had formed. With a brief touch of her hand to Frank's arm, Jackie interrupted them. "Frank, I know that you're probably working on the jewelry heist case too. The men that abducted me first were working for a guy named Mr. Smith, a loan shark in Charlotte. He is the mastermind behind the jewelry heist. I've actually met him before when he came to our house in Charlotte looking for Maurice. I didn't know then who or what he was."

"Jackie, what did you mean by the first people that abducted you? When did the second abduction take place?"

"Mr. Smith's people abducted me first. They only wanted the key to my storage facility where the jewels were stored. Luckily I had my storage key in Atlanta still on my keychain; otherwise I might not be standing here. After I gave that to them, they took us to another location where they handed us over to the guys that worked for the Chameleons. I believe that's what the group called themselves. I was slightly dazed from the chloroform but I believe that's what they said. Putting the pieces of the puzzle together, I think that Maurice may have hid the jewels in my handbags. They were the only things destroyed when the break-in occurred in Atlanta.

Ryan then interjected, "What break-in?"

"That's not important right now Ryan. We'll fill you in later. What will they find when they go to your storage facility in Atlanta, Jackie?" Malcolm asked.

"Only furniture and clothes."

Frank then spoke. "That poses a problem then. They will be back for you; this time with a vengeance. Where are the rest of your possessions that you didn't take with you to Atlanta?"

'They are at my house, in my garage," Ryan stated. "When Jackie left, she asked me to take care of packing her things and storing them. I didn't see the need to pay for a storage facility when I had all that room in my garage."

"Ryan, can you give us the keys to your house?"

Speaking with authority, Solomon advised, "David, you know what to do with Jackie since you've been part of the FBI Relocation Unit. She has to disappear until these guys are caught. We'll go over to Ryan's house and confiscate the handbags and search them for jewels. Any of the handbags that we have to destroy Jackie, the government will reimburse you."

"Solomon, I'm going right now to discuss this latest development with Max and then we'll contact Mr. B." Frank explained as he headed to the hospital room to talk to Max.

"I can't do that, Solomon. I refuse to live my life again in fear. Right now, I'm the only one who knows what Mr. Smith and his men look like."

"Jackie, I'm afraid you're not going to have a choice in this matter. If it's my responsibility to keep you safe, you're going to have to comply; government's orders."

"For how long?"

"Until we can capture those responsible."

"Give me a time frame."

"I can't, but what I can give you is one night before we have to move you to a safer place."

"One night. What if I choose not to participate?"

"What do you mean?"

"What if I choose not to go with you?"

"Jackie, this is not a game! It's not debatable."

"I'd rather stay and take my chances."

"And risk putting others lives in danger? What about Joshua? Do you want him to get hurt? What about your family? Do you want to put them at risk? Haven't they suffered enough?"

"Okay, I give up. Stop badgering me! I'll let you keep me safe for two weeks. That's all. Otherwise I walk away right now."

"Frank, Solomon, I'll make the necessary arrangements. You already have my secure telephone number. I'll touch base every two days."

"Where will you be tonight?" Frank asked Jackie.

"At Joshua's, if I have only one more night," replied Jackie as she and Ryan exited the waiting room.

Malcolm intended to follow them to their destination to make sure that they arrived safely. Then he would take his place that evening in guarding Jackie and Joshua to make sure that nothing happened before she was whisked off to safety.

As he was leaving, Frank thought it best to call Malcolm on his cellular phone to verify his whereabouts for the remainder of the evening. He didn't want any surprises. "Malcolm, from what vantage point will we be able to locate you this evening?"

"I thought that David and I could each take up residence in Joshua's neighbor's house. Where will you guys be?"

"Solomon will be up in the trees and I will be on the rooftop. We'll also setup a perimeter guard around the house and the backyard so that if anyone attempts to gain entry into the yard, they'll be fried."

"What about Caleb? Is he going to be there also?"

"No, he's checking out another aspect of the case in Charlotte."

Finally, after being at work for twelve hours, Dr. Kelley was finally able to leave the hospital. The injury in the emergency room was taken care of and he was now free to spend time with his woman. He had taken a week of vacation to show Jackie how much he loved her and also to protect her until her husband was captured. According to a message from Caleb, the case was heating up and her ex-husband would be forced to do something else drastic before they were able to capture him.

Sleep could wait, thought Dr. Kelley as he walked the corridors of the hospital on his way to the building's entrance. If he was going to retain his sanity, he had to see Jackie immediately. Pulling out his cellular phone, he was too intent on dialing his sweetheart's number to notice his surroundings. Moving steadily towards the door, he missed the two women that rose slowly from their seats to follow him.

Jackie and Ryan smiled as they watched Joshua heading towards the hospital's exit, with his entire focus on what appeared to be his Blackberry in his hand.

As he touched the screen to dial a number, another phone could be heard ringing in the background. Without even a curious look behind him, Joshua waited impatiently for Jackie to answer.

Ryan looked at Jackie, "Is that your telephone I hear ringing? Perhaps he's calling you. It appears that he can't wait to talk to you."

Jackie fumbled in her enormous bag in search of her telephone. *Where was the telephone when you needed it?* While she was fishing around in her bag, her loose tweezers that had fallen out of its pouch snagged the lining in her pocketbook. Just as she grabbed the small telephone, the diamonds that had been sewn into the lining spilled over into her purse without her knowledge.

Finally she held the telephone to her ear, as she breathlessly answered, "Hello."

"Sweetheart, I just finished at the hospital. Would it be possible for me to come over tonight? There are a couple of things that we should discuss. As a matter of fact, I'm headed to your house now and should be there within twenty minutes."

"Um, Joshua."

"What is it baby? Here I am running off with the mouth about what I want and I didn't give any thought that you might not be at home after all that's happened. I don't know what I was thinking. Can we start this conversation over again? Let's just blame this on my being extremely tired."

"Uh, Joshua."

"Yes, I'm listening. Where can I come to talk to you, even if it's just for a short period of time?"

"I'm at the hospital waiting on you."

"What? Why? How long? Please tell me that you're not by yourself."

"No, I'm not by myself. Ryan and Malcolm are here with me. I just arrived about thirty minutes ago after a brief shower and a change of clothes."

"Exactly where are you at the hospital?"

Feeling a tap on his shoulder, Joshua turned around and seeing Jackie apprehensively standing in front of him, opened his arms. Without hesitation, she walked into them and pressed a fervent kiss to his lips.

Releasing her mouth with reluctance, he apologized, "I hope I haven't kept you waiting too long."

Ryan spoke with merriment. "Not long for some of us and too long for others, if you know what I mean. Jackie, since you're in good hands, I will make myself scarce." Giving her sister a heartfelt hug, she whispered, "Be safe. May God and his angels encamp around you and all that you love. I'll see you in a couple of weeks."

To Joshua, she patted him on the arm, "Take good care of her."

Joshua looked expectantly at Ryan, trying to decipher what she meant by her remark. "I plan to do just that."

Together, they exited the building and waved at Malcolm, who was waiting at the entrance to take Ryan home and then to circle back to begin his vigil.

In the car, Joshua turned to Jackie and asked, "Where to sweetheart?"

"I just want to go home with you Joshua."

He liked the sound of that. "Then home it is. If it is within my power, I want to fulfill every wish that you have."

Caressing the side of his face, Jackie whispered, "You already have."

Pulling a blanket from his backseat, Joshua wrapped it around Jackie and told her to relax as soothing music played in the background on their drive to his house.

All of a sudden after driving for about ten minutes, Jackie spoke. "You realize that your house will have been searched by the time that we get there right?"

"Yes. If Caleb was here and not in Charlotte, he would have done the same and would still be there waiting. Will your brothers and friends be in the house with us? Joshua asked curiously. It didn't matter to him. He was going to make love to her, brand her to him forever, leaving his indelible possession upon her mind, body and soul, regardless of his surroundings.

"No, probably not in the house; but nearby. They take their responsibilities seriously."

"Then it won't bother you that I make you mine once again?"

"I'd be disappointed if you didn't." With a quick kiss at the stoplight, they soon arrived at Joshua's house.

When Joshua got out of the car, he surveyed his surroundings. With a keen eye, he looked up and down the street and catalogued everything that he saw. Nothing seemed out of the ordinary. Then he scanned his yard and the neighbors. Hearing a whistling in the trees, he glanced briefly to the trees then away. Satisfied that Jackie's brothers and friends were in place, he opened the passenger door.

Leaning forward, as if he couldn't help himself, Joshua slowly lowered his head and captured Jackie's lips in a long, lingering, intoxicating kiss. At the touch of her lips, he forgot that her brothers were nearby, watching them, watching the house for the enemy. Instinctively Jackie parted her lips to give him greater access. Sweet sensations began washing over her, causing her to close her eyes and savor the taste of his lips. Her eyes opened wide with shock, as Joshua lifted her in his arms and carried her to the house without breaking their heated kiss.

The house key was inserted into the lock and they barely made it inside before their passion began to spiral out of control. Memories of the kidnapping and what could have happened tore at Joshua's senses. Words at that moment couldn't express what was in his heart. He was operating on pure emotion. Setting Jackie on her feet, with breathless urgency, Joshua continued to devour her lips as he backed her against the wall, while his hands began a sensual onslaught, touching and caressing her body, bringing it to a fever pitch that caused her to whimper in ecstasy.

Shaking with need, he kissed his way down her body removing her pants and her lacy panties in the process. The warmth of his breath caressed her inner thigh as he rained kisses along her satin heat. Drinking the essence of her, he pleasured her until she cried out his name. Desire began to build, gathering speed as it tore through her body, pushing relentlessly for release, shattering her into a tiny million pieces.

Kissing his way back up her body, he lifted Jackie off the floor to bring her lips closer to his in a deep, scorching kiss. In response, Jackie wrapped her legs around his waist. With a fierceness born almost of desperation, he joined their bodies together with one quick thrust. She greedily accepted what his body offered. Her sensuous movements caused him to fasten his hands beneath her hips as he continued to plunder the depths of her feminine core. Again and again, he surged into her, sending waves of pleasure cascading over them.

He had hungered for her touch for so long that his passion became uncontainable. It was wild and urgent. With an insatiable appetite, he took them to the brink of rapture only to pull back and begin the ascent again. Over and over they rode the wave of ecstasy until they exploded together and blissful spasms racked their bodies.

Caught up in the excitement of exploring each other's bodies, they forgot that they were in the living room, half dressed, in a compromising position. Kissing her lips once, more, Joshua leaned his head on Jackie's forehead as he eased her down his body. Still holding her in his arms, he gently led them to the couch. "Sweetheart, I thank God for bringing you back to me! Can you ever forgive me for not protecting you and Taylor after you filed charges against your ex-husband?"

"It's not your fault. I was the one being stubborn. If you hadn't checked on me that morning, I might not be here now. I'm glad that you cared enough to follow what your heart was telling you to do. How did that happen when you were mad at me?"

"My love for you overrode my anger. I just wanted to understand what went wrong. What it was that I did to drive you away."

Cupping his face in her hands, Jackie placed a passionate kiss to his lips as she whispered, "You didn't drive me away." Since she only had this one night before she was sent into seclusion, she didn't want to waste any of the precious moments that she had talking with Joshua. Jackie parted her lips to tell him that she had to go away; for his safety and for her families safety; but not until the morning; not until she found heaven in his arms once again; not until she expressed her love again in the most elemental way possible.

The words died in her throat, as Joshua plundered her mouth once again. Swinging her into his arms, Joshua carried Jackie up the stairs to his bedroom where their passion once again flared out of control. It was as if they were making up for the week that they had spent apart.

Joshua gathered Jackie possessively to him as he settled her into the spoon position as their breathing became less ragged and their heart rates returned to normal. This is what she craved; the feeling of being wanted, loved and protected, as if she were the most important person in her man's life. Wanting to shore up enough memories to last a lifetime, Jackie refused to let the tears drop at the sweet if somewhat ferocious loving that they had just shared.

Never before had she experienced such wantonness, such boldness to finally feel free to express who she was and how she felt. It was amazing that even now, she wanted more and by the feel of Joshua's arousal, he wanted the same.

"Do I detect a hint of desperation in your lovemaking? Is this a goodbye?" Joshua asked as he angled his head to stare into her smoldering eyes.

Refusing to answer his question, Jackie sensuously arched her body backwards, letting her derriere slide across his arousal. With just the slightest of movements, he entered her again and proceeded to bring them to another earth-shattering climax more intense than ever before.

While they were still riding the waves of ecstasy, a sixth sense warred within him to be heard over the rampaging emotions that he was experiencing.

Something wasn't right; he could feel it. His spirit showed him images of Caleb in trouble as well as the danger that was imminent if they stayed in the house. Abruptly he withdrew from Jackie's secret garden, much to her dismay. At her stare of confusion, Joshua said, "We've got to get out of here, quickly! Here, put these on," he indicated of the sweatpants and shirt that he pulled from the drawer and threw to her.

Jumping quickly from the bed, Jackie donned the clothing without asking questions.

There could be only one reason for Joshua's urgency; the enemy had found her and had come to kill her. Obviously he had heard something outside that propelled him to act fast. She trusted him with her life.

Moving swiftly around the room, Joshua grabbed his Blackberry, a shirt and his gun that was in another drawer of the same dresser. Without stopping to put on the shirt, they ran out of the bedroom.

Chapter 21

Two cars in the distance were seen driving slowly down the street from Frank's vantage point on the roof behind the chimney. Sending a message via their headsets to Solomon, David and Malcolm, everyone was on alert. Frank had just enough time to send a text message to Joshua about the impending danger. Unfortunately, there wasn't enough time for them to get out of the house safely.

As the cars slowed down just before they reached Joshua's house, four men got out of each car, while the others continued down the street, leaning out of the car window with machine guns, intent on doing a drive-by shooting.

Spotting the car through the telescopic lens, Frank flipped a switch on his watch to arm the perimeter force field with artillery that was setup in the front and back yards. When the first shots were fired from the car towards the house, the force field rapidly returned heavy gunfire. To the men in the car, it seemed as if twenty men were shooting at them.

Malcolm, from the neighbor's house, shot two of the individuals that had gotten out of the car, with the intent of breaking into the house. David, who was covering the back entrance to the house, was able to take out two more men that had come across the yard from the other side of the street. Since the gunfire was fierce and rapid, they all had their hands full.

Solomon and Frank returned fire on the two moving vehicles, shooting out two of the tires and hitting the drivers in the middle of the head with a bullet, causing the cars to run into nearby poles and then to explode.

As the car exploded, Solomon concentrated on taking out the remaining men that were steadily firing shots at the house as they made their way closer to its entrance.

From the rooftop, Frank joined in, eliminating others by firing an M60 machine gun, from left to right, that was perched atop a tripod that he had quickly assembled once the cars exploded. Within fifteen minutes everything was over. The ground was littered with dead bodies. Once the perimeter grid has been deactivated, David raced towards the house to search for Jackie and Joshua.

Frightened out of her wits, Jackie numbly followed Joshua down the back stairway that would lead them directly into the kitchen. A rapid splatter of gunfire was heard hitting the windows in the kitchen and all the other areas on the ground floor of the house. Joshua paused on the steps and covered his body with Jackie's, to shield her from any danger.

When he felt a pause in the action, Joshua took that moment to propel them into the kitchen near the pantry. Quickly pushing a switch on the wall that was carefully hidden behind several groups of canned goods, the pantry doors swung open to reveal what looked like a small room.

As the gunshots intensified, hitting the walls within inches of where they stood, Joshua grabbed Jackie and dived into the room, just in time to avoid being shot. Swiftly standing to his feet, he pushed a circular knob that looked like a bottle opener and the doors closed. Keeping his arm around Jackie, he felt for his Blackberry that was attached to his hip, which would provide them enough illumination to see where they were going.

Thank God the previous owner had the foresight to build a wine cellar below ground or they might not be alive. Pulling Jackie closer to his heart, he held her trembling body as he whispered soothing words to comfort her.

"Baby, it's going to be alright. Please don't cry. We need to be as quite as possible until Frank or David lets us know it's safe to leave." Kissing her tears away he positioned himself in front of the door. On his Blackberry, he started to send a text message that they were okay but decided that it would be too dangerous. If the enemy had somehow managed to kill Frank and his group and then get into the house, he didn't want to give them any indication that they were still alive.

Joshua felt sure that Frank would let them know when all was clear. Jackie, who remained encircled within Joshua's arms, while frightened, felt very secure. Her honey had used his body to shield her on the stairs. Even now when danger was imminent, he was protecting her by putting her body behind his, in case someone was able to find the wine cellar. If the door opened, he would be the first one they saw and also the first one they killed.

Turning in his arms, Jackie slid her arms further around Joshua's waist. Quietly, she whispered, "I love you Joshua. Even if we don't get out of here alive, I want you to know that I love you with all of my heart; it just took me awhile to figure that out."

Unerringly his lips found hers in the darkness, delivering a sensual, riveting kiss. "Sweetheart, I love you more than life itself. I promise you that I'll protect you with every fiber of my being. Have faith in God that he will pull us through and that the enemy will be defeated."

Grasping her hands together in his, Joshua said a prayer for protection and thanked God that their love for each other was real and had weathered the storm that the devil had purposed for confusion. He also prayed that he could reach Caleb and help him before it was too late.

Trevor, after leaving the hospital, headed to Charlotte in the helicopter, to wrap up the Cymballas case. He had just received a text message from Caleb that the first of two meetings was set with a Mr. Smith, for the fencing of some jewels. Trevor knew that he would be the first to arrive as backup to Caleb. Frank, Solomon and Max would arrive at some point later that evening.

After arriving at the airport, he rented a car and drove to his house. Letting himself inside, he immediately checked his phone messages. There were none. He wondered why Cherita hadn't called. Ever since Mr. McAlston agreed to keep her on board at the bank, she had been flying constantly to San Francisco, working on the merger that she had put together.

Although they talked every day, they didn't get to spend a lot of time together because of her hectic schedule and his heavy caseload. However, at least twice a month they would spend three consecutive days together no matter what. This weekend she was supposed to come to Charlotte. He had given her a key to his house when she had to check into a hotel one weekend when he had been delayed a couple of hours in getting home. She adamantly refused to go back to her sister's house ever since she had her arrested.

Wondering if something was wrong, he picked up his phone to call her but reconsidered. He needed to touch base with Caleb and Max and he needed a shower to be alert for the evening's activities. Walking into his bedroom, he stripped naked then grabbed a towel from the linen closet. Just as he was about to go into the bathroom, he noticed the envelope resting upon his pillow.

Thinking that Cherita had already arrived and perhaps had left to pickup some dinner, he smiled as he opened the envelope. She was always leaving him little notes of love so the envelope resting upon the pillow didn't initially cause him any concern.

That changed when he read the contents of the letter.

She had left him.

After staring at the letter for about ten minutes, and reading it over for the umpteenth time, Trevor decided that the quicker he resolved this case, the quicker he could find his heart and slowly put the pieces back together again. *Cherita, I'm coming, so beware!*

After Max was released from the hospital, he wanted to spend the next couple of days with his wife and child, celebrating life and the wonderful blessings that God had returned to him but unfortunately, duty called. He had to identify the second mole and apprehend him so that he wouldn't keep looking over his shoulder for the rest of his life wondering when that person would strike again. Therefore, he only took a couple of hours to be with them before he had to leave.

He kept going over in his mind, how someone could know so much about their activities that they would constantly get the jump on them and never get caught. Randolph of course was the chief suspect but the main question remained, Who was the common denominator that tied him or her to the Chameleons? Now that they had eliminated the two leaders of the Chameleons, it was time to smoke out the remaining two individuals. Perhaps then they would secure the evidence needed to put Randolph away for life.

As he pondered all aspects of the case, using his laptop to access the timeline of events, he tried to locate anything that he might have missed. Only someone with inside information, like a police officer with close ties to the Bureau that was willing to make extra money, or an ex agent that had an ax to grind, would have access and the resources necessary to pull off this type of scheme.

Working the information like a puzzle, he listed the agents that were suspected of being dirty and the agents that were no longer with the Bureau onto a grid. With the touch of the screen, he was able to identify each agent's caseload over a two year, then a four year period, the type of contraband that was being smuggled, and the city of origin. Next he plotted those cities on a map. With another touch of a button, he ran an analysis to see if any of the agents were simultaneously in the same city. He plotted the cities were the Chameleons were known to operate. He then overlapped this map with the map of the agents and their caseloads.

Looking at the lines that crisscrossed on the computer screen, Max identified a match. The Chameleons were in the same city, Colombia, South America, when a former agent by the name of Shelby Thomas, was working on a drug smuggling operation. She had been an expert in computer communications which would have allowed her to tap into the Bureau's wire for confidential information, at will. Shelby had been fired from the Bureau because of a love affair with one of the drug lords, whom she let escape. Shelby had gone underground from that point forward. While she was believed to still be the drug lord's girlfriend, she remained on the FBI's most wanted list.

Max reviewed the file again on the last case that Shelby had worked, looking for anything that could lead to her whereabouts. It was noted that three months after the initial escape, the Bureau was successful in killing the drug lord in a massive shootout at his highly guarded home. Once the drug kingpin was eliminated, his remaining men fought to their deaths. It was believed that one of the men, before he was killed, sat fire to the main structure. C4 explosives must have been placed strategically within the house because it quickly exploded.

The agents barely had time to flee before the entire house burst into flames, causing a small mushroom cloud of smoke to infiltrate the air. It was enough smoke to cover an entire city block.

After searching the pillage of corpses, they located a female body, which was almost burned beyond recognition. According to the autopsy report, the only way they could positively identify the body was via the fingertips.

Rereading the information from the autopsy report, Max snapped his fingers. The person that completed the autopsy report must have been on "the take". The report never specified whether or not the body that was recovered was actually Shelby's. It just stated vaguely that the body was believed to be that of the kingpin's girlfriend, an ex-agent. Looking at the signature on the form, Max noticed that Randolph had signed off on the form.

It stood to reason that Shelby wasn't dead. That would explain how the Chameleons were so successful. Per the timeline, the Chameleons soon began killing operatives in other countries before any Bureau agent could come close to catching them. With Shelby's knowledge of computers and the ability to hack into the government's system, the information would be right at her fingertips of every known operative's overseas address and caseload.

Delving deeper, Max decided to follow his gut instinct. When starting over, people often did what was familiar to them. If that philosophy held true, then Shelby, who was used to the finer things in life, would want to continue that lifestyle. What better way to do that, than to find someone who could pose as the front man for a new drug territory in the States? Max assumed that she had found such a man in Michael, who had dibbled and dabbled in the drug scene since high school. Perhaps he had even worked for the kingpin at some point, which would make it easier for him to assume the role as leader.

The question became how would she accumulate enough cash to purchase the type of drugs needed to operate a territory? Did her dead boyfriend leave all of his money to her? No, according to the file, the money went to his mother. Was she somehow able to tap into his bank account to siphon money into an offshore account? Or was she planning a major heist on a bank? The answer, Max felt, was there somewhere in the file. As he continued to peruse the file, nothing jumped out at him until he came across a listing of items that were confiscated.

According to the report, several imaging machines were found that ordinarily would be used in a hospital for reconstructive surgery. Thinking back to how the Chameleons operated, he knew that they changed identities between jobs and that the fingerprints that they left behind when their jobs were over were never the same.

Picking up the telephone, Max dialed Dr. X, his inventor extraordinaire. "Talk to me."

"X, I need your help."

"Max, what type of invention do you need?"

"I need answers to a couple of questions first. What would a person attempt to create if they assembled the following items: a large quantity of scalp hair net, Alginate Impression Material, Petroleum Jelly, molding cement, and flesh-colored liquid latex?"

"My first thought would be a scalp or skin wig, which would be attached to the person's hairline to make it look more realistic than a regular weave, because they could blend the skin cap with their scalp."

"Is it possible that someone could use this method to create a facial mask to hide their identity?"

"Let me think about this for a minute. I guess it's possible but only for a temporary amount of time. Usually such a device would only be used in theatrical plays because of the ventilation needed for extended wear. Do you think this is how the Chameleons have been able to elude us thus far?"

"I'm just researching a hunch. I believe that the Chameleons used this method to adhere some type of skin material or latex to their fingertips to disguise their real identity. Is it possible that someone could make a skin wig and have some type of attachment in the wig that would secure the skin over an existing face? If my guess is correct, Shelby Thomas, a former FBI agent and possibly the female Chameleon, may have used this imaging technique to alter her facial identity."

"Let's assume that the ex-agent was there when the Bureau killed her boyfriend that she had previously let escape. In a fit of rage and also to fake her own death, she blows up his house, leaving a female body charred beyond recognition, making identification impossible for the coroner. Shelby is somehow wounded trying to leave the scene of the crime. She's in desperate need of skin graft surgery to repair the damage to her features."

Continuing the story, Max added, "While she is getting the skin grafts completed, she uses a temporary mask to conceal her injuries in public. If we search the database of all burn victims around that time, we should be able to locate where the surgery was done."

"As long as the clinic or hospital was credible, we would have access to that information. She couldn't go to a regular hospital because she obstructed justice when she let her boyfriend escape. Subsequently, a warrant was issued for her arrest. That would force her to go to a clinic in Mexico, that specializes in alternative treatments, where no questions would be asked as long as the money for the procedure was paid up front. If the doctor then became a good friend and knew that she had just come into a large portion of money and was in need of some investing advice, he would steer her to the firm that handled his affairs. I'm thinking that Cymballas was that firm."

"That would explain how she came to know Maurice, at least by telephone. Given her computer background, she could also have accessed the offshore bank accounts database. If she found that Maurice was laundering money from Cymballas, he would be the perfect person to help her acquire large amounts of money to fund the Chameleons drug territory. Since we know that he was messing around with the personal banker at McAlstons, depending on how deep she wanted her cover to be, she could have switched places with the personal banker if she used the skin mask and disguised her facial features."

"Good point Dr. X. That ties both participants to the case. I'm sending the pictures of the personal banker to you right now. Can you make a skin mask using Alexis' features?"

"Yes. It'll be ready in a few hours."

"Thanks. If you have any other gadgets that will be useful for this black market jewelry sale, send them by Alexis."

Picking up the telephone he dialed Trevor's number. Although what they had discussed was logical, he would feel better if Trevor could collaborate the sequence of events and verify his assumptions so that they wouldn't be walking into a trap. If anyone could find the ex-agent, it would be Trevor.

"Trevor, I think that I might have stumbled upon a connection to the Chameleons and an ex-agent." He proceeded to bring him up to speed on all the assumptions that they had come up with regarding the ex agent, Cymballas and the Chameleons. Max even sent him the maps that he had designed over the computer stored in his watch; a device that he and Trevor had invented.

With a heavy heart, while the maps were being uploaded, Trevor gave Max an update on everything else that had happened.

"The money has been transferred out of Maurice's account and he's now searching for a buyer for some of the jewels. As yet though, I don't believe that he has found them otherwise the sale would already have taken place. I just received a message from Caleb that contact has been made for a private sale with his parent's jewelry store for tomorrow night. So he must think that he can recoup them tonight otherwise, Caleb's jewelry store is going to be subjected to a jewelry heist. It is one of the more prominent stores in Charlotte."

"I'm on my way now. I should be there within an hour. Have you heard from Frank and Solomon?"

"Yes, they are camping out at Dr. Kelley's house. David gave Jackie one more night with Joshua before he takes her into seclusion until the case is over. The men that were looking for the jewels no doubt will be back, looking for retribution. Caleb left a message that he had received a tip on Maurice's whereabouts. He sent some agents in Washington to the address to verify the tip. By the time they got there, the place was empty."

"I'll touch base with Frank then I'll touch base with Caleb. You sound a little down, Trevor. What's wrong?"

"Cherita's gone. No forwarding address, no telephone number; nothing. She left me a note explaining that she too had found Maurice and Rasheeda. They were living at her house in Washington, can you believe that? She happened to go home to pickup some graphical supplies and stumbled upon them in bed. Luckily she was able to escape, but only after she heard them planning to make her the fall guy for all the crimes that they had committed. I believe that up until that point she had hoped that she was wrong about sister. She even resigned from McAlstons. I think that she's lost faith in humanity."

"I know how much she means to you. We'll find her. Let's concentrate on the next two days, then when this case is over, we'll search for her."

"Thanks Max. I really value your friendship more than you'll ever know."

"No more than what you've done for me, friend. You're family."

Switching gears, Trevor cleared his throat. "Give me about fifteen minutes and call me back after you've spoken to Caleb and Frank. I should have something for you then.

"Okay. I'm headed over to Joshua's to check in with Frank."

"Then I'll meet you at the jewelry store."

Chapter 22

David and Malcolm rushed into Joshua's house, fearing the worst. Pulling up short, they surveyed the damage done to the living room and the adjacent dining room. Every crevice possible had been hit by bullets. There was no way that Joshua and Jackie could have survived if they were downstairs when the shooting started.

Fearing the worst both sprung into action. Downstairs, David checked the family room, the kitchen and the sitting room. Motioning that he was going to check upstairs, Malcolm raced up the steps, taking them two at a time. Frantically, he searched every room. When he didn't find them, he growled in frustration and hit the wall with his bare hand, knocking a large hole in it.

Had someone come through the backyard and taken them away? No that was impossible. Frank had setup the perimeter force field around the entire house. If they had gone outside, they would have been fried; literally. There must be another explanation. Swiftly going back downstairs, he met Frank and Solomon as they came through the door.

"Where are Jackie and Joshua? We need to get out of here before they send reinforcements." Frank stated as he performed yet another reconnaissance throughout the house. Walking back outside, he studied the layout of the house and noticed some windows near the ground level. Since the house didn't have a basement, he could only surmise that the house had a wine cellar. Opening the door, he went back inside.

Turning to Solomon he requested, "Send a text message to Joshua that all is clear. Tell him to make haste and come out of the cellar so that we can jet before the reinforcements come."

Solomon sent the text as quickly as possible while walking towards the front of the house, to keep an eye on the activity on the street. He knew that they had only about fifteen minutes before things became very chaotic.

Suddenly a sound could be heard in the kitchen as the pantry doors sprung open. The barrels of six guns were trained on the opening, ready for fire, given the slightest provocation. Joshua came out first with his hands raised in the air, as he emphatically pleaded, "Don't shoot." Once the men saw that it was Joshua and Jackie walking out of the cellar, they put the safety back on their guns.

Joshua gave each of the men a quick embrace then stepped aside. Jackie then came from behind Joshua's back and embraced her brothers. After a quick hug for each one, she quietly walked back into Joshua's waiting arms. Over Jackie's head, Joshua said, "Thank you" to everyone present.

Taking the lead, Frank announced, "We need to leave right now, while we still can! Let's go! Everyone will be riding in the same vehicle. That way, we have enough firepower to stop anything that gets in our way. "

"Frank, where are you?" Max asked as he wrapped up his conversation with Trevor.

"We just finished a massive shootout at Joshua's house. Two cars tried to do a drive by shooting with some heavy artillery. Joshua and Jackie were rescued unharmed. They are gathering their things and within five minutes we are leaving."

"Frank! We've got company! A car and a F350 truck are headed this way and are slowing down to do another drive-by shooting," yelled Solomon as he noticed the barrel of a gun being pointed out of the car's window.

"Max, how far away are you? We sure could use some interference in order to get out of the driveway and away to safety." Frank asked.

Grabbing her purse from the cellar, Jackie and the men rushed through the house into the garage to get into the Yukon.

"I'm right around the corner. Alexis and I will run interference for you with the Blazer and the Mustang. Malcolm and David, take out the tires on the first car and the people in the back seat. Solomon will handle the driver. Let's do this expeditiously because we need to get to Charlotte as soon as possible. Alexis, what are your coordinates?"

"I'm several streets over. I should meet you at the four way intersection within two minutes." Having been the bodyguard for a Formula One race car driver, Alexis knew how to handle a car. In order to protect her client, it was safer if she knew how to drive like one of them in case the need arose where they needed to make a quick escape.

"Frank, raise the garage door and sit idle for two minutes then barrel out of the driveway onto the street at a rapid but controllable pace, then turn left. We've got your back."

Two minutes later, Frank gunned the motor and sped out of the garage at a very fast clip, just as the first car was coming abreast of the house. Malcolm and David, one by the window and the other standing up in the sunroof, broke the back windshield with two bullets, and eliminated the men in the back seat. Solomon took care of the front windshield and the guy in the passenger's seat.

The driver was too busy focusing on the road and the SUV in front of him to notice the car coming across the intersection from the opposite direction. When he did look up, it was in horror, to see another car intent on causing a head-on collision.

The Yukon slammed on brakes and just in the nick of time, at the very last minute, the car approaching them swerved, but by then it was too late. Mr. Smith's driver, fearful of being hit, frantically wrenched the wheel of his car to the left to avoid the on-coming car and slammed on brakes to avoid hitting the Yukon in front of him. He overcompensated for the near miss and sent the car into a tailspin causing the car to flip over several times. His last thought was that he should have hit the Yukon.

The second vehicle intensified their effort to shoot out the tires and the windows of the Yukon. With bulletproof glass and body armor it was virtually indestructible. When the bullets kept bouncing off the truck, the enemy then tried to ram it off the road. Speeding up, the F350 truck pulled alongside the Yukon.

One of the Yukon's tires could be heard popping as a bullet from the enemy's gun hit it. The Yukon's tire deflated; causing the truck to tilt before dropping the chassis to the ground. The other tires on the Yukon then collapsed to the size of the punctured tire, like a hydraulic custom car, in order to run more smoothly.

Max took advantage of the driver's momentary surprise to pull beside the truck and fire two bullets into the cab, hitting the passenger and the driver. Flooring his car, he sped off to allow Frank to make his next move.

As the car veered out of control, a man that had been hiding in the back part of the cab jumped up to grab the steering wheel. His actions proved futile.

The back part of the Yukon then swung in an arc allowing Malcolm to shoot a bullet at the F350's gas tank, three hundred feet away, blowing it to smithereens.

Max dialed the police chief to advise him of the carnage left behind. Wasting no time, they headed to the airport. Collectively the people in the Yukon breathed a sigh of relief.

"That was a close call. Is everyone okay?" Frank asked.

After their affirmative nods, David then began his relocation speech, much to Jackie's dismay. She never actually got around to telling Joshua about her upcoming exile.

"Jackie, when we get to the airport, Frank and Solomon are leaving to assist Max in Charlotte to their attempt to arrest Maurice after he either tries to participate in another jewelry heist or after he tries to fence the stolen jewelry on the Black Market. You're coming with me to an undisclosed location until he's brought to justice."

"Frank, does this impressive vehicle have a privacy barrier?" Joshua asked butting into David's dialogue.

"Yes Joshua." With the flip of a switch, the privacy barrier slid into place separating Joshua and Jackie from the rest of the occupants.

"Was that why you came back to the hospital to wait on me instead of going to your parent's house? Was that the sense of desperation that I felt when we were making love? Are you giving up on our love?"

"No! How can I give up on something that means everything to me? I love you Joshua and I'm only going away to protect you and my family. I don't want either of you senselessly being killed because my ex-husband owes some loan shark lots of money. Last night was my chance to store memories in my heart of you while I was away. I couldn't ask you to give up your career, your family and your life, to run around the world with me until Maurice is caught."

"Why couldn't you allow me to make that decision for myself? That's what you fail to understand. I love you more than life itself. Without you, nothing else matters." Tired of talking, Joshua pulled Jackie even closer to him, if that was possible and delivered another sensual kiss that took her breath away and made her long for something that she couldn't have.

Time to just be with him. Time to love him.

Finally needing to draw breath into his lungs, Joshua placed one final kiss to Jackie's forehead. "Sweetheart, Caleb's in trouble. While we were making love before the chaos started, I had a vision that he needed my help with the case that he's working on." He returned Jackie's smile. 'Yes, I have them too. Something passed on from our Indian ancestors. Now that you're going with David, I can go with Frank and Solomon to rescue him without feeling guilty about deserting you."

"Oh honey, I'm so sorry. Don't worry about me. David is very good at what he does. I'll be fine. Go find Caleb and hasten back to me." With one final kiss, she leaned her head on Joshua's shoulder and said a silent prayer. Tapping the window, Joshua let Frank know that the privacy shield could be lifted.

"Fellas, Caleb is in trouble. Something went wrong with the case. I had a premonition that he needs my help to track him. I'm going with you to Charlotte."

At Malcolm's protest of an inexperienced person going with them, possibly jeopardizing the mission, Frank interrupted him. "Malcolm, he's qualified. David, continue your last instructions."

Malcolm's first instinct was to argue but if Frank was satisfied with Joshua's background and street credibility then he would let it go.

"Jackie, I need your telephone in order to exchange it for a more secure one."

Reaching into her bag, she grabbed her phone then dropped it as she gasped in surprise when something pricked her finger.

"Honey, what's wrong? Did you hurt yourself? Let me see your hand." At the small trickle of blood that had started to form, Joshua put Jackie's finger into his mouth to suck the blood away.

"No, as you can see, I didn't hurt myself, something just pricked my finger." As Joshua released her hand, Jackie smiled at his demonstrative gesture as she reexamined her pocketbook for the offending object.

"Did you find out what it was?"

"Yes. It seems that my tweezers not only pricked my finger but also poked a hole in the lining of my pocketbook."

Turning on the overhead light, Jackie further inspected the damage. The lining that was coming apart wasn't the real lining of the pocketbook. She could still see the other lining behind it.

"Oh my God!" Jackie exclaimed.

"What is it? What's wrong?"

Speechless, she held up several large diamonds in her hand.

Reaching over the seat, Malcolm grabbed his sister's handbag. Taking the diamond out of his sweetheart's shaking fingers, Joshua examined it thoroughly.

"Without a loupe to verify its complete authenticity, I can guarantee that this diamond is flawless."

"How do you know so much about diamonds?"

"Caleb taught me everything that he knows. Besides being a doctor, I'm a certified gemologist. Making jewelry is kind of a hobby of ours, more like a family business."

"Malcolm, how many other diamonds are in the purse?" Frank asked as he turned a dial on his watch.

"Enough to fill a small pouch."

"Joshua, can you take a look at the diamonds and tell us an approximate market value?"

Taking the handbag that Malcolm extended, Joshua gathered the diamonds in one hand to estimate the weight of the diamonds. "I need more light and a loupe to determine the cut and clarity of the diamonds. Off-hand, I would estimate that the value is somewhere between five and ten million."

"That means that there's another ten million dollars worth of diamonds in another handbag at Ryan's house. Malcolm, once we get to the airport, I need you to circle back to Ryan's house and retrieve the box that contains Jackie's handbags."

"Knowing Ryan, everything is labeled and sorted so I shouldn't have a problem locating it. I'll then catch the next flight to Charlotte and meet you at the Kelley's jewelry store."

"Joshua, is there any way to put a small tracking device into one of the diamonds?"

"There might be, depending on the size of the tracking device."

At the airport, secluded in a room, before the diamonds were handed over to Maurice, a tracking device was placed inside the lining of the pouch. The device would allow Max's team to track Maurice when he sold the jewels and hopefully unearth the identity of the person that was bankrolling the heists.

On the way to Charlotte, breaking news surfaced about a double homicide that apparently stemmed from an altercation with a woman and her two lovers. The footage was being sent from a neighbor, an off-duty reporter that had videotaped the entire scene until his station crew arrived. The story unfolded that the two lovers were found dead on the premises, but that the woman was nowhere to be found. Rasheeda's face was then shown as a person of interest along with the clip.

Once the station crew arrived, footage was aired of the reporter talking with various neighbors about the incident. In the background, a woman dressed in all black, was shown walking quickly away from the crowd until another neighbor, in her haste to find out what was going on, bumped into her. The cameraman, sensing a story with the person leaving the scene of the crime so quickly, zeroed in on the two people that were having the altercation. Unknown to the reporter and the camera crew, the female in black was none other than Shelby Thomas, an ex-FBI agent. Turning her head away from the camera, she made a quick, hurried exit through one of the neighbor's back yards before the reporter could get an interview.

Seeing Rasheeda's and Shelby's face on the breaking news report that was airing on all the news stations, further collaborated Max' theory that Shelby was masquerading as Rasheeda Montgomery. Based on the pictures of the crime scene, it appeared that she had conveniently staged the two murders. Where was she headed to next?

Once the private jet landed in Charlotte, in rented cars they drove separately to the planned drop off area. One car was already there waiting, when Joshua pulled up. By using their telescopic lens, they assessed the entire area. With the earpiece that was almost invisible in his ear, Max told Joshua that Maurice was in one car and that another car with a suspected loan shark henchman was driving slowly into the area.

Getting out of the car, Joshua walked twenty feet away from the car. With the push of a button on the special watch that Max had given him on the plane, he activated the invisible force field that would protect him if shots were fired.

The message that Trevor sent, had gotten the desired effect because Maurice was present and so was one of the loan shark's representatives. The picture that the telescopic lens had captured when it scanned the area, confirmed the other occupant in the approaching car as a known criminal, by the name of Leon, Mr. Smith's second in command. It would seem that Mr. Smith wasn't leaving anything to chance.

Joshua was there to give Maurice the diamonds that were found in one of Jackie's handbags in exchange for leaving her alone and for identifying the guy that had been trying to kill her. Maurice showed up so that he could get his money back that was taken from his offshore account and to retrieve the diamonds.

As Joshua got out of his car, Maurice met him halfway across the expanse of the empty lot, with an envelope in his hand of the person and the contact numbers that were used for the jewelry heists and the person that bankrolled the entire event.

As arrogant as ever, Maurice was the first to speak. "Well, well, well; if it isn't the good doctor to the rescue. I assume that you enjoyed the pictures of my wife and I making love. It's such a shame that you weren't enough for her that she had to come back to me. Although she wasn't any good while we were married, with her frigid self, it seems that she's picked up a trick or two."

Before Joshua could contain his emotions, he had touched the dial on his watch and disengaged the force field. With a couple of jabs he broke Maurice's nose and his jaw. Several punches to his midsection resulted in at least three ribs also breaking. Writhing in pain, Maurice fell to the ground.

"Joshua, we need to leave," Max said into the earpiece.

Standing over Maurice, Joshua pressed his foot heavily into Maurice's sternum. "I could easily end your life right here. From this day forward, Jackie does not exist to you. If you ever try to contact her again, I will personally break every bone in your body." As if seeking to demonstrate his promise, Joshua, bending forward, grabbed Maurice's arm, and twisting it counter clockwise, broke it.

Releasing a loud groan, Maurice attempted to remove Joshua's foot from his chest with his good hand.

Pressing harder, Joshua asked, "Do you see how that feels? Now you know how she felt when you abused her. You'll feel this and much more if you ever attempt to contact her again."

"Joshua, activate the force field!" Max yelled.

Sensing that the fellow standing over Maurice was out of control, and was close to killing him, and possibly getting away with the diamonds, Leon drove his car straight towards the guy that was beating up Maurice. Aiming his gun out of the window, he fired successive shots at his target.

In the next instant chaos erupted. The men that Leon had paid to investigate the area, started to fire their weapons as soon as Leon gave them the command. Unfortunately for Leon, his men had been overpowered by Max's team. Alternating from different sides, Max and his team saturated the air with bullets, mimicking a carefully orchestrated sequence of events, allowing Joshua enough time to escape.

Grabbing the envelope, Joshua dived over Maurice as he flipped the dial on the watch, activating the force field, just in time to miss being hit by a bullet. Luckily the force field held as the bullets ricocheted off Joshua as he ran to the driver's side of the rental car. Within minutes, he was able to floor the gas pedal and speed away.

The diamonds were left lying in their pouch next to Maurice's dead body, which had been killed by a bullet from Leon's gun.

Chapter 23

Caleb was able to negotiate two meetings for the fencing of the jewels. The first meeting was to test the authenticity of the jewels that the seller was trying to fence. The second meeting was the actual exchange of the jewels and the money. Before the meeting took place though, Caleb received a visit from Shelby Thomas, an FBI agent, that was sent from the Bureau to help him until Max and his team could arrive.

Suspicions at the timing of her arrival, Caleb touched a button under the counter that would start videotaping the premises and would also take a live camera shot of the people that entered the store. Once their picture was taken, the image would be fed into the FBI, CIA and Scotland Yard databases for a match. If a hit was found, a picture would then printout in the back of the store of the person along with a complete dossier.

True enough, her profile showed up in the FBI database as an active operative assigned to Max's team when Caleb went to his office to check on some paperwork. Since neither his boss nor Max's boss had sent any information regarding any change in personnel, Caleb could only assume that she was working on the opposite side of the law. It would seem that the deal was going down before reinforcements could arrive.

Having been in similar situations in the past, Caleb squared his shoulders and revised his plan of action. First, he had to get his sister out of the building. Hopefully the videotape that was running would help in identifying the persons responsible for whatever was about to take place. Taking off his diamond encrusted cufflinks; he placed a microscopic tracking device in each one then placed only one cufflink back into the cuff of his shirt. The other, he placed on his worktable beside his tools.

Reaching for the remaining cufflink, he ran a critical eye over the replica that he had made of his favorite cufflinks. If something happened, Joshua would know what to do with the one that was left behind.

Shelby, meanwhile in the showroom, was taking in every nuance of the building as she pretended to scan the selection of bridal wedding rings. Under the watchful eye of the other sales person, she chose one or two rings to view before Caleb returned. The only way that she would get a jump on whoever was intent on exposing her, was to show up as her former self instead of the disguise of Rasheeda Montgomery that she had been wearing for the last six months.

If she was lucky, the person that scheduled this meeting could either be won over by her charm or eliminated. The question of the day remained; what did the person want? They had already taken more than a million dollars from her bank account. If the person wanted more money, she was sure that a jewelry heist of the current store would offer approximately five million.

When Caleb returned to the showroom, he told his sister to take the rest of the day off. His sister was getting ready to remind him that they still had to design the wedding set that was due in two weeks, until she met his eye. Something dangerous lurked within their depths. Grabbing her handbag, she exited the store. As soon as she was in her car and had pulled off, she placed a call to Joshua.

When he didn't answer immediately, she sent him a text message. *Joshua, Caleb is in trouble at the store. Staying to help.* After the message was sent, she circled the block and parked across the street to watch the building to see if anyone else went into the store.

Finally, Joshua sent a text response to his sister. *John and Anthony are on their way to help. Wait for them! I'll be there soon.*

Ten minutes later, Mr. Smith dressed in a business suit walked into the store along with five other men, one of whom, was sent to the backroom to guard the back entrance.

Spencer, who had remained in her watchful position, noticed that six dangerous looking men had just entered the store. Not good for Caleb. *The cavalry had better arrive soon, thought Spencer, or I'm going to have to help him on my own.* Pulling off into traffic, she drove down the street and then parked her car in the adjacent parking deck before walking back to the store on foot.

Walking directly to Shelby, as the other men stationed themselves strategically around the room, Mr. Smith embraced her as he leaned forward and kissed her fully on the lips. "Darling, I see that you've started without me. I apologize for being late. Sir, can we have a minute?"

Caleb discreetly walked a few feet away. What were they up too? Why the need for so many men? If she was a federal agent coming to help with the case, how does she know the guy that just walked in, who presumably was there to discuss selling illegal jewels? Positioning himself behind the counter, he had access to three weapons, in addition to the weapon tucked in his waist at the back.

Pressing a button on the counter, Caleb was able to lower the shades on the large expansive windows, isolating them from the outside world. Once the shades were lowered, the outer doors would lock automatically within five minutes to prevent other customers from coming in. This was a safety feature he had designed in case there was ever a robbery.

"Is there a need for the shades to be drawn?"

"For our custom consultations and fittings we ensure that our clients have complete privacy." Caleb explained as the shades whispered quietly into place.

Whispering in Shelby's ear, Mr. Smith acknowledged that he knew who she was and that if she wanted to stay alive she needed to get Maurice to meet her and hand over the jewels that he had stolen. As if on cue, Mr. Smith's telephone started ringing. Looking down at the display to ascertain the identity of the caller, he quickly answered the call.

With a quick nod of his head, his men pulled out automatic machine guns and aimed them at Shelby and Caleb. Only one side of the conversation could be heard as he started a dialogue with the caller.

"Yes, we're at the jewelry store. She's here and so is the store manager."

Randolph then advised him, "Is the store manager a male or a female?"

"It's a male. Why?" Mr. Smith turned his head to assess Caleb's position.

After describing Caleb's description, Randolph then stated, "The gentleman is an FBI agent. We need to change our plans. Try to get some information out of the agent. See what he knows. Take both of them to the designated place and hold them until I get there. Have we located the jewels yet?"

"No, however, we initiated a plan of action where we would bring Maurice out of hiding. We sent him an anonymous message, advising him that if he wanted the jewels, he would have to meet at a pre-arranged site in exchange for some type of information. Since he's guilty of several crimes and has a warrant out for his arrest, we know that he will not go to the police. According to Leon, who just called, Maurice went alone to the delivery."

"Just make sure that Leon retrieves the diamonds and kills Maurice so that there won't be any loose ends."

"Consider it done." Mr. Smith hung up the telephone and turned to assess the market value of the jewelry store.

Caleb pondered how he was going to get out of the current dilemma. Judging the distance between each man, he determined that he could eliminate all of the men but didn't relish the thought of killing seven people in cold blood. If they were good marksmen, they might even have him at a disadvantage. Plus the agency needed to know who the mole was, evidently the person that was on the other end of the call. The lives of their undercover operatives were at stake. If he stalled a little longer, he was sure that Spencer would have gone for help.

"It seems that you have me at a disadvantage. I was under the impression that this young lady was waiting on her fiancé to arrive to pick out your wedding rings. With all of our clients we afford them complete privacy when deciding on such an important piece of jewelry. "

"Let's cut to the chase shall we? You're an FBI agent by the name of Caleb Kelley. This little rendezvous was setup to capture the person that stole twenty million dollars in jewels in South Africa. How am I doing so far?"

"Actually you're a little off target. I am simply here to work in my parent's jewelry store while they are away on a trip. Nothing more, nothing less."

"Who do you actually think that you are kidding? I've just got word of who you are and now you're trying to play me like a fool!" Mr. Smith expostulated, walking closer to the counter where Caleb stood, pointing a gun in his face.

In the backroom at the private entrance, John, Anthony and Spencer had arrived. The police had not been called because of the nature of Caleb's job. Whatever that was going down, her family could handle it. Quickly and quietly they disarmed the guy that was guarding the back door. When he attempted to fire his weapon that had a silencer on it, he was eliminated.

Strategically positioning themselves behind the display case enclosures that led to the showroom, they were ready to eliminate the other men with the guns.

"Since it's obvious that you're not going to let me leave here alive, why don't you tell me how you were able to pull this off?" Caleb questioned to buy more time.

"Let's just say that I have friends in some very high places."

Thinking that he heard a small sound from the backroom, Caleb discreetly glanced down at the built-in computer screen that was attached to the main display case, which also served as a security camera. It allowed him a visual of the backroom. His cousins, his sister and his brother were seen ushering in a woman and several other guys.

Follow our lead. The man and woman that are coming into the showroom are undercover FBI agents. The woman that is with you is an ex-FBI agent and a known killer.

Walking into the room, Alexis and Frank, the FBI agents that were working undercover, posing as Rasheeda and Maurice entered the room from the back, hugging and kissing each other.

A startled gasp could be heard from Shelby as she watched her boyfriend materialize out of thin air to show up at the "secret meeting" with another woman who looked just like the woman that she had murdered and had assumed her identity.

Mr. Smith was astonished that Maurice was still alive. "Have you come to deliver the diamonds?"

At Maurice's nod, Mr. Smith extended his hand for the diamonds. As soon as the diamonds were exchanged, Shelby, who had thus far been quiet, came to life upon seeing her man, whom she had been through thick and thin with, hugging and kissing another woman.

"This lady is an imposter! She was killed over six months ago, and unless she has a twin, she's wearing a mask to disguise her real features. I'm the one that's going to expose you. It seems that I'm going to have to kill you again. I bet this time you won't resurface from the grave."

With a muttered expletive, she sprang into action. Going straight to Maurice, she took his lips in hers for a thorough kiss while disengaging the woman's arms from around her man. Then with an enraged cry, she attempted to throw several blows at the woman for encroaching on her property but didn't get very far.

Alexis smoothly deflected her blows and delivered several of her own. She was fighting mad that the woman had the audacity to put her lips on Frank. Determined not to blow her cover, she tried to compose herself. In a husky voice she asked, "Darling, who is this woman and is your debt now paid?"

Mr. Smith motioned for one of his men to restrain Shelby.

Frank shrugged his shoulders, while looking at Mr. Smith for confirmation.

With one finger held up requesting silence, Mr. Smith pulled a lupe out of his pocket to verify the authenticity of the diamond. "These are of great clarity and quality. Kill them all." Motioning to his men, he headed towards the door before turning around to fire his weapon amongst the remaining individuals.

All hell broke loose then. The men with the machine guns started firing their weapons just as John and Anthony, from the backroom, quickly shot four small miniscule poisonous darts at their necks. One by one, they collapsed to the floor. Five police officers then burst through the door and entered the frenzy, firing shots at Max's team. Since the policemen were obviously paid men, Max and Frank came from the back and finished them off.

Caleb grabbed the guns from the display case and aimed his firepower towards Mr. Smith who was swiftly edging out of the door. By that time, Shelby, with her weapon drawn, fired her gun at Alexis. Swiftly pushing her aside, Frank pulled the trigger and with one shot to the head, he sent Shelby crashing to the floor.

Everything was over within seconds. Unfortunately, Mr. Smith was able to escape since more policemen were coming on the scene. This time, the police chief, one of Max's friends, was able to halt his guys from shooting and possibly getting killed once he recognized Max in the background. Claiming jurisdiction, Max stepped forward and announced that the FBI was in charge of the operation.

Shaking hands with his friend, he stated, "Chief, Trevor will explain everything. Right now we've got to catch the man that just left, who we believe, holds the key to this entire series of events."

Max, Frank and Solomon raced out the back entrance to their SUV, where they used the tracking device in the pouch of the diamonds to locate what they assumed was the designated meeting with the FBI mole for the exchange of the diamonds.

Following the signal from the tracking device, they were led to the penthouse suite of a national hotel.

Too much traffic to wage a war. The mole was smart.

After picking the lock to the hotel room, instead of catching Mr. Smith with the diamonds, they caught Roger, a member of Max's team, in a compromising position with someone other than his wife. While he was doing his thing, he was talking to an unknown person via a web camera on a laptop computer that was sitting on the hotel desk. As soon as the door opened, the connection was severed. The identity of the person on the other end of the webcam was still mysterious.

There on the desk, lay the pouch with the diamonds. Upon closer inspection, Frank saw that all but three of the diamonds had been taken.

"Roger, if we may interrupt…"

Both Roger and the young lady scrambled to cover themselves. Roger then started stuttering an explanation while the young lady ran into the bathroom.

"Save it. You disgust me. I want to know who you were talking to and where did you get these diamonds"

"What diamonds? I was only playing a video." Roger managed to stammer.

"Then I guess you won't mind if we take this will you?" Solomon asked as he picked up the computer and tucked it under his arm as they headed out the door.

Two other agents entered the room to escort Roger to the Headquarters for questioning.

"I don't believe what I just saw. Apparently he was too occupied to hear someone enter his hotel room. He appeared clueless when we asked about the diamonds."

"Let's prepare a media release that half of the diamonds from the South African jewelry heist was recovered and sent back to the South African Corporation they were stolen from. That means that we've eliminated a reason for Mr. Smith to bother anyone in the family again. We will however, go after Roger and attempt to uncover the mole. After I talk with Mr. B, we'll setup a sting operation for Roger, who I think is a key player and see what or whom he leads us too. We'll take the computer to Trevor to see if he can work his magic to see where the connection came from. Let's head back to the jewelry store to help them clean up."

Epilogue

When Max and his team returned to the jewelry store, the FBI agents had carted off the bodies and had taken all the pictures necessary of the crime scene. The pieces of the puzzle of the day's events were quickly put into perspective. After storing all of the jewels in the vault, Caleb called in a cleaning crew to repair the damage done to the store. Since the damage was expansive, they decided to give their parents store a makeover.

Caleb then hugged his sister, his cousins, his brother, and Max's team; thanking them for coming to his rescue.

"How did you know that something was wrong?" Caleb asked Joshua.

"When Jackie and I were spending what she thought was our last night together, I saw you troubled, in my spirit. If it had not been for that vision and the sense of imminent danger, I would not be standing here today. The loan sharks men shot up my house while we were still in it. Luckily the wine cellar saved us."

"To God be the glory!" Spencer replied. "When are you going to make an honest woman of Jackie?" She asked curiously. As a sister, she couldn't have picked a better person for her brother to fall in love with, except of course for the extra baggage of her ex-husband and his drama.

Smiling, Joshua pulled his telephone out to contact Jackie on the secured telephone that David had given her. After several rings she picked up. "Sweetheart, it's over! How quickly can I see you again?"

With a loud squeal, Jackie started praying and crying, all at once. Finally when she was able to compose herself, she asked, "Are you hurt? Is everyone all right?"

"Everyone is fine. No one got hurt. When are you coming home to me?"

"Today! Hold on a moment and let me check with David."

Jackie handed David the telephone so that he could ask Max a couple of questions. "Joshua, can I talk to Max for a moment, before I make that decision?"

"Sure." Joshua extended the telephone to Max.

After discussing the events and the outcome, Max let David know that everything was okay and that Jackie was safe to return. Handing the telephone back to his future brother-in-law, Max patted him on the back.

Quickly Jackie and Joshua discussed her time of arrival. It would take them about four hours to return. After hanging up the telephone, Joshua looked at everyone that was assembled in the room and had an epiphany.

"Can I have everyone's attention? As you know by now, Jackie is my one true love, and I'm going to ask her to marry me tonight. I don't want to spend another night without her, especially after what we've all just been through. Would it be possible, since all of you have played a part in saving our lives that you join us in celebrating our life together as one?"

Everyone smiled and readily agreed that they would participate in the wedding except Solomon, who grudgingly agreed after coercing from Max.

"Spencer and Caleb, how soon can you finish the custom wedding ring designs that I gave you?"

"That's already taken care of Joshua." Spencer went back into the vault to pull out the rings that he had designed for his lady love.

Caleb then turned to Joshua, "Hadn't you better freshen up and gather everything that you'll need for your ultimate proposal tonight?"

Looking at his watch, Joshua grimaced as he recognized the time. "Oh my God! My house is tore up, what am I going to do?" he asked frantically.

Laughing, Spencer replied, "The unflappable doctor has just lost his cool points."

Everyone burst out laughing. "Just tell me what you want done and we'll take care of everything. My house is at your disposal. Caleb and I can just stay at John and Anthony's house for tonight, right?" Spencer asked her male cousins.

Pulling her closer, John replied, "As if we have a choice. Of course you can stay at our place."

After receiving the news that everything was over, David and Jackie headed to the airport to catch a flight back home. Unfortunately their connecting flight had been delayed due to bad weather. They ended up waiting an additional four hours for their connecting flight to arrive. Disappointed, Jackie telephone Joshua with the news.

"Hello sweetheart. Are you missing me already?" Joshua asked smiling.

Despondently Jackie replied, "It seems that I'll be missing you even more."

"Why? What's wrong? Has something else happened?" Joshua wanted to know with fear in his heart.

"No, only our connecting flight has been delayed for about four hours. We won't get in until around eight."

Releasing a deep sigh as his heart stopped racing, Joshua admitted, "Then I'll be waiting for you at the airport at eight o'clock. I love you and I can't wait until you're back in my arms, baby."

"I love you too and there's no place I'd rather be. See ya soon."

Four hours later…

At eight o'clock, Joshua was at the airport anxiously awaiting Jackie's arrival. As soon as the plane landed, he hurried forward to the ticket gate to greet her. Flying first class had its advantages. David and Jackie were the first ones to deplane.

Quickly walking forward, Joshua scooped Jackie into his arms as his lips captured hers in an intensely satisfying kiss.

They only stopped kissing when David commented, "You are so sprung," before laughing. Several people nearby, whistled and grinned at seeing a young couple so much in love.

"I'm glad that you're back. I've missed you."

"I've missed you too."

"Come on, let's go home. David, can we drop you off anywhere?"

"No, someone should be here any minute to pick me up. Go on. I know that you have some catching up to due."

After securing Jackie's luggage, Joshua led her to the waiting limousine. Inside the limousine, two dozen roses awaited her as she slid onto the seat. With an exclamation of surprise, Jackie bent to sniff the beautiful bouquet. Ever so gently, Joshua pulled her closer to his body, to give her a long, unhurried kiss.

Her lips instinctively parted to receive the invasion of his hot tongue. His mouth plundered her depths, teasing and tasting, causing shudders to race down her spine. Relentlessly he devoured her lips, his tongue bending and moving, caressing all the angles, pulling her deeper into the vortex of sensual delight.

Savoring the taste of her lips, he ended the kiss before he was tempted to show her the true depths of his passion, his love.

Looking out the window, he realized that they were almost at their destination.

Gazing out of the window in an attempt to compose her ragged emotions, Jackie asked curiously, "Where are we going?"

"Since my house hasn't been repaired yet, Spencer offered us the use of her house. Of course if you want to go home, I'll have the driver to turn around."

"No, Spencer's house is fine. I don't think that I will ever be comfortable in my house again."

"Let's not worry about that tonight. I just want to show you how much you were missed."

"Well you're off to a good start."

The car pulled into Spencer's driveway. Exiting the car, Joshua helped Jackie out then proceeded to unlock the door to the house. The chauffer deposited the bags in the foyer, then left.

"Hold still. Let me turn on some lights." With the flip of a switch, the living room was bathed in a soft, romantic glow. Rose petals covered every surface available on the floor and candles were lit around the entire room.

"Oh my," was all that Jackie could say, as tears welled in her eyes. This was the first time that someone had ever done something so romantic for her.

With his hand extended, Joshua pulled Jackie further into the room. Leaning forward, he gently placed a kiss to her lips. "This was supposed to make you happy, not cry."

"This is the most romantic thing anyone has ever done for me. Thank you!" She replied tremulously.

"Since I know that you've been on that long flight, why don't you freshen up in the bathroom while I get our food ready? There is a bubble bath waiting just for you."

Like a kid in a candy store, Jackie rushed off to the bathroom, only to stop dead in her tracks as she noticed that the rose petals continued throughout the house, to the dining room, the bathroom and to the bedroom. Joshua sure made a woman feel special with his attention to detail.

After soaking for twenty minutes, Jackie finally felt refreshed as she toweled herself dry. With a brief knock, Joshua came into the bathroom holding a garment bag from a distinctive, soon to be well-known clothier. "I wanted to spoil you so I picked out an outfit that I thought would look good on you. Wear it for me please?"

"Do I have to put something on?" Jackie asked mischievously?

"Yes, you do. Behave. There will be time for that later; after dinner. I know that you must be starved."

Her stomach chose that moment to agree with him. "Okay, you're right. Give me five minutes and I'll be ready." Pleasure swept through her as he gifted her with another long, lingering kiss.

Unzipping the bag that Pauletta had obviously designed, Jackie smiled at the simple, yet elegant, A-line dress with the flirty hem in the beautiful raw silk fabric. One that would show off her legs and look good while dancing.

Left on the bathroom granite countertop was a gift; a pretty, corked bottle with some type of paper inside. Peering closer, Jackie saw that the tag on the gift had her name emblazoned in Joshua's descriptive, cursive scrawl. Curious, Jackie pulled the cork from the bottle and shook the paper loose. Opening the paper, she read the poem that eloquently expressed his love.

Running from the room, Jackie went in search of Joshua. She found him in the dining room putting the finishing touches on an elaborate candlelit dinner for two with catered food that resembled everything that they had eaten on their first date.

"Joshua, what are you trying to do? Drown me in my tears?" Jackie asked as she embraced him from behind.

"No baby, I'm simply surrounding you with my love." Joshua explained as he turned around.

Jackie melted against his body as he gathered her possessively to his him, consuming her mouth like the meal set before them. "Before we get carried away, there's one more thing that I want to show you." Grabbing her hand, he led her to the bedroom.

In the center of the bed lay an oblong box tied with an extravagant bow with a rose on top. Feeling that she had better sit down, before she fell down, Jackie gingerly sat down on the bed. "Please open it."

Jackie pulled the bow from the box with shaking fingers. Opening the lid, all she could do was stare at the magnificent ring that was resting inside. It was a three carat, princess cut diamond, nestled in a platinum setting, with three smaller diamonds embedded along each side of the ring. It was astonishingly beautiful.

Tears again began to slide effortlessly down her face. With a gentle touch, bending down on one knee, Joshua raised her face to his, as he kissed her tears away. "If you read the words that I expressed from my message in a bottle, then you know how much I love and need you. My heart belongs to you. I don't want to spend another day without you in my life, by my side, for the rest of eternity. Will you marry me?"

Shaking her head, Jackie threw her arms around his neck. When she could breathe, she exclaimed, "Yes!" Taking a deep gulp of air into her lungs, she exhaled. "Joshua, you continue to make me feel special every time that we are together. I will always treasure this night. You taught me to love again; to believe in humanity. You've protected me and pulled me from harm's way. You would have even willingly died for me. For that you will always have my everlasting love."

Sealing their vows with a kiss, Joshua asked, "If that's how you feel, then will you marry me tonight?"

"Silly, it takes months to plan a wedding." Jackie laughingly stated until she saw that Joshua was utterly serious. How can we get married tonight?"

"Please don't think that it was presumptuous of me to plan our wedding without your knowledge or input but I knew that when you returned, I didn't want to spend another day without you. While I've been proposing, everyone that we love has been working to transform this house into the candlelit wedding of your dreams."

"Sweetheart, you've thought of everything. If the wedding is as carefully thought out as your proposal, I'm going to love it. Oh my gosh! What about a wedding dress?"

"If you'll look in the closet, there's another garment bag, with a wedding dress in it, designed by Toni, a good friend of Max's family." With a sweet kiss and a whispered, "I love you," Joshua left the bedroom before he was tempted to consummate the marriage and forget about the people that were in the house waiting on them.

While Joshua was proposing to Jackie in the bedroom, there was a flurry of activity throughout the rest of the house. Joshua had spared no expense in making his bride's fairy tale wedding come true. At least seventy five people were on hand to artfully move and arrange the furnishings. The roses that literally were sprinkled upon every surface and the candles that were strategically placed in every room set the ambience that Joshua wanted, for his candlelight wedding.

The sunroom had been designated, due to its open floor plan, as the room where the actual wedding would take place. Four rows of baguette seats were placed side by side for seating; enough to accommodate fifty people. The piano from the living room was moved to the den that was adjacent to the sunroom, so that the couple could be serenaded during the ceremony.

Caterers had whisked away the uneaten dinner for two that was cleverly arranged on the buffet tables that were draped in linen and silk, and replaced it with the food for the Reception. It was only fitting that the wedding cake would resemble a large diamond; a reminder of how God's grace and mercy had kept them alive. An extraordinary wedding would not be complete without the couple's first dance on the lanai patio covered in hundreds of rose petals.

Most of the preparations had been completed while they waited on Jackie's plane to land. Therefore it took less than an hour for everything to be rearranged and for everyone to be in their proper place. Soon the beginning strands of the song *Unconditional Love* could be heard as the wedding began.

Jackie kept her composure until she heard Joshua singing a hauntingly beautiful song that he had composed as she walked down the spiral staircase with her father. At the bottom of the staircase, Joshua waited for his bride. When she reached him, he took her in his arms and kissed her tears away while whispering, "I love you more than life itself."

In return, Jackie lovingly cupped his face as she replied, "You are my everything; for now, forever, for eternity. Our love shall never die."

A dry eye couldn't be found in the entire room; women and men alike.

The preacher smiled at the loving couple who had evidently forgotten that they were not alone. Clearing his throat, he joked, "I haven't performed a wedding yet for this family where the groom doesn't kiss the bride before the wedding vows are affirmed." Laughter could be heard around the room.

Smiling, Max looked at Chelsea and mouthed the words, "I love you." The same sentiment was being delivered by all of the married couples including: TJ and Erica, The Baileys and the Kelleys who had flown back early from their vacation.

The ceremony continued with beautifully chosen songs, *God's Gift, When God Gave Me You and This I Promise You;* that expressed how the couple felt towards each other and God. The wedding vows were simple yet carried a wealth of meaning; they repeated what was in their hearts that they had expressed when Joshua proposed.

As the preacher pronounced them man and wife, Joshua shed a couple of tears as he embraced his wife, his future, his soul mate and placed a searing kiss to her lips that had every single lady in the audience fanning themselves.

Discover exciting and intriguing romantic sagas where the hero/heroine through faith, overcomes adversity while producing a legacy for future generations.

Don't miss another saga in The Romance Chronicles...

Love's Purpose

Adrienne Woods

The flame is burning low in Sebastian and Dominique's marriage. Dominique's career as a boutique owner and jewelry designer has sky-rocketed. Sebastian, while supportive of his wife's endeavors, feels left out. He misses the love and camaraderie that they used to share. No longer able to spend quality time together, Sebastian devises a scheme that would put the sparkle, the passion and the sensuality back into their marriage by sending his wife on a scavenger hunt for his heart.

Available Spring 2009 from Pass It On Publishing!

Pass It On
Publishing
Dramatic. Sensual. Riveting.

Discover exciting and intriguing romantic sagas where the hero/heroine through faith, overcomes adversity while producing a legacy for future generations.

Don't miss another saga in The Romance Chronicles...

Lay it on the Line
Adrienne Woods

A Bailey Novel

Although David and Tamera have been dating exclusively for the past seven years, Tamera's clock is ticking and she wants to know where their relationship is headed. David has a ten year plan of accomplishments that he would like to achieve before settling down and doesn't understand what all the fuss is about. Tamera believes that he has commitment issues and delivers an ultimatum.

Available Summer 2009 from Pass It On Publishing!

Pass It On
Publishing
Dramatic. Sensual. Riveting.

Discover exciting and intriguing romantic sagas where the hero/heroine through faith, overcomes adversity while producing a legacy for future generations.

Don't miss another saga in The Romance Chronicles...

Delayed but not Denied

Adrienne Woods

After struggling as an entrepreneur, Dustin's charter boat business finally takes off. With his wife Janice by his side, all his dreams have finally come true. Returning from a long trip geared towards expanding the business, Dustin is stunned to learn that his wife has left him for another man. After she leaves, he also discovers that his business is all but destroyed, and that he is penniless. Left to pick up the pieces, with faith and determination, his dream that had been delayed, through the will of God, was not denied!

Available Fall 2009 from Pass It On Publishing!

Pass It On
Publishing
Dramatic. Sensual. Riveting.